# CAIN HIS BROTHER

*Books by Anne Perry*
*Published by Fawcett Books*

*Featuring Thomas and Charlotte Pitt*

The Cater Street Hangman
Callander Square
Paragon Walk
Resurrection Row
Rutland Place
Bluegate Fields
Death in the Devil's Acre
Cardington Crescent
Silence in Hanover Close
Bethlehem Road
Highgate Rise
Belgrave Square
Farriers' Lane
The Hyde Park Headsman
Traitors Gate

*Featuring William Monk*

The Face of a Stranger
A Dangerous Mourning
Defend and Betray
A Sudden, Fearful Death
The Sins of the Wolf
Cain His Brother

# CAIN HIS BROTHER

## Anne Perry

FAWCETT COLUMBINE
New York

A Fawcett Columbine Book
Published by Ballantine Books
Copyright © 1995 by Anne Perry

All rights reserved under International
and Pan-American Copyright Conventions. Published
in the United States by Ballantine Books, a division of Random
House, Inc., New York, and simultaneously in Canada
by Random House of Canada Limited, Toronto.

LIBRARY OF CONGRESS CATALOGING-IN-PUBLICATION DATA
Perry, Anne.
Cain his brother / Anne Perry
p. cm.
ISBN 0-449-90847-X
1. Monk, William (fictitious character)—Fiction. 2. Private
investigators—England—London—Fiction. 3. London (England)
—Fiction. I. Title.
PR6066.E693C25 1995
823'.914—dc20                                                      95-8680
                                                                   CIP

Text design by Holly Johnson

Manufactured in the United States of America

First Edition: October 1995

10 9 8 7 6 5 4 3

To the people of Portmahomack
for their great kindness

*"We have read each other as Cain his brother"*
— G. K. CHESTERTON

# CHAPTER
# ONE

---

"Mr. Monk?" she said, then took a deep breath. "Mr. William Monk?"

He turned from the desk where he had been sitting, and rose to his feet. The landlady must have let her through the outer chamber. "Yes ma'am?" he said inquiringly.

She took another step into the room, ignoring her huge crinoline skirts as they touched against the table. Her clothes were well cut and fashionable without ostentation, but she seemed to have donned them in some haste and without attention to detail. The bodice did not quite match the skirt, and the wide bow of her bonnet was knotted rather than tied. Her face with its short strong nose and brave mouth betrayed considerable nervousness.

But Monk was used to that. People who sought the services of an agent of inquiry were almost always in some predicament which was too serious, or too embarrassing, to have dealt with through the more ordinary channels.

"My name is Genevieve Stonefield," she began. Her voice quivered a little. "Mrs. Angus Stonefield," she amended. "It is about my husband that I must consult you."

With a woman of her age, which he placed between thirty and thirty-five, it most usually was, or else a minor theft, an unsatisfactory household servant, occasionally a debt. With older women it was an errant child or an unsuitable match in prospect. But Genevieve Stonefield was a most attractive woman, not only in her warm

1

coloring and dignified deportment, but in the frankness and humor suggested in her face. He imagined most men would find her greatly appealing. Indeed, his first instinct was to do so himself. He squashed it, knowing bitterly the cost of past misjudgments.

"Yes, Mrs. Stonefield," he replied, moving from the desk into the middle of the room, which he had designed to make people feel at ease—or more accurately, Hester Latterly had persuaded him to do so. "Please sit down." He indicated one of the large, padded armchairs across the red-and-blue Turkey rug from his own. It was a bitter January, and there was a fire burning briskly in the hearth, not only for warmth but for the sense of comfort it produced. "Tell me what disturbs you, and how you believe I may help." He sat in the other chair opposite her as soon as courtesy permitted.

She did not bother to rearrange her skirts; they billowed around her in exactly the way they had chanced to fall, hoops awry and showing one slender, high-booted ankle.

Having steeled herself to take the plunge, she had no need of further invitation, but began straightaway, leaning forward a little, staring at him gravely.

"Mr. Monk, in order for you to understand my anxiety, I must tell you something of my husband and his circumstances. I apologize for taking up your time in this manner, but without this knowledge, what I tell you will make little sense."

Monk made an effort to appear as if he listened. It was tedious, and in all probability quite unnecessary, but he had learned, through error, to allow people to say what they wished before reaching the purpose of their visit. If nothing else, it permitted them a certain element of self-respect in a circumstance where they found themselves obliged to ask for help in an acutely private matter, and of someone most of them regarded as socially inferior by dint of the very fact that he earned his living. Their reasons were usually painful, and they would have preferred to have kept the secret.

When he had been a policeman such delicacy would have been

2

irrelevant, but now he had no authority, and he would be paid only according to his client's estimate of his success.

Mrs. Stonefield began in a low voice. "My husband and I have been married for fourteen years, Mr. Monk, and I knew him for a year before that. He was always the gentlest and most considerate of men, without giving the impression of being easily swayed. No one has ever found him less than honorable in all his dealings, both personal and professional, and he has never sought to take advantage of others or gain by their misfortune." She stopped, realizing—perhaps from Monk's face—that she was speaking too much. His features had never concealed his feelings, especially those of impatience, anger or scorn. It had served him ill at times.

"Do you suspect him of some breach in his otherwise excellent character, Mrs. Stonefield?" he asked with as much concern as he was able to pretend. It was beginning to appear that her interesting face covered a most uninteresting mind.

"No, Mr. Monk," she said a little more sharply, but the fear was dark in her eyes. "I am afraid he has been done to death. I wish you to find out for me." In spite of her desperate words, she did not look up at him. "Nothing you can do will help Angus now," she continued quietly. "But since he has disappeared, and there is no trace of him, he is presumed by the law simply to have deserted us. I have five children, Mr. Monk, and without Angus, his business will very rapidly cease to provide for us."

Suddenly the matter became real, and genuinely urgent. He no longer saw her as an overwordy woman fussing over some fancied offense, but one with a profound cause for the fear in her eyes.

"Have you reported his absence to the police?" he asked.

Her eyes flickered up to his. "Oh yes. I spoke to a Sergeant Evan. He was most kind, but he could do nothing to help me, because I have no proof that Angus did not go of his own will. It was Sergeant Evan who gave me your name."

"I see." John Evan had been Monk's most loyal friend at the time of his own trouble, and would not have dismissed this woman could he have helped her. "How long since you saw or heard from your husband, Mrs. Stonefield?" he asked gravely.

The shadow of a smile crossed her features and was gone. Perhaps it was a reflection in the change in his own expression.

"Three days, Mr. Monk," she said quietly. "I know that is not long, and he has been away from home often before, and for longer, sometimes up to a week. But this is different. Always before he has informed me, and left provision for us, and of course he left instructions for Mr. Arbuthnot at his place of business. Never before has he missed an appointment, or failed to leave authority and direction so Mr. Arbuthnot might act in his absence." She leaned forward, almost unaware of the charming tilting of the hoops of her skirt. "He did not expect to be gone, Mr. Monk, and he has contacted no one!"

He felt a considerable sympathy for her, but the most practical way he could help was to learn as many of the facts as she was able to give him.

"At what time of the day did you last see him?" he asked.

"At breakfast, about eight o'clock in the morning," she replied. "That was January the eighteenth."

It was now the twenty-first.

"Did he say where he intended going, Mrs. Stonefield?"

She took a deep breath, and he saw her folded hands in her lap clasp each other more firmly in their neat white gloves. "Yes, Mr. Monk. He went from home to his place of business. From there he told Mr. Arbuthnot that he was going to see his brother."

"Did he call upon his brother often?" he asked. It seemed an unremarkable occurrence.

"He was in the habit of visiting him at irregular intervals," she replied. She looked up, staring at him intently, as if the meaning of this were so vital to her she could not believe it would not have the same impact on him. "As long as I have known him," she added, her voice dropping and becoming husky. "You see, they are twins."

"It is not uncommon for brothers to visit each other, Mrs.

4

Stonefield." He remarked it only because he could see no reason for her white face, or her tense body as she sat uncomfortably on the edge of her chair. "Of course, you have been in touch with the other Mr. Stonefield and asked if your husband arrived safely, at what time, and in what circumstances he left?" It was barely a question. He had already assumed the answer.

"No ..." The word was no more than a whisper.

"What?"

"No," she repeated with despair, her eyes wide, blue-gray and burningly direct. "Angus's brother Caleb is everything he is not—violent, brutal, dangerous, an outcast even among the underworld along the river beyond Limehouse, where he lives." She gave a shuddering sigh. "I used to beg Angus not to keep seeing him, but in spite of everything Caleb did, he felt that he could not abandon him." A shadow crossed her face. "There is something very special about being a twin, I suppose. I confess, it is not something I understand." She shook her head a little, as if denying her own anguish. "Please, Mr. Monk, will you find out what happened to my husband for me? I ..." She bit her lip, but her eyes did not waver. "I shall need to know your terms in advance. My resources are limited."

"I will make inquiries, Mrs. Stonefield." He spoke before he considered the implications for his own financial status. "Then when I report their results to you, we can make arrangements accordingly. I shall need certain information from you in order to begin."

"Of course. I understand. I am sorry I do not have a picture of him to show you. He did not care to sit for a portrait." She smiled with a sudden tenderness that was desperate with pain. "I think he felt it a trifle vain." She took a deep breath and steadied herself. "He was tall, at least as tall as you are." She was concentrating fiercely, as if bitterly aware she might not see him again, and all too soon would she find his appearance fading from its present clarity in her mind. "His hair was dark, indeed his coloring was not unlike yours, except that his eyes were not gray, but a most beautiful shade of green. He had very good features, a strong nose and a generous mouth. He was quite gentle in manner, not at all arrogant, but yet no one ever supposed him to be a person with whom one might take liberties."

He was aware that already she spoke of him in the past. The room was full of her fear and the sense of grief to come. He considered asking her of Stonefield's business affairs, or the likelihood of his having another woman, but he doubted he would receive an answer from her which would be accurate enough to be of any value. It would only distress her unnecessarily. It would be better to seek some tangible evidence and form his own judgment.

He rose to his feet and she rose also, her face tight with apprehension, her chin high, ready to argue with him, plead if necessary.

"I shall begin inquiries, Mrs. Stonefield," he promised.

Immediately she relaxed, coming as close to a smile as she was capable in her present mind. "Thank you. . . ."

"If you will give me your address?" he asked.

She fished in her reticule and brought out two cards, offering them to him in her gloved hand. "I'm afraid I did not think of a letter of authority. . . ." She looked embarrassed. "Have you any paper?"

He went to the desk, opened it and took out a plain white sheet of notepaper, a pen, ink and blotting paper. He pulled out the chair where she might sit. While she was writing he glanced at the cards she had given him and saw that the home was on the borders of Mayfair, a very acceptable area for the gentry. The business was south of the river on the Waterloo Road on the edge of Lambeth.

She finished the letter, signed it, blotted it carefully and handed it to him, looking up at him anxiously while he read it.

"It is excellent, thank you." He folded it, reached for an envelope and placed it inside, to keep it from becoming soiled, then put it in his pocket.

She rose to her feet again. "When shall you begin?"

"Immediately," he replied. "There is no time to be lost. Mr. Stonefield may be in some danger or difficulty but still able to be rescued from it."

"Do you think so?" For a moment hope flared in her eyes, then reality returned, and with it renewed pain. She turned away to hide her emotion from him, to save them both embarrassment. "Thank you, Mr. Monk. I know you mean to offer me comfort." She went to the door, and he only just reached it in time to open it for her. "I shall await news." She went out and down the step into the street, then walked away, northwards, without looking back.

Monk closed the door and returned to his room. He put more coal on the fire, then sat down in his armchair and began to consider the problem and what he knew of it.

It was common enough for a man to desert his wife and children. The possibilities were endless, without even considering his having come to harm—let alone anything so bizarre and tragic as having been murdered by his own brother. Mrs. Stonefield had clearly wanted to believe that. Monk observed to himself that it was the solution least harmful to her. Without entirely dismissing it out of hand, he was inclined to relegate it to the bottom of the list of possibilities. The most obvious answers were that he had simply found his responsibilities overweighing him and run off, or that he had fallen in love with another woman and decided to live with her. The next most probable was some financial disaster, either already occurred or pending in the near future. He might have gambled and finally lost more than he could meet, or borrowed from a usurer and been unable to repay the interest, which would grow day by day. Monk had seen more than a few victims of such practice and he hated moneylenders with a cold and unremitting passion.

Stonefield might have made some enemy he had good reason to fear, or be the victim of blackmail for an indiscretion or even a crime. He might be fleeing the law for some misappropriation not yet uncovered, or any other offense, an accident or a sudden violence not so far traced to him.

He might have suffered an accident and be lying in hospital or in a workhouse somewhere, too ill to have sent his family word.

It was even conceivable that, like Monk himself, he had been struck on the head with a blow which had obliterated his memory.

He broke out in a prickle of sweat which a moment after was cold on his skin as he remembered waking up two years before in what he had taken to be a workhouse without the slightest idea who or where he was. His past had been an utter blank to him. Even his face in the glass had been unrecognizable.

Slowly he had pieced together fragments here and there, scenes of his youth, his journey south from Northumberland to London, probably when he was nineteen or twenty—roughly about the time of the accession of Queen Victoria, although he could not remember it. The coronation he knew only from pictures and other people's descriptions.

Even this much was deduced, because he supposed himself to be now in his early forties, and it was January 1859.

Of course, it was absurd to suppose Angus Stonefield was in a similar situation. Such things must happen exceedingly rarely. But then murder was fortunately not so common either. It was far more probably some sad but ordinary domestic circumstance or a financial disaster.

He always disliked having to tell a woman such a thing. In this case it would be harder than usual because already he had formed a certain respect for her. There was a femininity to her which was charming, and yet a defiant courage, and in all she had told him, in spite of her grief and thinly concealed desperation, there was no self-pity. She had asked for his professional services, not begged his compassion. If Angus Stonefield had left her for another woman, he was a man whose taste Monk did not understand, or share.

Still turning the matter over in his mind, he rose, stoked the fire and set up the guard, then put on his coat and hat and took a hansom cab south from his rooms in Fitzroy Street, down Tottenham Court Road, Charing Cross Road, then the Strand, right at Wellington Street and across Waterloo Bridge to the business address on the card Mrs. Stonefield had given him. He alighted, paid the driver and dismissed him. He turned to look at the building. The outside appeared prosperous, in a discreet fashion, either from old money so well known it had no need to advertise or money newly earned but with the tact to remain unostentatious.

He pushed the front door, which was open to the public, and was greeted in the room inside by a smart young clerk dressed in stiff wing collar, cutaway jacket and shining boots.

"Yes sir?" he inquired, summing up Monk's sartorial elegance and concluding he was a gentleman. "May I be of service?"

Monk was too proud to introduce himself as an agent of inquiry. It equated him with the policeman he had been until his irreparable quarrel with his superior, only now he had not the authority.

"Good morning," he replied. "Mrs. Stonefield has requested me to be of what assistance I may in contacting her husband since he left last Tuesday morning." He allowed the ghost of a smile to cross his face. "I hope she is mistaken, but she fears some harm may have come to him." As he spoke he produced the letter of authority.

The clerk accepted it, read it at a glance, and returned it to him. The anxiety which he had been holding in check now flooded his face and he looked at Monk almost pleadingly. "I wish we could help you, sir. Indeed, I wish with all my heart we knew where he was. We require him for the business. His presence is essential." His voice was rising in earnestness. "There are decisions to be made for which Mr. Arbuthnot and myself have neither the legal power nor the professional knowledge." He glanced around to make sure none of the three young ledger clerks were within earshot, and moved a step closer. "We are at our wits' end to know what to do next, or how to put people off any longer without their guessing that something is most seriously amiss. Business is most competitive, sir. Others will seize the chance to profit from our indecision." His face grew pinker and he bit his lip. "Do you think that he could have been kidnapped, sir?"

It was not among the possibilities that had occurred to Monk.

"It would be a most extreme step," he replied, watching the young man's face. He saw nothing in it but fear and sympathy. If he knew anything more, he was an actor to rival Henry Irving and had missed a career on the stage.

"Then he must have been taken ill," the clerk said with concern. "And is even now lying in some hospital, unable to contact us. He would never wittingly leave us in this way." He grew even pinker. "Nor his family either, of course! That I need hardly say." His expression indicated he knew he should have said it to begin with.

"Does he have business rivals who might think to profit if he were out of the way?" Monk asked, casting his eye discreetly around the tidy, well-furnished room with its desks and shelves of books and files of ledgers. The winter sun came in through high, narrow windows. He still thought a domestic answer more likely.

"Oh yes, sir," the clerk replied with assurance. "Mr. Stonefield is most successful, sir. A rare gift he has for knowing what will sell, and for precisely how much. Made a profit where quite a few others would have burned their fingers ... and did!" There was a lift of pride in his voice, then as he looked at Monk, a sudden anxiety. "But always strictly honest!" he added, regarding Monk gravely to make sure he understood that. "There's never been a whisper against him anywhere! Not in the City, not on the Exchange."

"The Stock Exchange?" Monk asked.

"Oh no, sir, the Corn Exchange."

He should have asked before he spoke.

"These rivals of Mr. Stonefield's," he said quickly, his voice harder. "Whose business in particular has he taken lately, or whose does he threaten?"

"Well ..." The clerk hesitated unhappily.

For a moment there was no sound but the scratching of pens and someone shifting his feet.

"I don't like to speak ill ..." the clerk resumed.

"If there is a possibility Mr. Stonefield has been kidnapped, then you will do him little service if you remain silent!" Monk snapped.

The clerk colored. "Yes. I understand. I'm sorry, sir. Mr. Marchmont, of Marchmont and Squires, lost out to him rather badly last month, but they are large enough they will ride that out." He thought hard. "Mr. Peabody, of Goodenough and Jones, took it very badly when we beat them to a very good price about six weeks ago. But the only person I know who really suffered was poor Mr. Niven. He is no longer in business, I am sorry to say. Took it like a gentleman, but very hard for him, it was, especially with him and Mr. Stonefield being acquaintances socially. Very sad." He shook his head very slightly. "But having said that, sir, I cannot imagine Mr. Niven wishing Mr. Stonefield any harm. He's not like that at all. Very decent sort of gentleman, just not as clever as Mr. Stonefield. Perhaps I shouldn't have said anything. It's . . . it's really very hard to know what to do for the best." He looked at Monk miserably, seeking some kind of indication.

"You have done quite the right thing," Monk assured him. "Without information we cannot even make a judgment, let alone pursue the best course." As he was speaking he was looking beyond the young man and around the offices. The place had every appearance of prosperity. Several clerks were busy with ledgers, accounts, business letters to other houses, possibly overseas as well. They were all smartly dressed with stiff white collars and tidy hair, and they looked diligent, and content enough in their work. Nothing was shabby or obviously mended. There was no air of discouragement; only anxiety, a discreet glance one to another.

He returned his attention to the immediate.

"When was the last occasion on which Mr. Stonefield came into the office?"

"Three days ago, sir. The morning of the last day in which"—he bit his lip—"on which he was seen." He eased his neck in his rather tight collar. "But you will have to ask Mr. Arbuthnot what transpired, and he is not here at present. I really do not feel able to tell you anything further. It is . . . well, company business, sir." He was apologetic and obviously uncomfortable, shifting his weight from one foot to the other.

Monk doubted it would have any relevance anyway, and was

quite content to leave it for the time being. But before he took his leave, he obtained the address of Mr. Titus Niven, now no longer in business because of the skill of Angus Stonefield.

Monk left the offices and walked briskly back along the Waterloo Road in the sharp wind.

It still remained the strongest possibility that the answer to Angus Stonefield's disappearance lay in his personal life, therefore it was necessary for Monk to learn as much about it as he was able. However, he had no possible grounds to call upon neighbors, still less to question them as to Stonefield's habits or his comings and goings. It would hardly be in the best interest of his client. Having her neighbors gossiping about the fact that her husband was missing, and she had called in a person to try to find him, was the very last thing she would wish.

But the fact that there was no crime—in fact, no acknowledged problem at all—was extremely restricting. The only course open to him in that direction would be to pursue servants' chatter from nearby houses. Servants frequently knew a great deal more than their masters or mistresses supposed. They were most often regarded in much the same light as a favorite piece of furniture, without which one would be lost but in front of which discretion was not a consideration.

He was approaching the river. It shone pale under the winter sky, the mist rising in wreaths, softening the dark shingles' edges and carrying the raw smell of sewage on the outgoing tide. Dark barges and ferries moved up and down. It was not the season for pleasure boats.

He wished he had John Evan with him, as he had had when he first returned to the police force after his accident, and before he had quarreled finally and irreparably with Runcorn, storming out the instant before Runcorn dismissed him. Evan, with his charm and gentleness of manner, was so much better at eliciting confidences from people. They forgot their natural reticence and shared their thoughts.

But Evan was still with the police, so Monk could not call upon him for help except when there was an investigation in which he too was involved and was prepared to disclose his information, at great risk to himself. Runcorn would never forgive such an act. He would see it as a personal and professional betrayal.

It had often crossed Monk's mind that he would like to offer Evan a position as his assistant in some future day when he earned sufficient to support a second person. But that was only a dream, and perhaps a foolish one. At present he did not always make enough even for himself. There were weeks when he was profoundly grateful for his patroness, Lady Callandra Daviot, who made up the difference in his income. All she asked in return was that he share with her all those cases which had elements of interest for her . . . and they were considerable. She was a woman of high intelligence and curiosity, decisive opinions, and a consuming and generally tolerant interest in human nature in all its manifestations. In the past, Monk had inquired into matters solely at her behest, when she felt that an injustice was threatened or had been done.

To begin with, he caught a cab to see Mrs. Stonefield in her own home, as he had said he would. It would give him a clearer impression of her, of the family's well-being, both financial and social, and—if he were perceptive enough—also of the relationships beneath the surface of what she had told him.

The house was on Upper George Street, on the corner of Seymour Place just east of the Edgware Road. It took him more than an hour in heavy traffic and a hard, soaking rain, from the far side of the river to arrive at the other side of Mayfair, alight, and pay the driver. It was nearly four o'clock, and the lamplighters were already out in the thickening dusk.

He turned his coat collar up and crossed the footpath to knock on the front door. At this hour any formal callers would have been and gone, if indeed she were receiving callers.

He shivered and turned to look back at the street. It was quiet and eminently respectable. Rows of similar windows looked out onto neat front gardens. Areaways were swept clean. Behind closed back gates would be cellar chutes for coal, dustbins, scrubbed scullery steps and back door entrances for tradesmen and deliveries.

Was this what Angus Stonefield wanted? Or had he become suffocated by its predictability and discretion? Had his soul yearned for something wilder, more exhilarating, something that challenged the mind and disturbed the heart? And had he been prepared to sacrifice safety, the warmth of family, as its price? Had he grown to loathe being known by his neighbors, relied upon by his dependents; every day, every year mapped out before him to a decent and uneventful old age?

Monk felt a sharp sadness that it was such a vivid possibility. Stonefield would not be the first man to have run away from the reality of love and its responsibilities, to grasp instead the illusion and excitement of lust and what might seem like freedom, only later to realize it was loneliness.

Another gust of rain soaked him just as he turned back to the door and it opened. The fair-haired parlormaid looked at him inquiringly.

"William Monk, to call upon Mrs. Stonefield," he announced, dropping his card on the tray she held. "I believe she is expecting me."

"Yes sir. If you care to wait in the morning room, I shall see if Mrs. Stonefield is at home," she replied, stepping back for him to enter.

Monk walked through the pleasant hall behind her to wait in the room which he was shown. It gave him an opportunity to glance around and make some estimate of Stonefield's character and circumstances—although if he were in difficulties, the front rooms where guests were received would be the last to show it. Monk had known families to live without heat, and eat little more than bread and gruel, and yet keep up the facade of prosperity the moment visitors called. Generosity, even extravagance, was displayed to foster the pretense. Sometimes it aroused his contempt for the ridiculousness of it. At others he was moved to a strange, hurting pity that they found it necessary, that they believed their worth to their friends lay in such things.

He stood in the small, tidy room in which the maid had left him, and looked around it. To the outward eye it presented every sign of comfort and good taste. It was a little overcrowded, but that was the fashion, and there was no fire lit, in spite of the weather.

The furniture was solid and the upholstery of good quality and, as far as he could see, not overly worn. He looked more closely at the antimacassars on the backs of the chairs, but they were clean and un-faded or rubbed. The gas mantles on the walls were immaculate, the curtains unfaded in the folds. The red-and-cream Turkey carpet was only slightly worn in a passage from doorway to hearth. There were no darker patches on the wallpaper to indicate a picture missing. The fine china and glass ornaments were unchipped. He could see no hairline cracks carefully glued together. Everything was of good qual-ity and individual taste. It reaffirmed the impression of Genevieve Stonefield he had already formed.

He was about to begin reading the titles of the books in the oak case when he was interrupted by the return of the maid to conduct him to the withdrawing room.

He had intended to make a discreet assessment of that room also, but as soon as he was through the doorway his entire attention was taken by Genevieve Stonefield herself. She was dressed in a smoky blue gown with darker stripes of velvet around the skirt. Perhaps it was an obvious choice for a woman of her warm skin and rich hair, but nonetheless, it was extraordinarily flattering. She was not lovely in the classical mold, and certainly she had not the pallor and child-like daintiness which was currently admired. There was an earthy, more immediate quality to her, as if in other circumstances she would have been full of laughter, imagination, even hunger. Her features were those of a woman who threw herself wholeheartedly into what-ever she espoused. Monk could not imagine what sort of a man Angus Stonefield could be to have won her love in the first place and then to have left her willingly. It precluded his being any kind of coward, or a retreater from life.

The room and its furnishings dissolved into irrelevance.

"Mr. Monk," she said eagerly. "Please do sit down. Thank you, Janet." She lifted one hand in dismissal of the maid. "If anyone else should call, I am not at home."

"Yes ma'am." Janet went out obediently, closing the door behind her.

As soon as they were alone, Genevieve turned to Monk, then realized it was far too soon for him to have learned anything. She attempted to disguise her disappointment and her foolishness for having allowed hope in the first place.

He wanted to tell her that his initial suspicions seemed less and less likely, but to do so he would have to tell her what they were, and he was not prepared to do that.

"I have been to Mr. Stonefield's place of business," he began. "Only briefly, as yet, but I can see nothing out of order. I shall return when Mr. Arbuthnot is present and see what more he can tell me."

"I doubt there will be anything," she said sadly. "Poor Mr. Arbuthnot is as confused as I. Of course, he does not know what I do of Caleb." Her mouth tightened, and she turned half away towards the very small fire glimmering in the hearth. "It is something I prefer not to make public, unless I am left no alternative whatever. One does not like to air one's family tragedies for all to know. Poor Angus tried to keep it as discreet as he could, and I don't believe his friends or colleagues were aware." She lifted one shoulder very slightly in a gesture of despair. "It is most embarrassing that one's relatives are . . . criminal." She looked back at him as if it had been a kind of relief to her to speak the truth aloud. Perhaps she saw a shred of incredulity in his eyes.

"I do not blame you for finding it hard to believe, Mr. Monk, that two brothers could be so different. I found it hard myself. I used to fear Angus had conceived some jealousy or fancy which made him see his brother in such a light. But a little investigation will show you that far from painting Caleb black, Angus was, if anything, too kind in his judgment."

He did not doubt her sincerity, but he still held his reservations as to what Caleb Stonefield might really be like ... probably no more than a rake or a gambler, someone Angus did not wish to bring to his charming and comfortable home, perhaps least of all leave in the company of his wife. If Caleb were a womanizer, he could never resist trying to awaken in this woman the fires which might so easily lie nascent beneath her proper exterior. Monk himself could feel the temptation. There was a richness in her mouth, a daring in her eyes, and strength in the angle at which she carried her head.

"Why do you believe your brother-in-law might have harmed your husband, Mrs. Stonefield?" he said aloud. "After all the long years of relationship between them, and your husband's loyalty, why should he now hate so deeply as to commit violence against him? What has changed?"

"Nothing that I know," she said unhappily, staring now at the fire. There was no doubt in her voice, no lessening of the emotion.

"Did your husband threaten him in any way, financially or profes-sionally?" Monk went on. "Is it likely that he became aware of some misdemeanor, or even crime, that Caleb may have been involved with? And if he did, would he have reported it?"

Her eyes flickered up quickly, meeting his with sudden light. "I don't know, Mr. Monk. You must think me very vague, and most un-charitable to a man I don't even know. Of course what you suggest is possible. Caleb lives in a way which would make it likely he is in-volved in many crimes. But it is not that which causes my fear."

Had she said anything else he would have known she lied. He had seen the spark of realization in her eyes, and the doubt.

"What is it?" he said with a gentleness unusual to him.

"I wish I could tell you more precisely," she answered with a tiny, self-deprecating smile. Then she looked up at him and her expression was startlingly intense. "My husband was not a cowardly man, Mr.

Monk, neither morally nor physically, but he lived in dread of his brother. For all that he pitied him, and tried all the years I have known him to bridge the gulf between them, he was deeply afraid."

Monk waited for her to continue.

She looked into the distances within her own mind. "I have seen the change come over his face when he spoke of Caleb, how his eyes darkened and his mouth showed lines of pain." She took a deep breath and he could see that she was shaking very slightly, as if mastering a deep shock within herself. "I am not exaggerating, Mr. Monk. Please believe me, Caleb is both evil and dangerous. My worst fear is that his hatred has finally driven him mad and he has killed Angus. Of course, I hope he is alive . . . and yet I am terrified it is already too late. My heart tells me one thing, and my mind another." At last she looked at him, her eyes wide and direct. "I need to know. Please leave no effort untried for as long as I have any means with which to recompense you. For my children's sake, as well as my own, I have to know what has happened to Angus." She stopped. She would not repeat herself or beg for pity beyond his labor that she could hire. She stood very straight in the room he still merely observed only as a kind of elegance behind her. He was unaware even of the ash settling in the fire.

Not only for her, but for the man whose wife and home this was, he had no hesitation in accepting the task wholeheartedly.

"I will do everything in my power, Mrs. Stonefield, I promise you," he answered. "May I continue by speaking to some of your servants who may have noticed letters or callers?"

She looked puzzled, and a flicker of disillusion shadowed her eyes.

"How will that help?"

"It may not," he conceded. "But without some kind of indication that some of the more obvious answers are untrue, I cannot request the help I shall need from the River Police to conduct a search of the docks or of the quarter where you say Caleb lives. If he has indeed killed his brother, it will not be easy to prove."

"Oh . . ." She let out her breath in a jerky little sigh. "Of course." She was very pale. "I had not thought of that. I'm sorry, Mr. Monk. I shall not interfere again. Whom would you like to see first?"

He spent the rest of the afternoon and early evening questioning the staff from the butler and the cook through to the between-maid and the bootboy, and learned nothing to contradict his first impression that Angus Stonefield was a diligent and prosperous man of excellent taste and very ordinary habits, with a wife to whom he was devoted, and five children ranging in age from three to thirteen years.

The butler had heard of the brother, Caleb, but had never seen him. He knew only that Mr. Stonefield would go quite regularly to the East End to meet with him, that he seemed nervous and unhappy prior to going and sad on his return. On almost every occasion he had sustained both personal injury and severe damage to his clothes, sometimes beyond repair. Mr. Stonefield had refused to call a doctor, insisting that the matter not be reported, and Mrs. Stonefield had cared for him herself. None of it helped to explain where Angus Stonefield was now or what had happened to him. Even his effects, and the few letters in the top drawer of his tallboy, were precise, each in its place, and exactly what Monk would have expected.

"Did you learn anything?" Genevieve asked when he returned to the withdrawing room to take his leave.

He would have disliked disappointing her, but there was no hope in her face.

"No," he confessed. "It was simply an avenue I dared not leave unexplored."

She looked down at her hands, twisting together in front of her dress, the only betrayal of the emotion within her.

"I received a letter today from Angus's guardian, Lord Ravensbrook, offering to assist us until we can . . . until . . . You might care to see if he can . . . help . . . with information, I mean." She looked up at him. "I have written his address for you. I am sure he will receive you whenever you care to call."

"You are going to accept his offer?" he said urgently.

The moment he asked he saw her face shadow, and knew he had been intrusive. It was not his concern. She had promised to pay him, and he wondered now if she assumed that concern for money was the reason he had asked.

"No," she said, before he could apologize and find some excuse to moderate his discourtesy. "I would very much prefer not to be"—she hesitated—"indebted to him, if it can be avoided. He is a good man, of course!" She went on quickly. "He raised Angus and Caleb when their own parents died. They are only distant relatives. He had no real obligation, but he gave them every opportunity, as if they were his own. His first wife died very young. He has married again now. I am sure he would give you any assistance he can."

"Thank you," he accepted, grateful that she had apparently taken no more offense at his clumsiness. "As soon as I learn anything, I promise I will let you know."

"I am most obliged," she said quietly. She seemed about to add something, then changed her mind. He wondered if it had been about the depth of her fears for her husband, or the urgency with which she needed an answer. "Good evening, Mr. Monk."


It was not a courteous time to call upon Lord and Lady Ravensbrook, but Genevieve's plight struck deep into him, and he was perfectly prepared to disturb them at dinner, or draw them away from guests if need be, and offer the truth as explanation.

As it was, when the hansom dropped him at Ravensbrook House in the rain and he splashed across the footpath through the arc of the streetlight and up the marble steps, he was prepared for whatever battle faced him. But his forethought proved unnecessary. The door was opened by a footman in livery who accepted his card and the letter Genevieve had given him, leaving him in the hall while he went to present them to his master.

Ravensbrook House was magnificent. Monk judged it to date back to Queen Anne, a far more elegant period of architecture than that of the present queen. Here nothing was overcrowded. Ornamentation was simple, giving an air of space and perfect proportion. There were rather good portraits, presumably of the past Ravensbrooks, on three of the four walls. They all either had been of handsome appearance or had been highly flattered by the various artists.

The staircase was gray marble, like the front steps, and swept in a curve up the right-hand wall to a landing balustraded in the same stone. A chandelier of at least eighty candles illuminated the whole, and hothouse hyacinths flowered in a blue delft bowl, scenting the air.

It occurred to Monk that perhaps Angus Stonefield had been given an excellent start in his business, both financially and socially. It was a peculiar and rather harsh pride of Genevieve's that would not allow her to accept help now, at least for her children's sake, if not her own. Or did she really believe, in spite of what she said, that Angus would somehow return?

The footman came back, showing only the mildest surprise by the lifting of an eyebrow, and conducted Monk to the library. Lord Ravensbrook awaited him, apparently having left his dinner to receive this unexpected guest.

The door closed behind the retreating footman.

"I apologize, my lord, for the unseemliness of the hour," Monk said immediately.

Ravensbrook dismissed it with a wave of his hand. He was a tall man, perhaps an inch or two taller than Monk, and extremely handsome. His face was lean and narrow, but with fine, dark eyes, a long nose and a chiseled mouth. Apart from his features, there was a quickness of intelligence in him, lines of wit and laughter around his mouth and a hint of temper between his brows. It was the face of a proud man of unusual charm and, Monk guessed, a considerable ability to command others.

However, on this occasion he made no attempt to impress.

"I gather from Mrs. Stonefield's letter that she has sought your help to discover what has happened." He made it a statement, not a question. "I admit, I am close to my wits' end to think what can have befallen him, and would be glad of any assistance you can give."

"Thank you, my lord," Monk acknowledged. "I have been to his offices and they appear to know nothing, although I have not yet been able to question Mr. Arbuthnot, whom I am told is in charge and would have the authority to speak more frankly to me. However, if there is any financial hardship, it is certainly not evident—"

Ravensbrook's black eyebrows rose fractionally. "Financial hardship? Yes—I suppose you have to consider that. To one who does not know Angus, it would seem a possibility. However . . ." He turned very slightly, indicating where Monk might sit, and walked over to the mantelshelf, where two exquisite Georgian silver candlesticks sat on either end and an Irish crystal vase a little to the left of center held a spray of golden winter jasmine. "As Mrs. Stonefield will have told you," he continued, "I have known Angus since he was a child. He was five when his parents died. He has always been ambitious, and prudent, and he had the skill to bring dreams into reality. He has never been one to seek shortcuts to success, or easy paths. He would not have gambled."

He turned to face Monk, his eyes very dark, absolutely level. "He was of a nature which hated risks, and was totally honest down to the slightest detail. I happen to know that his business is flourishing. Of course, if you wish to satisfy yourself in the matter, it will be perfectly possible for you to examine the accounts, but it will be a waste of time, as far as finding him is concerned."

His voice was tight with emotion, but his expression was unreadable. "Mr. Monk, it is of the utmost urgency that you learn the truth, whatever it may be. The business requires his presence, his judgments." He took a deep breath. Behind him the fire roared up the chimney. "When it becomes known that he is missing, not merely on some journey, then confidence will crumble. For his family's sake, if something . . . appalling has happened to him, the business must be sold or a new manager appointed before it is known, and prestige and the value of his reputation are squandered. I have already offered Genevieve and her children my protection, here in my home, as I did Angus before them, but so far she has declined. But the time will come, and quite shortly, when she can no longer manage."

Monk made a rapid decision as to whether he should be candid. He regarded Ravensbrook's lean, intelligent face, the sophisticated taste in the room, the slight drawl in his voice, the steadiness of his gaze.

"After financial difficulty, the other most obvious possibility is another woman," he said aloud.

"Of course," Ravensbrook agreed with a slight downturning of his lips and the barest flicker of distaste. "You have to consider it, but you have met Mrs. Stonefield. She is not a woman a man would leave out of boredom. I rather wish I could believe it was something . . . forgive me"—a muscle twitched in his jaw—"so pedestrian. Then you could find him, bring him to his senses, and return him home. It would be most unpleasant, but in the end it would make no permanent difference, except perhaps to his wife's regard for him. But she is a sensible woman. She would get over it. And of course she would be discreet. No one else need know."

"But you think it unlikely, sir?" Monk was not surprised. He found it less easy to believe than he would were it any other woman than Genevieve Stonefield. But then he did not know her. The warmth and the imagination which seemed to lie behind her eyes might be an illusion. And perhaps Angus had gone seeking the reality.

Ravensbrook shifted his weight. The heart of the fire fell in with a shower of sparks and the heat from it grew more intense. "I do. Let me be frank, Mr. Monk. This is not a time for euphemisms. I fear some serious harm has come to him. He has long been in the habit of going to the most insalubrious parts of the East End of the city, down by the docks . . . Ide, Limehouse and Blackwall regions. If he has been attacked and robbed he may be lying injured, insensible or worse." His voice dropped. "It will take all your skill to find him." He moved a step away from the fire, but still did not invite Monk to sit, nor did he sit himself.

"Mrs. Stonefield says that he goes to visit his twin brother, Caleb," Monk continued, "who she says is of a totally different nature, and both hates him and is uncontrollably jealous. She believes that he may have murdered her husband." He watched Ravensbrook's face intensely. He saw a fear cross it, and deep distress. He could not believe it was feigned.

"I deeply regret having to admit, Mr. Monk, that that is so. I have no reason to believe there is any other cause which takes Angus to the slums of the dockside. I have long begged him to desist, and leave Caleb to his own devices. It is quite futile to hope to change him. He hates Angus for his success, but he has no wish to be like him, only to have the profits of his labor. Angus's affection and loyalty towards him is in no way returned." He drew in his breath and let it out in a slow sigh. "But there is something in Angus which will not let go."

It was a painful subject. It must be especially bitter for a man who had watched the two brothers since childhood, but he did not equivocate or make excuses, and Monk admired him for that. It must have taken an iron self-discipline not to indulge in anger or a sense of injustice now.

"Do you believe Mrs. Stonefield is right, and Caleb could have killed Angus, either intentionally or by accident in a struggle?"

Ravensbrook met his eyes with a long, level stare.

"Yes," he said quietly. "I am afraid I believe it is possible." His lips tightened. "Of course, I should prefer to think it is an accident, but murder is also believable. I am sorry, Mr. Monk. It is a bitter case we have given you, and one which may take you into some personal danger. You will not catch Caleb easily." There was a harsh twist of his mouth, less than a smile. "Nor will you easily prove what has happened. Whatever help I can be, you have but to call upon me."

Monk was about to thank him when there was a light rap on the door.

"Come!" Ravensbrook said with surprise.

The door opened and a woman of extraordinary presence entered. She was of little more than average height, though her bearing made her seem taller. But it was her face which commanded Monk's attention. She had high, wide cheekbones, a short, jutting aquiline nose and a wide, beautifully shaped mouth. She was not traditionally lovely, yet the longer he looked at her, the more she pleased him, because of the balance and honesty in her. She was every bit as candid as Genevieve, and more commanding. It was the face of a woman born to power.

Ravensbrook lifted his hand very slightly.

"My dear, this is Mr. Monk, whom Genevieve has engaged to help us find out—what has happened to poor Angus." From the way he touched her and his expression as he regarded her, it was unnecessary to announce her identity.

"How do you do, Lady Ravensbrook." Monk bowed very slightly. It was not something he normally did, but it came to him without thought when he spoke to her.

"I am very glad." She regarded Monk with interest. "It is time something was done. I should like to think otherwise, but I know Caleb may be at the root of it. I am sorry, Mr. Monk, we have asked of you a most unpleasant task. Caleb is a violent man, and will not welcome any attention from the police, or any other authority. And as you may already be aware, there is also a serious outbreak of typhoid fever in the south area of Limehouse at the moment. We are most grateful that you should have accepted the case."

She turned to her husband. "Milo, I think we should offer to meet Mr. Monk's expenses, rather than allow Genevieve to do it.

She is hardly in a position . . . The estate will be frozen, she will have only whatever funds—"

"Of course." He stopped her with a gesture. To speak of such things was indelicate in front of a hired person. He returned his attention to Monk. "Naturally we shall do so. If you submit whatever accounts you give, we shall see that they are met. Is there anything else we can do?"

"Do you have a likeness of Mr. Stonefield?"

Lady Ravensbrook frowned, thinking on the subject.

"No," Ravensbrook replied immediately. "Unfortunately not. Childhood likenesses would be of little use, and we have not seen Caleb in fifteen years or more. Angus did not care to have pictures made of him. He considered it vain, and always preferred to have such portraits as there were made of Genevieve or the children. He meant to have one done one day, but now it seems he may have left it too late. I'm sorry."

"I can make a sketch for you," Lady Ravensbrook offered quickly, then the color flushed up her cheeks. "It would not be of any artistic merit, but it would give you some notion of his appearance."

"Thank you," Monk accepted before Ravensbrook could interpose any objection. "That would be extremely helpful. If I am to trace his movements, it would make it immeasurably easier."

She went to the bureau over at the far side of the room, opened it and took out a pencil and a sheet of notepaper, then sat down to draw. After about five minutes, during which time both Monk and Ravensbrook remained in silence, she returned and proffered it to Monk.

He took it and looked at it, then stared more closely with surprise and considerable interest. It was not the rough, tentative impression he had expected, but a face which leaped out at him, executed in bold lines. The nose was long and straight, the brows winged, the eyes narrow but bright with intelligence. The jaw was broad under the ears, but going to a pointed chin, the mouth wide, poised between humor and gravity. Suddenly Angus Stonefield was real, a man of flesh and blood, of dreams and passions, someone he would grieve to find destroyed in a wanton act of violence and thrown into some dockyard sewer or passageway to the river.

"Thank you," he said softly. "I shall begin again at first light, tomorrow. Good night my lady, my lord."

# CHAPTER
# TWO

———

Monk spent a restless night and was up early the next morning to resume his search for Angus Stonefield, although he realized grimly
that he had already assumed Genevieve was right in her fears, and
what he was truly seeking was proof of his death. But whatever he
found, it was unlikely to bring her any happiness. If Angus had absconded with money, or another woman, that would not only rob her
of the future but, in a sense, of the past as well, of all that was good
and she had believed to be true.

The hansom set him down on the Waterloo Road.

The rain had stopped and it was a brisk, chilly day with fast
scudding clouds. A cutting east wind came up from the river with a
smell of salt from the incoming tide, and the soot and smoke of
countless chimneys. He stepped smartly out of the way of a carriage
and leaped for the footpath.

He pulled his coat collar a little higher and strode out towards
Angus Stonefield's place of business. The domestic servants yesterday
evening had told him nothing of use. No one had noticed any behavior out of the very ordinary routine of rising at seven and taking
breakfast with his wife while his children ate in the nursery. After
reading the newspaper, and any post that may have been delivered,
he left in sufficient time to arrive at his office by half past eight. He
did not keep a carriage but traveled by hansom cab.

The day of his disappearance he had followed exactly that pattern. The morning's post had contained a couple of small household

bills, an invitation, and a polite letter from an acquaintance. No one had called at the house other than the usual tradesmen and a woman friend of Genevieve's who came for afternoon tea.

Monk arrived at Stonefield's offices too early, and was obliged to wait a quarter of an hour before Mr. Arbuthnot appeared walking along the pavement from the north, carrying an umbrella in his hand and looking hurried and unhappy. He was a small man with thick gray hair and a gray, immaculately trimmed mustache.

Monk introduced himself.

"Ah!" Arbuthnot said anxiously. "Yes. I suppose it was inevitable." He took out a key from the pocket of his coat and inserted it into the outer door. He turned it with some effort.

"You believe so?" Monk said with some surprise. "You foresaw such a thing?"

Arbuthnot pushed the door open.

"Well, something has to be done," he said sadly. "We can't go on like this. Do come in. Allow me to close this wretched door."

"It needs oiling," Monk observed, realizing Arbuthnot was referring to his own inquiries as inevitable, not his employer's disappearance.

"Yes, yes," Arbuthnot agreed. "I keep telling Jenkins to do it, but he doesn't listen." He led the way into the main office, empty still, and dark before the lamps were lit, the gray light through the windows being inadequate to work by.

Monk followed him through the glass-paned doors and into his own more comfortably furnished room. With a murmur of apology Arbuthnot bent and put a match to the fire, already carefully laid in the hearth, then let out a sigh of satisfaction as the flames took hold. He lit the lamps also, then took off his coat and invited Monk to do the same.

"What can I tell you that may be of service?" he said, knitting his brows together unhappily. "I have no idea what has happened, or I should already have told the authorities, and we should not now be in this terrible position."

Monk sat in the rather uncomfortable upright chair opposite him. "I presume you have checked the accounts, Mr. Arbuthnot, and any monies which may be kept here?"

"This is really very unpleasant, sir," Arbuthnot said in a tight, quiet voice. "But yes, I felt obliged to do that, even though I was quite certain I should find them in perfect order."

"And did you?" Monk pressed.

"Indeed, sir, to the farthing. Everything is accounted for and as it should be." He did not hesitate, nor did his eyes waver. Perhaps it was his perfect steadiness which made Monk believe there was something else to add, some qualification.

"What time did Mr. Stonefield arrive that morning?" he asked. "Perhaps you would tell me everything you recall of that day, in the order it happened."

"Yes . . . er, of course." Arbuthnot shivered a little and turned aside to pick up the poker from the hearth and prod at the fire. He continued with his back to Monk. "He arrived at quarter to nine, as usual. The first delivery of post was already here. He took it into his office and read it—"

"Do you know what was in it?" Monk interrupted.

Arbuthnot finished his administrations to the fire and laid the poker back on its rest. "Orders, delivery notices, advice of shipments, an application for a position as clerk." He sighed. "A very promising young man, but if Mr. Stonefield does not return, I doubt we should be able to keep those we have, much less employ additional staff."

"And that was all? Are you quite sure?" Monk avoided the subject of Stonefield's return and the dismissing of staff. There was nothing helpful he could say.

"Yes, I am," Arbuthnot said firmly. "I asked young Barton about it, and he remembered precisely. You can ask him yourself if you wish, but there was nothing in the post to occasion Mr. Stonefield's departure, of that I am quite certain."

"Visitors?" Monk asked, watching Arbuthnot's face.

"Ah . . ." He hesitated. "Yes."

Monk looked at him steadily. Arbuthnot was distinctly uncomfortable, but Monk had no way of knowing whether it was embarrassment, guilt, or just the general distress of talking about someone he had liked and respected and who was in all probability now dead. And, of course, if the business had to be sold or closed down, he too would lose his livelihood.

"Who?" Monk prompted him.

Arbuthnot gazed at the floor between them.

"Mr. Niven. He's in a similar line of trade himself. At least . . . he . . . he was."

"And now?"

Arbuthnot took a deep breath. "I fear he is on hard times."

"Why did he come here? I understood from your clerk when I was here yesterday that it was largely Mr. Stonefield's superior skill which was responsible for his misfortune."

Arbuthnot looked up quickly, his long face full of reproach. "If you think Mr. Stonefield did him out of business on purpose, sir, you are quite wrong, quite wrong indeed! It was never his intention at all. It's just that you have to do the best you can if you want to survive yourself. And Mr. Stonefield was quicker in his judgment, and more accurate. Never exactly took chances"—he shook his head—"if you understand me? But he was very diligent in his studies of trends, and well liked in the business. People trusted him when they might not someone else." There was a furrow of concern between his brows and he searched Monk's face to be certain he took his meaning exactly.

Was his scrupulous honesty a safeguarding of his position in case Stonefield should return after all, or a protection for Niven for any of a dozen reasons, including some nature of collusion?

"Why did Mr. Niven come?" Monk repeated. "How was he dressed? What was his demeanor?" As Arbuthnot hesitated again, he became impatient. "If you wish me to have any chance whatever of finding Mr. Stonefield, you must tell me the exact truth!"

Arbuthnot caught the hard edge of Monk's voice, and his prevarication dropped like a mask to reveal acute pity and discomfort.

"He came to see if we could put any work his way, sir. I'm afraid things are most difficult for him. He knew Mr. Stonefield would help him if he could, but I'm afraid there was nothing at present. He did give him a letter of commendation for his honesty and diligence, though, in case that might be of use to him." He swallowed with an effort.

"And his demeanor?" Monk insisted.

"Distressed," Arbuthnot said quietly. "At the end of his strength, poor man." His eyes flicked up at Monk's again. "But a complete gentleman, sir. Never for a moment did he indulge in self-pity or anger against Mr. Stonefield. The simple truth is he made an error of judgment in trade which Mr. Stonefield avoided, and at a juncture in the ebb and flow of business when it cost him very dear. He understood that, I believe, and took it like a man."

Monk was inclined to believe him, but he would still see Titus Niven for himself.

"Was he the only visitor?" he asked.

Arbuthnot colored painfully and took several moments to compose his answer. His hands were clenched together in front of him, and he looked anywhere but at Monk's eyes.

"No, sir. There was also a lady . . . at least, a female person. I don't know how to describe her. . . ."

"Honestly!" Monk said tersely.

Arbuthnot drew in his breath, then let it out again.

Monk waited.

Arbuthnot took him very literally, as if it were an escape from expressing a more personal judgment.

"Ordinary sort of height, a trifle thin maybe, but that's a matter of opinion I suppose. Quite well built, really, considering where she came from—"

"Where did she come from?" Monk interrupted. The man was rambling.

"Oh, Limehouse way, I should think, from her speech." Unconsciously Arbuthnot was widening his nostrils and tightening his lips, as though he smelled something distasteful. But then if he were correct and she had come from the slums of the East End dockside, he may well have. The damp overcrowded rooms, the open middens, and the sewage from the river made any alternative impossible.

"Handsome," Arbuthnot said sadly. "At least nature gave her that, even if she did her best to hide it with paint and garish clothes. Very immodest."

"A prostitute?" Monk said bluntly.

Arbuthnot winced. "I have no idea. She said nothing to indicate so."

"What did she say? For heaven's sake, man, don't make me draw answers from you like teeth! Who was she and what did she want? Not to buy or sell corn futures!"

"Of course not!" Arbuthnot blushed furiously. "She asked for Mr. Stonefield, and when I informed him of her presence, he saw her immediately." He took another deep breath. "She had been here before. Twice, that I am aware of. She gave her name as Selina, just that, no surname."

"Thank you. What did Mr. Stonefield say about her? Did he explain her presence?"

Arbuthnot's eyes widened. "No, sir. It was not our business to inquire into who she was."

"And he felt no wish to tell you?" Monk let his surprise show. "Who did you suppose her to be? Don't say you did not think of it."

"Well, yes," Arbuthnot admitted. "Naturally we did wonder who she was. I assumed it was something to do with his brother, since as you observe, it could not be business."

The first flush of fire settled down now that the kindling was burned, and Arbuthnot put more coal on.

"What was Mr. Stonefield's manner after she left?" Monk pursued.

"Disturbed. He was somewhat agitated," Arbuthnot answered unhappily. "He withdrew what money there was in the safe—five pounds, twelve shillings and sixpence. He signed a receipt for it, and then he left."

"How long after Selina was this?"

"As near as I can remember, about ten or fifteen minutes."

"Did he say where he was going, or when he expected to return?" He watched Arbuthnot closely.

"No, sir." Arbuthnot shook his head slowly, his eyes sad and anxious. "He said some urgent matter needed his attention, and I should see Mr. Hurley in his stead. Mr. Hurley was a broker who was expected that afternoon. I assumed he thought he might be out all day, but I fully expected him the following morning. He gave no instructions for the next day, and there were most important matters to attend to. He would not have forgotten." Suddenly his face filled with grief and an agonizing fear and bewilderment, and Monk realized with a jolt how Arbuthnot's own world had been damaged by Stonefield's disappearance. One day everything had been safe and assured, predictable, if a little pedestrian. The next it was overturned, filled with mystery. Even his livelihood and perhaps his home were jeopardized. There was uncertainty in every direction. It was he who would have to tell Genevieve that they could no longer continue, and then he would have to dismiss all the rest of the staff and try to wind up the company and salvage what was left, pay the debts and leave a name of honor behind, if little else.

Monk searched his mind for something comforting or helpful to say, and found nothing.

"What time did he leave, as closely as you can recall?" he asked. The question was dry and literal, reflecting nothing of what he felt.

"About half past ten," Arbuthnot said bleakly, his mild eyes reflecting a dislike Monk understood only too easily.

"Do you know how?"

Arbuthnot stared at him. "I beg your pardon?"

"Do you know how?" Monk repeated. "If I am to trace him, it

would be helpful to know if he went on foot or took a hansom, what he was wearing, if he turned left or right upon leaving . . ."

"I see, yes, I see." Arbuthnot looked relieved. "Of course. I beg your pardon. I misunderstood you. He was wearing an overcoat and carrying an umbrella. It was a most inclement day. He always wore a hat, naturally, a black high hat. He took a hansom, down towards the Waterloo Bridge." He searched Monk's face. "Do you think you have some chance of finding him?"

A lie sprang to Monk's mind. It would have been easier. He would have liked to leave him with hope, but habit was too strong.

"Not a great deal. But I may learn what became of him, which will be of practical use to Mrs. Stonefield, though of little comfort. I am sorry."

A succession of emotions played across Arbuthnot's face—pain, resignation, pity, ending in a kind of grudging respect.

"Thank you for your candor, sir. If there is anything else I can do to be of assistance, you have but to inform me." He rose to his feet. "Now there is a great deal I must attend to." He gulped and coughed. "Just in case Mr. Stonefield should return, things must be kept going. . . ."

Monk nodded and said nothing. He stood up and put on his coat. Arbuthnot showed him out through the office, now filled with clerks busy with letters, ledgers, and messages. The room was brightly lit, every lamp burning, neat heads bent over quills, ink and paper. There was no sound but the scratching of nibs and the gentle hissing of the gas. No one looked up as he passed, but he knew there would be whispers and the exchanging of glances the moment he was gone.

Monk assumed Stonefield had gone to the East End in answer to some message either directly from Caleb or at least concerning him. There was no other explanation suggested. It did cross his mind as he went down the steps into the windy street, fastening his coat again, that the woman, Selina, might have some relationship with Stonefield which had nothing to do with Caleb. Some eminently respectable men with faultless domestic lives still had a taste for the rougher charms of street women, and kept a second establishment quite separate from, and unknown to, the first. He discounted it because he did not believe Stonefield would have been rash enough to allow such a woman, if she existed, to know of his business address. It would be absurdly dangerous and completely unnecessary. Such arrangements survived only if total secrecy were observed.

He walked briskly down as far as the bridge. Perhaps it was unprofessional, but he believed Genevieve that Angus Stonefield had gone to see his brother and that this time the quarrel between them had ended in violence which had either injured Angus so seriously he had been unable to return home, or even to send a message, or else he was dead, and the best Monk could do would be to find proof of it adequate to entitle his widow to his estate.

He must begin by finding the cabby who had picked Angus up on the morning he disappeared. It would most probably be one from the nearest stables; if not, he would move outward from there.

Actually it took him five cold and exhausting hours, and more than one false trail, before he was certain he had the man. He caught up with him at mid-afternoon, in Stamford Street, near the river. He was standing over a brazier, thawing out his fingers and shifting from one foot to the other, trying to keep warm. Behind him, his horse was snorting breath into the cold air, waiting impatiently, head down, for the next fare and the chance of movement.

"Goin' somewhere, guv?" the cabby asked hopefully.

"Depends," Monk replied, stopping beside him. "Did you pick up a fare on the Waterloo Road, about half past ten in the morning, last Tuesday, and take him probably east? Tall, dark gentleman with an overcoat, high hat and an umbrella." He showed him Lady Ravensbrook's drawing.

"Wot's it to yer if I did?" the cabby asked guardedly.

"Hot cup of tea laced with something stronger, and a fare to wherever you set him off," Monk replied. "And a great deal of unpleasantness if you lie to me."

The cabby swiveled around from the brazier and eyed Monk narrowly.

"Well now, if it in't Inspector Monk," he said with surprise. "Left the rozzers, 'ave we? 'Eard about that." Neither his voice nor his face gave any indication as to his feelings on the subject.

It was a sore one to Monk. His departure from the police force had been forced upon him by that final quarrel with Runcorn. The fact that he had been proved right and Runcorn wrong had helped nothing. With no livelihood anymore, he had been obliged to take up private inquiries, since detection was the only marketable skill he possessed. But he no longer had either the authority of the police force nor the facilities of its vast network and specialist abilities, as the cabby had so pertinently reminded him.

"Well, why d'yer want the poor geezer as I took, then? Wot's 'e done? Took the funds with 'im, did 'e?" the cabby asked. "An' if 'e did, why do you care?"

"No, he didn't," Monk said truthfully. "He's missing. His wife is afraid some harm may have befallen him."

"Likely gorn off with some tart or other, stupid sod," the cabby said dismissively. "Gorn private then, 'ave yer? Chasin' runaway 'usbands for women as 'ave lorst 'em." He grinned, showing gapped teeth. "Bit of a comedown for yer, in't it—Hinspector Monk?"

"Warmer than driving a cab!" Monk snapped, then remembered he needed the man's goodwill. The words choked in his throat to be civil. "Sometimes," he added between clenched jaws.

"Well now, Mr. Monk." The cabby sniffed and wiped his nose on his sleeve, looking at Monk maliciously. "If yer asks me, polite like, I might tell yer w'ere I took 'im. Mind I want me cup of char as well, an' me drop o' brandy in it. Don't want no cheap gin. An' I can tell the diff'rence, so don't go fobbin' me orff."

"How shall I know if you're telling me the truth?" Monk asked bluntly.

"Yer won't," the cabby said with satisfaction. " 'Ceptin' I don't suppose as yer've changed all that. Don't want yer on my tail fer ever more. Right narsty yer can be if'n yer crorssed, an' no mistake. Best suits me if yer pays me fair an I tells yer fair."

"Good." Monk fished in his pocket and brought out a sixpence. "Take me to where you let him off, and I'll get your tea and brandy at the nearest pub."

The cabby took the sixpence as earnest of his intent, bit on it automatically to test its genuineness, then slipped it into his pocket.

"Come on then," he said cheerfully, walking towards his horse and untying the reins as he mounted the box.

Monk stepped up into the cab and took his seat. They set off at a fast walk, then a trot.

They crossed the Blackfriars Bridge, then moved steadily eastwards through the City, then Whitechapel and into Limehouse. The streets became narrower and grimier, the brick darker, the windows smaller, and the smell of midden and pigsty more pervasive. Drains overflowed into gutters, and there had obviously been no crossing sweepers or dung carts near for weeks. In Bridge Road cattle had passed on the way to the abattoir. The smell brought back sharp memories to Monk's mind, but of emotions, not faces or events. He remembered overwhelming anger and urgency, but not the reasons for them. He could recall his heart pounding and the smell sticking in his throat. It could have been three years ago or twenty. Past time had no meaning, nothing to relate to.

"'Ere y' are!" the cabby said loudly, pulling his horse to a halt and tapping on the hatch.

Monk returned his mind to the present and climbed out. They were in a narrow, dirty street running parallel to the river in an area known as Limehouse Reach. He fished in his pocket and pulled out the fare, adding it to the sixpence he had already given.

"An' me drink," the cabby reminded him.

Monk added another sixpence.

"Ta," the cabby said cheerfully. "Anyfink else as I can do for yer?"

"Ever picked up the same man before?" Monk asked.

"Couple o' times. Why?"

"Where did you take him?"

"Once 'ere, once up west. Oh, an' once ter someplace orff the Edgware Road, to an 'ouse. Reckon as maybe 'e lived there. Rum, innit? I mean, why do a proper sort o' gent like that wanna come 'ere? In't nuffin' 'ere as anybody'd want. Even got the typhus less than 'alf a mile away." He gestured with his mittened thumb eastwards. "An' someone told me as they'd got the cholera in Whitechapel too, or mebbe it were Mile End. Or Blackwall, or summink."

"I don't know," Monk replied. "It wants explaining. I don't suppose you saw which way he went?"

The cabby grinned. "Wondered if yer'd think o' that. Yeah, 'e went that way." He jerked his thumb again. "'Long there t'wards the Isle o' Dogs."

"Thank you." Monk closed the conversation and set out along the road the cabby had indicated.

"If 'e went in there yer won't never find 'im!" the cabby called out. "Poor sod," he added under his breath.

Monk feared he was right, but he did not turn or alter his stride. It was going to be difficult to trace Angus, except that dressed as he was he would have stood out from the regular inhabitants, just as Monk did now. But he was unlikely to have stopped to purchase anything in the various shops that were spaced sporadically along the street. There were no newspaper vendors. People in Limehouse Reach had no spare money for such luxuries, even supposing they could read. They learned of such events that interested them by word of mouth, or from the running patterers, men whose trade was to put into endless doggerel whatever bulletin or gossip they heard and relay it in a kind of one-man musical sideshow from place to place, collecting a few coppers from appreciative listeners. Here and there billboards were posted for the few who were literate, but no one stood about selling. Even peddlers went farther west, where custom was more likely.

He went into a grocer's shop selling tea, dried beans, flour, molasses and candles. It was dark and smelled of dust, tallow and camphor. He produced the drawing of Angus and received a blank stare of incomprehension. He also tried an apothecary, a pawnbroker, a rag and bone merchant and an ironmonger, all with similar results. They stared at Monk's expensive clothes, his warm, well-cut overcoat and polished boots which kept out the wet, and knew he was alien. Children in layers of rags, some of them barefoot, faces gap-toothed and dirty, followed him, begging for money, alternately whistling and catcalling. He gave what pennies he had, but when he asked after Caleb Stonefield, they fell silent and ran away.

On Union Road, which sloped down towards the river with pavement so narrow he could hardly stand on it, its cobbles chipped and uneven, simply because he knew nothing else to do, he tried a cobbler who made new shoes from old.

"Have you ever seen this man, dressed in a good coat and high hat, maybe carrying an umbrella?" he asked flatly.

The cobbler, a narrow-chested little man with a wheeze, took the paper in one hand and squinted at it.

"Looks a bit like Caleb Stone ter me. And I only seen 'im a couple o' times, an' that were a couple too many. But it in't a face as yer'd forget. 'Cept this gent looks sane enough, and real tidy. Dressed like a toff, yer said?"

Monk felt a leap of excitement in spite of all common sense telling him otherwise.

"Yes," he said quickly. "That's only a drawing. Forget Caleb Stonefield—"

"Stone," the cobbler corrected.

"Sorry, Stone." Monk brushed it aside. "This man is related to him, so there will be a resemblance. Have you ever seen him? Specifically, did you see him four days ago? He probably passed this way."

"Dressed like a toff, an' with an 'at an' all?"

"Yes."

"Didn't 'ave no 'at as I recall, but yeah, I reckon as I saw 'im."

Monk sighed with relief. He must not overpraise the man or he might be tempted to embroider the truth.

"Thank you," he said as gravely as he could, squashing the elation rising inside him. "I'm obliged to you." He fished in his pocket and brought out threepence, the price of a pint of ale. "Remember me at the pub," he offered.

The cobbler hesitated only a second. "I'll do that, guv," he agreed, and shot out a strong, misshapen and callused hand before Monk could change his mind.

"Which way did he go?" Monk asked the final question.

"West," the cobbler replied instantly. "T'ward the South Dock."

Monk had already turned the handle of the door to leave when another question occurred to him, perhaps the most obvious of all.

"Where does Caleb Stone live?"

The cobbler turned pale under the layer of grime on his face.

"I dunno, mister, an' I'm real 'appy ter keep it that way. An' if yer'd any sense yer'd not ask neither. W'ere some folks is concerned, iggerance is a blessin'."

"I see. Thank you anyway." Monk smiled at him briefly, then turned and went out into the cold street and the stench of salt tide, raw sewage and overloaded drains.

He tried for the rest of the day, but by five o'clock it was dark, bitterly cold with a rime of ice forming on the slimy cobbles of the footpaths, and he had achieved nothing further. It was not safe to remain here alone and unarmed. He walked rapidly, head down and collar up, back toward the West India Dock Road and regular street lamps and a hansom back home again. He was stupid to have come here in good clothes. He'd never get the smell out of them. Another hole in his memory! He should have thought of that before he set out! It was not only the gaping voids in his life—an entire childhood, youth and early manhood which were a mystery to him, his triumphs and failures, his loves, if there had been any which were of lasting value—it was the stupid little pieces of practical knowledge he had forgotten, the mistakes which were like splinters under the skin every day.

41

---

The cobbler had been almost correct in his information about the fever in Limehouse. It was not the respiratory disease of typhus, but the intestinal typhoid, which raged through the tenements and rookeries, carried from one inadequate and overflowing midden to the next.

Hester Latterly had been a nurse serving with Florence Nightingale in the Scutari hospital in the Crimea and on the battlefield. She was more than used to disease, cold, filth and the sight of suffering. She could not count the deaths she had seen from injury or fever. But still the plight of the poor and the sick in Limehouse touched her, until the only way she could bear it and shut out the nightmares was to work with her close friend and Monk's patroness, Lady Callandra Daviot, and Dr. Kristian Beck to do all she could, both to relieve the distress in whatever small way was possible and to fight for some alleviation of the conditions which made these diseases endemic.

On the day that Monk was searching the streets for someone who had seen Angus Stonefield, Hester was on her hands and knees scrubbing the floor of a warehouse which Enid Ravensbrook, another woman of wealth and compassion, had obtained, at least temporarily, so that it might be used as a fever hospital after the order of the military hospital in Scutari. Hester had a feeling that the water she was using was as full of infection as any of the patients, but she had added plenty of vinegar and hoped it might serve the purpose. Dr. Beck had also obtained half a dozen open braziers in which they were going to burn tobacco leaves, a practice much followed in the navy to fumigate between decks and help to fight against yellow fever. Callandra had purchased several bottles of gin, which were firmly locked in the medicine cabinet and which could be used to clean pans, cups and any instruments. Since they had no others who were nurses by trade, there was a diminished chance of it being drunk.

Hester had just finished the last yard of floor and stood up, easing her back from its stiffness by bending back and forth a few times, when Callandra came in. She was a broad-hipped woman well into middle-age. Her hair was habitually untidy, but today it had exceeded even its usual wildness. It poked and looped in every direction, several of its pins threatening to fall out completely. Even in her youth she could not have been thought beautiful, but there was such intelligence and humor in her face it had a unique charm.

"Finished?" she asked cheerfully. "Excellent. I'm afraid we're going to need every foot of space we can find. And, of course, blankets." She surveyed the room for a moment, then proceeded to pace the floor out carefully, measuring precisely how many people might lie on it without touching each other. "I would like to get pallets," she went on, her back to Hester. "And pans or buckets of some type. Typhoid is such a beastly disease. So much waste to dispose of, and heaven only knows how we are going to do that." She was now at the far end of the space and almost inaudible to Hester. She turned and started to pace the width. "There isn't a midden or a cesspit within miles of here that isn't overflowing already."

"Has Dr. Beck spoken to the local council of authority yet?" Hester asked, picking up her bucket and going over to the window to tip it out. There were no drains, and the water was full of vinegar anyway, so it would be more likely to improve the gutters than harm them.

Callandra reached the far side and lost count. She had loved Kristian Beck since before the wretched business at the Royal Free Hospital the previous summer. Hester was aware of it, but it was something they never discussed. It was too delicate, and too painful. The depth of Kristian's feeling in return only added to the poignancy of the situation. Callandra was a widow, but Kristian's wife was still alive. She had long ceased to care for him, if indeed she ever had in the manner he longed for, but she clung to her rights and all the status and the comfort they afforded. To Callandra he could give nothing but an intense friendship, humor, warmth, admiration, and shared passions for causes in which they both believed with ardor and dedication.

Even the mention of his name could still jar her concentration, so vulnerable was she even now. She turned and began to pace back, beginning to count the width again.

Hester looked out of the window to make sure no one was passing beneath, then emptied the bucket.

"I think we could get about ninety people in here," Callandra announced. Then her face pinched. "I wish to God I could think that was all we should need. We have forty-seven cases already, not counting seventeen dead and another thirteen too ill to move. I'll be surprised if they live the night." Her voice rose. "I feel so helpless! It's like fighting the incoming tide with a mop and bucket!"

The door opened behind Hester and a striking-looking woman came in, a bottle of gin under one arm and another in each hand. It was Enid Ravensbrook.

"I suppose it's better than nothing," she said with a tight smile. "I've sent Mary out to get some clean straw. She can try the ostler at the end of the lane. His mother's one of the victims. He'll do what he can." She set the gin down on the floor. "I don't know what to do about the well. I've pumped the water, but it smells like next-door's pigsty."

"Probably with good reason," Hester said, tightening her lips. "There's a well in Phoebe Street that smells all right, but it'll be an awful nuisance to carry water over. And we're desperately short of buckets."

"We'll have to borrow them," Enid said resolutely. "If every family spared us one, we'd quickly have sufficient for all purposes."

"They haven't got them," Hester pointed out, setting her bucket, scrubbing brush and cloth away tidily. "Most families around here have only one pan between them anyway."

"One pan for what?" Enid pressed. "Perhaps they can use their night bucket for scrubbing the floor as well?"

"One pan for everything," Hester explained. "The same one for scrubbing the floor, for bathing the baby, for waste at night, and for cooking in."

"Oh God!" Enid stood still, then blushed, robbed of speech for an instant. She took a deep breath. "I'm sorry. I suppose I'm still very ignorant. I'll go out and buy some." She turned on her heel and was about to leave when she almost bumped into Kristian Beck coming in. His face was set in anger, his cheeks burned with color which had nothing to do with the cold outside, and his beautiful mouth was set in a tight line. There was no need to ask if he had met with success or failure with the local authority.

Callandra was the first to speak.

"Nothing?" she said softly, no criticism in her voice.

"Nothing," he conceded. Even in the single word there was a trace of some European accent, very slight, only an extra preciseness which marked English as not his mother tongue. His voice was rich and very deep, and at the moment expressive of his utter contempt. "They have a hundred prevarications, but they all amount to the same thing. They don't care enough!"

"What excuses?" Enid demanded. "What could there possibly be? People are dying, scores of people, and it could be hundreds before it's over. It's monstrous!"

Hester had spent nearly two years as an army nurse. She was used to the workings of the institutional mind. No local authority could be worse than military command, or in her opinion more stubborn or totally fossilized in its thinking. Callandra's late husband had been an army surgeon; she too was familiar with ritual and the almost insuperable force of precedent.

"Money," Kristian said with disgust. He looked up and down at the length of the now-scrubbed warehouse with satisfaction. It was cold and bare, but it was clean. "To build proper drains would add at least a penny to the rates, and none of them want that," he added.

"But don't they understand . . ." Enid began.

"Only a penny . . ." Callandra snorted.

"At least half of the members are shopkeepers," Kristian explained with weary patience. "A penny on the rates will hurt their business."

"Half shopkeepers?" Hester screwed up her face. "That's ridiculous! Why so many of one occupation? Where are the builders, the cobblers or bakers, or ordinary people?"

"Working," Kristian said simply. "You cannot sit on the council unless you have money, and time to spare. Ordinary men are at their jobs; they cannot afford not to be."

Hester drew in breath to argue.

Kristian preempted her. "You cannot even vote for council members unless you own property worth over one thousand pounds," he pointed out. "Or rental of over one hundred a year. That excludes the vast majority of the men, and naturally all the women."

"So only those with a vested interest can be elected anyway!" Hester said, her voice rising in fury.

"That's right," Kristian agreed. "But it helps no one to waste your energy on what you cannot change. Rage is an emotional luxury for which we have no time to spare."

"Then we must change it!" Callandra almost choked on the words, her frustration was so consuming. She swung around to stare at the empty barn of a place, tears of impotence in her eyes. "We should never have to fill something like this with people we can't save because some damnable little shopkeepers won't pay an extra penny on the rates for us to get the sewage out of the streets!"

Kristian looked at her with an affection so naked that Hester, standing between them, felt an intruder.

"My dear," he said patiently. "It is very much more complicated than that. To begin with, what should we do with it? Some people argue for a water-carried system, but then it has to empty somewhere, and what of the river? It would become one vast cesspool. And there are problems with water. If it rains heavily may it not back up, and people's houses would become awash with everyone's waste?"

She stared at him, as much of her emotion drinking in his face, his eyes, his mouth, as thinking of the bitter problem. "But in the summer the dry middens blow all over the place," she said. "The very air is filled with the dust of manure and worse."

"I know," he replied.

There was a noise on the staircase. Mary returned with an under-sized little man in a shiny hat and a jacket several sizes too large for his narrow shoulders.

"This is Mr. Stabb," she introduced him. "And he will rent us two dozen pots and pans at a penny a day."

"Each, o' course," Mr. Stabb put in quickly. "I got a family to feed. But me ma died o' the cholera back in forty-eight, an' I wouldn't want as not ter do me bit, like."

Hester drew in her breath to bargain with him.

"Thank you," Callandra said quickly, cutting her off. "We'll have them immediately. And if you know of any other tradesman who would be prepared to assist, please send him to us."

"Yeah," Mr. Stabb agreed thoughtfully, his face failing to mask a few rapid calculations.

Further deliberations were prevented by the arrival of several bales of straw and canvas sheets, old sails and sacking, anything that might be used to form acceptable beds, and blankets to cover them.

Hester left to set about procuring fuel for the two potbellied black stoves, which must be kept alight as much of the time as possible, not only for warmth but in order to boil water and cook gruel, or whatever other food was obtainable for anyone who might be well enough to take nourishment. Typhoid being a disease of the intestines, that might not be many, but if any survived the worst of it, they would need strengthening after the crisis. And fluid of any sort was of the utmost importance. Frequently it was what made the difference between life and death.

Meat, milk and fruit were unobtainable, as were green vegetables. They might be fortunate with potatoes, although it was a difficult season for them. They would probably have to make do with bread, dried peas and tea, like everyone else in the area. They might find a little bacon, although one had to be very careful. Frequently meat of any sort came from animals which had died of disease, but even then it was extremely scarce. In most families it was only the working man who had such luxuries. It was necessary for everyone's survival that he maintain as much of his strength as he could.

Patients were brought in over the next hours, and indeed all through the night, sometimes one at a time, sometimes several. There was little even Kristian could do for them, except try to keep them as clean and as comfortable as possible with such limited facilities, to wash them with cool water and vinegar to keep the fever down. Several quite quickly lapsed into delirium.

All night, Hester, Callandra and Enid Ravensbrook walked between the makeshift pallets carrying bowls of water and cloths. Kristian had returned to the hospital where he practiced. Mary and another woman went back and forth emptying the ironmonger's buckets into the cesspool and returning. At about half past one there was some easing and Hester took the opportunity to prepare a hot gruel and use half of one of the bottles of gin to clean some dishes and utensils.

There was a noise in the doorway and she looked up to see Mary come limping in carrying two pails of water she had drawn from the well in the next street. In the candlelight she looked like a grotesque milkmaid, her shoulders bent, her hair blowing over her face from the wind and rain outside. Her plain stuff dress was wet across the top and her skirts trailed in the mud. She lived locally and had come to help because her sister was one of those afflicted. She set the pails down with an involuntary grunt of relief, then smiled at Hester.

"There y'are, miss. Bit o' rain in 'em, but I s'pose that don't 'urt none. Yer want them 'ot?"

"Yes, I'll add them to this," Hester accepted, indicating the cauldron she was stirring on top of one of the potbellied stoves.

"Were it like this in the Crimea?" Mary asked in a husky whisper, just in case some poor creature should be sleeping rather than insensible.

"Yes, a bit," Hester replied. "Except, of course, we had gunshot wounds as well, and amputations, and gangrene. But we had lots of fever too."

"Think I'd like to 'ave bin there," Mary said, stretching and bending her back after the weight of the water. "Gotta be better than 'ere. Nearly married a sol'jer once." She smiled fleetingly at the memory of romance. "Then I went and married Ernie instead. Just a brickie, 'e were, but sort o' gentle." She sniffed. " 'E'd a' never made the army. 'Is legs was bad. Rickets w'en 'e were a kid. Does that to yer, rickets does." She stretched again and moved closer to the stove, her wet skirts slapping against her legs, her boots squelching. "Died o' consumption, 'e did. 'E could read, could Ernie. Captain o' the Men o' Death, 'e called it. Consumption, I mean. Read that somewhere, 'e did." She eyed the gruel and lifted one of the pails to pour in a gallon of water to thin it.

"Thank you," Hester acknowledged. "He sounds special."

" 'E were," Mary said stoically. "Miss 'im I do, poor bleeder. Me sister Dora wanted to get out of 'ere. Never thought it'd be in a coffin, leastways not yet. Not that there's many as gets out ter anythink much different. There were Ginny Motson. Pretty, she were, an' smart as yer like. Dunno wot 'appened to 'er, nor w'ere she went, but up west somewhere. Real bettered 'erself, she did. Learned ter talk proper, an' be'ave like a lady, or least summink like."

Hester refrained from speculating that it was probably into a brothel. The dream of freedom was too precious to destroy.

"Reckon as she got married," Mary went on. " 'Ope so. Liked 'er I did. D'yer want more water, miss?"

"Not yet, thank you."

"Oh—there's someone sick, poor devil." Mary darted forward to pick up a pan and go to assist. Enid came out of the shadows on the far side, her face white, her thick and naturally wavy hair piled a little crooked, and a long splash of candle tallow on the bosom of her dress.

"The little boy at the end is very weak," she said huskily. "I don't think he'll last the night. I almost wish he'd go quickly, to ease his suffering, and yet when he does, I'll wish he hadn't." She sniffed and pushed her hair out of her eyes. "Isn't it ridiculous? I first saw him only a few hours ago, and yet I care so much it twists inside me. I've never even heard him speak."

"Time has nothing to do with it," Hester replied in a whisper, adding salt and sugar liberally to the gruel. It was necessary to replenish what the body lost. Her own memories crowded her mind, soldiers she had seen for perhaps only an hour or two, and yet their agonized faces remained in her memory, the courage with which some of them bore their wounds and the breaking of their own bodies. One was sharp before her vision even now. She could see his blood-smeared features superimposed in the cauldron of gruel she was stirring, the smile he forced on his lips, his fair mustache and the mangled mass where his right shoulder had been. He had bled to death, and there had been nothing she could do to help him.

"I suppose not." Enid picked up the dishes, wrinkled her nose at the lingering odor of the gin, and began to ladle out a little gruel into about six of them. "I don't know who can eat, but we'd better try." She regarded it unhappily. "It's very thin. Haven't we any more oatmeal?"

"It's better thin," Hester answered. "They can't take much nourishment; it's just the liquid that's of value."

Enid drew in her breath, then perhaps realized why they did not simply use water. She would have gagged to drink it herself, more especially knowing where it came from. In silence she took the dishes and spoons and began the slow, distressing task of helping one person after another to swallow a mouthful and try to keep it.

The night wore on slowly. The smells and sounds of illness filled the huge room. Shadows passed to and fro in the flickering candlelight as the tallow burned down. About three in the morning Kristian returned. Callandra came over to Hester. There were dark smudges of weariness under her eyes and her skirts were soiled where she had been helping someone in extreme distress.

"Go and take a few hours' sleep," she said quietly. "Kristian and

I can manage." She said it so naturally, and yet Hester knew what it meant to her to be able to speak their names together in such a way. "We'll call you towards morning."

"A couple of hours," Hester insisted. "Call me about five. What about Enid?"

"I've persuaded her." Callandra smiled faintly. "Now go on. You can't stay up indefinitely. If you don't rest you'll be no use. You've told me that often enough."

Hester gave a rueful little shrug. There was no honesty or purpose in denial.

"Watch the boy over there on the left." She gestured towards a figure lying crumpled, half on one side, about twenty feet away. "He's got a dislocated shoulder. I've put it back, but it slips out if he leans on it when he sits up to retch."

"Poor little creature." Callandra sighed. "He looks no more than ten or twelve, but it's hard to tell."

"He said he was sixteen," Hester replied. "But I don't suppose he can count."

"Did it happen recently? The shoulder, I mean?"

"I asked him. He said he got across Caleb Stone and got beaten for his cheek."

Callandra winced. "There's a woman on the far end with a knife scar on her face. She said that was Caleb Stone too. She didn't say why. He seems to be a very violent man. She sounded still afraid of him."

"Well, I don't suppose we'll see him in here," Hester said dryly. "Unless he gets typhoid. Nobody comes to pesthouses to collect debts, however large—or to exact revenge either." She glanced down the dark cavern of the warehouse. "No revenge could be worse than this," she said softly.

"Go and rest," Callandra ordered. "Or you won't be fit to work when I sleep."

Hester obeyed gratefully. She had not dared to think how tired she was, or she could not have continued. Now at last she was free to go into the small outer room, where there was a pile of extra straw, and let herself sink into it in the darkness, away from duty, the sounds of distress and the constant awareness of other people's suffering. For a moment she could forget it all and let exhaustion and oblivion overtake her.

But the straw prickled. It had been a long time since Scutari, and she had forgotten the feeling of overwhelming helplessness in the face of such enormity of pain, and she could not so easily blank it from her mind. Her ears still strained for the sounds and her body tensed, as if in spite of everything Callandra could say, she really ought to go and do what she could to help.

That would be futile. She would become too worn out to take her turn when Callandra and Kristian needed to sleep. She must fill her mind with something else deliberately, force herself to think of some subject which would overtake even this.

It came unbidden to her mind, in spite of all her intentions to the contrary. Perhaps it was the fact that she was lying awkwardly in a small, strange room, close to the end of her strength, both physically and emotionally, but thoughts of Monk filled her, almost as if she could feel the warmth of his body beside her, smell his skin, and for once in their lives, know that there was no quarrel, no gulf, no barrier between them. She flushed hot to remember how utterly she had given herself to him in that one consuming kiss. All her heart and mind and will had been in it, all the things she could never ever have said to him. She had not seen him since the end of the Farraline case. They had continued in the heat of that desperate conclusion, so involved in it that there had been no time to feel more than a glancing moment of awkwardness.

Now if they met again it would be different. There would be memories neither of them could ever discard or forget. Whatever he might say, whatever his manner now, she knew that for that moment when they had faced death in the closed room, he had left behind all pretense, all his precious and careful self-protection, and had admitted in touch of aching and desperate tenderness that he too knew what it was to love.

Not that she deluded herself the barriers would not return. Of course they would. Rescue, and a taking up of life again, had brought back all the differences, the shadows which kept them apart. She was not the kind of woman who excited him. She was too quarrelsome, too independent, too direct. She did not even know how to flirt or to charm, to make him feel gallant and protective, let alone romantic.

And he was too often ill-tempered. He was certainly ruthless, highly critical, and his past was full of darkness and fears and ties which even he did not know, perhaps of violence he only half thought in nightmare, of cruelties he imagined but for which he had no proof—except what others told him, not in words but in the way they reacted to him, the flicker of old pain, humiliations from his keener, faster mind and his sharper tongue.

She knew all the arguments, just like the prickling straw ends poking into her arms now, scratching her cheek and spearing through the thin stuff of her dress. And yet just like the sweet oblivion closing around her, the memory of his touch obliterated it all until she was so tired she could sleep.

# CHAPTER
# THREE

———

Monk was confused by the Stonefield case. It was not that he seriously doubted what had happened to Angus Stonefield. He very much feared that Genevieve was correct and he had indeed received some kind of summons from Caleb and had gone immediately to meet him. In all probability that was why he had taken the five pounds, twelve shillings and sixpence that Arbuthnot had spoken of, and for which he had left the receipt. Monk's difficulty was now to prove his death so that the authorities would grant Genevieve the legal status of widow and allow her to inherit his estate. Then she might sell the business before it was ruined by speculation and neglect, and no doubt the advantage his rivals would take of his absence.

It would be good to talk to Callandra. It was part of their bargain that he share with her any case which was difficult or of particular interest.

He was not sure if this one would catch her emotions or not, but he knew from experience that even the act of explaining it to her would clarify it in his own mind. It had happened that way more often than not. She asked pertinent questions and allowed him to escape with no generalizations or inexactitudes. Her understanding of people, especially women, was often far more acute than his. She had a perception of relationships which made him realize, with some pain and a new sense of loneliness, how little he knew of the emotions of interdependence and the closeness of daily friendship and family ties. There were so many gaps in his life, and he did not know if those things had never existed for him or if it was simply that his memory of them was gone. And if he had lived such a narrow and solitary life, was that of his own choosing? Or had some circumstance forced it upon him? What had happened to him—and more urgently by far, what had he done—in all those lost years?

Of course, he had learned fragments, flashes of recollection prompted by some present sight or sound, the glimpse of a face. Some things he had deduced. But there were still vast, empty reaches, only a glimmer of light here and there, and he did not always like what it showed. He had been cruel of tongue, harsh of judgment, but clever . . . always clever.

But if he had not truly loved anyone, or been loved, why not? What ghosts walked in that darkness? What injuries might there be, and would he ever know? Might they return to horrify him with guilt . . . or offer him a chance to repay? Might he after all discover acts of generosity and warmth, companionship he would want to recall, sweetness that was precious even in hindsight?

But no matter how hard he searched, nothing returned. There was no shred of memory there, not a face, a smell, or sound that was familiar. The only friends he knew were those of the present. The rest was a void.

Perhaps that was why when he reached Callandra's house he was absurdly disappointed to be told by the maid that she was not in.

"When will she return?" he demanded.

"I couldn't say, sir," the maid replied gravely. "Maybe tonight, but more likely not. Maybe tomorrow, but I couldn't say so for sure."

"That's ridiculous!" Monk snapped. "You must know! For heaven's sake, be honest with me. I'm not some social climbing lady friend she doesn't want either to see or to offend."

The maid drew in her breath and let it out in a sigh of politeness. She knew Monk from many previous visits.

"There's an outbreak of the typhoid in Limehouse, sir. She's gone there to help with Dr. Beck, and I expect a good few others. I really couldn't say when she'll be back. No one can."

Typhoid. Monk had no personal knowledge that he could recall, but he had heard the fear and the pity in other people's voices, and saw both in the maid's face now.

"Limehouse?" It must have been typhoid the cobbler had meant, not typhus. He knew where it was, down by the river along the Reach. "Thank you." He turned to leave. "Oh . . ."

"Yes sir?"

"Is there anything I could take for her, a change of clothes perhaps?"

"Well . . . yes sir, if you're going that way, I'm sure it'd be appreciated. And per'aps for Miss Hester too?"

"Miss Hester?"

"Yes sir. Miss Hester went as well."

"Of course." He should have known she would be there. It was an admirable thing to do, and obvious, with her professional training. So why was he angry? And he was! He stood in the porch entrance while the maid went to fetch the articles and put them in a soft-sided bag for him to carry, and his body was stiff and his hands clenched almost to fists. She rushed into things without thought. Her own opinions were all that mattered. She never listened to anyone else or took advice. She was the most willful and arbitrary person he knew, vacillating where she should be firm, and dogmatic where she should be flexible. He had tried to reason with her, but she only argued. He could not count the quarrels they had had over one issue or another.

The maid returned with the bag and he took it from her smartly with a brief word of thanks. A moment later he was back in the street, striding out towards the square, where he knew there would be a hansom.

In Limehouse it did not take him long to trace the warehouse on Park Street now converted into a fever hospital. He could see the fear of it in people's faces and the drop in the tone of voice as they spoke of it. He spent all the change he had on half a dozen hot meat pies.

He went in the wide door and up the shallow steps with the pies wrapped in newspaper under his arm and the soft-sided case in the other hand. The smells of human waste, wet wood, coal smoke and vinegar met him before he was into the main room, which must originally have been designed to accommodate bales of wool, cotton, or other similar merchandise. Now it was ill lit with tallow candles and the entire floor was covered with straw, and blankets under which he could make out the forms of at least eighty people lying in various states of exhaustion and distress.

"Yer got them buckets?"

"What?" He turned around sharply to see a woman with a tired, smut-dirtied face staring at him. She could have been any age from eighteen to forty. Her fair hair was greasy and screwed into a knot somewhere at the back of her head. Her figure was broad-chested and broad-hipped but her shoulders sagged. It was impossible to tell whether it was from habit or weariness. Her expression was almost blank. She had seen too much to invest emotion in anything but hope, or grief. A stranger who might or might not have buckets was not worth the effort. Disappointments were expected.

"'Ave yer got the buckets?" she repeated, her voice dropping as she knew already that the answer was negative.

"No. I came to see Lady Callandra Daviot. I'm sorry." He let the case drop to the floor. "Do you want a hot pie?"

Her eyes widened a little.

He unrolled the newspaper and handed her one. It was still warm and the pastry was crisp. A tiny piece flaked off and fell to the floor.

She hesitated only a moment, her nostrils widening as she caught the aroma.

"Yeah. I do." She took it and bit into it quickly before he could change his mind. She could not remember the last time she had had such a delicacy, let alone a whole one to herself.

"Is Lady Callandra here?" he asked.

"Yeah," she said with her mouth full. "I'll get 'er for yer." She did not ask his name. Anyone who brought meat pies needed no further credentials.

He smiled in spite of himself.

A moment later Callandra came down the length of the room, also tired and dirty, but a lift in her step and a quickening in her face.

"William?" she said softly when she reached him. "What is it? Why have you come here?"

"Hot pie?" he offered.

She took it with thanks, wiping her hands briefly on her apron. Her eyes searched his, waiting for him to explain himself.

"I have a difficult case," he answered. "Have you time to listen? It won't take more than ten or fifteen minutes. You have to rest sometime. Come and sit down while you eat the pie."

"Have you one for Kristian?" she asked, still having taken only a bite from the one he had given her. "And Hester? And Enid? And. Mary, of course?"

"I don't know Enid or Mary," he answered. "But I gave one to a young woman with straight hair who expected me to have buckets."

"Mary. Good. The poor soul has worked herself to dropping. Have you any more? If not, I'll share this one."

"Yes, I have." He proffered the rolled-up newspaper. "There are another four in there."

Callandra took them with a quick smile and carried them back up the dim room to pass them to figures Monk could recognize only with difficulty. The thin, very upright one with the square shoulders and uplifted chin was Hester. He would have known her outline anywhere. No one else held her head at quite that angle. The masculine one had to be Kristian Beck, barely average height, slim-shouldered and strong. The third looked reminiscent of someone he had seen only lately, but in the poor light and the smoke from the stoves and the smell stinging his eyes, he did not know whom.

Callandra returned, eating her own pie before it got cold. She led him into a small room to the side which presumably had once been an office when the building was used for its original purpose. Now it boasted a table piled with blankets, four bottles of gin, three un-opened and one half empty, several casks of vinegar, a flagon of Hun-garian wine and a candle. Two very rickety chairs were also piled with blankets. Callandra cleared them off and offered him a seat.

"What's the gin for?" he asked. "Desperation?"

"It wouldn't be sitting there unopened if it were," she replied grimly. "Tell me about your case."

He hesitated, uncertain how much to say about Genevieve. Perhaps he should give Callandra only facts and omit his own impressions.

"To clean things with," she answered his question. "Alcohol is better than water, especially from the wells around here. Not the floors, of course. The vinegar's for that. I mean plates and spoons."

He acknowledged the explanation.

"The case . . ." she prompted, sitting heavily on one of the chairs, which rocked, tilted and righted itself at an angle.

He sat on the other gingerly, but it supported his weight, albeit with an alarming creak.

"A man has disappeared, a businessman, comfortably off and em-inently respectable," he began. "He seems happily married, with five children. It was his wife who came to me."

Callandra was watching him, so far without interest.

"His wife says he has a twin brother," Monk continued with a ghost of a smile, "who is in every way opposite. He is violent, ruth-less, and lives alone, somewhere in this area."

"Limehouse?" Callandra said in surprise. "Why here?"

"Apparently choice. He lives by his wits, and occasional gifts from Angus, the missing brother. In spite of their differences, Angus insisted on keeping in touch, although his wife says he was afraid of Caleb."

"And it is Angus who has disappeared?"

The candle on the table flickered for a moment. It was stuck in the top of an empty bottle and the tallow ran down the side.

"Yes. His wife is deeply afraid that Caleb has murdered him. In fact, I think she is convinced of it."

She frowned. "Did you say Caleb?" She reached out absently and righted the candle.

"Yes. Why?" he asked.

"It's an unusual name," she replied. "Not unknown, but not common. I heard only a few hours ago of a brutal man in this area named Caleb Stone. He injured a youth and slashed the face of a woman."

"The same man!" he said quickly, leaning forward a little. "The brother is Angus Stonefield, but Caleb may well have dropped the second half of his name. It fits with what Genevieve said of him." He realized as he spoke how he had been hoping inside himself that it was not true, that perhaps her view of Caleb was exaggerated. Now in a sentence that was ended.

Callandra shook her head. "I am afraid if that is so, then you have not only a greater task ahead of you but perhaps an exceedingly difficult one. Caleb Stone may be guilty, but it will be very hard to prove. There is little love lost for him around here, but fear may hold people silent. I assume you have already inquired into the more usual explanations for the brother's absence?"

"How delicately put," he said with a sharp edge to his voice. He was not angry with her, only with the circumstances and his own helplessness. "You mean debt, theft or another woman?"

"Something like that . . ."

"I haven't proved them impossible, simply unlikely. I traced him the last day he was seen. He came as far as Union Road, about a mile from here."

"Oh—"

Before he could add anything further he caught a movement out of the corner of his eye, and turned to see Hester standing in the doorway. Even though he had already seen her dimly in the main room, it had not prepared him for meeting her face-to-face. He had thought a dozen times exactly what he was going to say, how casual he was going to be, as if nothing had changed between them since the conclusion of the trial in Edinburgh. On reflection, that was about the best time to go back to. They could hardly pretend that had not occurred. If she referred to the Farralines, that was acceptable, although the subject might be sensitive to her, and he would respect that.

She would not mention the small room in which they had been trapped, or anything that had happened between them there. That would be so indelicate as to be inexcusable. She knew it had been occasioned by what had seemed the knowledge of certain death, and not an emotion which could be carried into their succeeding lives. To refer to it would be both clumsy and painful.

But women were peculiar where emotions were concerned, especially emotions that had anything to do with love. They were unpredictable and illogical.

How did he know that? Was that some submerged memory, or simply assumption?

Not that Hester was very feminine. He would find her more appealing if she were. She had no art to charm, or the kind of subtle flattery that is only a selection and amplification of the truth. She was much too direct . . . almost to the point of challenge. She had no idea when to keep her own counsel and defer to others. Intellectual women were remarkably unattractive. It was not a pleasing quality to be right all the time, most particularly in matters of logic, judgment and military history. She was at once very clever and remarkably stupid.

"Is something wrong?" Her voice interrupted his thoughts. She looked from Callandra to Monk and back again.

"Does something have to be wrong for me to come here?" he said defensively, rising to his feet.

"Here?" Her eyebrows rose. "Yes."

"Then you've answered your own question, haven't you," he said tartly. She was quite right. No one would come to a pesthouse in the

East End without a desperate reason. Apart from the physical un-pleasantness of the smell, the cold, the drab, damp surroundings and the sounds of pain, it was the best way in the world to contract the disease yourself. He looked at her face. She must be exhausted. She was so pale her skin was almost gray, her hair was filthy and her clothes too thin for the barely heated room. She would not have the strength to resist illness.

She bit her lip in irritation. It always annoyed her to be verbally outmaneuvered.

"You've come for Callandra's help." Her tone was waspish. "Or mine?"

He knew that was meant sarcastically. He was also aware how of-ten she had helped him; sometimes, as in the first occasion they had met, when he was truly desperate and his life hung in the balance. He had never been able to forget how it was her courage and her be-lief in him which had given him the strength to fight.

Several answers flashed through his head, most of them offensive. In the end, largely for Callandra's sake, he settled for the truth, or close to it.

"I have a case which seems to fade out two streets away," he said, looking at her coldly. "But since the man I am trying to trace was the brother of a well-known local character, and presumably on his way to see him, I thought you might be of assistance."

Whatever other thoughts were in her mind—and she looked both irritable and unhappy beneath the weariness—she chose to ac-knowledge the interest.

"Who is the local character? We haven't had much time for conversation, but we could ask." She sat down on the chair he had vacated, not bothering to rearrange her skirts.

"Caleb Stone, or Stonefield. I don't suppose—" He stopped. He had been about to say that she would know nothing of him, but the changed expression in her face made it perfectly obvious that she did know, and that it was ill. "What?" he demanded.

"Only that he is violent," she replied. "Callandra will already have told you that. We were discussing it last night. Who are you looking for?"

"Angus Stonefield, who is his brother."

"Why?"

"Because he's disappeared," he said tartly. It was absurd to allow her to make him feel so uncomfortable, almost guilty, as if he were denying part of himself. And it was not so. He liked and admired many of her qualities, but there were others which he deplored and which were a constant source of annoyance to him. And he had always been perfectly frank about it, as indeed so had she. There were certain debts of honor between them, on both sides, but that was all. And for heaven's sake, that was all she wished also. But perhaps part of that obligation was to tell her of the dangers she faced spending her time in a pesthouse like this.

"Is he wanted for something?" she said, interrupting his thoughts.

His temper broke. "Of course he's wanted," he said. "His wife wants him, his children, his employees want him. That's an idiotic question!"

The color washed up her pale cheeks as she sat hunched a little with cold, her shoulders rigid.

"I had meant was he required by the law," she said icily. "I had temporarily forgotten that you also chase after errant husbands for their wives' sakes."

"He is not errant," he responded with equal venom. "The poor devil is almost certainly dead. And I would do that for anybody . . . his wife is out of her mind with grief and worry. She has every bit as much right to be pitied as any of your unfortunates here." He jabbed angrily with his finger towards the great hall filled with its straw and blankets, although even as he said it, pity of a far harsher sort twisted inside him for its occupants. Not many of them would live through it, and he knew that. He was angry with Hester, not with them.

"If her husband is dead, William, there is nothing you can do to help her except find proof of it," Callandra interposed calmly. "Even if Caleb killed him, you may never find evidence of that. What will the police require to accept death? Do they have to see a corpse?"

"Not if we can find witnesses adequate to assume death," he replied. "They know perfectly well that the tide may carry bodies out and they are never seen again." He faced Callandra, ignoring Hester. The dim lights, the smells of tallow, gin, vinegar and damp stone permeating through everything, were sickening. And through it all the consciousness of illness was making him even more tense. He was not afraid in his brain. He would despise that in himself. Callandra and Hester were here day and night. But his body knew it, and all his instinct told him to go, quickly, before it could reach out and touch him. Hester's courage awoke emotions in him he did not want. They were painful, contradictory and frightening. And he loathed her for making him vulnerable.

"If we learn anything, we shall let you know," Callandra promised, rising to her feet with something of an effort. "I am afraid Caleb Stone's reputation makes your theories more than possible. I'm sorry."

Monk had not said all he intended. He would like to have spent longer in her company, but this was not the time. He thanked her a little stiffly, nodded to Hester but could think of nothing he wanted to say. He took his leave, feeling as if he had left something undone that would matter to him later. He had found none of the easing of his mind that he had hoped.

On leaving the warehouse, Monk steeled himself to go to the River Police at the Thames Police Station by Wapping Stairs, and ask if they had recovered any bodies in the last five days which might answer the description of Angus Stonefield.

The sergeant looked at him patiently. As always, Monk did not recognize him but had no knowledge of whether the man knew him or not. More than once he had realized he was familiar, and disliked. At first he had been at a loss as to why. Gradually he had learned his own quick brain and hard tongue had earned the fear of men less gifted, less able to defend themselves or retaliate with words. It had not been pleasant.

Now he regarded the sergeant steadily, hiding his own misgivings behind a steady, unblinking gaze.

"Description?" the sergeant said with a sigh. If he had ever seen Monk before he did not seem to remember it. Of course, Monk would have been in uniform then. That might make all the difference. Monk would not remind him.

"About my height," he replied quietly. "Dark hair, strong features, green eyes. His clothes would be good quality, well cut, expensive cloth."

The sergeant blinked. "Relative, sir?" A quiet flicker of sympathy crossed his blunt face, and Monk realized with a start how close the description was to his own, except for the color of the eyes. And yet he did not look like the picture Enid Ravensbrook had drawn. There was a rakishness in that face which set it at odds with what both Genevieve and Arbuthnot had said of Angus Stonefield, but not of his brother Caleb. Had Enid unintentionally caught more of the spirit of Caleb? Or was Angus not the sedate man his family and employees supposed? Had he a secret other life?

The sergeant was waiting.

"No," Monk answered. "I am inquiring on behalf of his wife. This is not something a woman should have to do."

The sergeant winced. He had seen too many pale-faced, frightened women doing exactly that; wives, mothers, even daughters, standing as Monk was now, afraid, and yet half hoping the long agony of uncertainty was over.

" 'Ow old?" the sergeant asked.

"Forty-one."

The sergeant shook his head. "No sir. No one answering to that. Got two men, one not more'n twenty, the other fat wi' ginger 'air. Though 'ed be late thirties or thereabouts, poor devil."

"Thank you." Monk was suddenly relieved, which was absurd. He was no further forward. If Angus Stonefield was dead, he needed to find proof of it for Genevieve. If he had simply absconded, that would be a worse blow for her, leaving her both destitute and robbed even of the comfort of the past. "Thank you," he repeated, his voice grimmer.

The sergeant frowned, at a loss to understand.

Monk did not owe him an explanation. On the other hand, he might very well need him again. A friend was more valuable than an enemy. He winced at his own stupidity in the past.

Arrogance was self-defeating. He bit his lip and smiled dourly at the sergeant. "I think the poor man is dead. To have found his body would be a relief . . . in a way. Of course, I would like to hope he is alive, but it is not realistic."

"I see." The sergeant sniffed. Monk had no doubt from the expression in his mild eyes that he did indeed understand. He had probably met many similar cases before.

"I'll come back," Monk said briefly. "He may yet turn up."

"If yer like," the sergeant agreed.

Monk left the East End and traveled west again to resume investigation into other possibilities. The more he thought of the face Enid Ravensbrook had drawn, the more he thought he would be remiss simply to accept Genevieve's word for Angus's probity and almost boringly respectable life. The sergeant of the River Police had thought him, for a moment, to be a relative of Monk's because of the similarity of description. What words would Monk have used of his own face? How did you convey anything of the essence of a man? Not by the color of his eyes or hair, his age, his height or weight. There was something reckless in his own face. He remembered the shock with which he had first seen it in the glass after his return from hospital. Then it had been the face of a stranger, a man about whom he knew nothing. But the strength had been there in the nose, the smooth cheeks, the thin mouth, the steadiness of the eyes.

In what way was Angus Stonefield different, that they could not be brothers? It was there, but he could not place it, it was something elusive, something he thought was vulnerable.

Was it in the man? Or only in Enid Ravensbrook's sketch?

He spent a further day and a half trying to establish a clearer picture of Angus. What emerged was an eminently decent man, not only respected by all who knew him but also quite genuinely liked. If he had offended anyone, Monk could not find him. He was a regular attender at church. His employees thought him generous, his business rivals considered him fair in every respect. Even those whom he had beaten to a good deal could find no serious fault with him. If anyone had a criticism, it lay in the fact that his sense of humor was a little slow and he was overformal with women, which probably sprang from shyness. On occasion he spoiled his children and lacked the type of discipline considered proper. All the faults of a careful and gentle man.

Monk went to see Titus Niven. He didn't know what he expected to learn, but it was an avenue which should not be overlooked. Possibly Niven might have some insight into Angus Stonefield that no one else had felt comfortable to speak.

Genevieve had supplied him with Niven's address, about a mile away, off the Marylebone Road. She had looked somewhat anxious, but she refrained from asking him if he expected to learn anything.

The first time Monk called there was no one at home except one small maid-of-all-work who said Mr. Niven was out, but she had no idea where or at what time he might be back.

Monk could see the strain of poverty staring at him from every surface, the girl's face, the hemp mat on the floor, the unheated air smelling of damp and soot. It was not a poor neighborhood; it was a very comfortable one in which this individual house had fallen upon greatly reduced circumstances. It stirred memories in him, but they were indistinct, emotions of anger and pity rather than fear.

When he called in the evening, Titus Niven himself opened the door. He was a tall man, slender, with a long-nosed, sensitive face full of humor and, at the moment, a mixture of self-deprecation and hope struggling against despair. Monk's instinct was to like the man, but his intelligence told him to be suspicious. He was the one person known to have a grudge against Angus Stonefield, perhaps a legitimate one, certainly one that was very real. How successful he had been previously Monk could not estimate until he was inside the house, but he certainly was in dire straits now.

"Good evening, sir?" Niven said tentatively, his eyes on Monk's face.

"Mr. Titus Niven?" Monk inquired, although he was in no doubt.

"Yes sir?"

"My name is Monk. I have been retained by Mrs. Stonefield to inquire into Mr. Stonefield's present whereabouts." There was no point in evasion any longer. To ask only such questions as would leave it concealed would be a waste of time, which was short enough, and he had accomplished nothing so far. It was already seven days since Angus had last been seen.

"Come in, sir." Niven opened the door wide and stood back to allow Monk to pass. "It is a cruel night to stand on the step."

"Thank you." Monk went into the house, and almost immediately was aware just how far Titus Niven had fallen. The architecture was gracious and designed for better times. It had been decorated within the last year or two and was in excellent condition. The curtains were splendid, and presumably would be the last things to be sacrificed to necessity, for the privacy they offered when drawn but even more for their warmth across the cold, rain-streaked glass. But there were no pictures on the walls, although he could see with a practiced eye where the picture hooks had been. There were no ornaments except a simple, cheap clock—to judge from the curtains, not Niven's taste at all. The furniture was of good quality, but there was far too little of it. There were bare spaces which leaped to the eye, and the fire in the large hearth was a mere smoldering of a couple of pieces of coal, a gesture rather than a warmth.

Monk looked at Niven and saw from his face that words were unnecessary. Niven had seen that he understood. Neither comment nor excuse would serve purpose, only add weight to the pain that was real enough.

Monk stood in the center of the room. It would somehow be a presumption to sit down before he was invited, as if the man's poverty reduced his status as host.

"I daresay you are aware," he began, "or have deduced, that Angus Stonefield is missing. No one knows why. It is now of some urgency, for his family's sake, that he is found. Quite naturally, Mrs. Stonefield is alarmed that he may have been taken ill, attacked, or in some other way met with harm."

Niven looked genuinely concerned. If it was spurious, he was a master actor. But that was possible. Monk had seen such before.

"I'm sorry," Niven said quietly. "Poor Mrs. Stonefield. I wish I were in a position to offer her help." He shrugged and smiled. "But as you can see, I can scarcely help myself. I have not seen Angus since—oh—the eighteenth. I went to his place of business. But I daresay you know that. . . ."

"Yes. Mr. Arbuthnot told me. How did Mr. Stonefield seem to you then? What was his manner?"

Niven waved towards the sofa, and himself sat in one of the two remaining large chairs. "Just as usual," he answered as soon as Monk was seated. "Quite composed, courteous, very much in command of himself and of his affairs." He frowned and regarded Monk anxiously. "You understand, I do not mean that in any critical sense. I do not intend to imply he was arbitrary. Far from it. He was always most courteous. And his staff will have told you, he was a generous master and neither an unreasonable man nor given to rudeness."

"What *did* you mean, Mr. Niven?"

Monk watched him closely, but he saw no embarrassment, no hint of deviousness, only a searching for words, and the same glint of humor and self-mockery.

"I meant, I suppose, that Angus ordered his life very well. He hardly ever made mistakes nor lost his ability to govern himself and much of what happened around him. He never seemed out of his depth."

"Did you know his brother?" Monk was suddenly very curious.

69

"His brother?" Niven was surprised. "I didn't know he had a brother. In the same line of business? Surely not. I would have known. Genevieve ... Mrs. Stonefield ..." He colored slightly and was instantly aware that he had given himself away. "Mrs. Stonefield never mentioned any relative other than his childhood guardian, Lord Ravensbrook," he went on. "And as far as I can recollect, she spoke of him only once or twice. They seemed a family very sufficient unto themselves." There was the faintest shadow of pain in his face, or was it envy? Monk was reminded again, sharply, how very attractive Genevieve was, how alive. She did not talk a great deal, or move vivaciously, yet there was a quality of emotion in her which made other women seem dull in comparison.

"Yes," Monk replied, watching him closely. "He had a twin brother, Caleb, who is violent and disreputable, a waster bordering on the criminal, if not actually so." That was something of an understatement, but he wanted to see what Niven made of it.

"I think you are mistaken, sir," Niven said softly. "If there were such a man, the City would know of it. Angus's reputation would be compromised by the existence of another with his name, and whose character was so unfortunate. I have been in the City for fifteen years. Word would have spread. Whoever told you this is misleading you, or you have misunderstood. And why do you say 'had'? Is this brother supposed to be dead? In which case, why raise the fellow's name when it can only hurt Angus?" His body tensed where he sat in the large chair beside the cold hearth. "Or do you also fear Angus may have met with some profound harm?"

"It was a slip of the tongue," Monk confessed. "I allowed Mrs. Stonefield's anxieties to influence me. I am afraid she is concerned that he is no longer alive, or he would have returned home, or at the very least sent some message to her of his whereabouts."

Niven remained silent for several moments, deep in thought.

Monk waited.

"Why did you mention this brother, Mr. Monk?" Niven asked at length. "Is he a fabrication, or do you believe him to be real?"

70

"Oh, he is real," Monk affirmed. "There is no doubt of that. You have not encountered him because he neither works in the City nor lives in the suburbs. He occupies himself entirely in the East End and calls himself Stone, rather than Stonefield. But Angus kept in touch with him. It seems the old loyalties died hard."

Niven smiled. "That sounds like Angus. He could not abandon a friend, much less a brother. I assume you have been in touch with this man, and he can tell you nothing?"

"I have not found him yet," Monk replied. "He is elusive, and I fear he may be at the heart of the problem, even perhaps responsible for it. I am investigating all other possibilities as well. Regrettable as it is, others do come to mind."

"One is frequently surprised by people," Niven agreed. "Nevertheless, I think you will not find that Angus had financial problems, nor will you discover that he has a mistress, or a bigamous wife somewhere else. If you had known him as I did, none of these thoughts would come to your mind." Niven's face was earnest in concentration. "Angus was the most honest of men, not only in deed but even in thought. I have learned much from him, Mr. Monk. His integrity was something I admired intensely, and I wished to pattern myself upon it. He was truly a man to whom true goodness was the highest aim, above wealth or status or the pleasures of his success." He leaned towards Monk. "And he understood goodness! He did not mistake it for some new absence of outward vice. He knew it for honor, generosity, loyalty, tolerance of others and the gift of gratitude without a shred of arrogance."

Monk was surprised, not only by what he said but by the depth of his emotion.

"You speak very well of him, Mr. Niven, considering that he is largely responsible for your present misfortune," he said, rising to his feet.

Niven stood also, his face flushed pink.

"I have lost my wealth and my position, sir, but not my honor. What I say is no less than I have observed."

"That is apparent," Monk acknowledged with an inclination of his head. "Thank you for your time."

"I fear I have been of little service." Niven moved towards the door.

Monk did not explain that he had not expected to learn anything of Angus from him, but only to make some estimate as to the likelihood of Niven's having harmed Angus himself. Niven was a man of quick intelligence, but also a certain naïveté. It would be an unnecessary cruelty to suggest that now.

Monk expended some further effort trying to learn more of Angus from various social and professional acquaintances, but nothing varied from the picture already painted. The Stonefields had enjoyed several pleasant friendships but entertained little. Enjoyment seemed to be within the family, with the exception of the occasional evenings at concerts or the theater. Certainly their manner of living was very well within their means, although those means must now be growing considerably thinner as she was unable to draw from the business. And since he was nominally still in charge, Genevieve was unable to exercise any jurisdiction herself, or to claim any inheritance.

"What am I to do?" she said desperately when Monk called on her at the end of a long and fruitless day, now nine days since Angus's disappearance. "What if you never find ... Angus's body?" There was a crack in her voice and she was keeping her composure only with a visible effort.

Monk longed to comfort her, and yet he could not lie. He toyed with it. He turned over in his mind all the possibilities, seriously considering each. And yet he could not force the words out.

"There are other ways of satisfying the authorities of death, Mrs. Stonefield," he answered her. "Especially where a tidal river like the Thames is concerned. But they will require that all other avenues are explored as well."

"You will not find anything, Mr. Monk," she said flatly. They were standing in the withdrawing room. It was cold. The fire was not lit, nor were the lamps. "I understand why you must do it, but it is a waste of your time, and mine," she continued. "And I have less and less left as each day goes by." She turned away. "I dare not spend money on anything but necessities, food and coal. I do not know how long that will last. I cannot think of things like boots, and James is growing out of his. Already his toes press against the leather. I was about to purchase them . . ." She did not add the rest; it was obvious, and she did not wish to say it again.

"Will you not consider accepting Lord Ravensbrook's offer, at least temporarily?" Monk asked. He could understand her reluctance to be dependent upon someone else's kindness, but this was not a time to allow pride to dictate.

She took a deep breath. The muscles tightened in her neck and shoulders, pulling the fabric of her blue, checked dress till he could see the line of stitches at the seam.

"I don't believe it is what Angus would have wished," she said so quietly he barely heard her. She seemed to be speaking as much to herself as to him. "On the other hand," she went on, scowling in concentration, "he would not wish us to be in want." She shivered as if the thought made her cold, and not the room.

"It is only just over a week, Mrs. Stonefield," he pointed out as gently as he could. "I am sure Lord Ravensbrook would advance you sufficient funds for immediate necessities, against the estate, if you do not wish to accept a gift. There cannot be much else that will not wait. If the boots have served until now—"

She swung around to him, her eyes frightened, her hands clenched. "You don't understand!" Her voice rose with a high pitch of fear in it. She was accusing, angry with him. "Angus isn't going to come back! Caleb has finally murdered him, and we shall be left on our own with nothing! Today it is just a matter of being a little careful with food. No meat except on Sundays, a little herring or bloater, onions, oatmeal, sometimes cheese. Apples if we are lucky." She glanced at the fire, then back at him. "Be careful with the coal. Sit in the kitchen where the stove is, instead of lighting the parlor fire.

Use tallow candles instead of wax. Don't burn the lights until you absolutely cannot see. Patch your clothes. Pass from the elder children to the younger. Never buy new." Her voice was growing harsher as panic rose inside her. "But it will get a lot worse. I have no family to help me. It will come to selling the house while I can still afford to bargain and get a fair price. Move to lodgings, two rooms if we are fortunate. Live on bread and tea, and maybe a pig's head or a sheep's head once a month if we are lucky, or a little tripe or offal. The children won't have school anymore—they'll have to work at whatever they can, as will I." She swallowed convulsively. "I cannot even reasonably hope they will all live to grow up. In poverty one doesn't. One or two may, and that will be a blessing, at least for me to have them with me. Only God knows what awaits them!"

He looked at her in amazement. Her imagination had carried her close to hysteria. He could see it in her eyes and in her body. Part of him was moved by pity for her. Her grief was real and she had cause for anxiety, but the wildness in her was out of character, and he was surprised how it repelled him.

"You are leaping too far ahead, Mrs. Stonefield," he said without the gentleness he had intended. "You—"

"I won't let it happen!" she interrupted him furiously. "I won't!"

He saw the tears in her eyes, and glimpsed how fragile she was under the mask of courage. He had never had to be responsible for other people, for children who trusted and were so vulnerable. At least as far as he knew he had not. Even the idea of it had no familiarity to him. He realized it only partially, as a stranger might catch sight through a window.

"The situation need never arise," he said softly, taking a step closer to her. "I shall do everything I can to find out what happened to your husband and to prove it to the authorities' satisfaction. Then either your husband will be returned to you or you will inherit the business, which is doing well. In that case you may appoint someone to manage it for you, and at least your financial welfare will be taken care of." That was an overstatement, but he made it without compunction. "Until then, Lord Ravensbrook will care for you as he did for Angus and Caleb when they were left to misfortune. After all, you are, by his own choice, family. Your children are his only grandchildren. It is natural he should wish to provide for them."

She made a visible effort to control herself, straightening her back and lifting her chin. She took a deep breath and swallowed.

"Of course," she said more steadily. "I am sure you will do all you can, Mr. Monk, and I pray God it will be sufficient. Although you do not know Caleb's cunning or his cruelty, or you would not be so confident. As for Lord Ravensbrook, I expect I must steel myself to accept his charity." She tried to smile and failed. "You must think me very ungrateful, but I do not care for his ways a great deal, and I am not prepared lightly to give the upbringing of my children into his hands." She looked at him very steadily. "When one lives in someone else's house, Mr. Monk, one loses a great deal of the rights of decision one is used to. It is a hundred small things, each of which are trivial in themselves, but together they amount to a loss of freedom which is very hard."

He tried to imagine it, and could not. He had never lived with anyone else except in childhood, at least as far as he knew. To him home was a solitary place, a retreat, but also an isolation. Its freedom had never occurred to him.

She gave a little shrug. "You think it is foolish of me. I can see it in your face. Perhaps it is. But I dislike not being able to decide whether to have the window open or closed, what time to rise or retire, at what hour I shall eat. And that is absurd, when the alternative may be not to eat at all, I know that. But the things that matter are how I shall discipline my children, what they shall be permitted to do and what not, whether my girls may learn what they wish, or if it must be music and painting and how to sew. And above all, I care to choose for myself what I shall read. I care very much. This house is mine! Here I am my own mistress."

The anger was back in her face, and the spirit he had seen the first day he met her.

He smiled. "That is not absurd, Mrs. Stonefield. We should be poor creatures if we did not care about such things. Perhaps Lord Ravensbrook may be prevailed upon to make you an allowance. You could remain here, albeit in straitened circumstances, but with autonomy."

She smiled patiently and made no reply, but her silence and the tension in her face were eloquent enough.

Monk continued to eliminate the possibilities other than violence at the hands of Caleb. He began to trace Angus's actions over the weeks immediately previous to his disappearance. Arbuthnot had a business diary and allowed Monk free access to it, and assisted him with all his own recollections. From Genevieve, Monk learned of Angus's comings and goings from the home.

They had dined once with friends, and been to the theater twice. There were also events to which Angus had gone alone, mostly as a matter of improving his professional alliances.

Monk pieced all his information together carefully, and found one or two periods of time still unaccounted for. Had he indeed gone to see Caleb, as Genevieve believed? Or had he led some alternate existence of which she knew nothing, a vice of which he was so ashamed he kept it an utterly separate life?

The most obvious thought was another woman, although even the most scrupulous examination of the accounts revealed not a farthing's discrepancy. Whatever it was, it apparently cost him nothing in terms of money.

Monk grew more and more puzzled, and unhappier.

It was while pursuing Angus Stonefield's path over the previous month that he went to the Geographic Society in Sackville Street. Angus had said he attended, but there was no record of him there. Monk was leaving, somewhat preoccupied with his thoughts, when he bumped into a young woman who was just mounting the steps. Her companions had gone on ahead of her and were already inside.

He looked up absentmindedly to apologize, then found his attention grasped most firmly. She was quite small and delicately shaped, but there was a fire and charm in her face unlike any other, and she was staring at him intently, searching his features.

"I'm sorry," he said with a sincerity which surprised him. "I was not looking where I was going. I beg your pardon, ma'am."

She smiled with what seemed genuine amusement.

"You were a little preoccupied with your thoughts, sir. I hope they were not as gloomy as they seemed." Her voice was rich and a little husky.

"I'm afraid they were." Why on earth had he said that? He should have been cautious instead of so frank. Was it too late to retreat? "I was on an unpleasant errand," he added, by way of explanation.

"I'm sorry." Her face filled with concern. "I hope at least you can now say it is concluded."

It was mid-afternoon. He could not abandon the chase for the day, although he was enjoying it less and less. There were certainly gaps in Angus Stonefield's life, whether he was as blameless as his wife believed or not. Some of them might have been accounted for by visits to Caleb, but were they all?

"Not concluded," he replied unhappily. "Simply come to another blind alley."

She did not move. She made a delightful picture standing on the steps in the winter sun. Her hair was the color of warm honey, and thickly coiled. It looked as if it would be soft to the touch and he imagined it would smell sweet, perhaps faintly of flowers, or musk. Her eyes were wide and hazel-brown, her nose straight and strong enough to speak of character, her mouth full-lipped.

A stout gentleman with a rubicund face came down the steps and tipped his hat to her. She smiled back, then turned to Monk again.

"You are seeking something?" she asked with quick perception.

He might as well tell her the truth.

"Did you ever meet a man named Angus Stonefield?"

Her winged eyebrows rose. "Here? Is he a member?"

He changed his mind rapidly. "I believe so."

"What was he like?" she countered.

"About my height, dark hair, green eyes." He was about to add that he was probably well dressed and sober of temperament, then he realized that possibly he was denying himself an entire avenue of exploration. Instead he fished in his pocket and brought out Enid Ravensbrook's drawing and passed it to her.

She accepted it with a slender hand, delicately gloved, and inspected it with considerable thought.

"What an interesting face," she said at last, looking up at Monk. "Why do you want to know? Or is that a tactless question?"

"He has been absent from his home, and his family are concerned," he said noncommittally. "Have you seen him?" He found himself hoping that she had, not only for his investigation but because it would allow him further time in her company.

"I am not sure," she said slowly. "There is something familiar about him, but I cannot think from where. Isn't it odd how one can think one knows a face but cannot tell from where? Do you have that happen to you? I am sorry to be so vague. I promise I will search my memory, Mr. . . ."

"Monk," he said quickly. "William Monk." He inclined his head in something resembling a bow.

"Drusilla Wyndham," she replied with a smile which touched not only her lips but her eyes. She was beautiful, and she could not be unaware of it, but neither did it make her arrogant or cold. Indeed, there was a warmth in her and an ability to laugh which he found not only attractive but eminently comfortable. She was sure of herself, she would not need constant flattery and small attentions, nor would she be simplemindedly focused upon marriage. With her beauty, she could afford to pick and choose and await her fancy.

"How do you do, Miss Wyndham," he replied.

A gentleman wearing a dark suit and carrying a newspaper

brushed past them, his mustache bristling. Without knowing why, Monk glanced at Drusilla Wyndham and saw amusement flash in her eyes, and they both smiled as if understanding some secret joke.

"Are you about to keep some appointment inside?" he asked, hoping fervently that she was not. Already his mind turned over plans to meet her again in less hasty circumstances.

"Yes, but it is not of the slightest importance," she replied airily, then dropped her lashes quite deliberately, laughing at both herself and him.

"Then would it be acceptable for me to invite you to accompany me for a cup of coffee or hot chocolate?" he said impulsively. "It is damnably cold out here, and there is a most respectable coffeehouse about a hundred yards along the street. And we might sit near the window, so as to be well observed." Her gaiety and charm were so infectious they reached out to him like the aroma of food to a hungry man. He was ineffably weary of the smell and sound of distress, of knowing everything he pursued would end in someone's misery. Whatever he found out about Angus Stonefield, it was going to be wretched for Genevieve and her children. There was no happy ending.

And the last thing he wanted to think of was Hester, laboring in the makeshift fever hospital, trying to relieve some tiny measure of the sea of agony around her. They would not alter the dirt or the despair of people. If typhoid did not kill them, poverty, hunger or some other disease would. Even turning it over in his mind made him angry and vulnerable. He did not even like Hester. She was certainly little enough pleasure to be with. Every encounter ended in a quarrel. Except, of course, the last one in Edinburgh. But that was only brought about by impending disaster. It held no truth in it.

"Should I not be taking you out of your way, Mr. Monk?" Drusilla said cheerfully.

"Yes," he agreed. "And I should be delighted to be out of it. It is a most unhappy and unrewarding way at the moment."

"Then let us go out of it." She swung around, her huge, smartly checked crinoline skirts brushing the steps.

He offered his arm, and she took it.

They walked together along the footpath in the brisk wind, he on the outside, sheltering her from the splashes of the passing carriages. He walked slowly, to keep pace with her easily.

"I wish I could remember where I have seen that man," she said with a little shake of her head. "Do you know him well, Mr. Monk?"

Several answers flashed through his mind that would impress her, cut before her the figure he would wish. But lies would catch up with him, and he wanted to know her for more than a few hours. Anything but the truth would jeopardize the future.

"Not at all," he replied. "His wife asked me to help her. I used to be with the police."

"You left?" she asked with extraordinary interest. "Why was that? What do you do now?"

A hansom bowled past them, the draught of its passage sending his coattails flying and making her bend her head and turn a little aside.

"A disagreement of principle," he said briefly.

She looked at him with fascination, her face reflecting amusement and disbelief.

"Please don't tantalize me so. Over what?" she begged.

"Prosecuting an innocent man," he answered.

"Well, I never," she said quietly, her face reflecting a dozen different and conflicting emotions. "That concerned you! And did your resignation save him?"

"No."

She walked in silence for about twenty yards. She seemed to be thinking deeply. Then suddenly she turned to face him, and her eyes were bright, her expression relaxed.

"And what is it you do now, Mr. Monk? You didn't tell me. You help ladies in distress because their husbands are missing?" She had a most attractive and individual voice.

"Among other things." He stopped and indicated the coffeehouse, stepping ahead and opening the door for her. Inside was warm and noisy, and smelled of the delicious aroma of coffee beans grinding, the sweetness of chocolate, and the close, clinging odor of damp coats, wool and fur and wet leather boots.

They were shown straightaway to a table. He asked her what she wished, and on her reply ordered them both hot coffee. When it came the conversation was resumed, although in truth she was such a pleasure to look at he would not have minded silence. He was also aware of the slight hush around them, and the admiring glances of many of the other guests. If Drusilla noticed, she was so accustomed to it, it had no effect upon her.

"It must be a most interesting occupation you have," she said, sipping at her coffee. "I suppose you meet all sorts of people? Of course you do. It is a foolish question." She sipped again. "I don't suppose you even remember them all when a case is over. It must be like a magic lantern slide of life, all passions and mysteries. And then it is solved, and you leave it and begin the next."

"I am not sure that I would have phrased it like that," he replied, smiling at her over the rim of his own cup.

"Of course you would. It is fascinating, and so unlike my life, where I know the same tedious people year after year. Now please tell me more of this man who is missing. What manner of person is he?"

Quite unwillingly he told her all he knew that was not in confidence, and watched with pleasure both her intelligence and the smooth, unharassed expression of her face, as if her mind were engaged but she was not going to permit another woman's tragedy to spoil the pleasure or ease of their encounter.

"It seems to me," she said thoughtfully, drinking the last of her coffee, "that the first thing you need to determine is whether he has a secret habit of some sort, be it another woman or some vice or other; or if he did as his wife feared, and went to visit his brother in the East End, and met with violence."

"Quite," he agreed. "That is why I am pursuing all I can in an effort to trace him during the last two or three weeks before his disappearance."

"Hence the Geographical Society." She nodded. "Where else might you try? Perhaps I may be of some assistance?" She bit her lip. "This is, if I am not being too presumptuous?" She looked at him candidly with her wide, hazel eyes, but there was amusement and confidence in them. He knew that if he had refused her she would not have been hurt or offended, simply philosophical, and turned her attention to something else.

Not for a moment did he hesitate.

"Thank you. The matter is urgent, for Mrs. Stonefield's sake, so I should be grateful for any help at all. As you say, the first thing is to eliminate the most obvious alternative. His business affairs seem to be in excellent order, and his personal finances, so I cannot believe he gambled or indulged in any other vice which cost him money. Would you care for more coffee?"

"Thank you. I should like it very much," she accepted.

It took him a moment to attract the waiter's attention, then when the man weaved his way through the tables to them, he ordered and paid. When the coffee came it was as steaming and fragrant as the first.

"Perhaps he was a successful gambler?" Drusilla raised her eyebrows.

"Then why disappear?" he countered.

"Oh, yes, I see." She wrinkled her nose at him. "Well . . . naughty theater? Peep shows? Some forbidden religion? Séances or black magic?"

He started to laugh. It was wonderful to be able to wander into the realms of the absurd and forget poverty, disease and all the wretchedness he had seen.

"I can't see the man I've discovered so far indulging in anything so frivolous," he said candidly.

She was laughing too. "Is black magic frivolous?"

"I don't honestly know," he confessed. "It sounds pretty irrelevant to reality to me, a sort of escape from responsibility and the daily round of duties, particularly for a man who spends his working hours considering the price of corn and other commodities."

"And leads family prayers," she added, "for a good wife and five children, and however many servants they have, not to mention goes to church every Sunday and observes the Sabbath with all diligence."

There was a burst of laughter from the next table, and they both ignored it.

"Did you find out if they eat cold meals only, don't permit singing, whistling, games of any nature, and reading of fiction, taking of sugar in his tea or the eating of sweets or chocolates, in case it causes inappropriate love of luxury? And of course no laughing."

He groaned. It was not the picture he had formed of Genevieve, but he had not asked. Perhaps Angus was as sober and worthy as that. She had certainly spoken of him in glowing, but rather formal and reverent, words.

"Poor devil," he said aloud. "If he lived like that, there would be little wonder if he took leave of reality on occasion and did something totally bizarre. It might save his sanity."

She finished her coffee the second time and sat back.

"Then permit me to discover what I can of such societies, and if anyone I know has met this Angus Stonefield." Her eyes flickered down and then up again. "And of course there is the other possibility, which seems indelicate to mention, but we are speaking to each other without pretense—I do get so tired of pretense all the time, don't you? He may have met another woman, one who offers him laughter and affection without demanding anything from him at all, except the same in return. He may long for the freedom from the responsibility of children and the sobriety and decorum of family life. Many men find a liberty to express themselves to another woman in a way they cannot to their wives, if nothing else, simply because they do not have to face her every day across the breakfast table. If they make a fool of themselves, they may walk away and never meet again."

He looked at her where she sat smiling at him, her slender shoulders so feminine and delicate, her thick shining hair, her lively face with its wide eyes, and always the air of composed amusement about her, as if she knew some secret happiness. He could well understand if Angus Stonefield, or any other man, found such a woman irresistible, a blazing, delicious freedom from the restrictions of the domestic round, the wife who was harassed by the duties of household and children, who did not feel it proper to laugh too easily or too loudly, who was conscious of her duty to him, and her dependence, and very probably who also knew him too well, and had expectations of what he should be, and how it was proper for him to behave.

Yes, perhaps Angus Stonefield had done precisely that. And if he had, Monk, for one, would not entirely blame him. On the other hand, he also felt a very sharp spur of envy which took him completely by surprise. Was Drusilla speaking from supposition? Or had she been that exquisite, delightful "other woman" for Stonefield, or for someone else? He would resent it profoundly if she had—which was both painful and absurd, but if he were as honest with himself as he was with others, still real.

"Of course," he said at last, finishing his coffee also. "I shall look into that as well."

# CHAPTER
# FOUR

---

Every hour or two brought more cases of fever to the makeshift hospital in Limehouse. The only blessing was that it also brought more volunteers to help with what little practical nursing could be done, and willing hands to help with the endless tasks of emptying, cleaning, laundering what sheets and blankets they had, and changing the soiled straw and fetching in new. Local men came and carried away the bodies of the dead.

"Where do they take them?" Enid Ravensbrook asked as they sat together in the small room where Monk had spoken with Callandra and Hester. It was late afternoon, dark and cold. Three people had died the previous night. Kristian had been there since the previous evening, and he had taken a short break to go home, wash and change his clothes and get a few hours of sleep before going back to his own hospital. There was little enough he could do at the best of times. There was no known medicine against typhoid, only constant nursing to ease the distress, keep the temperature down and some fluid in the body, and the will of the victim to live.

Callandra looked up with surprise. "I don't know," she said. "I admit I hadn't thought about it. I suppose to—" she stopped. "No, that's ridiculous. No undertaker's going to handle fever victims. Anyway, there are too many of them."

"They've got to be buried," Enid pointed out, sitting in the rickety chair where Monk had sat. Callandra was on the other, Hester on the floor. "If not undertakers, then who? You can't expect gravediggers to lay out bodies properly and observe the decencies. All they know is to bury coffins. Coffin makers will be the only people profiting out of this." She took a deep breath and let it out slowly. "At least it has got warmer. Or is it just that we have more fuel in the stove?"

"I'm frozen." Callandra shivered and hugged her arms around herself. "Hester, have you put more on the fires?"

"No." Hester shook her head. "I daren't, or we'll run out. We've only got enough for two more days anyway. I meant to speak to Bert about that, and I forgot."

"I'll ask him next time I see him." Callandra dismissed it.

"I don't know where he's gone." Enid was staring at her. She looked very pale except for spots of color in her cheeks. She must be exhausted. She had not been home for two days, just sleeping on the floor in this room when she had the chance. "He went out over two hours ago," she added. "I asked him about going to the undertaker, but I don't think he heard me."

Hester glanced at Callandra.

"There must be so many funerals," Enid went on, speaking more to herself than to either of them. Her face was very pale and there was a gleam of sweat across her brow and upper lip. She looked up. "What graveyard are they putting them in, do you know?" She turned, first to Callandra, then to Hester.

"I don't know," Callandra said quietly.

"I should find out." Enid sighed and pushed her hand across her brow, brushing away her falling hair.

"It doesn't matter!" Callandra said, looking past her to Hester.

"Yes it does," Enid insisted. "People may ask, relations may."

"They are not burying them separately anymore." Hester gave the answer Callandra had been avoiding.

"What?" Enid swiveled around. She looked bleached of all color but for a feverish stain on her cheeks, and her eyes were hollow, as though bruised.

"They are in common graves," Hester explained quietly. "Don't grieve over it." She reached over and touched Enid's arm very lightly. On the table the candle flickered, almost went out, then burned up again. "The dead won't mind."

"What about the living?" Enid protested. "What about when all this is over and they need to grieve, need a place to remember those they lost?"

"There isn't one," Hester answered. "It happens in war. All you can say to the family of a soldier is that he died bravely, and if it was in hospital, that there was someone there to care for him. There isn't anything more."

"Yes, there is," Callandra said quickly. "You can tell them he died fighting for a cause, serving his country. Here all you can say is they died because the damnable council would not build sewers, and they were too poor to do it themselves. That's hardly a comfort to anyone." She looked across at Enid and frowned. "They also died because they are half starved and cold all winter, half of them have rickets or tuberculosis, or are stunted by some other childhood disease. But you can hardly put on a tombstone, if you had one, that they died of having been born in the wrong time and place. Are you all right? You don't look well."

"I have a headache," Enid confessed. "I thought I was just tired, but I do feel rather worse now than I did before I sat down. I thought I was hot, but perhaps I'm cold. I'm sorry—I sound ridiculous. . . ."

Hester stood up and crossed the short space between them, bending down in front of Enid, searching her face, her eyes. She reached up her hand and placed it on her brow. It was burning.

"Is it . . .?" Enid whispered, the question too dreadful to ask.

Hester nodded. "Come on. I'll take you home."

"But . . ." Enid began, then realized it was pointless. She clambered to her feet, swayed, and buckled at the knees. Hester and Callandra only just caught her in time to ease her back down into the chair.

"You must go home," Callandra said firmly. "We can manage here."

"But I can't just leave!" Enid argued. "There's so much to do! I . . ."

"Yes you can." Callandra forced a smile; there was tiredness, patience and a deep grief in it. She touched Enid very gently, but without the least indecision. "You will only distract us here, because we can't look after you as we would wish. Hester will take you."

"But . . ." Enid swallowed hard and began to writhe deeply, gasping, and in obvious distress. "I'm sorry . . . I think I may be sick."

Callandra looked across and met Hester's eyes.

"Fetch a pail," she ordered. "Then go and tell Mary. You'd better find a hansom and bring it back here."

"Of course." There was nothing to discuss or with which to take issue. She went into the main room and returned within seconds with a pail, then went to find Mary, who was up at the far end of the room, sponging down a woman who was almost insensible with fever. The rush torches on the walls threw shifting shadows over the straw and the dim shapes of bodies under the blankets. There were no sounds but the rustling of feverish movement and the murmurs and cries of delirium, and close to the windows, the thrumming of the rain outside.

"I fink she's a little better," Mary said hopefully when she realized Hester was beside her.

"Good." Hester did not argue. "Lady Ravensbrook's got the fever now. I'm going to find a hansom to take her home. Lady Callandra will stay here, and Dr. Beck will be back later this evening. See what you can do about some more wood. Alf said there was some rotten timber on the dockside. It'll be wet, but if we stick it in here it may dry out a bit. It will spark badly, but in the stoves that won't matter."

"Yes, miss. I . . ."

"What?"

"I'm sorry about Lady Ravensbrook." Mary's face was pinched with concern. Hester could see it even in this uncertain light. "That's a real shame." Mary shook her head. "Didn't think a strong lady like that'd catch it. You take care, miss. In't much ter you neither." She looked up and down Hester's rather thin figure with kindly honesty. "Yer ain't got much ter fight agin it wif. You lose 'alf yer weight an' there won't be nuffink left."

Hester did not agree with that piece of logic, but she did not argue. She pulled her shawl closer around herself and retraced her steps back between the straw beds and the entrance, and went down the stairs to the outside door and the street.

Outside was pitch-dark and gusting rain on the blustery wind. The solitary gas lamp just around the corner shed a haze of light through the rain, guiding her towards Park Place. She would probably have to round the narrow Limehouse Causeway up to the West India Dock Road before she could find a hansom. She pulled her shawl tighter around herself and bent her head against the rain. It was less than half a mile.

She passed several people. It was still early evening and men were returning from work in factories, dockyards and warehouses. One or two nodded to her as their paths crossed in the misty arc of a streetlight. She had become a familiar figure to far too many who knew or loved someone stricken with typhoid, but to most she was just another drab woman about her business.

The West India Dock Road was busier. There was plenty of general traffic, goods carts, drays, wagons laden with bales for the docks or warehouses, loads taken off barges or ready to go on in the morning, horse-drawn omnibuses, an ambulance, and all manner of coach and carriage of the more ordinary type. There were no hansoms, broughams or fashionable pairs.

It was ten minutes before she managed to stop a hansom looking for a fare.

"The corner of Park Street and Gill Street, please," she requested.

"It's less 'n five minutes away," the cabby protested, seeing her wet shawl, worn boots and dull dress. "Lost the use o' yer legs, 'ave yer? Look, luv, i'nt worth your money. You can walk it, an' sure as 'ell's a waitin', yer i'nt goin' ter get any wetter than y'are!"

"I know, thank you." She forced herself to smile at him. "I've got a friend there who needs to go up west, all the way to Mayfair. That's what I need you for."

"Mayfair?" he said with disbelief. "What'd anybody from 'ere be doin' in Mayfair?"

She debated whether to tell him to mind his own business, and decided swiftly against it. She needed him too much. Enid was too ill to wait until she found another cabby who was less skeptical or inquisitive.

"She lives there. She's been helping us organize the hospital for the fever!" She said it in her own most cultured accent.

" 'Ad enough o' Limehouse, 'as she?" he said dryly, but there was no unkindness in his voice, and she could not see his face since he had his back to the light.

"For a while," she replied. "Change of clothes and some more money." It was a lie, but one to serve a better purpose. If she told him the truth, he might well whip up his horse and she'd never see him again.

"Get in!" he said agreeably.

She climbed in without hesitation, ignoring her wet skirts slapping around her ankles, and immediately the cab lurched forward.

As he had said, it was less than five minutes before they were outside the fever hospital, and she went inside to fetch Enid, who was by now so dizzy and faint she was unable to walk unaided. Hester and Callandra were obliged to come, one on either side of her to support her, and Hester thanked God in a silent prayer that the street lamp was around the corner and the cabby could see only the lurching figures of three women and not how ghostly the center one looked with her ashen face and half-closed eyes, and the sweat streaming off her, making her skin wetter even than the fine rain of the night could explain.

He peered at them in the gloom, and snorted. He had seen gentry drunk before, but the sight of a drunken woman always disturbed him. Somehow it was worse for a woman than a man, and the quality had not the same excuses. Still, if she gave money for the sick, he would reserve judgment . . . this once.

" 'Yal in," he said, holding the horse steady as it smelled fear and threw its head up and took a step sideways. " 'Old 'ard!" he ordered, pulling the rein tighter. "Come on!" He turned back to his passengers again. "I'll take yer 'ome."

The journey was a nightmare. By the time they reached Ravensbrook House, Enid was hot and cold by turns, and seemed unable to keep her body from shaking violently. Her mind wandered as if she were half waking and half in dream.

As soon as they drew up, Hester threw open the door and almost fell to the pavement, calling out commands to the cabby to wait exactly where he was. She rushed up the steps and rang the bell violently, then again and then a third time. She heard it jingling in the hall.

A footman came to the door, his expression fixed in furious disapproval. When he saw a white-faced, bedraggled young woman with wild eyes and no hat, his offense knew no bounds. He was a good six feet tall, as a footman should be, and with excellent legs and a suitably supercilious mouth.

"Lady Ravensbrook is extremely ill in that hansom!" Hester said curtly. "Will you please assist me to carry her inside, and then send for her maid and anyone else necessary to make her comfortable."

"And who are you, may I ask?" He was shaken, but not to be stampeded by anyone.

"Hester Latterly," she snapped back. "I am a nurse. Lady Ravensbrook is very ill. Will you please hurry, instead of standing there like a doorpost!"

He knew where she had been, and why. He wavered on the edge of argument.

"Are you hard of hearing?" she demanded more loudly. "Go and fetch your mistress before she falls insensible faint and may injure herself."

"Yes, ma'am." He galvanized into action, striding past her down the steps and across the pavement gleaming wet in the lamplight to the hansom where the cabby was fingering the reins nervously, staring down at the doorway as if it were an open grave.

The footman flung the door open and with the expression of a man about to spur his horse into battle, poked his head and shoulders inside to lift Enid, who was now fallen sideways and almost unconscious. As soon as he had grasped her, which even for a man of his strength was not easy, he pulled her out and straightened up, bearing her in his arms back across the footpath towards the door.

Hester took a step down, fishing in her reticule for money to pay the cabby, but he stood up in his urgency to get his horse going, flicking the long whip over its ears, and was already away from the curb and increasing pace before she could go any farther.

She was surprised only for a moment. He knew where he had picked up his fare, and seeing the address to which he brought her, and the liveried footman, he had guessed the truth. He did not want her close enough to touch, or to take anything, even money, from her hand.

Hester sighed and followed the footman, closing the door behind her.

He was standing in the center of the hall helplessly, Enid in his arms as lifeless as a rag doll.

Hester looked for a bell rope to pull.

"Bell?" she asked sharply.

He indicated with his head to where the ornamental rope hung. No other staff had come because presumably they knew it was his duty to answer the door. She strode over and yanked the rope more roughly than she had intended.

Almost immediately a parlormaid appeared, saw the footman, then Enid, and her face went white.

"An accident?" she said with a slight stammer.

"Fever," Hester answered, going toward her. "She should go straight to bed. I am a nurse. If Lord Ravensbrook is willing, I shall stay and look after her. Is he at home?"

"No ma'am."

"I think you should send for him. She is very ill."

"You should have brought her sooner," the footman said critically. "You had no right to leave her till she was in this state."

"It came on very suddenly." Hester held her tongue with difficulty. She was too tired and too distressed for Enid to have patience to argue with anyone, least of all a footman. "For heaven's sake, don't stand there, take her upstairs, and show me where I can find clean water, a nightgown for her, and plenty of towels and cloths, and a basin—in fact, two basins. Get on with it, man!"

"I'll get Dingle," the parlormaid said hastily. And without explaining who that was, she turned on her heel and left, going back through the green baize door and leaving it swinging. Hester followed the footman up the broad, curved staircase and across the landing to the door of Enid's bedroom. She opened it for him and he went inside and laid Enid on the bed. It was a beautiful room, full of pinks and greens, and with several Chinese paintings of flowers on the walls.

But there was no time to observe anything but the necessities, the ewer of water on the dresser, the china bowl and two towels.

"Fill it with tepid water," Hester ordered.

"We have hot—"

"I don't want hot! I'm trying to bring her fever down, not send it up. And another bowl. Any sort will do. And please hurry up."

With a flash of irritation at her manner, he took the ewer and left with the door ajar behind him.

He had been gone only long enough for Hester to sit on the bed beside Enid and regard her anxiously as she began to toss and turn, when the door swung wide again and a woman of about forty came in. She was plain and dowdy, and wore a gray stuff dress of rigid design, but extremely well cut to show an upright and well-shaped figure. At the present she looked in a state of considerable distress.

"I am Dingle, Lady Ravensbrook's maid," she announced, staring not at Hester but at Enid. "What has happened to her? Is it the typhoid?"

"Yes, I'm afraid so. Can you help me to undress her and make her as comfortable as possible?"

They worked together, but it was not an easy task. Enid now ached all over, her bones, her joints, even her skin was painful to the touch, and she had such a headache she could not bear to open her eyes. She seemed to be drifting in and out of consciousness, suffocatingly hot one moment and shivering the next.

There was nothing to be done for her except bathe her in cool water at regular intervals to moderate the fever at least to some degree. There were moments when she was aware of them, but much of the time she was not, as if the room swayed, ballooned, and disappeared like some ghastly vision in mirrors, distorted beyond reality.

It was nearly two hours before there was a knock at the door and a small and very frightened maid, standing well back, informed Hester that his lordship was home, and would miss please attend on him in the library straightaway.

Leaving Dingle with Enid until she returned, when it would be necessary to do the first laundry, Hester followed the maid as she was bid. The library was downstairs and at the far side of the hall, around a corner. It was a quiet room, comfortably furnished, lined with oak bookcases and with a large fire burning in the hearth. It took barely a glance to notice the polished wood, the warmth, the faint smell of lavender, beeswax and leather, to know its luxury.

Milo Ravensbrook was standing by the window, but he turned the moment he heard Hester's step.

"Close the door, Miss . . ."

"Latterly."

"Yes, Miss Latterly." He waited while she did so. He was a tall man, extraordinarily handsome in a dark, highly patrician way. His was a face in which both temper and charm were equally balanced. He might be an excellent friend, entertaining, intelligent and quick to understand, but also she judged he would be an implacable enemy.

"I understand you brought Lady Ravensbrook home, having observed she was taken ill," he said, allowing it to be half a question.

"Yes, my lord." She waited for him to continue, watching his expression to see the fear or the pity in it. It was not a mobile face. There was a stiffness in him, both of nature and of a rigid upbringing of self-mastery, extending perhaps as far back as the nursery. She had known many such men before, both in the aristocracy and in the army. They were born into families used to power and its responsibilities as much as its privileges. They took for granted the respect and obedience of others, and expected to pay for them in the self-discipline taught from the nursery onwards, the mastery of indulgence to the softer things, either emotional or physical. He stood to attention, like a soldier, in the warm library, surrounded by the deep color of the old wood, velvet and leather, and she could judge nothing of him at all. If he was racked by pity for his wife, he masked it in front of her. If he was wary of hiring her, or afraid of catching the illness himself, it was too well hidden for her to see.

"My footman said you are a nurse. Is that correct?" He moved his lips so very slightly it was barely discernible, but there was an inflexion in his voice when he spoke the word *nurse* that betrayed his feelings. Nurses were generally women of the roughest sort; very often they were drunken, dishonest, and of a physical appearance where the more lucrative occupation of prostitute was not open to them. Their duties were largely those of scrubbing, emptying slops and on occasion disposing of dressings or rolling new bandages and tending to linen. Actual care of patients lay with doctors, and most certainly all decisions, attention to wounds or giving of medicines.

Of course, since Florence Nightingale's fame in the Crimea, many people were aware that a nurse could be much more, but it was very far from the normal case. Lord Ravensbrook was obviously among the skeptics. He would not be openly offensive without provocation, but his view of her was the same as his view would have been of Mary, or any of the other East End women who helped in the pesthouse. Hester found her body stiffening and her jaws tight with anger. For all her ignorance and dirt, Mary had a compassion which was eminently worthy of his respect.

She made an effort to stand even straighter.

"Yes, I am." She did not add "sir." "I learned my craft in the Crimea, with Miss Nightingale. My family did not approve, which was not unexpected. They considered I should remain at home and marry someone suitable. But that was not the path I wished." She saw in his face that he was not in the slightest interested in her life or the reasons for her choice, but reluctantly he had a certain respect. The mention of the Crimea held a credit he could not deny.

"I see. Presumably you have tended fever before, other than in Limehouse?"

"Regrettably—yes."

He raised black eyebrows, straight and level above deep set eyes.

"Regrettably? Does that not give you an advantage of experience?"

"It is not pleasant. I saw too many men die who need not have."

His expression closed over. "I am not concerned with your political opinions, Miss—er—Latterly. My only interest is in your ability to nurse my wife, and your willingness."

"Of course I am willing. And I have as much ability as anyone."

"Then it remains only to discuss your remuneration."

"I consider Lady Ravensbrook my friend," she said icily. "I do not require remuneration." She could regret that later. She most assuredly required funds from somewhere, but she had enormous satisfaction in denying him now. It would be worth a little chill or hunger.

He was taken aback. She could see it in his face. He regarded her soiled and crumpled clothes, of very mediocre quality, and her weary face and straggly hair, and a minuscule flicker of amusement crossed his mouth and vanished.

"I'm obliged to you," he accepted. "Dingle will attend to any laundry that may be necessary and prepare and bring to you whatever food you desire, but since she will be in the company of other servants, she will not enter the sickroom. I have a responsibility to do what I can to keep the fever from spreading throughout the household, and then God knows where."

"Of course," she said levelly, wondering how much he was thinking of himself, whether he would visit the sickroom . . . or not.

"We will have a cot put into the dressing room where you may rest," he went on. "May we send to your home for any change of clothes you require? If that is not suitable, I am sure Dingle could find you something. You look not dissimilar in build."

Remembering Dingle's scrubbed, middle-aged face and meticulously plain clothes, Hester found it not a flattering thought, but then on the other hand, she was of a surprisingly comely figure for such a dour woman, so perhaps she should not be downhearted about it.

"Thank you," she said briefly. "I am afraid I have little available at home. I have been in Limehouse for so many days I have had no opportunity to launder."

"Just so." At the mention of Limehouse his face tightened, and his disapproval of Enid's participation was plain enough not to need words, not that he would have spoken them in front of her. "Then it is agreed? You will remain here as long as it is required." It was an assumption, and as far as he was concerned, the matter was finished.

"She may need nursing all the time," she pointed out. "Night as well as day, when the crisis comes."

"Is that more than you can cope with, Miss—Latterly?"

She dimly heard someone's footsteps crossing the hall behind her and fading away as they went into another room.

"Yes it is," she said decisively. "Especially since I still have some moral commitment to the hospital in Limehouse. I cannot leave Lady Callandra totally without experienced assistance."

A flash of temper crossed his face and he drew in his breath sharply.

"My wife is a great deal more important to me, Miss Latterly, than a score of paupers in the East End who will almost assuredly die anyway, if not of this, then of something else. If you require some remuneration, then please say so. It is not dishonorable to be rewarded for one's labor."

She curbed the answer that rose to her lips, although with difficulty. She was too tired to be bothered with such trivialities of arrogance and misjudgment.

"She is also personally more important to me, my lord." She met his eyes very levelly. "But matters of duty can exceed one's own emotional ties and certainly one's individual wishes. I imagine you believe that as thoroughly as I do? I am a nurse, and I do not abandon one patient for another, no matter what my personal feelings might be."

A dull color flushed up his face and his eyes looked hot and angry. But she had shamed him, and they both knew it.

"Have you some friend or relative who could watch while I am absent?" she asked quietly. "I can show them what is to be done."

He thought for a moment. "I imagine that will be possible. I will not have Dingle coming and going, spreading it through the house. But Genevieve may be willing to spend the necessary time here. She can bring her children with her, and they can be cared for by the staff. That will serve very well. It will benefit her for the time being, and she will know she is of service, and not feel obliged. She is a very proud woman."

"Genevieve?" It did not really matter who he was referring to, but she would like to know.

"A relative," he replied coldly. "By marriage. An agreeable young woman who is presently in a difficult circumstance. It is an excellent solution. I shall attend to it."

And so it was that by that evening Hester was established in Ravensbrook House, with the promised cot in the dressing room, and changes of clothes from Dingle which fitted adequately.

Enid was extremely ill. Her entire body ached so severely it was painful to the touch. She was running so high a fever she seemed unsure of where she was and did not recognize Hester even when she spoke to her gently, held a cool cloth on her brow and called her by name. She was perpetually thirsty, and so weak she could not sit up sufficiently to drink without assistance, but she did manage to keep on her stomach the boiled water mixed with honey and salt which Hester gave her. From her face it was obvious that the taste of it was most unpleasant, but Hester knew from experience that plain water did not give the body some element it needed, and so she insisted in spite of Enid's whispered protest.

At about half past nine in the evening there was a knock on the bedroom door, and when she went to open it, she found on the threshold a woman perhaps a year or two older than herself but with a face she knew to be far prettier than her own, with a frank and earthy openness to it which she could not but like.

"Yes?" she inquired. The woman was plainly dressed, but both the cut and fabric were excellent, and the style was more flattering than any servant would be permitted. She knew before she spoke that this must be the relative Lord Ravensbrook had promised.

"I'm Genevieve Stonefield," the woman introduced herself. "I've come to help you nurse Aunt Enid. I hear she is dreadfully ill."

Hester opened the doors wider. "Yes, I'm afraid she is. I'm very grateful you have come, Mrs.—Stonefield, did you say?" The name was familiar, but for the moment she could not place it.

"Yes." She came in through the door nervously, almost immediately glancing across to the big bed where Enid lay, white-faced, her hair wet and straggling over her brow. The room was lit only by the gas bracket on the farther wall, hissing gently, casting long shadows from the bedside chair and the jug on the table. "What can I do to help?" she asked. "I—I've never nursed anyone before, except my own children, and that was only for colds and chills—nothing like this. Robert once had tonsillitis, but that is hardly the same."

Hester could see that she was profoundly afraid, and she could not blame her. Only experience made it tolerable for her. She could well remember her first night in the wards in Scutari. She had felt so inadequate, so aware of each moan or rustle of movement. The minutes had dragged by as if daylight would never come. The next night had been even worse, because she had known in advance how long and desperate it would be. If she could have run away, she would have. Only pity for the men and shame for herself kept her there.

"There is nothing you can give her that will help, except the water from that jug." Hester closed the door and indicated the small blue china jug on the side table. "The other is just clear water for the cloths to keep her as cool as you can. Wash her brow and hands and neck as often as you please. Every ten minutes, if it seems it may help. She has not vomited since the very beginning, but if she should seem distressed in that way, be prepared for it. There is a dish over there." Again she pointed.

"Thank you," Genevieve said huskily. She looked alarmed. "You're not going just yet, are you?"

"No," Hester assured her. "And when I do, I will simply be in the next room to sleep for a few hours." She indicated the dressing room door. "I can't remember when I last lay down, but it seems like the day before yesterday, although I don't suppose it can be."

"I didn't know she had been ill so long!" Genevieve was aghast. "Why did Lord Ravensbrook not send for me before?"

"Oh no, she was only taken ill today. We have been down in Limehouse, with the typhoid outbreak there," Hester replied, leading the way to the bed. "I'm sorry, I'm not being very clear."

Genevieve swallowed, her throat tight as if she would choke. "Limehouse?"

"Yes. There is a very bad outbreak there at the moment. We have converted a disused warehouse into a temporary hospital."

"Oh. That is very good of you. I believe it is not a pleasant area at all. Not that I know it, of course," she added hastily.

"No," Hester agreed. She could not imagine how any relative of Lord Ravensbrook would know Limehouse, or anywhere else in the East End. "Before I go, we should change the bed linen. It will be much easier with two of us. Dingle will take the soiled sheets and attend to them."

Together they changed the bed. Hester had said good night and was almost at the dressing room door when Genevieve's voice stopped her.

"Miss Latterly! What—what can you do for them in Limehouse? It isn't like this, is it? And won't there be—well—lots of them ill?"

"Yes. And no, it isn't like this." Genevieve, with her charming face and well-cut gowns, could not have any conception of the makeshift fever hospital in Limehouse, the stench of it, the suffering, the stupid unnecessary dirt, the overflowing middens, the hunger and the hopelessness. There was no point in trying to tell her, and no kindness. "We do what we can," she said briefly. "It does help. Even someone there to try to keep you cool and clean and feed you a little gruel is better than nothing."

"Yes. Of course." She seemed to want to discuss the subject, but as if she regretted asking. "Good night."

"Good night, Mrs. Stonefield."

It was only when Hester was washing her face in the bowl of water which had been left for her that she suddenly remembered the name. Stonefield. It was the name of the man Monk was searching for in Limehouse! He had said he was a respectable man who had suddenly disappeared, for no apparent reason other than to visit his brother in the East End. And his wife feared him dead.

Surely Enid would have said something, if she had overheard Monk? But Enid had not been in the room, only Monk, Callandra and herself. She was too tired now to turn it over in her mind any further. All she wished was to wash the grit out of her eyes, feel the warm clean water on her skin, and then lie down and at last stop fighting exhaustion and allow it to overcome her.

She was wakened by a persistent rocking and a voice in her ear whispering her name over and over. She struggled to consciousness to find a gray light seeping into the room and Genevieve Stonefield's white and anxious face only a foot from hers.

"Yes?" she mumbled, fighting to clear her mind and free herself from the shreds of sleep. Surely it couldn't be morning already? It seemed she had just lain down.

"Miss Latterly! Aunt Enid seems—worse. I dare not leave calling you any longer. I know how tired you must be—but . . ."

Hester hauled herself up, reaching out blindly for her robe, then remembered she did not have one. Even her nightgown was Dingle's. Ignoring the cold—there was no fire in the dressing room, although there was a fireplace—she went past Genevieve into the bedroom.

Enid was tossing and turning and crying out with pain in a soft, almost childlike whimpering, as if she were completely unaware of her surroundings. She seemed completely delirious. The perspiration stood out on her skin, even though the jug of water and a cloth were on the bedside table and the cloth was still cool and damp when Hester picked it up. A good deal of the sugar water was gone.

"What can we do?" Genevieve asked desperately from just behind her.

There was little enough, but Hester heard the fear and the grief in her voice, and felt a quick pity for her. If she was indeed Monk's client, then she had enough tragedy to contend with, without this bereavement added to it.

"Just try to bring the fever down," she replied. "Ring for some more water, at least two jugs of it, and cool, no more than hand heat at the most. And perhaps we'd better have clean cloths and towels as well."

Genevieve went to obey, glad to have something specific to do. The relief was naked in her face.

When the water and towels came Hester put them on the table and pulled back the bedcovers, ready to begin. Enid's nightgown was soaked with perspiration and clung to her body.

"We'll change her into a shift, I think," Hester suggested. "And change that lower sheet again. It's very rumpled." She reached out her hand. "And damp."

"I'll get the clean ones," Genevieve said instantly, and before Hester could agree or disagree, she darted away and started opening the drawers of the linen press and searching.

She brought the shift, and then went back straightaway to find a sheet, leaving Hester holding Enid and trying alone to take off the soiled nightgown. Enid did what she could, but she was barely conscious, and it was only too apparent that every touch hurt her and every movement sent pain right through her bones and joints. Added to which, her vision was so distorted by fever she could not focus on anything and kept misjudging where her hands could grasp.

Hester was intent upon causing her as little additional distress as possible.

"Genevieve!" she called. "Please help me here. Never mind the sheet yet."

Genevieve turned around from the drawers where she was standing. Her face was white, her hair straggling out of its pins. She looked desperately tired.

"Please?" Hester said again.

Genevieve hesitated. The silence hung between them as if she had not heard, or not understood what was said. Then as if with a great effort, she came over and stood at the far side of the bed, leaned forward, her head down, and took Enid's limp body in her arms.

"Thank you," Hester acknowledged, and pulled the nightgown off and put it away. Quickly and as gently as she could, she bathed Enid all over with cool water. Genevieve stood back again, taking the used cloths from her and rinsing them out and wringing them, then passing them back. Over and over she washed her own hands, once or twice right up to the elbows.

"I'll get the clean sheet," she offered as soon as the task was completed.

"Help me put the shift on her first, will you?" Hester asked.

Genevieve took a deep breath, gulping awkwardly, but she did as she was bid. She stretched out her arms, and Hester saw the muscles tense, and saw that her hands were shaking. It was only then that she realized how terrified Genevieve was of catching the disease herself. She was trembling and almost sick with the sheer fear of it.

Hester was not sure how she felt. A tangle of emotions rose in her. She could understand it easily! She had felt the same overwhelming horror in her own early experiences. Now time had taught her a more philosophical view. She had seen hundreds of cases, by far the majority of them dying of it, and yet she had never been touched by it herself. She had suffered the occasional chest fever or chill, but nothing worse, although they could certainly make one feel badly enough at the time.

"You are not likely to get it," she said aloud. "I never have."

The color burned hot up Genevieve's face.

"I—I'm ashamed to be so afraid," she said haltingly. "It's not for myself—it's my children. There is no one to care for them if anything happened to me."

"You are a widow?" Hester asked more gently. Perhaps in her place she would have felt the same. It was more than natural, it would be hard to understand any other feeling.

"I . . ." Genevieve took a deep breath. "I don't know. I know that sounds absurd, but I am not sure. My husband is missing. . . ."

"I'm sorry." Hester meant it profoundly. "That must be dreadful for you—the uncertainty and the loneliness."

"Yes." Genevieve took a deep breath and steadied herself. Very deliberately she slid the clean cotton shift over Enid's body, watching every movement in her attempt not to jolt or bump her.

"How long?" Hester asked as they took off the old sheet.

"Twelve days," Genevieve replied. "I—I know this sounds as if I have given up all faith, but I believe he is dead, because I know where he went, and he would have been back long ago if he were able."

Hester went over to the linen press and fetched the clean sheet. Together they put it on the bed, moving Enid gently as they did so.

"Where did he go?" Hester asked.

"To Limehouse, to see his brother," Genevieve answered.

"Caleb Stone . . ." Hester said slowly. "I've heard of him."

Genevieve's eyes widened. "Then you know I am not foolish in my fear."

"No," Hester agreed honestly. "From the little I have learned, he is a violent man. Are you sure that is where he went?"

"Yes." There was no hesitation in Genevieve's voice. "He went quite often. I know it seems hard to understand, when Caleb was so dreadful, he seems to have nothing to commend him at all, but you see they were twins. Their parents died when they were very young, and they grew up together." She smoothed the blanket and tucked it in with quick, careful hands. "Lord Ravensbrook took them in, but he is only a distant cousin, and that was before he married Aunt Enid. They were cared for by servants. They had only each other to show any kind of affection to, any laughter—or tears. If they were ill, or afraid, they had no one else. Caleb was different then. Angus doesn't say a great deal, I think he finds it too hurtful." Her face was pinched with imagination of pain, and the child she could not comfort within the man she loved. Now even the man was beyond her reach, and there was nothing she could do, except wait.

Hester longed to offer her some ease or hope, but there was none, and to invent it would be cruel. It would force her through the agony of realization, acceptance and grief twice, instead of once.

"You must be tired," she said instead. "Have Dingle bring us some breakfast, then you should change your clothes and go to your room and sleep."

They had barely finished eating when there was a brisk tap on the door, and before either of them could answer, it opened and Milo Ravensbrook came in. He closed it behind him and stepped a couple of yards inside. He spared only a glance at Hester and Genevieve, staring past them to Enid, his face bleak. From his pallor and the red rims to his eyes, he could have lain awake most of the night.

"How is she?" he asked, looking at neither of them.

Genevieve said nothing.

"She is very ill," Hester answered gently. "But the fact that she is still alive gives good cause for hope."

He swung around to her, his face tight and hard.

"You don't mince with words, do you! I hope you are kinder with your patients than you are with their families!"

Hester had seen fear lead to anger too often to respond with anger herself.

"I told you the truth, my lord. Would you rather I had told you she was better, when she is not?"

"It is not what you say, ma'am, it is your manner in saying it," he retorted. He would not retreat. He had criticized her, therefore she must be wrong. He would forgive her in his own time. "I will have the physician attend as soon as possible—within the hour. I shall be obliged if you will remain on duty until he has been. Thereafter, if he deems it acceptable, you may go back to your patients in Limehouse for a spell, providing he is not of the opinion you may return further infection here with you. I am sure you yourself would not wish to do that."

She was about to argue, but he gave her no opportunity. He turned instead to Genevieve.

"I am delighted you saw fit to come, my dear. Not only are you of the greatest help to poor Enid, but it gives me the chance to offer you some measure of assistance in your present difficulty." His face softened a fraction, a tenderness above the mouth, there, and then gone again. "And as family, we should be together in this anxiety, and support each other, should it come to be a bereavement." His expression flickered, unreadily. "I sincerely hope it will not. We may yet discover there has been some form of accident—retrievable. Caleb is violent—indeed, he has lost almost every redeeming feature of his youth—but I find it hard to believe he would willfully injure Angus."

"He hates him," Genevieve said, her voice thick with an inner exhaustion far deeper than the one night nursing Enid, the sleeplessness or the fear of disease. "You don't know how much!"

"Nor do you, my dear," he said, without making any move towards her. "All you have heard is Angus's fear speaking, and his very natural grief at the situation, and the degradation he has seen in his brother's nature. I refuse to believe it is irredeemable."

"Thank you," she whispered. For an instant her face was bright with gratitude, and vulnerable as a child's with sudden new hope.

Hester did not know whether to be furious with him for wakening such thoughts again in her or to pity him because of his own need. She imagined the young man he must have been, taking in two orphaned boys and learning to think of them as his own, clothing them in his dreams, teaching them the arts and truths of life, sharing his experiences and beliefs. And then must have come the disillusion as one of them slowly became bitter, vicious, and began step by tragic step to destroy himself. He had burned out all that was good, all the gentleness and the aspiration towards virtue, until at last he had cut himself off completely and given way to a kind of despair. Surely such a man as Caleb Stone had become could only result from despair?

No wonder Milo Ravensbrook stood in his wife's sickroom and refused to believe one son could have murdered the other. He was facing the loss of all those he loved, except Genevieve and her children, who, through Angus, were his last blood left.

He turned slowly and looked at Enid, then pale-faced, stiff-backed, he walked out, unable to bring himself to speak.


By midday the doctor had been and gone, offering little more than sympathy. Hester was about to leave for Limehouse, when she almost ran into Monk in the hallway of Ravensbrook House. She stopped abruptly, the instant after he also had seen her.

"What are you doing here?" he demanded, but his face was full of relief.

In spite of all her intentions, she felt a surge of pleasure inside her. She refused to explain or excuse it to herself.

"Lady Ravensbrook is ill. I am caring for her," she replied.

There was a flicker of black humor in him, almost a kind of perverse satisfaction. "You got tired of Limehouse rather quickly, didn't you? What about Callandra? Is she there all by herself now that you and Lady Ravensbrook have left?"

"I'm on my way there," she said tartly, anger welling up inside her.

"Very intelligent," Monk said sarcastically. "Then you can bring the typhoid back here with you, to add to whatever Lady Ravensbrook already has. I hadn't thought you so stupid! Does Lord Ravensbrook know? Perhaps he doesn't realize, but I would have thought better of you."

"It is typhoid she has," she replied, looking him straight in the eyes. "It is a risk one runs, nursing fever patients. But as you also pointed out, Callandra has very little other help, except a few local women who are willing but have no experience. The only other one there is Kristian. They have to get some rest, so I imagine they are taking turns. They need someone else to help for a while, even if only so they can leave to buy more supplies."

His face was pale and he looked considerably shaken, as if what she had said distressed him.

"Is she going to recover?" he asked after a moment.

"I hope so. She'll be very tired, of course, but Kristian will do all he can to—"

"Not Callandra, you fool," he cut across her. "Lady Ravensbrook. You said she has typhoid."

"Yes. You seem very slow to grasp the point, but that is why I am here looking after her."

"So why are you leaving her then?" He jerked his head towards the front door, where she had been going. "Is she well enough to be left alone?"

"For heaven's sake, she's not alone," she snapped furiously. "Genevieve Stonefield is here while I am gone. We are taking turns to do all we can. Do you think I would walk out and leave a patient?

I am used to you being gratuitously offensive, but even you know better than that."

"Genevieve?" He was surprised.

"That is what I said. Presumably she is your client? Have you proceeded any further? You seemed to have had no success at all when I last saw you."

"I have considerably more information," he answered.

"In other words, no," she interpreted.

"Do you really think you have time and talent enough to spare to do your own work and mine too?" he asked with a lift of sarcasm. "You rate yourself higher than the evidence supports."

"If you want Genevieve," she retorted, "you will have to wait. She cannot leave Lady Ravensbrook until I return." And with that she brushed past him and strode towards the front door, yanking it open and leaving it swinging behind her for the footman to close.

"I came to see Lord Ravensbrook," Monk said between his teeth. "You monumentally stupid woman!"


Nevertheless on the evening of the day after, tired as she was, Hester went to Monk's rooms in Fitzroy Street to give him the general information she had learned about Angus and Caleb Stonefield from her time in Ravensbrook House. It was not a great deal, but it might help. She was not concerned so much for him as for Genevieve.

It was a wintry night and she held the collar of her cloak up around her neck and chin as she crossed the pavement and mounted the step. She rapped smartly on the door, before she could change her mind.

She stepped back, and was about to decide that he was not in and she had done all duty demanded of her, when the latch turned and the door swung open. Monk stood just inside, outlined by the light behind him. From what she could see of his face he was tired and discouraged. He did not hide his surprise at seeing her.

She felt sorry for him, and was suddenly glad she had come.

"I thought I should tell you the little I have learned about Angus and Caleb," she explained her presence.

"You've learned something?" he said quickly, stepping back for her to enter.

Perhaps she had overstated it and given him unjustified hope. She felt foolish.

"Only a few facts, or perhaps I should more correctly say a few people's opinions."

"Whose opinions? For heaven's sake, come in! I don't want to stand here on the step, even if you don't mind." He pulled the door wider, and then as she passed him, closed it behind her.

"Why are you so angry?" She decided to stop retreating and attack instead. It was more in her nature. She should not allow him to make her feel as if she had to justify herself all the time. "If your case is going badly, that is unfortunate," she continued, walking past him through the outer chamber to the inner one. "But being offensive will not help it, and it is very childish. You should learn to control yourself."

"Have you come all the way, at this time of the evening, to tell me that?" he said incredulously, following her in. "You interfering, opinionated, monumentally arrogant woman! Treating the sick has gone to your brain! Even in your futile field, surely you must have something more useful to do? Go and empty some slops, or scrub a floor. Stoke a fire somewhere. Comfort someone, if you have the faintest idea how."

She took off her wet cloak and handed it to him.

"Do you want to know about Angus and Caleb, or not?" It was almost a relief to be just as rude in return. She had guarded her tongue for so long, all sorts of emotions were knotted up inside her, memories of loneliness and fear, of horror and exhaustion in the past, pain she could not ease, deaths she had been helpless to prevent. All of it came back to her so much more vividly and easily than she had expected. And she did not want to care about Monk. It was nice, al-

110

most like a familiar pleasure, to quarrel with him. "Are you actually interested in helping poor Genevieve, or are you just taking her money?"

His face went white. She had hurt him with that last suggestion. For all his faults, she knew with absolute certainty he would never have done that. Perhaps she should not have said it. But then he had insulted her professionally just as much.

"I'm sorry," he said tightly. "I had not realized that this time you had something useful to say. What is it?" He put her cloak absent-mindedly over the back of one of the chairs.

Now she felt foolish. It was not truly useful. Maybe he knew that too? She took a deep breath and faced him. His gray eyes were cold and level, full of anger.

"Lord Ravensbrook does not think Caleb would have harmed Angus," she began. "Because for all his violence, they are brothers, and grew up together, sharing their loneliness and grief when they lost their parents. But he thinks that because he loves them, and cannot bear to think otherwise. He has already lost his first wife, and then the boys' parents, and now Enid is terribly ill, and Angus is missing."

He was staring at her, waiting for her to conclude.

Her voice sounded thin even in her own ears. "But Genevieve is convinced Caleb has killed him. She told me that in the past Angus has come home with knife scars that no one else knows about. He would not call a doctor. He was ashamed of them. I think that is why she did not tell you. She does not wish anyone to think Angus was not able to stand up for himself, or that he was a coward. Angus . . ." She did not know how to phrase what she thought and make it seem sensible. She could almost hear Monk's sarcastic dismissal even before she spoke. "Angus loved Caleb," she went on hastily. "They were very close as children. Perhaps that bond still existed, for him, and he could never believe Caleb would hurt him. Maybe he could even have felt guilty for his own success, when Caleb had so little. That could be why he kept going back—to try to help him—for his own conscience's sake. And pity can be a very hard thing to take. It can eat more deeply into the soul than being hated or ignored."

He looked at her in silence for a long time. She did not look away, but stared back.

"Perhaps," he conceded at length. For the first time his imagination could conceive of the emotions within Caleb, the explosion of rage which could end in such violence. "It could explain both why Angus did not simply leave him to rot, which is what it would seem he both wanted and deserved, and why Caleb was stupid enough to kill the one man on the earth who still cared about him. But it doesn't help me find Angus."

"Well, if it was Caleb who killed him, at least you have some idea where to look," she pointed out. "You can stop wasting your time trying to find out if Angus had a secret mistress or gambling debts. He was probably just as decent as he seemed, but even if he wasn't, you don't need to find out, and you certainly don't need to tell Genevieve—or Lord Ravensbrook. They are both convinced he was an extraordinarily good man. Everything they knew of him was honorable, generous, patient, loyal and innately decent. He read stories to his children, brought his wife flowers, liked to sing around the piano, and was good at flying a kite. If he is dead, isn't that loss enough? You don't have to find his weaknesses too, do you, simply in the name of truth?"

"I'm not doing it in the name of truth," he said, his face screwed up with irritation and pain at the thought. "I want, in the name of truth, to find out what happened to him."

"He went to the East End to see his twin brother, who in a fit of violence, which he is prone to, killed him! Ask the people of Limehouse—they are terrified of him!" she went on urgently. "I've seen two of his victims myself, a boy and a woman. Angus crossed him one time too many, and Caleb killed him—either by accident or on purpose. You have to prove it, for the sake of justice, and so Genevieve can know what happened and find some peace of heart— and know what to do next."

"I know what I have to do." he said curtly. "It is a great deal harder to know how. Can you be as quick to tell me that?"

She would have loved to reply succinctly and brilliantly, but nothing came to her mind, and before she had time to consider the matter for long, there was a sharp, light rap on the door.

Monk looked surprised, but he went straight over to answer it, and returned a moment later accompanied by a woman who was beautifully dressed and quite charming. Everything about her was feminine in a casual and unaffected way, from her soft, honey-colored hair, under her bonnet, to her small, gloved hands and dainty boots. Her face was beautiful. Her large hazel eyes under winged brows looked at Monk with pleasure, and at Hester with surprise.

"Am I intruding upon you with a client?" she said apologetically. "I am so sorry. I can quite easily wait."

Somehow the suggestion was painful. Why had the woman automatically assumed that Hester could not be a friend?

"No, I am not a client," Hester said more sharply than she would have wished the moment she heard her own voice. "I called to give Mr. Monk some information I thought might be of assistance."

"How kind of you, Miss ... ?"

"Latterly," Hester supplied.

"Drusilla Wyndham." The woman introduced herself before Monk had the opportunity. "How do you do."

Hester stared at her. She seemed very composed and her attitude made it apparent that in spite of the fact that this was Monk's office, her call was social. Monk had never mentioned her before, but there was no question that he knew her, and every evidence he also liked her. It was there in his expression. The way he stood with his shoulders straight, the very slight smile on his lips, unlike the hard-eyed look of the moment before she came.

Perhaps he had known her in the past? She seemed extraordinarily comfortable with him. Hester felt a sudden, awful sinking in her stomach, as if there were nothing inside her. Of course, he must have known women in the past, probably loved them. For heaven's sake.

It was not impossible he had been married! Could a man forget such a thing? If he had really loved . . . ?

But would Monk really love anybody? Had he that capacity in him to love utterly and totally, sharing all of himself?

Yes. For a few moments in that closed room in Edinburgh he had. It was precious, like a brilliant star inside her memory. And yet it hurt, because she could not forget or dismiss it. She could never think of him as she had before that, never completely believe the anger or the coldness, and never tell herself with any honesty that there was nothing in him she really wanted.

Drusilla Wyndham stopped talking to Monk, and had swung around to look at Hester again, her lovely eyes wide and inquiring.

"Would you care for me to wait somewhere else while you conclude your business, Miss Latterly?" she asked politely. "I do not wish to intrude, or to hold you from what else you plan for this evening. I am sure you must have friends to call upon, or family awaiting you." It was a remark, not a question. It was also a very plain dismissal.

Hester felt her neck and shoulders tighten in anger and a bitter resentment. How dare this woman take charge like this, as if in some way she owned Monk? Hester knew him far better than she ever could. She had shared desperate battles with him, hope and courage, pity and fear, victory and defeat. They had stood beside each other when both honor and life were threatened. Drusilla Wyndham knew nothing of that!

But she might know all manner of other things. Perhaps she could even tell Monk his lost past? And if Hester loved him—no, that was absurd! If she was a true friend, an honorable person, she could not wish to deny him that.

"Of course," she said coldly. "But there is no need to retire, Miss Wyndham. All that is confidential has already been said." She must let her know that there were confidential things. "I wish you a pleasant evening." She turned to Monk and saw amusement in his face, which infuriated her and sent the color burning up her cheeks.

Drusilla smiled. Perhaps she too had read Hester more accurately than she wished. She felt horribly naked.

"Good night, Mr. Monk," she said with a forced smile in return. "I hope you have more success in the future than you have found so far." And she went to the door and opened it before he could get there and do it for her. She stepped out into the cold street, and left him to close the door after her.

As soon as Hester had gone, Drusilla turned to Monk.

"I do hope my calling was not inopportune? I did not mean to embarrass her. The poor creature looked quite disconcerted. She said it was not a personal matter, but was she simply being polite?" Her words were concerned, but there was a sparkle in her eyes that looked close to laughter, and a glow in her face.

"Not at all," Monk said firmly, although he knew Hester had been upset. It was quite extraordinary. He would never have suspected her of being vulnerable to such a feminine emotion as jealousy. He was angry on her behalf. It was such a gap in her armor it was uncharacteristic. And yet he was also undeniably pleased. "She had given me the information," he said to Drusilla, stepping back so she could come closer to the fire. "She had no call, and no desire to remain. She was about to leave when you arrived." He did not add that he was delighted to see her, but it was plain in his manner, and he meant it to be.

"Are you working on another case, beside the one you told me of?" she inquired.

"No. May I offer you some refreshment? A cup of tea? Or a cup of hot chocolate? It is a cold evening."

"Thank you," she accepted. "That would be most welcome. I admit I became very chilled in the hansom. It was a rash thing to do to come here, when I did not even know if you would be at home, let alone prepared to receive company. I blushed for myself, when it was rather late, and I was already halfway here. Thank you." She handed him her cape and took off her bonnet, running her fingers delicately through the soft curls at the edge of her brow. "I admit to being interested, in a most unladylike fashion, in the story you told me of your investigation of the unfortunate man who has been missing." She looked at him with a smile. "I have asked among the few acquaintances I have in the Geographical Society, and also in a musical society I know and a debating association, but I learned nothing, except that Mr. Stonefield attended the Geographical Society once, as a guest, and seemed a quiet and charming man who claimed too many family and business obligations on his time to attend more often." Her glance strayed around the room, taking in the gracious but well-worn furnishings, the polished wood, the rich dark colors of the eastern carpet, the absolute lack of any photographs or personal mementos.

"The others did not know him at all," she continued. "Except by repute, and as a most honorable man, very upright, given to charitable donations of a modest sort, a regular attender at church, and in every way a pillar of the community." There was a vividness in her eyes and a faint flush in her cheeks. "It is very strange, is it not? I fear greatly that his poor wife is correct, and he has met with some harm."

"Yes," Monk agreed gravely. He stood by the mantelshelf, close to the fire. She sat in the chair opposite, her wide skirts almost touching the fender. Almost absently he rang the bell for his landlady. "Yes, I am afraid it looks more and more as if that is so."

"What are you going to do next?" she asked, looking up at him. "Surely you will try to prove it? How else can any sort of justice be done?"

"Yes, of course I will."

There was a sharp knock on the door and his landlady appeared. She was a cheerful soul who had overcome her scruples at having an agent of inquiry in the establishment, and now took a certain kind of pride in it, suggesting all kinds of intrigue and glamour to other less fortunate keepers of similar establishments in the neighborhood whose lodgers followed more pedestrian callings.

"Yes, Mr. Monk. And what can I do for you?" She eyed Drusilla with interest. A lady of such beauty must either be in a marvelous distress or be a very wicked woman and highly dangerous. Either way, it was of the utmost interest. Not that she would repeat a word of it, of course, should she chance to overhear anything.

"Two cups of hot chocolate, if you please, Mrs. Mundy," he replied. "It is a very inclement evening."

"Indeed it is that," Mrs. Mundy agreed. "Only one in dire need would be out at this hour of a winter's evening. Two cups of hot chocolate it is, Mr. Monk." And she withdrew to set about preparing them, her imagination whirling.

"What are you going to do next?" Drusilla asked the moment the door was closed. "How will you set about finding where he went, and finding Caleb Stone? That surely must be the answer, mustn't it?"

"I think so," he agreed, amused by her eagerness and, in spite of himself, somewhat flattered. She was attracted to him, no matter how modest he might want to be, that much was apparent. He found himself responding because he too found her everything which appealed to him in a woman: charming, intelligent, confident, amusing and feminine with just the hint of vulnerability which complimented him. It was not a completely unfamiliar feeling. He had no specific memory, but he responded by instinct, with assurance and quite definite pleasure.

"So you will go to the East End?" she urged, her eyes shining.

"Yes," he said, looking at her with amusement, baiting her gently. He knew she was bored, looking for adventure, something utterly different from anything her friends could boast. She had courage, that he did not doubt, and possibly even a desire to broaden her experience and to help someone for whom she felt a certain pity. He knew what she was going to say.

"I'll help you," she offered. "I am a very good judge of whether someone is lying or telling the truth, and together we can speak to twice as many people as you could alone."

"You can't come dressed like that." He looked her up and down with open appreciation. She was delightful to the eye, a perfect blend of spirit and good taste, enough beauty displayed to hold any man's attention, and yet sufficiently modest and with that measure of dignity and self-possession to make it plain she was her own person and there was immeasurably more concealed than any man could learn unless he gave a great deal of himself in return. He found he most definitely wanted her to come, whether she was of the slightest use or not. Her company would be delightful.

"I shall borrow my maid's clothing," she promised. "When may we begin?"

"Tomorrow morning," he answered with no more than a hint of a smile, his eyebrows raised. "Is eight o'clock too early for you?"

"Not in the slightest," she rejoined, her chin high. "I shall be here at eight o'clock, on the dot."

He grinned. "Excellent!"

Mrs. Mundy knocked on the door and brought in the hot chocolate. Monk accepted it as if it were champagne.

# CHAPTER
# FIVE

———

In Bloomsbury, where they set off the next morning, it was a still, cold morning, but as they went east, and drew nearer to the river, they came into fog. It grew thick in the throat and sour with the smell of smoke from house and factory chimneys. Eventually, short of the Isle of Dogs they could go at no greater pace than a careful walk. The hansom stopped in Three Colt Street. Monk paid the cabby and held out his hand to help Drusilla down. As she had promised, she was dressed in her maid's clothes: a dark-colored skirt and pale undistinguished blouse under a jacket top and a cloak which could have been either brown or gray. In the thin half-light of the fog it was impossible to tell. She had put a shawl over her bright hair and even one or two smuts and smears on her cheeks, but nothing could mask her natural beauty, or the white evenness of her teeth when she smiled.

The cab moved off into the gloom, and with a little shiver she linked her arm in his and they began the long task. At first she stood well back as Monk spoke to peddlers, a running patterer and a rag-and-bone man, and learned nothing of use. He was not surprised that she found them alien and frightening. Their accents must have been hard for her to follow, and their faces, matted under the grime, were haunted by a permanent wariness, a mixture of anger and fear.

Within a hundred yards a troop of children now joined them, thin-faced, wide-eyed, several of them barefoot, even in the bitter cold of the wet cobbles. They were inquisitive, and eager for any odd

119

halfpenny or farthing that might be given. Dirty little hands plucked at Monk's sleeves and at Drusilla's skirts, which were less than half the size of her usual crinoline.

Gradually they moved eastward. In Rope-Makers' Field Monk tried several shopkeepers. Drusilla even plucked up courage to make several suggestions herself. But still they met with nothing useful. There were references to Caleb Stone, few of them flattering, many of them spoken with overt fear.

Emmett Street was the same. The fog from the river was even denser here, hanging in thick curtains, blocking out the light. There was no color to drain from the drab streets with their high, narrow walls, sooty and damp-stained, the chimneys dribbling out thin wreaths of smoke. Middens ran out into the gutters and the smell was choking. The fog deadened sound; even other footsteps on the wet stones were hardly audible. Now and then the wail of a foghorn came from the river a street away.

Several times Drusilla looked at Monk, question and horror in her eyes.

"Do you want to go back?" he asked, knowing the pity and the dismay she must feel, a woman who had never seen or imagined such things before. It said much for her courage that she had come this far.

"We haven't learned anything yet," she said doggedly, gritting her teeth. "Thank you, but I can continue."

He smiled at her with a warmth he had no need to affect. He held her arm a little closer as they went on past the West India Docks towards the Isle of Dogs.

On West Ferry Road Monk stopped a woman with a large bosom and short, very bowed legs. She was carrying a bundle of rags and was about to go through a doorway which emitted a smell of burned fat and blocked drains.

"Hey!" Monk called out.

The woman stopped and turned, too tired for curiosity. "Yeah?"

"I'm looking for someone," Monk began, as he had so many times before. "It's worth something to me to find him."

"Oh yeah?" There was a slight flicker across the impassivity of the woman's face. " 'Oo yer lookin' fer, then?"

Drusilla passed her Enid's drawing of Angus. She peered at it in the gray light. Then her face tightened and she thrust the drawing back at Monk, anger harsh in her voice.

"If yer wants Caleb Stone, yer'll find 'im wivaht my 'elp! Stuff yer money. In't no use ter mie in me grave!"

"It isn't Caleb Stone," Monk said quickly.

"Yeah 'tis!" The woman thrust the picture back at him. "Wotcha take me fer? I know Caleb Stone w'en I sees 'im!"

"It isn't Caleb," Drusilla said urgently, stepping forward for the first time. "He is related to him, that's why there is such a resemblance. But look more closely." She took the picture back from Monk and passed it to the woman. "Look at his face again. Look at his expression. Does he appear the sort of man Caleb Stone is?"

The woman screwed up her face in concentration. "Looks like Caleb Stone ter me. All got up like a toff, but got them same eyes, an' nose."

"But he isn't the same," Drusilla insisted. "This is his brother."

"Garn! 'E in't got no bruvver."

"Yes, he has."

"Well ..." the woman said dubiously. "Mebbe 'e do look a bit different, abaht the marf, partic'lar. But I in't seen 'im!"

"He'd be well-dressed and well-spoken," Drusilla added.

"I tol'jer, I in't seen 'im, an' wot's more, I don' wanter!" She shoved the picture back.

But before Drusilla could take it the door swung open and a lean man with a swarthy, unshaven face poked his head out.

"In't yer ever goin' ter stop yer yappin', yer fat cow? W'ere's me dinner? I don' work me guts aht ter come 'ome an' listen ter yer yap, yap, yap in the street wi' some tart! Get in 'ere!"

"Shut yer face an' come an' look at this pikcher, will yer?" the woman yelled back, no particular venom in her voice at being thus spoken to.

"Still worf money ter yer?" she asked Monk.

"Yes," Monk agreed.

The man came out reluctantly, his face creased with suspicion. He glared at Drusilla, looked at Monk narrowly, then finally at the picture.

"Yeah," he said finally. "I seen 'im. So wot's it ter yer? 'Ad a pint down the Artichoke, then went dahn towards the river. W'y?"

"It wasn't Caleb Stone you saw?" Monk said doubtfully.

"No, it wasn't Caleb Stone I saw." The man mimicked his voice viciously. "I know the difference 'atween Caleb Stone an' some gee-zer wi' fancy manners an' dressed like a toff."

"When was this?" Monk asked.

" 'Ow do I know?" the man said irritably. "Las' week, or week afore."

Monk put both hands harder into his pockets.

" 'Course yer knows, yer stupid sod!" the woman said sharply. "Fink, an' it will come back ter yer. Wot day was it? Was it afore or arter Aunt give yer them socks?"

"It were the same day," he said sullenly. "Or the day afore." He belched. "It were the day afore, which makes it two weeks ago, 'zac'ly! An' all I kin tell yer." He turned to go back inside.

The woman shot out her hand, and Monk gave her a shilling. That was the day Angus Stonefield had disappeared. It was worth a shilling.

"Thank you," he said graciously.

She grasped the money, hid it in her voluminous skirts, and followed her husband inside, slamming the door.

Monk turned to Drusilla. There was a look of triumph in her face, her eyes were bright, her skin glowing. Delighted as he was with having traced Angus to the Isle of Dogs on the day of his disappearance, even to a specific tavern, his foremost emotion was pleasure in her company, a lift of excitement as he looked at her and he thought how lovely she was.

"Shall we adjourn to the Artichoke and take some luncheon?" he said with a wide smile. "I think we deserve it."

"Indeed we do," she agreed heartily, taking his arm. "The very best they have to offer."


They ate at the Artichoke and Monk attempted to question the landlord, a burly man with a red face and a magnificent nose, squashed sideways from some ancient injury. But he was busy and highly disinclined to answer any questions that were not to do with the bill of fare. Monk learned nothing, except that it would be an excellent place in which two men might meet unnoticed.

Afterwards they tried a few more shops and passersby; there were few idlers in the thick fog and darkening afternoon. By three o'clock Monk offered to take her home. It was bitterly cold with a rawness that chilled to the bone, and she must be weary.

"Thank you, but you don't need to come with me," she said with a smile. "I know you want to go on until darkness."

"Of course I shall take you," he persisted. "You should not be alone anywhere near here!"

"Nonsense!" she said briskly. "We are equals in this. Courtesy I accept, but I refuse to be treated as an incompetent. Call me a hansom, and I shall be home within the hour. If you make me feel a burden to you, you will rob me of all the pleasure I feel now." She smiled at him dazzlingly, laughter in her voice. "And the very considerable feeling of accomplishment. Please, William?" She had not used his name before. He found it peculiarly pleasing to hear it on her lips.

And the argument was telling. He conceded, and took her to the nearest main thoroughfare, where he stopped a hansom and helped her in, paid the driver, and watched it retreat into the looming fog. It was quickly swallowed, even its lights engulfed within minutes.

Then he turned back and spent one more hour asking, probing, seeking. But he learned nothing more, only fear and rumor of Caleb Stone, all of it ugly. He seemed an elusive man, appearing and disappearing at will, always angry, always on the edge of violence.

Everything that he knew convinced him the more that Angus Stonefield was indeed dead and that Caleb had murdered him when the hatred and jealousy of years had finally exploded.

But how to prove it to a jury? How to create more than a moral certainty, a crushing sense of injustice, of wrong done, and all answer for it defied? There was no corpse. Maybe there never would be. Everything he knew of Caleb depicted him as a man of cruelty and absolute selfishness, but also of considerable cunning, with many friends along the waterfront who would hide him—who did, whenever he was threatened.

But surely Monk had the intelligence and the imagination to outwit him? He was walking slowly, almost feeling his way as the fog turned to darkness.

He could barely hear the muffled footsteps of others returning home in the late afternoon. Carriage lamps hung like moons suspended in the shrouds of mist. The sound of horses' hooves had no sharpness on the freezing cobbles.

There was so much of himself he did not know, but at least since the accident he had never been permanently defeated in a case that really mattered—a few thefts, never a murder. Before the accident he knew only from what he had read of his own case notes in the police files.

But every case he read showed a man of relentless tenacity, broad imagination and a passion for truth. There had been other adversaries as harsh and violent as Caleb Stone, and none of them had beaten him.

He had walked a mile and a half along the West India Dock Road before he finally found a hansom and directed it to take him home to Fitzroy Street. He was expecting Genevieve Stonefield. He had promised her some report of his progress, and he must be there when she arrived. He settled back in the seat and closed his eyes for the long, slow journey. It would be well over an hour at this time of night, and in this weather, even as far as Bloomsbury.

By the time he had changed his clothes and had a hot cup of tea, and Genevieve had arrived, he was set in his determination not only to find the truth but to prove it.

"Come in, Mrs. Stonefield." He closed the door behind her and helped her with her wet cloak and bonnet. She looked extremely tired. There were fine lines in her face which had not been there a few days earlier.

"Thank you," she accepted, sitting down reluctantly, perched on the edge of the chair as if to relax would somehow leave her vulnerable.

"How is Lady Ravensbrook?" he asked.

"Ill," she answered, her eyes dark with distress. "Very ill. We do not know if she will live. Miss Latterly is doing everything for her that can be done, but it may not be enough. Mr. Monk, have you learned anything about my husband? My situation is growing desperate."

"I am very sorry about Lady Ravensbrook," Monk said quietly, and he meant it. He had liked her in the brief moment they had met. Her face had had courage and intelligence. It hurt to think of her dying so pointlessly. He looked at Genevieve. How much more must she feel a helpless sense of loss. She was sitting rigidly on the edge of her chair, face earnest, waiting for him to answer her questions.

"I am afraid it begins to look increasingly as if you are right," he said gravely. "I wish I could hold out a more helpful answer, but I have traced him into Limehouse on the day of his disappearance, and there seems no reason to doubt he went to see Caleb, as he had so often before."

She bit her lip and her hands tightened in her lap, but she did not interrupt him.

"I am still looking, but I have not yet found anyone who has seen him since then," he went on.

"But Mr. Monk, what I need is proof!" She took a deep breath. "I know in my heart what has happened. I have known since he did not return home at the time he said he would. I have feared it for long enough, but I could not dissuade him. But the authorities will not accept that!" Her voice was rising in desperation as she could not make him understand. "Without proof I am simply an abandoned woman, and God knows, London is full of them." She shook her head as if in despair. "I cannot make any decisions. I cannot dispose of property, because as long as he is legally supposed to be alive, it is his, not mine or my children's. We cannot even appoint a new person to manage the business. And willing as Mr. Arbuthnot is, he has neither the confidence nor the experience to do it adequately himself. Mr. Monk, I must have proof!"

He stared at her earnest, anguished face and saw the fear in it. That was all he could see, it was so sharp and urgent. Did it mask grief she could not bear to allow herself, least of all now when there was so much to be done, and she was not alone where she could weep in private? Or was something less attractive behind it—a driving concern for money, property, a very thriving business which would be hers alone as a widow?

Perhaps if Monk were doing his duty to Angus as well as to her, he would look a little closer at Genevieve as well. It was an ugly thought, and he would far rather it had not entered his head, but now that it was there he could not ignore it.

"Previously you spoke of selling the business while it is still profitable and of excellent reputation," he pointed out. It was irrelevant—she could do neither—but he was interested in her change of mind. "Have you a manager in mind?"

"I don't know!" She leaned forward and her full skirts touched and spilled over the fender. She seemed not to notice. "Perhaps it would be better than selling. Then all our present employees could remain. There is that to consider." She was ardent to convince him. "And it would be a continued source of security for us . . . something for my sons to inherit. That is better than a sum of money which can disappear alarmingly quickly. A piece of misguided advice, a young man willful, unwilling to be counseled by those who are older and he considers staid and unimaginative. I have heard of it happening."

He bent over and moved her skirt, in case a coal should fall or spark and set it alight.

She barely noticed.

"Aren't you looking rather far ahead?" he said a little coolly.

"I have to, Mr. Monk. There is no one to take care of me but myself. I have five children. They must be provided for."

"There is Lord Ravensbrook," he reminded her. "He has both means and influence, and seems more than willing to be of every assistance. I think your anxiety is greater than it need be, Mrs. Stonefield." He hated it, but his suspicions were wakened. Perhaps the relationship between herself and her husband was not as ideal as she had said. Possibly it was she whose affections had wandered elsewhere, not he? She was an extremely attractive woman. There was in her an element of passion and daring far deeper than mere physical charm. He found himself drawn to her, watching her with fascination, even while his mind was weighing and judging facts.

"And I have already tried to explain, Mr. Monk, that I do not wish to forfeit my freedom and become dependent upon the goodwill of Lord Ravensbrook," she went on, her voice thick with emotion she could not hide. "I won't have that, Mr. Monk, as long as I have any way at all of preventing it. I am growing more afraid day by day, but I am not yet beyond my wits' end. And whether you believe it or not, I am doing what my husband would have wished. I knew him well, for all that you may think perhaps I did not."

"I don't doubt you did, Mrs. Stonefield." It was quite out of character for him to lie. He barely knew why he did it, except some need to comfort her. He could hardly touch her and he had no instinct to. It did not come to him naturally to express himself by touch. Whether it ever had, he could not know.

"Yes you do," she said with a pinched smile, a bitter humor of knowledge. "You have explored every other possibility than the one

127

that Caleb killed him, because you think it more likely." She leaned back in her chair again, and finally became aware of her skirt near the fender and almost automatically tweaked it away. "And I suppose I cannot blame you. Every day I daresay some man deserts his wife and children, either for money or another woman. But I knew Angus. He was a man to whom dishonor was not only abhorrent, it was frightening. He avoided it as another might have the touch of leprosy or the plague." Her voice at last lost its steadiness and cracked with effort of control. "He was a truly good man, Mr. Monk, a man who knew evil for the ugliness and the ruin it is. It had no disguise of charm for him."

His intelligence told him it was a bereaved woman speaking with the hindsight of love, and his instinct told him it was the truth. This is how he had always looked in her eyes, and although she admired it wholeheartedly, it also exasperated or oppressed her at times also.

"Now so many days have passed," she said very quietly, "I fear it may be beyond anyone's ability to prove what has happened to him."

He felt guilty, which was unreasonable. Even if he had followed Angus on the very day he disappeared, he might still not have been able to prove murder against Caleb. There were enough ways of disposing of a body in Limehouse. The river was deep there, with its ebb tide to carry flotsam out and its cargo boats coming and going. At the moment there were also the common graves for the victims of typhoid, to name only a few.

He put half a dozen more coals on the fire.

"You do not always need a body to presume death," he said carefully, watching her face. "Although it may be a good deal harder to prove murder—and Caleb's guilt."

"I don't care about Caleb's guilt." Her eyes did not deviate from his face. "God will take care of him."

"But not of you?" he asked. "I would have thought you a great deal more deserving . . . and more urgent."

"I cannot wait for charity, Mr. Monk," she answered with some asperity.

He smiled. "I apologize. Of course not. But I should like to deal with Caleb before waiting for God. I am doing all I can, and I am much closer than I was last time we spoke. I have found a witness who saw Angus in Limehouse, on the day of his disappearance, in a tavern where he might easily have met Caleb. I'll find others. It takes time, but people will talk. It is just a matter of finding the right ones and persuading them to speak. I'll get Caleb himself, in the end."

"Will you . . ." She was on the edge of hope, but not allowing herself to grasp it. "I really don't care if you cannot prove it was Caleb." The shadow of a smile touched her mouth. "I don't even know what Angus would want. Isn't that absurd? For all that they were so utterly different, and Caleb hated him, he still loved Caleb. It seemed as if he would not forget the child he had been and the good times they had spent together before they quarreled. It hurt him every time he went to Limehouse after Caleb, yet he would not give up."

She looked away. "Sometimes it would be weeks, especially after a particularly wretched visit, but then he would relent and go back again. On those times he'd be gone even longer, as if it were necessary to make up the difference. I suppose childhood bonds are very deep."

"Did he tell you much of his visits to Caleb?" Monk asked. "Did he give you any indication of where they met, or where they might have been? If you can think of any description at all, it might help."

"No," she said with a slight frown, as though it puzzled her on recollection. "He never spoke of it at all. I think perhaps it was his silence which made me wonder if it was as much guilt as love which took him."

"Guilt?"

There was a gentle pride in her face when she replied, a very slight, unconscious lift of her chin. "Angus had made a success of everything, his profession, his family and his place in society. Caleb had nothing. He was feared and hated where Angus was loved and respected. He lived from hand to mouth, never knowing where the next meal would come from. He had no home, no family, nothing in his whole life of which to be proud."

It was a grim picture. Suddenly, with a jolt as if he had opened a door into a different, icy world, Monk perceived the loneliness of Caleb Stone, the failure that ate at his soul every time he saw his brother, the happy, smooth successful mirror image of what he might have been. And Angus's pity and his guilt would only make it worse.

And yet for Angus too, perhaps the memory of love and trust, the times when all things were equal for them and the divisions and griefs of the future still unknown, held a kind of sweetness that bound them together.

Why should it boil over into violence now? What had happened to change it? He looked at Genevieve. The strain was clearly marked in her face now. There were tiny lines in the skin around her mouth and eyes, visible even in the gaslight. Angus had been gone fifteen days. She was also using at least half her time nursing Enid Ravensbrook. No wonder she was tired and riven with fear.

"Have you someone in mind you can appoint to manage the business in Mr. Stonefield's absence?" he asked. It was hardly relevant to him, and yet he found himself waiting for the answer, willing that she had not. It seemed so coldly practical for a woman not yet surely a widow.

"I thought Mr. Niven," she answered frankly. "In spite of the error of judgment which brought him to his present state, he is of absolute honesty, and of unusual skill and knowledge in the business. I think he would not be so rash or so lenient in another's cause. Mr. Arbuthnot has always thought well of him, and might not be averse to continuing with us if it was in Mr. Niven's service. Mr. Niven is also very agreeable, and I should not mind thinking of him in Angus's place, since there needs must be someone. He has no family of his own, and would not be seeking to put me, or my sons, from their place."

It should have made no difference whatever, and yet he found himself chilled by the readiness of her reply.

"I had not realized you knew him personally," he said.

"Of course. He and Angus had a most cordial relationship. He has dined with us on many occasions. He is one of the few people we entertain in our home." The shadow crossed her features again. "But naturally I cannot approach him yet. It would be quite improper until I have some proof of Angus's fate that will satisfy the law." She sat very straight and sighed, as if controlling herself with an effort.

He wondered exactly what emotion it was that lay so powerfully just beneath the surface of her composure. There was a strength in her at odds with her gentle, very womanly appearance, the aura of obedient wife and devoted mother, some depth to her far out of the ordinary. It troubled him, because he had liked what he had first believed of her; even her quiet strength was appealing. He did not want to think of it as ruthlessness.

"I will do all I can, Mrs. Stonefield," he promised, his tone of voice unwittingly putting some distance between them. "As you suggest, I shall concentrate my efforts upon satisfying the authorities that your husband is dead, and leave the manner of his death for others to worry about. In the meantime, since it may not be an easy task, or a quick one, I advise you to consider Lord Ravensbrook's offer of a home for yourself and your family, even if it is upon temporary terms."

She sensed his thoughts and stood up gracefully, gathering her cape around her with a quick movement, but her face registered distaste and a hardening stubbornness of resistance.

"It will be a last resort, Mr. Monk, and I am not yet come to that pass. I think I shall call upon Mr. Niven, and test his feelings in the matter, before I return to Lady Ravensbrook. Good day to you."


The next few hours passed with agonizing slowness for Hester. She sat by Enid's bedside watching her haggard face, which was white, sweat-soaked, with two blotches of hectic color on the cheekbones. Her hair was tangled, her body tensed, turning and shivering with pain, too sore to touch. Hester could do little but keep patting her softly with cool cloths, but still her fever rose. She was delirious, seldom wholly aware of where she was.

Genevieve returned some time in the evening and looked in for a few moments. She was not due to take her turn until morning, when Hester would go to the dressing room for a few hours' sleep.

They exchanged glances. Genevieve was flushed. Hester presumed it to be from the chill outside, until she spoke.

"I have just been to see Mr. Monk. I am afraid he does not understand my urgency to know of Angus's fate." She stopped just inside the door, her voice low in case she should disturb Enid. "Sometimes I think the suspense is more than I can bear. Then I went to call upon Mr. Niven . . . Titus Niven . . . he used to prosper in the same business as my husband, until very lately. He was also a friend."

Even though she had spoken so softly, Enid started and tried to sit up. Quickly Hester eased her down again, smoothing her hair off her brow and speaking softly to her, although she was uncertain if Enid heard her or not.

Genevieve looked at Hester, her face tight with fear. The question was so plain it needed no speech. She was afraid the crisis was coming, and Enid might not survive the night.

Hester had no answer. Anything she could say would be only a guess, and a hope.

Genevieve let out her breath slowly. The ghost of a smile returned to her face, but it was only a reaching across pain in a moment's closeness; there was no happiness in it. Whatever comfort or ray of light Titus Niven had been able to give, it was gone again. Even the gentleness with which she had spoken his name seemed forgotten.

"There is no point in your remaining," Hester told her honestly. "It might be tonight, it might not be until tomorrow. There's nothing you can do, except be ready to take over in the morning." She tried to smile, and failed.

"I will," Genevieve promised, touching her lightly on the shoulder. Then she turned and went out of the door, closing it behind her with barely a click.

The early evening was dark, rain battering against the windows behind the thick drawn curtains. The clock on the mantel was the only other sound except for the soft hissing of the gas, and every now and again a moan or whimper from Enid.

A little after half past seven, Lord Ravensbrook knocked on the door and immediately came in. He looked worn and there was a flicker of fear in the back of his eyes, thinly masked by pride.

"How is she?" he asked. Perhaps it was a pointless question, but he knew of nothing else to say, and it was expected. He needed to say something.

"I think the crisis may be tonight," she answered. She saw his face pinch, almost as if she had struck him. She regretted for a moment that she had been so forthright. Maybe it was brutal. But what if Enid died tonight, and she had not told him? There was nothing he could do for her, but afterwards his grief would be allied with guilt. She would have treated him as if he were a child, not able to stand the truth, not worthy to be told it. The healing would be harder, and perhaps never completed.

"I see." He stood still in the middle of the room, with its shadows and florals, its femininity, isolated by his inability to speak, the social conventions that bound them to their separate roles. He was a peer of the realm, a man expected to have courage both physical and moral, absolute mastery of his emotions. She was a woman, the weaker vessel, expected to weep, to lean on others, and above all she was an employee. The fact that he did not actually pay her was irrelevant. He was as incapable of crossing the chasm between them as she. Very possibly it had not even occurred to him. He simply stood still and suffered.

When he turned slowly, his eyes were very dark and there was almost an opaque look in them, as if he could not focus his gaze. He took a deep breath.

"You mean would I like to be here at the end? Yes . . . yes, of course I would. You must send for me." He stopped, uncertain whether to offer to remain now. He looked across the bed. It had been changed only two hours ago, but it was badly rumpled now, in spite of Hester's frequent straightening of it. He drew in his breath sharply. "Does . . . does she know I am here?"

"I don't know," Hester said honestly. "Even if she doesn't seem to, she may. Please don't think it is futile. She might be much comforted."

His hands were clenched by his sides. "Should I remain?" He did not move towards the bed, but looked at Hester.

"It is not necessary," she said with instant certainty. "Better to rest, then you will have the strength when it is needed."

He breathed out slowly. "You will call me?"

"Yes, as soon as there is any change, I promise you." She inclined her head towards the bell rope near the bed. "As long as there is someone awake to answer, they will come to you within moments."

"Thank you. I'm most obliged, Miss . . . Latterly." He went to the door and turned again. "You . . . you do a very fine work." And before she had time to respond, he was gone.

Some twenty minutes later Enid began to be more troubled. She tossed and turned in the bed, crying out in pain.

Hester touched her brow. It was burning hot, even hotter than before. Her eyes were open, although she did not seem to be aware of the room but stared beyond Hester, as if there were someone behind her.

"Gerald?" she said huskily, ". . . not here." She gasped and was silent for a moment. "My dear, you really must not come—Papa will . . ." She gave a little gasp and then tried to smile. "You know Mama favors Alexander."

Hester wrung out the cloth in cool water again and laid it across Enid's brow, then moved the sheet and put it gently on her throat and chest. She had tried to get her to drink, and failed. She must at least do all she could to reduce her temperature. She seemed now completely delirious.

"All right," Enid said suddenly. "Don't tell Papa ... he is such a ..." She tossed and pulled away, then suddenly seemed overtaken by sadness. "Poor George. But I simply couldn't! Such a bore. Don't understand that, do you?" She was quiet for several minutes, then tried to sit up, peering at Hester. "Milo? Don't be so angry with him. He didn't mean—"

"Hush." Hester put her arms around Enid. "He's not angry, I promise you. Lie down again. Rest."

But Enid's body was rigid and she was breathing heavily, gasping with distress.

"Milo! My dear, I'm so sorry! I know it hurt you ... but you really shouldn't ..."

"He isn't," Hester repeated. "He isn't upset. He only wants you to rest and get better." She held Enid closer. Her body was burning, shivering, her clothes sodden with perspiration. Through the thin cotton she felt light, as if the flesh had already shrunken and her bones were brittle. Only days ago she had been a strong woman.

"So angry!" Enid cried, her voice now harsh with distress. "Why? Why, Milo?"

Hester held her gently. "He's not angry, my dear. He really isn't. If he was, it was a long time ago. It's all over now. Lie still and rest."

For several minutes there was peace. Enid seemed to be easy.

Hester had seen many people in delirium, and she knew that past and present became muddled in the mind. Sometimes people seemed to retreat as far as childhood. The delusions of fever were terrifying: huge faces ballooned, then retreated; features were distorted, became hideous and threatening, full of deformities.

She ached to be able to help, to relieve any of the anguish, even to avert the crises, but there was nothing she knew to do. There was no medicine, no treatment. All anyone could do was wait and hope.

135

The gas hissed gently in the single light that was still burning. The clock ticked on the mantel. The fire was so low in the grate the coals were hot and red, but there was no flame whickering, no sound of collapsing embers.

Enid stirred again.

"Milo?" she whispered.

"Shall I send for him?" Hester asked. "He's only a few rooms away. He'll come."

"I know it troubles you, my dear," Enid went on as if she had not heard Hester's question. "But you really must let it go. It was only a letter. He shouldn't have written . . ." There was worry in her voice, and something that could even have been pity. "I shouldn't have laughed . . ." She trailed off and her words were lost in a mumble, and then suddenly she gave a giggle of pure delight before she fell silent.

Hester wrung out the cloth again. It was time she pulled the bell and had it changed to new water, clean and cool. But to reach it she would have to let go of Enid.

Very gently she tried to ease herself out, but Enid suddenly clung to her, her hand weak but desperate.

"Milo! Don't go! Of course it hurts. It was shameful of him. I understand, my dear . . . but . . ." Again her words became jumbled and made no more sense. Her mind began to wander. She seemed to be a young woman again, mentioning dancing, parties. Sometimes her words were indistinguishable, but occasionally one or two would come through clearly, a man's name, a word of endearment, a chiding or a farewell. It seemed that either in imagination or reality, Enid had had many admirers, and from the intimacy of her voice and the snatched references here and there, some had loved her very much. Milo's name was spoken once with a cry of frustration, almost despair, and then again later two or three times in a row, as if she were fascinated by it, and it was both tenderness and exasperation to her.

Towards midnight she became quieter, and Hester feared she was slipping away. She was very weak, and the fever seemed, if anything, worse. She left her for a moment to pull the bell rope. Dingle came almost immediately, still fully dressed, her face pale with distress, eyes wide. Hester asked her to fetch Lord Ravensbrook and take away the water and bring fresh, and clean towels.

"Is it . . ." Dingle started, then changed her mind. "Is it time to change the bed linen, do you think, before his lordship comes?"

"No, thank you," Hester declined. "I'll not disturb her."

"I'll help you, miss."

"It won't make any difference now."

"Is it . . . the end?" Dingle forced the words between stiff lips. She looked very close to weeping. Hester wondered how long she had been with Enid . . . possibly all her adult life, maybe thirty years or more. If she were fortunate, Lord Ravensbrook would have allowed Enid to make provisions for her, or he would do so himself. Otherwise she would be without a position—although from her white face and brimming eyes, that was far from her thoughts now.

"I think it is the crisis," Hester answered. "But she is a strong woman, and she has courage. It may not be the end."

" 'Course she has," Dingle said with intensity. "Never know'd anybody like her for spirit. But typhoid's a terrible illness. It's took so many."

On the bed Enid gave a little moan, then lay perfectly still.

Dingle gasped.

"It's all right," Hester said quickly, seeing the faint rise and fall of Enid's breast. "But you had better fetch his lordship without delay. Then don't forget the water—and cool, not hot. Just take the chill off it, that's all."

Dingle hesitated. "I know you done all the nursing, but I'll lay her out, if you please."

"Of course," Hester agreed. "If it's necessary. But the battle isn't lost yet. Now please send for the water. It may make a difference."

Dingle whirled around and almost ran to the door. Perhaps she had thought it simply cosmetic. Now her feet flew along the passage and she returned in less than five minutes with a great ewer full of water barely off the chill, and a clean towel over her arm.

"Thank you." Hester took the ewer with the briefest smile and immediately dipped the towel. Then she laid it, still wet, across Enid's brow and her throat, then sponged her hands and lower arms.

"Help me hold her up a little," she asked. "And I'll place it in the back of her neck for a moment or two."

Dingle obliged instantly.

"Lord Ravensbrook is taking a long time," Hester murmured, laying Enid back again. "Was he very deeply asleep?"

"Oh!" Dingle stared at her, aghast. "I forgot 'im! Oh dear—I'd better go and fetch him now!" She did not ask Hester to keep silent about the omission, but her eyes made the plea for her.

"The water was more important," Hester said by way of agreement.

"I'll get 'im now." Dingle was already on her way to the door. "An' I'd better tell Miss Genevieve . . ."

Milo Ravensbrook came in within moments. He had dressed, but little more. His hair was uncombed and lay in thick, untidy curls most women would have envied with a passion. His eyes were hollow and his cheeks pinched and dark with stubble. He looked angry, frightened and extraordinarily vulnerable. He ignored Hester and went up to the bed and stood staring at his wife.

The clock on the mantelshelf gave a faint chime of quarter past midnight.

"It's cold in here," he said without turning, accusation flaring in his voice. "You've let it get cold. Stoke the fire."

She did not bother to argue. It probably did not matter now, and he was not in a mood to listen. Obediently she went to the coal bucket, picked up the tongs and placed two pieces on the hot embers. They were slow to ignite.

"Use the bellows," he commanded.

She had seen grief take people in many different ways. Sometimes it was dread of the loneliness which would follow, the long days and years of no one with whom to share their inner thoughts, the feelings which could not be explained, the belief that no one else would love them as that person had, and accept and understand their faults as well as their virtues. For some it was guilt that somehow or other they had not said or done all that they might, and now it was already too late. The minutes were slipping by, and still they could think of nothing adequate to say to make up for all the mistakes and missed opportunities. "Thank you" or "I love you" was too hard to say, and too simple.

And for many it was the fear of death itself, the absolute knowledge that one day they must face it too, and in spite of even profound religious faith, they did not really know what lay beyond. An hour a week of formal ritual was no comfort to the mind or the soul when faced with reality. Faith must be part of the daily web of life, a trust tested in a myriad smaller things, before it can be a bridge over the chasm of such a passage from the known to the unknown. If Milo Ravensbrook was afraid for himself, she did not blame him.

"You can speak to her," she said to him from the end of the bed to where he stood beside it, still looking down at Enid without touching her. "Even if she does not respond, she may hear you."

He raised his head, his expression impatient, almost accusatory.

"It may comfort her," she added.

Suddenly the anger drained out of him. He looked at Hester steadily, not so much at her face as at her gray dress and white apron, which were not Dingle's clothes but her own again. She realized how used he must be to women in such attire. She probably did not appear very different from the nursery maid or the nanny who would have brought him up, told him stories, given him his food and sat with him at mealtimes and made sure he ate what was put before him, disciplined him, nursed him when he was sick, accompanied him when he went out for walks in the park or for rides in the carriage. There was a lifetime's association with the gray, starched dress, and a score of others like it.

He turned away again and obeyed her, sitting on the bed, his back to her.

"Enid," he said a little awkwardly. "Enid?"

For several minutes there was no response. He shifted and seemed about to move away again, when she muttered something.

He leaned forward. "Enid!"

"Milo?" Her voice was barely audible, a whisper with a dry wheeze in the middle. "Don't be so angry . . . you frighten me!"

"I'm not angry, my dear," he said gently. "You are dreaming! I'm not angry in the slightest."

"He didn't mean to . . ." She sighed and was silent for several minutes. Ravensbrook turned to look at Hester, his eyes demanding an answer.

Hester moved to the other side of the bed. Enid was very white, her skin stretched over her cheekbones, her eyes far back in her head as if the sockets were too large for them. But she was still breathing, barely visibly, perhaps too lightly for Ravensbrook to be certain.

"It hasn't comforted her at all!" He choked on the words. "It's made it worse! She thinks I'm angry!" It was a charge, a blame against Hester for her misjudgment.

"And you have assured her you are not. Surely that must be of comfort," Hester replied.

He looked away impatiently, temper darkening his face.

"Angus," Enid said suddenly. "You must forgive him, Milo, however hard it is. He tried, I swear he tried!"

"I know he tried!" Ravensbrook said quickly, turning towards her, his own fear of the disease temporarily forgotten. "It is all past, I promise you."

Enid let out her breath in a long sigh and the faintest shadow of a smile touched her lips and then faded away.

"Enid!" he cried out, taking her hand roughly.

Hester picked up the damp cloth again and wiped Enid's brow, then her cheeks, then her lips and throat.

"That's bloody useless, woman!" Ravensbrook said loudly, lurching backwards and standing up. "Don't go through your damned rituals in front of me. Can't you at least have the decency to wait until I am out of the room. She was my wife, for God's sake!"

Hester held her hand on Enid's throat, high, under the chin, and pressed hard. She felt the skin cooler, the pulse weak but steady.

"She's asleep," she said with certainty.

"I don't want your bloody euphemisms!" His voice was cracking, but close to a shout, and filled with helpless rage. "I won't be treated like a child by some damn servant, and in my own house!"

"She is asleep!" Hester repeated firmly. "The fever has broken. When she wakens she will begin to get better. It may take some time. She has been very ill, but with care she will make a full recovery. That is if you don't distress her now and break her rest with your temper!"

"What?" he said, still angry, confused.

"Do you wish me to repeat it?" she asked.

"No! No." He stood perfectly still—just inside the door. "Are you sure? Do you know what you are talking about?"

"Yes. I have seen a great deal of typhoid fever before."

"In the East End?" he said derisively. "They're dying like flies!"

"In the Crimea," she corrected him. "And hundreds of the men died there too, but not all."

"Oh." His face ironed out. "Yes, I forgot about the Crimea."

"You wouldn't had you been there!" she snapped.

He made no remark, nor did he thank her, but went out, closing the door behind him.

She rang the bell, to tell Dingle that Enid was past the crisis and have her take away the bowl of used water. She also asked for a cup of tea. Until that moment she had not realized how devastatingly tired she was.

Dingle brought her tea, hot buttered toast, a fresh stone hot water bottle and a blanket warmed next to the kitchen fire.

"But you will stay with her, won't you?" she asked urgently. "Just in case?"

"Yes I will," Hester promised.

For the first time since Hester had arrived, Dingle's face relaxed into a smile.

"Thank you, miss. God bless you."

Monk was now certain in his own mind that there was no other course but to find Caleb Stone. None of his doubts about Genevieve warranted any delay or gave rise to anything more than a suspicion at the back of his mind, an awareness, haunting and painful, of other possibilities. But whatever they might be, they still led back to Caleb. There would be both time and need to apportion guilt once Angus's fate was known, or so deeply implicated that the authorities were obliged to investigate it. He dressed in old clothes which he must have purchased some time ago for such a task. His own wardrobe was immaculate. He had the tailor's bills from past years as testament to that, and to his vanity. The quality and cut of it, the perfectly fitting shoulders, the smooth, flat lapels made him wince at the expense, at the same time as giving him an acute satisfaction. The feel of the cloth pleased him every time he dressed, as did his elegant reflection in the glass.

However, today he was bound for Limehouse, and possibly the Isle of Dogs, in search of Caleb Stone, and he did not wish to be obvious as a stranger. As such he would be both disliked and despised, and most certainly lied to. Therefore he put on a torn striped shirt without a collar, then baggy, ill-fitting brownish-black trousers, and grimaced at the figure he cut. Then a stained waistcoat (largely for warmth) and an outer jacket of brown wool with several moth holes in it. He crowned it with a tall hat, and—refusing to look at himself again—he set out into the light drizzle of early morning.

He took a cab as far as the end of Commercial Road East in the heart of Limehouse, then continued on foot. He already knew it was going to be difficult to find Caleb. He had tried tentatively before. No one was eager to talk about him.

He turned his coat collar up and walked across Britannia Bridge over the dark water of Limehouse Cut, past the town hall and onto the West India Dock Road, then turned sharp right down Three Colt Street towards the river and Gun Lane. He had several places in mind to pursue the serious quest for Caleb. From what he had already learned of him, his life was a precarious balance on the edge of survival. He had been involved in various acts of violence and duplicity. He had a razor-edge temper and was spoken of in anxious and whispered tones. But so far, Monk had not been able to learn exactly how he made his money, nor where he lived, except most approximately that it was east, downriver from the West India Dock.

He began with the pawnbroker in Gun Lane. He had been there before. He could not remember anything about either the man himself or the small room no doubt crowded with domestic objects of every kind, grim reminders of the degree of poverty in the area. But the man's expression of alarm when he stood over the counter and the light from the oil lamps caught his face, was proof that some time in the past they had met before, and Monk had had the best of it.

Of course, he no longer had the power of the police to use, and Wiggins, the proprietor, was a hard man. He could not have plied his trade for long if he were taken advantage of often.

"Yes?" he said guardedly as Monk came in empty-handed. Then he recognized him. "I dunno nuffink ter tell yer," he said defensively. "I in't got nuffin 'ot, an' I don' do no bis'ness wi' thieves." He set his fat jaw hard. It was a lie, and they both knew it. Proving it was the issue.

Monk had already decided his course.

"I don't believe you, but then on the other hand, I don't care either."

"Yeah? Since when?" Wiggins's face registered profound disbelief.

"Since you're more use to me in business than in gaol," Monk replied.

"Oh, yeah?" He leaned over the counter in the space between two stone jars on one side and a pile of pans and kettles on the other. "Gorn inter a bit o' tradin' on the side, 'ave yer?" It was meant as an insult, then as Monk failed to be angry, his expression suddenly changed to one of amazement. "Gorn a bit bent, 'ave we? Well I never. 'Oo'd a' thought. Mr. Monk, an' all, reduced ter a bit on the side. 'Urts does it, not gettin' a reg'lar wage fer 'ounding folks? 'Ungry, are we, an' cold now an' agin? Must say as yer don' look the dandy as yer used ter. Right come down in the world, we 'ave." His smile grew with each new thought. "If yer wanter 'ock some o' that fancy rig o' yours, I daresay as I could see me way ter a fair price. Sell 'em up west, I could, for a nice penny. O' course, that's if yer don' wanna be seen doin' it yerself, like? Catches yer pride, do it?"

Monk made a powerful effort to control his temper. He considered returning at a later date in the very best clothes he had, and giving Wiggins a gold sovereign just to make the point.

"I'm a bad enemy when I'm hard-pressed," he replied between his teeth. "And I'm hard-pressed now."

"You was always a bad enemy," Wiggins said sourly. "An' a bad friend too, for all I know. D'jer wanna 'ock summink or not?"

"I want to do a little business," Monk said carefully. "Not with you, with Caleb Stone."

Wiggins's face tightened.

"I've got a job for him," Monk lied. "One I'll pay him for, and from what I hear, he could use the money. I need to know where to find him, and you seem a good place to start."

"I dunno w'ere ter find 'im, nor I wouldn't tell you if I did." Wiggins's eyes were cold and hard. They did not flinch a fraction as they met Monk's.

The door opened and an undersized woman came in, a thin shawl held around her hunched shoulders, a pair of boots in her hand. She peered at Monk anxiously to determine whether to wait for him to finish his affairs or not.

"Wotcher want, Maisie?" Wiggins asked, cutting across Monk. "Them your Billy's boots again? I'll give yer sixpence. If'n I gives yer more, yer'll not raise enough ter get 'em back."

" 'E'll get paid Friday," she said tentatively, as if she were saying it more in hope than belief. " 'E's got a bit o' work. But I gotter feed the kids. Gimme a shilling, Mr. Wiggins. I'll get it back to yer."

"They in't worth a shillin'," Wiggins said immediately. "Got 'oles in 'em. I know them boots like the back o' me 'and. Sevenpence. That's the lot! Take it or leave it."

"What work does Billy do?" Monk asked suddenly.

Wiggins drew in his breath to interrupt, but the woman was too quick.

" 'E'll do anyfink, mister. Yer got summink as yer wants done, my Billy'll do it for yer." Her thin face was full of hope.

"I want to find Caleb Stone," Monk replied. "I just want to know where he lives, that's all. I'll speak to him myself. His brother has died, and I want to inform him officially. They were close, even though his brother lived up in the West End."

"I kin tell yer w'ere Selina lives," she said after taking a deep breath. "She's 'is woman, like."

Monk fished in his pocket and brought out a shilling. "That's for you now, and there's another when you take me to her doorstep. Keep the boots."

She grasped the shilling in a thin, dirty hand, shot Wiggins a look halfway between triumph and the knowledge that she would certainly need him again, then led the way out of the door with Monk close behind her. Wiggins swore and spat into a brass cuspidor on the floor.

Monk was led through lined and grimy streets down to the river and eastward, as he had expected, towards the Isle of Dogs. A raw wind blew up from the water, carrying the smell of salt, stale fish, the overspill of sewage and the cold dampness of the outgoing tide sweeping down from the Pool of London towards the estuary and the sea. Across the gray water endless strings of barges made their heavy way downstream, laden with merchandise for half the earth. Ships passed them outward bound, down towards the docks of Greenwich and beyond.

A brewers' dray kept pace with them along the road, its wheels rumbling over the uneven cobbles. A rag-and-bone man called out dolefully, as if expecting an answer. Two women on the corner launched into a fierce quarrel and a cat scuttered across an alleyway with a rat in its mouth.

They were going down Bridge Street, with Limehouse Reach on one side and the West India Docks on the other. Tall masts broke the skyline, barely moving against the clouds. Chimneys belched thin streams of smoke up into the air. Maisie kept walking on past Cuba Street, then at Manilla Street she stopped.

"Fird 'ouse along ere," she said huskily. "Dahn ve steps. On'y one door. Vat's 'er. Selina, 'er name is." She held out her hand tentatively, not sure if she would get the second shilling or not.

"What does she look like?" He wanted to see if her description tallied with Mr. Arbuthnot's. If it did he would trust her, for a shilling.

"A tart," she said quickly, then bit her lip. "Quite 'andsome, really, in a flashy sort o' way. Thin, I suppose, sharp nose, but good eyes, real good eyes." She looked at Monk to see if that was sufficient, and saw that it was not. "Sort o' brownish 'air, good an' thick. Always kind o' sure of 'erself, least w'en I sees 'er. Walks cocky, wi' a swing to 'er 'ips. Like I says, a tart." She sniffed. "But she's got guts, I'll give 'er that. Never 'eard 'er moan, not like some. Put a good face on it, no matter wot. An' she can't 'ave an easy time, wi' Caleb Stone bein' like 'e is."

"Thank you." Monk gave her the shilling. "Have you seen Caleb Stone?"

"Me? I don't go looking fer folks like that. I got enough o' me own troubles. I reckon as mebbe I seen 'im once. Though I'll deny it if yer asks in front o' anyone."

"I never saw you before," Monk said easily. "And if I were to see you again, I don't suppose I should know you. What's your name?"

She smiled conspiratorially, showing chipped teeth.

"In't got no name."

"That's what I thought. Third house along?"

"Yeah."

He turned and walked down the narrow footpath, barely wide enough to keep his feet out of the gutter, and at the third house went down the steps to the door which led off the small, rubbish-filled areaway. He knocked sharply, and had just raised his hand to repeat it when a window covered with sacking opened above him and an old woman stuck her head out.

"She in't there! Come back later ifn' yer want 'er."

Monk leaned back to look up. "How much later?"

"I dunno. Middle o' the day, mebbe." She ducked back in again without closing the window, and Monk stepped away only just in time to avoid being drenched by a pail of bedroom slops.

He waited in the street about twenty yards along, half sheltered by an overhanging wall, but from where he could still see the steps down to Selina's rooms. He grew steadily colder, and towards noon it began to rain. Many people passed him, perhaps taking him for a beggar or simply someone with nowhere else to be, one of the thousands who lived on scraps and slept in doorways. The workhouse provided food of a sort, a shelter, but little heat, and the rigid rules were almost as harsh as those in prison. There were some who thought it an even worse place.

No one regarded him with more than a passing observation, not even curiosity, and he avoided the challenge of meeting their eyes. Paupers, such as he was pretending to be, cast their glances down, wary, ashamed and frightened of everything.

Shortly after noon he saw a woman approaching from West Ferry Road, where Bridge Street swept around the curve of the river which formed the Isle of Dogs. She was of average height, but she strode with her head high and a kind of swing in her step. Even across the street he could see that her face was highly individual. Her cheekbones were high, giving her eyes a slanted look, her nose well formed, if a little sharp, and her mouth generous. He had no doubt that this was Selina. Her face had the courage and the originality to hold the attention of men like Caleb Stone, who might be violent and degraded now, but who had been born to better things.

He moved from his position, his legs aching, joints locked from having maintained his stillness for so long. He almost stumbled off the curb; his feet were so cold he had lost sensation in them. He made his way across the street, stepping in the filth and regaining his balance by flailing his arms. Furious with himself, he caught up with her just as she started down the steps.

She swung around when he was a yard away from her, a knife in her hand.

"You watch yerself, mister!" she warned. "Try anyfink, an' I'll cut yer gizzard out, I warn yer!"

Monk stood his ground, though she had taken him by surprise. If he backed away she would tell him nothing.

"I don't pay for women," he said with a tight smile. "And I've never had to take one who wasn't willing. I want to talk to you."

"Oh yeah?" Disbelief was plain in her face, and yet she was looking at him squarely. There was no broken spirit behind her dark eyes, and her fear was only physical.

"I've come from your sister-in-law."

"Well, that's a new one." She arched her fine brows with amusement. "I in't got no sister-in-law, so that's a lie. Best try again."

"I was being polite," he said between his teeth. "The benefit of the doubt. She is certainly married to Angus. I thought it possible you might be married to Caleb."

Her body tightened. Her slim hands on the broken railing were grasping it till the knuckles were white. But her face barely changed.

"Did yer. So wot if I are? 'Oo are yer?"

"I told you, I represent Angus's wife."

"No yer don't." She looked him up and down with immeasurable scorn. "She wouldn't give yer 'ouse room! She'd call the rozzers if summink like you even spoke to 'er, less'n it were to ask her for an 'alfpenny's charity."

Monk enunciated very carefully in his best diction.

"And if I were to come here in my usual clothes, I would be as obvious as you would be dressed like that at a presentation to the Queen. Young ladies wear white for such occasions," he added.

"An' o' course yer invited ter such fings, so you'd know!" she said sarcastically, but her eyes were searching his face, and the disbelief was waning.

He put out a strong, clean hand, slim-fingered, immaculate-nailed, and grasped the railing near hers, but did not touch her.

She looked at his hand a moment, then back at his face.

"Wotcher want?" she said slowly.

"Do you want to discuss it on the step? You've got nosy neighbors—upstairs, if nowhere else."

"Fanny Bragg? Jealous ol' cow. Yeah, she'd love the chance ter throw a bucket o' slops over me. Come on inside." And she took out a key and inserted it in the door, turned it and led him in.

The room was dark, being lit by only one window, and that below street level, but it was larger than he would have guessed from outside, and surprisingly clean. The black potbellied stove gave out a considerable warmth, and there was a rug of knotted rags on the floor. There were three chairs of various colors and in different states of repair, but all of them comfortable enough, and the large bed in the shadows at the farther end was made up and covered with a ragged quilt.

He closed the door behind him and looked at her with a new regard. Whatever else she was, she had done her best to make a home of this.

"Well?" she demanded. "So yer come from Angus's wife. Wot abaht it? Why? Wot does she want wi' me?" Her lips tightened into an unreadable grimace. Her voice altered tone. "Or is it Caleb yer wants?" There was a world of emotion behind the simple pronunciation of his name. She was afraid of it, and yet her tongue lingered over it as if it were precious and she wanted an excuse to say it again.

"Yes, Caleb too," he agreed. She would not have believed him had he denied it.

"Why?" She did not move. "She never bothered wi' me afore. Why now? Angus comes 'ere now an' agin, but she never come."

"But Angus does?" he said gently.

She stared at him. There was fear in the back of her eyes, but also defiance. She would not betray Caleb, whether from love of him, self-interest because in some way he provided for her, or because she knew the violence in him and what he might do to her if she let him down. Monk had no way of knowing. And he would like to have known. In spite of the contempt with which he had begun, he found himself regarding her as more than just a means to find Caleb, or a woman who had attached herself to a bestial man simply to survive.

He had assumed she was not going to answer when finally she spoke.

" 'E in't got no love for Angus," she said carefully. " 'E don' understand 'im."

There was something in her inflexion, the lack of anger in it, which made him think that she did not include herself in the feeling, but it was too subtle to press, and far too delicate.

"Does he ever go uptown to see him?" he said instead.

"Caleb?" Her eyes widened. "No, not 'im. Caleb never goes uptown. Least, never that I knows. Look, mister, Caleb don't live 'ere. 'E just comes 'ere w'en 'e feels like it. I in't 'is keeper."

"But you are his woman. . . ."

Suddenly there was a softness in her face. The harsh lines of anger and defence melted, taking years away from her, leaving her, for an instant in the uncertain light, the twenty-five-year-old woman she should have been, would have been in Genevieve's place, or Drusilla's.

"Yeah," she agreed, lifting her chin a fraction.

"So when he asks you, you go uptown to see Angus." He made it a conclusion, not a question.

Again she was guarded. "Yeah. 'E told me ter go if he's short on the rent. But I in't never bin ter 'is 'ouse. Wouldn't know w'ere to look fer it."

"But you know his place of business."

"Yeah. So?"

"You went on the eighteenth of January, in the morning."

She hesitated only fractionally. Her eyes never left his, and she knew he must have spoken to Arbuthnot.

"So wot if I did? 'E in't complainin'."

"Caleb asked you?"

"Like I told yer, I goes up if the rent's up an' Caleb or I in't got it."

"So you go and ask Angus for it and he pays? Why, when Caleb despises him so much?"

Her jaw tightened again. "Caleb don' tell me. In't my business. Jus' wan'ed ter see 'is bruvver. They's twins, yer know. That in't like ordinary bruvvers. 'Is wife won't never stop that, not if she tries till 'er dyin' day. Caleb in't got no love for Angus, like Angus 'as for Caleb. Come if Caleb snaps 'is fingers, 'e does." She said it with a kind of pride, and something towards Angus which could almost have been pity, were her loyalties not so plainly defined.

"And Angus came this time?"

"Yeah. Why? I tol' yer, she won't stop 'im!"

"Did you see him that day?"

"Yeah!"

"I don't mean in the office, I mean here in the Isle of Dogs."

"Not 'ere. I saw 'im in Lime'ouse, but 'e were comin' this way. I s'pose 'e went over the West India Docks t'wards Blackwall an' the river again." She bent and put a piece of rotten wood into the stove and closed the door with a clatter.

"But you saw him?" he persisted.

"I jus' said I saw 'im. Don't yer 'ear good?"

"Did you see him with Caleb?"

She tipped some water out of a pail into a kettle and set it on the stove to boil.

"I tol' jer, I saw 'im goin' inter the Docks t'wards Blackwall, an' that's w'ere Caleb said 'e were goin' ter be. In't that enough for yer?"

"Is that where Caleb said to meet him?" he asked. "What instructions did you give Angus? Or did they always meet in the same place?"

"Down by the Cattle Wharf at Cold'arbour, often as not," she replied. "Any'ow, that's wot 'e said that time, why?" She looked back at him. " 'Oo cares? 'E in't there now! Why yer askin' me all these things? Ask 'im! 'E knows w'ere 'e went!"

"Maybe he is still there," Monk said, raising his eyebrows.

She drew breath to mock him, then saw the seriousness beneath his tone, and suddenly doubt entered her.

"Wot jer mean? Yer talkin' daft!" She put her hands on her hips. "Look, wot jer come 'ere fer anyway? Wot jer want? If yer want Caleb, the more fool you! Go look fer 'im! If Angus sent yer, then tell me wot fer, an' I'll tell Caleb. 'E'll come if 'e wants ter, and not if 'e don't."

There was no point in trying to trick her.

"No one has seen Angus since you did." He looked her straight in the eyes—large, dark eyes with long lashes. "He never returned home."

" 'E never went ..." Her face paled under its dirt and paint. "Wotcher sayin'? 'E never ran orff! 'E's got everyfink 'ere. 'As 'e done summink? Is 'e on the run from the rozzers, then?" A flicker of both amusement and pity touched her mouth.

"I think it very unlikely," he replied with an answering gleam of black laughter. Although even as he did so, he realized it was not a total impossibility, though it had never occurred to him before. "Far more probably that he is dead."

"Dead!" Her face blanched. "Why would 'e be dead?"

"Ask Caleb!"

"Caleb?" Her eyes widened and she gulped hard. "That's wot yer 'ere fer!" Her voice rose shrilly. "You fink as Caleb murdered 'im! 'E never! Why? Why'd 'e kill 'im arter all these years? It don't make no sense." But her mouth was dry and there was terror in her eyes. She stared at him, searching for some argument to convince him, but even as she did so, the hope faded and disappeared. She knew from his face that he had seen the knowledge in her. Caleb could very easily have killed his brother, and they both knew it—she from knowing Caleb, he from her eyes.

The kettle started to jiggle from the heat of the stove.

"Yer'll never get 'im!" she said desperately, fear and protection equal in her now. "Yer'll never take Caleb Stone."

"Perhaps not. I'm more interested in proving Angus is dead."

"Why?" she demanded. "That won't prove it were Caleb, an' it sure as 'ellfire won't catch 'im . . . or 'ang 'im." Her face was stricken and her voice had a thickness of emotion in it.

"So his wife can be treated like a widow," he replied. "And his children be fed."

She let out her breath. "Well in't nuffin' I can do, even if I were minded to." She was struggling to convince him, and herself. She put too much certainty into it, torn by loyalties.

"You already have," he replied. "I knew Angus was last seen here, going towards Blackwall Reach. No one ever saw him after that."

"I'll deny it!"

"Of course you will. Caleb's your man. Even if he weren't, you wouldn't dare say it if he didn't want you to."

"I 'int afraid o' Caleb," she said defiantly. " 'E wouldn't 'urt me."

He did not bother to argue. It was another thing they both knew was a lie.

"Thank you," he said quietly. "Good-bye . . . for the moment."

She did not answer. On the stove the kettle started to steam.


Monk left Manilla Street and went east through the West India Docks, the way Angus Stonefield must have gone, and spent all afternoon combing the docks and slums along the Isle of Dogs and the Blackwall Reach. Caleb Stone was known well enough, but no one was willing to say where he was. Most of them would not even commit themselves to when they had last seen him.

A knife grinder admitted to having spoken with him two days before, a chandler to having sold him rope a week ago, the keeper of the Folly House Tavern to seeing him regularly, but none of them knew where he was to be found at any specific time, and all spoke his name carefully, not necessarily with fear, but not lightly. Monk had no doubt whose side they would be on if there were ever a necessity to choose.

He left Blackwall at dusk, and was pleased to get back to Fitzroy Street to wash and change into his more customary attire. He would go to Ravensbrook House to report to Genevieve. After all, he had something to say this time. Then he had a dinner engagement with Drusilla Wyndham. The very thought of it made him smile. It was like a sweet smell after the dirt and stench of the Isle of Dogs, like laughter and bright colors after the gray misery.

He wore his very best jacket, perhaps partly because of the memory of Selina and her opinion of him, but mostly it was the mood he felt every time he thought of Drusilla. He could see her face in his mind's eye: the wide hazel eyes, the delicate brows, the soft mass of honey-shaded hair, the way her cheeks dimpled when she smiled. She had grace and charm, assurance, wit. She took nothing too seriously. She was a joy to the eye and to the ear, to the mind and the emotions. She seemed to have the perfect judgment of exactly what to say, and even when to remain silent.

He looked at himself in the glass, adjusting his cravat to perfection. Then, taking his overcoat and his hat, he went out of the door and walked smartly to find a hansom, humming a little tune to himself.

Of course Hester was likely to be at Ravensbrook House, but that was something he could not avoid. He would almost certainly not run into her. She would be in the sickroom, where he would not be permitted, even had he wished to go, which he certainly did not.

He tipped his hat to a woman he passed in the arc of the street lamp. The knowledge that he would not see Hester was an instant relief. He was in no mood to have his present happiness spoiled by her criticism, her constant reminder of the pain and injustices of life. She was so one-sided about everything. She had no sense of proportion. It was a fault possessed by many women. They took everything both literally and personally. Those like Drusilla, who could see the realities and yet had the courage to laugh and carry herself with consummate grace, were rare indeed. He was extraordinarily fortunate that she was so obviously enjoying his company every bit as much as he did hers.

Unconsciously he increased his pace, striding out over the wet pavement. He was quite aware that women found him attractive. He did not have to work at it; there was an element in his nature which drew their fascination. Perhaps it was a sense of danger, of emotions suppressed beneath the surface. It was of no importance. He simply realized it was there, and from time to time had taken some slight advantage of it. To use it fully would be stupid. The last thing he wanted was some woman pursuing him, thinking of romance, even marriage.

He could marry no one. He had no idea what lay in his past beyond the last couple of years, and perhaps even more frightening than that, what lay in his character. He had very nearly killed one man in a blinding rage. That he knew beyond question. Memories of those awful moments were still there, buried in his mind, sometimes troubling his dreams.

The fact that the man was one of the worst blackguards he had ever known was immaterial. It was not the evil in the man he feared. He was dead now, killed by another hand. It was the darkness within himself.

But Drusilla knew nothing of that, which was part of her allure.

Hester did, of course. But then he did not want the thought of Hester in his mind, especially tonight, or of the typhoid fever, its anguish or its bitter realities. He would tell Genevieve Stonefield he had made a considerable stride forward today, then he would leave and spend a bright, witty and elegant evening with Drusilla.

He stepped off the curb and hailed a hansom cab, his voice bright with anticipation.

# CHAPTER
# SIX

———

The next morning, Monk woke with a smile and arose early. The February morning was dark and windy and there was a hard frost in the sheltered hollows of the streets, but he set out before eight for the East End again, and the Blackwall Reach. He meant to find Caleb Stone, and he would not cease until he did, today, tomorrow, or the day after. If the man were alive, he was too angry, too distinctive and too well known to disappear.

By nine he was standing in thin daylight on the banks of the Blackwall Reach on the Isle of Dogs. This time he did not bother with pawnbrokers or street peddlers, but went straight to the places where Caleb might have eaten or slept. He tried hot pie sellers, alehouses and taverns, other vagrants who slept rough in old packing cases and discarded sails or awnings, piles of rotting rope, with timbers rigged to make some kind of shelter.

Yes, one old man had seen him the night before last, striding down Coldharbour towards the Blackwall Stairs. He had been wearing a huge coat, and the tails of it had flapped wide around his legs, like broken wings.

Was he sure it was Caleb?

The answer was a hollow laugh.

He did not ask anyone else if they were sure. Their faces told it for them. A young woman, perhaps eighteen or nineteen, simply ran away. A one-legged man sitting awkwardly, splicing ropes with horny hands, said he had seen him yesterday going toward the Folly House

Tavern. He was walking rapidly against the wind, and looked pleased with himself.

Monk took himself to the Folly House Tavern, a surprisingly clean establishment full of dark oak paneling and the smell of tallow candles whose flickering lights reflected in a mirror over the bar. Even at this hour of the morning there were a dozen people about, either drinking ale or busy with some chore of fetching or cleaning.

"Yeah?" the landlord inquired cautiously. Monk looked ordinary enough, but he was a stranger.

"Ale." Monk leaned against the bar casually.

The landlord pulled it and presented him with the tankard.

Monk handed over threepence, and a penny for the landlord, who took it without comment.

"Do you know Caleb Stone?" Monk said after a few minutes.

"I might," the landlord said guardedly.

"Think he'll be in today?" Monk went on.

"Dunno," the landlord replied expressionlessly.

Monk took half a crown out of his pocket and played with it in his fingers. Along the bar counter several other drinkers ceased moving and the dull background chatter stopped.

"Pity." Monk took another sip of his ale.

"Don't never know wiv 'im," the landlord said carefully. " 'E comes w'en 'e suits, an' goes w'en 'e suits."

"He was here yesterday." Monk made it a statement.

"So wot if 'e were? 'E comes 'ere now an' then."

"Did you see him when he was here two weeks ago last Tuesday?"

" 'Ow do I know?" the landlord said in amazement. "D'yer fink I write down everyone wot comes in 'ere every day? Fink I got nuffink better ter do?"

" 'E were." Another little man leaned forward, bright gray eyes in a narrow face. " 'Im an' 'is bruvver, both."

"Garn! 'Ow jer know?" a short man said derisively. " 'Ow jer know it were Tuesday?"

" 'Cos it were same day as ol' Winnie fell orff the dray an' broke 'is 'ead," the little man replied with triumph. "That were Tuesday, an' it were Tuesday as Caleb an' 'is bruvver were 'ere. Lookin' at each other fit to kill, they was, both of 'em blazin' mad, faces like death, they 'ad."

Monk could hardly believe his luck.

"Thank you, Mr. . . ."

"Bickerstaff," the man replied, pleased with the attention.

"Thank you, Mr. Bickerstaff," Monk amended. "Have a drink, sir. You have been of great assistance to me." He passed over the half crown, and Bickerstaff grabbed it before such largesse could prove a mirage.

"I will," he said magniloquently. "Mr. Putney, hif you please, we'll 'ave drinks all 'round for them gents as is me friends. An' fer me new friend 'ere too. An' fer yerself, o' course. Not forgettin' yerself."

The landlord obliged.

Monk stayed another half hour, but even in the conviviality of free-flowing beer, he learned nothing further of use, except a more detailed description of precisely where Bickerstaff had seen Caleb and Angus, and their obvious quarrel.

The early afternoon found him pursuing an ephemeral trail downriver towards the East India Docks and Canning Town. Twice it seemed he was almost on Caleb's heels, then the trail petered out and he was left in the gray, wind-driven rain staring at an empty dockside. Dark-mounded barges moved silently up the river through the haze, voices calling across the water in strange, echoing singsong, and the incoming tide whispering in the shingle.

He started again, coat collar turned up, feet soaked, face set. Caleb Stone would not escape him if he combed every rookery and tenement along the river's edge; every rickety, overlapping wooden house; every dock and wharf; every flight of dark, water-slimed and sodden steps down to the incoming tide. He questioned, bullied, argued and bribed.

By half past three the light was beginning to weaken and he was standing on the Canal Dock Yard looking across the river at the chemical works and the Greenwich marshes beyond, veiled in misty rain. He had just missed Caleb again, this time by no more than half an hour. He swore long and viciously.

A bargee, broad-chested and bow-legged, swayed along the path towards him, chewing on the stem of a clay pipe.

"Gonna throw yourself in, are ye?" he said cheerfully. "Wi' a face like that it wouldn'a surprise me. Ye'll find it powerful cold. Take yer breath away, it will."

"It's bloody cold out here," Monk said ungraciously.

"In't nothing compared with the water," the bargee said, still with a smile. He fished in the pocket of his blue coat and brought out a bottle. " 'Ave a drop o' this. It don't cure much but the cold, but that's somethin'!"

Monk hesitated. It could be any rotgut, but he was frozen and bitterly angry. He had come so close.

"Not if yer goin' to jump, mind," the bargee said, pulling a face. "Waste o' good rum. Jamaickey, that is. Nothin' else like it. Ever bin ter Jamaickey?"

"No. No, I haven't." It was probably true, and it hardly mattered.

The man held out the bottle again.

Monk took it and put it to his lips. It was rum, a good rum too. He took a swig and felt the fire go down his throat. He passed it back.

"Thank you."

"Why don't ye come away from the water an' have a bite ter eat. I got a pie. Ye can have half."

Monk knew how precious the pie was, a whole pie. The man's kindness made him feel suddenly vulnerable again. There was too much that was worth caring about.

"That's good of you," he said gently. "But I have to catch up with a man, and I keep just missing him."

"What sort of a man?" the bargee said doubtfully, although he must have heard the change in Monk's voice, even if he could not see his expression in the waning light.

"Caleb Stone," Monk replied. "A violent sort of man, who almost certainly murdered his brother. I don't suppose I can prove that, not when the body could be anywhere. But I want to know if he's dead, for the widow's sake. I don't give a damn about Caleb."

"Don't ye? He murdered his brother, and ye don't care?" the bargee said with a sideways squint.

"I'd prove it if I could," Monk admitted. "But I'm hired to prove the brother's dead, so she can at least have what's hers and feed his children. I think she'd sooner have that than revenge. Wouldn't you?"

"Aye," the bargee agreed. "Aye, I would that. So ye want Caleb?"

"Yes." Monk stared fixedly at the darkening river. Was it worth trying to get across to the other side now? He had no idea where to start looking, or even if Caleb might have doubled back and by now be safe in some comfortable public house in the Isle of Dogs.

"I'll take ye," the bargee offered suddenly. "I know where 'e's gone. Leastways, I know where 'e's likely gone. I don't do wi' leavin' bairns without a father. He's a bad one, Caleb."

"Thank you," Monk accepted before the man had time to change his mind. "What's your name? Mine's Monk."

"Oh, aye. Don't suit ye, less it be one o' them inquisitor monks what used to burn folks. Mine's Archie McLeish. Ye'd better come wi' me. I've a boat a few paces along. Not much, cold and wet, but it'll get us across." And he turned and ambled off, walking on the sides of his feet with a sway as if the dockside were moving.

Monk caught up with him. "The inquisitors burned people for their beliefs," he said waspishly. "I don't give a sod what people believe, only what they do to each other."

"Ye have the face o' a man who cares," Archie replied without looking at him. "I wouldn'a want ye after me. I'd as soon have the de'il himself." He stopped at the top of a narrow flight of steps leading down to the water where a very small boat was rising gently as the tide rose. "It's a hard thing to care," he added.

Monk was about to deny that he cared, but Archie was not listening to him. He had bent his broad back and was loosening the moorings, which seemed to be in an extraordinarily complicated knot.

Monk climbed in and Archie settled to the oars. He pulled out skillfully, twisting the boat around, propelling it and steering it at the same time. The bank and the steps disappeared into the gray rain within yards. The thought crossed Monk's mind that no one knew where he was. He had accepted the offer without taking the slightest precaution. Archie McLeish could have been paid by Caleb to do precisely this! He must know Monk was after him. Monk could go overboard in the darkness and mist of the river and be swept out with the ebb tide, his body washed up days later, or never. Caleb Stone might be blamed, but no one could prove it. It would be one more accident. Maybe Archie McLeish would even say Monk threw himself in.

He sat gripping the gunwales, determined if it came to that, he would make a damned good fight of it. Archie McLeish would go over with him.

They passed barges moving steadily, dark mounds in the mist, riding lights to port and starboard, hundreds of tons of cargo making them juggernauts on the tide. If they were caught in front of one of those they would be splintered like matchwood. There was no sound but the water, the dismal hoot far off of a foghorn, and now and then someone shouting.

They passed a square-rigger coming down from the Pool of London, its bare spars looming above them in the mist, reminding Monk of a row of gibbets. It was growing perceptibly colder. The raw wind blew through his coat as if it had been cotton shoddy, and touched his bones.

"Afraid o' Caleb Stone, then, are ye?" Archie McLeish said cheerfully.

"No," Monk snapped.

"Well, ye look it." Archie pulled hard on the oars, leaning his weight into them. "Feel like I was rowing a man to 'is 'anging wi' a face like that, an' grippin' me boat like it'd escape ye if ye let it go."

Monk realized grimly how he must look, and made an effort to smile. It might well be worse.

"Goin' ter kill 'im, are ye?" Archie said conversationally. "It'd surely be one way. Then ye'd have a corpse ter pass off. I daresay no one'd know it wasn't his brother. Alike as two peas, they say."

Monk laughed abruptly. "I hadn't thought of it—but it sounds like a good idea . . . in fact, a brilliant one. Accomplish justice for everyone in one blow. Only trouble is, I don't know if Angus is dead. He might not be."

"Angus'd be the brother," Archie said with wide eyes. "Well, I don't know either, I'm glad to say. So I'll not be havin' to take ye back, because I'll no be party to murder . . . even o' the likes o' Caleb Stone."

Monk started to laugh.

"And why'll that be so funny?" Archie asked crossly. "I may be a rough man and not the gentleman ye seem to be, although God knows, ye look hard enough . . . but I've me standards, same as ye!"

"Maybe better," Monk granted. "It had just occurred to me you might murder me out here in the middle of this godforsaken waste of water . . . on Caleb's account."

Archie grunted, but his anger appeared to evaporate.

"Oh, aye," he said quietly. "Well . . . I could have an' all."

He rowed in silence for several minutes. The shadows of the chemical works on the farther shore loomed through the mist, and Archie had to change course with a wrench of the oars to avoid a barge moving out from the dim wharves as the rain drove in their faces.

"Ye'll be needing a spot o' help then," Archie said after several more minutes. "Ye'll no catch the like o' Caleb on your own."

"Possibly," Monk conceded. "But I'm not trying to take him into custody, only to speak with him."

"Oh, aye," Archie said skeptically. "An' ye suppose he'll believe that, do ye?"

On the face of it, it was unlikely, and Monk was indisposed to attempt explanation, partly because it was unclear in his mind anyway. He simply had no alternative but to pursue Caleb.

"If you are offering to help, I'm obliged," he said tartly. "What do you want for it? It won't be easy, or pleasant. Not necessarily even safe."

Archie grunted with disgust. "Think I'm a fool? I know what it'll be a sight better than you do, laddie. I'll come for the satisfaction o' it. I dinna need payin' for every damn thing I do!"

Monk smiled, although in the darkness he was not sure if Archie could see him.

"Thank you," he said graciously.

Archie grunted.

They came ashore on the mudflats and moored the boat to a post sticking up like a broken tooth, then Archie led the way up the bank to the rough grass, tussock and mud, now heavily shrouded in lessening rain and near darkness. There were lights ahead of them across the fields, if one could call them such, although from the squelch and suck on his boots, Monk thought it was bogland.

"Where are we?" he asked quietly.

"Headin' for Blackwall Lane," Archie answered. "Keep quiet. Sound travels, even when ye don't think it."

"He's here?"

"Aye, he came this way not ten minutes before us."

"Why? What's here?" Monk struggled to keep up with him, feeling the ground cling to his feet and the freezing rain drift against his face.

"Is it him ye're after, or summat else?" Archie asked from just ahead of him in the gloom.

"Him. I don't care what else is going on," Monk replied.

"Then be quiet, an' follow me!"

For what seemed like a quarter of an hour, Monk trudged through the darkness, first from marshland to the road, then along harder surface towards the lights of small cottages huddled on the black landscape, marked out only by the dim eye of oil lamps in windows.

Archie knocked at one door, and when it was opened, spoke for a few moments, but so quietly Monk heard no words. He withdrew and the door closed, leaving them in the bitter night. Archie waited a few minutes until his eyes grew accustomed again, then led the way towards the other side of the neck of land and the far curve of the river.

Monk opened his mouth to ask where they were going, then changed his mind. It was pointless. He pulled his collar even closer, jammed his hat down again and thrust his hands into his coat pockets and trudged on. The raw fog tasted of salt, sewage and the sour water that lies stagnant in fens and pools beyond the tide's reach. The cold seemed to penetrate the bone.

At last they came to the dry dock at the farthest end and Archie put out his hand in warning.

Monk caught the smell of wood smoke.

Ahead of them was a lean-to made of planking and patched with canvas. Archie pointed to it, and then stepped aside, making for the far end, disappearing into the darkness, almost instantly swallowed up.

Monk took a deep breath, steadying himself. He had no weapon. Then he flung open the wood-and-canvas flap.

Inside was about a dozen square yards of space, bare but for wooden boxes piled against all of the walls except the farther one, where there was another doorway. It was impossible to tell what the boxes contained. There was a pile of rope forming a rough seat and more unraveled hemp for a bed. In the center a fire was burning briskly, sending smoke and flames up a roughly made chimney. It was blessedly warm after the raw night outside, and Monk was aware of it on the front of his body even as he looked at the one man who squatted beside the fire, a coal in his black-gloved hand, clutched like a weapon. He was tall, loosely built, agile, but it was his face that commanded the attention. It was Enid Ravensbrook's drawing come to life, and yet it was not. The bones were the same, the wide jaw and pointed chin, the strong nose, the high cheekbones, even the green eyes. But the flesh of the face was different, the mouth, the lines from nose to corner of lips. The expression was one of anger and mockery, and at this instant, poised on the edge of violence.

It was unnecessary to ask if he were Caleb Stone.

"Genevieve sent me looking for Angus," Monk said simply, standing square in the entrance, blocking it.

Caleb rose very slowly to his feet.

"Looking for Angus, are you?" He said the words as if they were curious and amusing, but he was balanced to move suddenly.

Monk watched him, aware of his weight, the coal in his hand. "He hasn't returned home. . . ."

Caleb laughed jerkily. "Oh, hasn't he, then! And does Genevieve think I don't know that?"

"She thinks you know it very well," Monk said levelly. "She thinks you are responsible for it."

"Kept him here, have I?" Caleb's smile was derisive, full of rage. "Thieving and brawling along the river! Is that what she thinks?" He almost spat the words. It was odd to see him, dressed in clothes so old and soiled they had lost all color and most of their shape, and yet he wore leather gloves. His hair was curly and overlong, matted with dirt, a stubble on his chin. And yet for all his hatred, his words were pronounced with the clarity and diction of his youth and the education Milo Ravensbrook had given him. Monk was aware, even through the contempt he felt for him, of the dual nature of the man, and how the promise of his youth had ended in such utter ruin. Had he not destroyed Angus, Monk could have pitied him, even seen some dim, different reflection of himself. He understood both the rage and the helplessness.

"Have you?" Monk asked. "I hadn't thought so. I rather thought you'd killed him."

"Killed him." Caleb smiled, this time showing fine teeth. He weighed the coal in his hand without taking his eyes off Monk. "Killed Angus?" He laughed again, a hard, almost choking, sound. "Yes—I suppose she's right. I killed Angus!" He started to laugh harder, throwing back his head and letting the noise tear out of him, rising almost hysterically, as if letting go of it hurt.

Monk took a step forward.

Caleb stopped laughing instantly, cut off as if someone had put a hand over his face. He glanced at Monk, his hand raised a little higher.

Monk froze. Caleb had already murdered his brother. If he were to kill Monk here in these desolate marshes, his body might not be found till it was rotted and unrecognizable, if ever. He would fight hard, but Caleb was strong and used to violence, perhaps even to killing, and he had nothing to lose.

Without the slightest warning, Caleb spun around on his heel and lunged for the farther end of the hut, crashing through the makeshift door and sending Archie sprawling in the mud.

By the time Monk had pushed his way through, Archie was scrambling to his feet again, and Caleb had disappeared into the rain and the darkness. They could hear the squelching sound of his feet, and another burst of laughter, then nothing at all.

Oliver Rathbone was one of the most outstanding barristers of the decade. He had eloquence, discernment and an excellent sense of timing. And better than that, he had the kind of courage which enabled him to take up controversial and desperate cases.

He was at his office in Vere Street, off Lincoln's Inn Fields, when his clerk announced, with a dubious expression, that Mr. Monk was here to see him on a matter of some urgency.

"Of course," Rathbone said with only the faintest of smiles on his lips. "Nothing ordinary would bring Monk here. You had better show him in."

"Yes, Mr. Rathbone." The clerk retreated and closed the door behind him.

Rathbone folded away the papers he had been reading and tied the file they had come from. He had mixed feelings himself. He had always admired Monk's professional abilities—they were beyond question—and also his courage in dealing with his loss of memory and the identity that went with it. But he also found his manner difficult—abrasive, to say the least. And there was the matter of Hester Latterly. Her fondness for Monk irritated Rathbone, although he was loath to admit it. Monk did not treat her with anything like the respect or regard she warranted. Monk brought out the worst in Rathbone, the greatest intolerance, shortest temper and most ill-considered judgment.

The door opened and Monk came in. He was immaculately dressed, as usual, but he looked tired and harassed. The skin under his eyes was shadowed and his muscles tense.

"Good morning, Monk." Rathbone rose as an automatic gesture of courtesy. "What may I do for you?"

Monk closed the door behind himself, not bothering with the trivialities. He began to speak as he moved to sit down in the chair opposite the desk, crossing his legs.

"I have a case upon which I need your advice." He did not hesitate for Rathbone to make any comment, but continued straight on, taking for granted that he would accept. "A woman consulted me concerning her husband, who is missing. I have traced him as far as Blackwall, on the Isle of Dogs, where he was last seen, in the company of his twin brother, who lives there, more or less . . ."

"Just a moment." Rathbone held up his hand. "I do not deal in cases of desertion or divorce. . . ."

"Neither do I!" Monk said tersely, although Rathbone knew that if that were true at all, it was only so of the last few months. "If you permit me to finish," Monk continued, "I will reach the point a great deal sooner."

Rathbone sighed and let his hand fall. From the expression on Monk's face, he was going to continue anyway. It crossed Rathbone's mind to remark that if Monk were taking clients from the Isle of Dogs, he had no occasion to be supercilious, but it would serve no purpose. Conceivably, the case could still be of interest.

"The brothers have long hated each other," Monk said, staring at Rathbone. "Caleb, the one who lives in the Blackwall area, survives by theft, intimidation and violence. Angus, my client's husband, lives on the edge of Mayfair, and is a pillar of respectability and orderly family life. He kept in touch with his brother out of loyalty, a feeling which was not returned. Caleb was furiously jealous."

Deliberately Rathbone said nothing.

Monk had hesitated only a second. After the silence he swept on. "The wife is convinced Caleb has murdered Angus. He has often attacked him before. I tracked Caleb to the Greenwich marshes, and he admitted having killed Angus, but I can find no corpse." His face was hard and tight with anger. "There are a dozen ways it could have been disposed of: down the river is one of the most obvious, buried and left to rot in the marshes, stuffed in the hold of some outgoing ship, or even taken to sea by Caleb himself as far as the estuary and put overboard. Or he could be buried in a common grave with the typhoid victims in Limehouse. Nobody's going to dig them up for a count and identification!"

Rathbone sat back in his large comfortable chair and made a steeple out of his fingers.

"I assume no one else heard this confession of Caleb's?"

"Of course not."

"And what evidence have you that it may be true, apart from the wife's conviction?" Rathbone asked him. "She is not an impartial witness. By the way, how was he placed financially? And what other . . . interests . . . might his wife have?"

A look of contempt crossed Monk's face. "He is doing nicely, as long as he is present in his business. It depends upon his personal judgment. It will fall into decline very rapidly if he remains absent, and the estate cannot be resolved. And as for the other question, as far as I can determine, she seems a most virtuous woman, and handsome, but now very anxious for the welfare of her children."

The irritation in Monk's voice might mean that he resented having his judgment questioned. On the other hand, Rathbone thought, from the level of intensity in Monk's eyes, that he felt some pity for the woman and believed her plight. But then he was uncertain that Monk, who was an excellent judge of men, was equally as good a judge of women.

"Witness to quarrels?" he asked, returning to the immediate issue. "Some specific contention between the two brothers over possessions, a woman, an inheritance, an old injury?"

"A witness who saw them together on the day Angus disappeared," Monk replied. "They were quarreling then."

"Hardly damning," Rathbone said dryly.

"What do I have to have, legally?" Monk's face was like ice. Something of the weariness and frustration showed in it, and Rathbone guessed he had been pursuing the case profitlessly for many days and knew his chances were slight, if any.

"Not necessarily a corpse." Rathbone leaned forward a little, granting Monk the seriousness he wished. "If you can prove Angus went to the Isle of Dogs, that there was ill feeling between the two, that they were in the habit of quarreling or fighting, that they were seen together that day, and no one at all has seen Angus since then, it may be sufficient to cause the police to institute a search. It will be highly unlikely to convict anyone of murder. It is conceivable Angus may have had an accident and fallen in the river, and the body been carried out to sea. He may even deliberately have lost himself, taken a boat elsewhere. I assume you have checked all his private and business finances?"

"Of course! There is nothing whatever amiss."

"Then you had better see if you can find some evidence of a

quarrel, and much tighter witnesses as to Angus not leaving the scene of their last meeting. So far you have insufficient to warrant the police investigating. I'm sorry."

Monk swore, and rose to his feet, his face set in anger and misery.

"Thank you," he said grimly, and went to the door, leaving without turning around or looking at Rathbone again.

Rathbone sat motionless for nearly a quarter of an hour before reopening the tied file. It was a delicate problem, and in spite of himself, Monk's dilemma intrigued him. Monk seemed morally certain that murder had been committed. He knew who was killed, by whom, where and why, and yet he could prove nothing. It was legally correct—and ethically monstrous. Rathbone racked his brain how he might help.

He lay awake that night, and still nothing came to his mind.

Monk was furious. He had never felt more desperately frustrated. He knew Caleb had murdered Angus—he had admitted as much—and yet he was powerless to do anything about it. He could not even prove death to help Genevieve. It was a most appalling injustice, and it burned like acid inside him.

But he must report to Genevieve. She deserved to know at least as much as he did.

She was not at Ravensbrook House. A prim maid in a crisp apron and cap informed him Mrs. Stonefield had returned home, and now came only during the day.

"Then Lady Ravensbrook is better?" Monk said quickly, and with a pleasure that surprised him.

"Yes sir, she is past the worst, thank the Lord. Miss Latterly is still here. Would you care to speak to her?"

He hesitated only a moment, Hester's face coming to his mind with such clarity it startled him.

"No—thank you. My business is with Mrs. Stonefield. I shall try her home. Good day."

———

Genevieve's door was opened by a between-maid who looked about fifteen years old, round-faced and harassed. Monk gave his name and asked for Genevieve. He was shown into the front parlor and requested to wait. A moment later the maid returned and he was taken to the small, neat withdrawing room with its portrait of the Queen, a pianoforte, legs decently skirted, some embroidered samplers and a few watercolors of the Bay of Naples.

What took him aback completely was Titus Niven standing in front of it, his coat as elegantly cut as before, and as threadbare, his boots polished and paper thin, his face still with the same expression of wry, self-deprecating humor. Genevieve was close beside him, as if they had been in conversation until the moment the door had opened. Monk had the powerful feeling that he had intruded.

Genevieve came forward, her face full of interest and concern. She was still pale and the marks of strain were still visible around her eyes and lips, but there was less tension in her, less overwhelming sense of desperation. She was an extremely attractive woman. Had he not met Drusilla Wyndham, his mind might have dwelt on that fact longer.

"Good morning, Mr. Monk. Have you some news for me?"

"Not what I would have wished, Mrs. Stonefield, but yes, I found Caleb, down in the Greenwich marshes."

She swallowed hastily, her eyes wide. As if almost unconsciously, Titus Niven moved a step closer to her, also staring at Monk, fear flickering across his face, and then resolution taking its place.

"What did he say?" Genevieve asked.

"That he had killed Angus but I would never prove it." He hesitated. "I'm sorry." He wished there were more he could add, but there was nothing which was either true or would be of any help or comfort. All his news offered was an end to the exhaustion of veering between hope and terror. There was no justice in it, nothing fair.

Titus Niven reached out his hand and touched Genevieve very gently on the arm, and, as if hardly aware of it, her hand sought his.

"You mean there is no more you can do?" she said in a whisper, struggling to keep her voice level and under control.

"No, that isn't what I mean," Monk replied, thinking carefully what he said so he did not mislead her. His mind was racing away with ugly thoughts about Titus Niven, barely yet taking shape. "I don't hold great hope of proving his guilt, although it is not impossible, but I shall certainly continue to try to prove Angus's death—if not directly, then indirectly. Assuming, of course, that that is still what you wish?"

There was an instant's silence so intense Monk could hear the gentle settling of ash in the fireplace.

"Yes," Genevieve said very quietly. "Yes. I wish you to continue, at least for the present. Although I don't know how long Lord Ravensbrook will be willing to pay you and I would be obliged if you would keep the financial accountancy up to date. I regret to ask you such a thing, it seems so tasteless, but I am obliged by circumstances to do so."

Monk thought of Callandra Daviot, and wondered if she would be prepared to support him if he continued the case without payment from Genevieve or Lord Ravensbrook. He determined at the first possible moment to ask her. He must know the truth. If Caleb Stone had murdered his brother out of jealousy, Genevieve deserved to have it proven, and Monk could almost taste his own keenness to see Caleb answer first. And if there were some other resolution, even one that involved Titus Niven, Monk wanted to know it. Or perhaps it would be more honest to say that Monk wanted to prove that it was not so. The possibility haunted his mind, too nebulous to grasp, too ugly to forget.

"Of course I will, Mrs. Stonefield," he said aloud. "It may be possible for one to offer sufficient proof or at least a serious case for the police to take over the investigation. Then there will naturally be no private cost."

"I see."

"I understand Lady Ravensbrook is past the worst and is expected to recover?" he went on.

She smiled, and Titus Niven also relaxed, although he remained close to her.

"Yes indeed, thank the good Lord. She was most dreadfully ill, and it will take her a long time to be back to herself again, but at least she is alive, and two days ago I had not dared hope for that."

"And you have moved out of Ravensbrook House?"

Her face tightened, a shadow crossed over her eyes.

"My presence is no longer necessary all the time. Miss Latterly is most competent, and naturally there are maids to take care of the domestic duties. I go every day, but it is far better for my children to be at home."

Monk was about to argue the issue, thinking of the expense of heating, food, even the retention of her own servants, but Titus Niven cut across him.

"It is good of you to be concerned, Mr. Monk, but with Mr. Stonefield's disappearance, there has been more than enough distress and disturbance in their lives. To leave home again, I am sure you agree, is a trial that is best avoided, as long as that is possible."

Many answers flashed in Monk's mind: the comfort of Ravensbrook House, particularly in the middle of winter; the warmth; the excellent food; the absence of a hundred worries and responsibilities; and on the other hand the lack of privacy for Genevieve to receive Titus Niven whenever she chose. Perhaps it would even make it easier for her, in time, to move him into Angus's business or install him as its new manager.

"Yes, I suppose it is," he conceded somewhat ungraciously. "I will continue to pursue such evidence as I can find. Can you recall, Mrs. Stonefield, any remark your husband may have made about where he met his brother, any comment upon surroundings, circumstances which may help me to find further proof?" He watched her face closely for the slightest flicker of forethought, guarding her tongue or feeding him information which she knew but should not have were she innocent.

"I don't understand you, Mr. Monk." She blinked.

He saw nothing but confusion in her.

"Did they eat together, take a pint of ale, for example?" he elaborated. "Did they meet inside or outside, on the river or ashore? In company with others, or alone?"

"Yes, I see." Understanding was quick in her face, then distress. "You want to know where to look for . . . a body. . . ."

Titus Niven winced and his sensitive mouth was pulled crooked with distaste. He shot Monk a look of pleading, but he did not interrupt, though the effort obviously cost him.

"Or a witness," Monk amended.

"I am afraid he didn't, or I should have told you." She shook her head. "He never discussed his meetings with Caleb. It always upset him. But once or twice his clothes were damp and smelled of salt and fish." She took a breath. "And other things I cannot identify for you, but most unpleasant."

"I see. Thank you." He had wondered if she would gently lead him to where Angus was. If she knew, then sooner or later she would. She needed his death proved. Standing in this gracious room, knowing it to be slowly denuded of its treasures, seeing the tiny heap of coals glowing in the hearth, her pale face smudged with weariness and anxiety, he found it almost impossible to believe she harbored any deceit at all. But he had been wrong before. And the fact that he liked Niven meant nothing either. He must pursue it. "Then I shall take my leave. Good day, ma'am. Mr. Niven."

He followed his hunch diligently for the rest of that day, and half of the next, and learned nothing at all. According to even the most critical of neighborhood gossip, Genevieve was as worthy as her husband, a virtuous woman in every outward regard, even to the point of being a trifle tedious. If she had any failings they were a carefulness with money, an extreme regard for it, and a rather unreliable sense of humor. She had been known to laugh more often than was entirely suitable, and on quite inappropriate occasions.

Titus Niven was a friend of the family, at least as much of Angus's as hers. And no, no one knew any occasion when he had called at the house when Angus was not also present.

If there had been any secret relationship then it was hidden superbly well. Titus Niven had cause to be envious of Angus Stonefield, both professionally and personally, perhaps even to hate him, but there was no evidence that indeed he did so.

In the early afternoon Monk went back to the East End, to Limehouse and the makeshift typhoid hospital to see Callandra Daviot. He wanted to see her for several reasons, but paramount in his mind was the matter of funds. It was obvious to Monk that if Lord Ravensbrook withdrew his funds Genevieve could not afford to employ him and the hope of being able to find proof was slight. Yet he was determined to follow the case to the bitter end.

Also he needed help, and the fever hospital was a good place to begin seeking more detailed local knowledge. He cursed his own inadequacy. If he had his memory he would probably know all kinds of people he could call upon.

He trudged along Gill Street, collar up against the wind, the stink of soot and middens thick in his nose. The massive outline of the old warehouse was ahead of him, gray against a gray sky. He increased his pace just as it began to rain, and was inside the entrance before he got wet.

The smell of illness caught in his nostrils and his throat immediately, different from the usual sour, rank smell outside, which he was now accustomed to. This was harsher and more intimate, and in spite of all the will he could exercise, it frightened him. This was not the business of life; it was pain, death and the closeness of death. It closed around him like a fog, and he had to grit his teeth and master his body not to turn and run back out of the door into the air again. He was ashamed of it and despised himself.

He saw the woman Mary coming towards him, a covered pail in her hand. He knew what would be in it and his stomach knotted.

"Is Lady Callandra here?" he asked her. His voice sounded brittle.

"Yeah." Her hair was plastered to her head with rain and sweat and her skin was pasty with exhaustion. She had no strength left for politeness, or even for awe of authority. "In there." She jerked her head sideways, indicating the vast space of the warehouse floor, then continued on her way.

"Thank you." Monk went reluctantly into the cavern of the room. It looked exactly the same, dimly lit by candles, floor covered with straw and canvas, the humps of bodies visible under blankets. At either end the black, potbellied stoves gave off heat and the odor of coal and steam from cauldrons. There was also a sharp catch in his throat from the burning tobacco leaves. He remembered Hester saying something about using it in the army for fumigation.

It took a moment for his eyes to adjust, then he saw Callandra standing close to one of the hunched figures on the straw. Kristian Beck was opposite her, and they were absorbed in conversation.

He was aware of movement to his left, and turned to see Hester coming towards him. She seemed even thinner in the candlelight and the severe gray dress, her hair screwed back unflatteringly. Her eyes looked larger than he had remembered, her mouth softer and more capable of passion, or pain. He wished intensely that he had not come. He did not want to see her, especially here. Enid Ravensbrook had caught typhoid here and nearly died. That thought crushed his mind, closing out almost everything else.

"Has something happened in your case?" she asked as soon as she was close enough to him to speak without being overheard.

"Nothing conclusive," he replied. "I've found Caleb, but not Angus."

"What happened?" Her expression was sharp with interest.

He did not want to tell her, because he did not want to stand here in this fearful place, talking to her. If he had had any luck, she would have been at Ravensbrook House.

"Why aren't you with Lady Ravensbrook?" he said curtly. "She can't be fully recovered yet."

"It's Genevieve's turn," she said with surprise. "Callandra needs help here. I would have thought you might see that for yourself. I assume from your temper that your conversation with Caleb Stone was unsatisfactory? I don't know what else you expected. He was hardly going to confess and lead you to the body."

"On the contrary," he said impatiently. "He did confess!"

She raised her eyebrows. "And led you to the body?"

"No . . ."

"Then confession wasn't much use, was it? Did he tell you how he killed him, or where?"

"No."

"Or even why?"

He was thoroughly annoyed. It would not be so infuriating if she were always so obstructive and unintelligent, but memories kept coming to his mind of other times, when she had been so different, full of perception and courage. He should make some allowance. She must be very tired. Perhaps it was only natural that she should be a little slow-witted in the circumstances. But then he wished intensely that she was not here anyway. He hated having to admire her for it. It was like gall in his mouth, and the hotter taste of fear. In fact, perhaps that was what it was—fear.

And that was natural. It was hard to lose a friend, even one you only partially liked. No decent man could view it with equanimity.

"Did he tell you why?" she demanded, cutting across his thoughts. "It might be some help."

The dim hump of the body nearest them groaned and moved restlessly in the straw.

"No," Monk said abruptly. "No, he didn't."

"I suppose it doesn't matter, except insofar as it might have been a clue to—" She stopped. "I don't know what."

"Of course it matters," he contradicted her instantly. "He might not have acted alone. Maybe Genevieve put him up to it."

She was startled. "Genevieve! That's ridiculous! Why would she? She has everything to lose and nothing to gain from Angus's death."

"She has a tidy inheritance to gain," he pointed out. "And the freedom, after a decent period, to marry again."

"Whatever makes you think she wants to?" she demanded hotly. It was apparent the idea was new to her, and repugnant. "There is every evidence she loved her husband deeply. What makes you think otherwise?" That was a challenge. It was quick in her eyes and her voice.

He responded with a similar sharpness. "Her close friendship with Titus Niven, which is quite remarkable for a woman hardly on the brink of widowhood. Her husband is not even pronounced dead yet, never mind in his grave."

"You have a vicious mind." She looked at him witheringly. "Mr. Niven is a family friend. For most people it is very natural to comfort a friend in time of bereavement. I'm surprised you haven't observed it in others, even if you wouldn't have thought it yourself."

"If I had just lost my wife, I wouldn't turn to the most attractive woman I could find," he retorted. "I would turn to another man."

Her contempt only increased. "Don't be naive. If you were a woman, you would turn to a man rather than a woman, for the practical matters. Not that they are any better at it, simply that they are taken seriously by others. People always assume women are incompetent, whether they are or not. And of course they have no legal standing anyway."

Before he could make exactly the right crushing remark, Callandra came over to them. She too looked tired and untidy, her clothes soiled, but there was a look of pleasure in her face at seeing him.

"Hello, William. How is your case progressing? I assume that is why you are here?" She brushed her hair out of her eyes absently, at the same time smearing her face with soot from the stove, but there was a lift in her voice and a calmness in her eyes as of some inner radiance. She met his glance absolutely squarely. "Is there something with which we can help you? We have heard quite a lot more about this wretched man, Caleb Stone. I am not sure of what use it could be."

"It might be of much use," he said quickly. "I found him myself, and he admitted having killed Angus, but I still have no corpse. Even if I can never prove Caleb's guilt, much as I would like to, the important thing is that the authorities will assume Angus's death, for the widow's sake."

"Yes, of course. I understand."

"Is there somewhere we can talk more privately?" he asked, looking away from Hester.

Callandra hid the faintest smile, then excused herself and led Monk to the small storeroom where they had spoken earlier, leaving Hester to return to her duties.

"You look in an ill temper, William," she observed as soon as the door was closed. She sat on the only chair and he sat half sideways on the bench. "Is it the frustration of your case, or have you been quarreling with Hester again?"

"She gets more arbitrary and set in her ways every time I see her," he responded. "And unbearably self-righteous. It is an extraordinarily unattractive quality, especially in a woman. She seems to be utterly without humor or the ability to charm, which is a woman's greatest asset."

"I see." Callandra nodded, poking the last stray end of hair into a pin behind her ear. "How fortunate that you feel that way. Now, if she should catch typhoid, like poor Enid Ravensbrook, you will not be so distressed as if you were fond of her, or found her pleasing."

It was a monstrous thing to say! The idea of Hester as desperately ill as Enid Ravensbrook, or these poor souls around him, was appalling. It chilled his flesh as if he were frozen from the inside. And she would not be cared for in luxury as Enid had been. There would be no one to sit with her day and night, to nurse her with the skill and

179

dedication to keep her alive. He could try, of course, and he would. But he had not the knowledge. How could Callandra speak so utterly heartlessly?

"Now, about this case," she said cheerfully, ignoring his feelings altogether. "It sounds most frustrating. What do you propose to do next? Or have you abandoned it?"

He was about to make an extremely tart reply when he realized there was humor in her eyes, and suddenly he felt foolish, and had a brilliant memory, barely a second long, of standing at the kitchen table, resting his chin on it, watching his mother rolling pastry. She had just told him something which made him realize that she knew almost everything and he knew nothing at all. It had been a revelation, both humiliating and at the same time comforting.

"No, I have not abandoned it," he said, and his voice sounded far more meek than he had intended. "I will continue it as long as I am able to, until I find proof, at the very least, that Angus is dead. I would dearly like to prove Caleb murdered him, but that may be impossible."

Her rather erratic eyebrows rose. "Has Mrs. Stonefield got funds for that? I gathered she was in some difficulty, or expected to be very shortly."

"No, she hasn't and though Lord Ravensbrook has agreed to pay for the investigation, Mrs. Stonefield seems worried that he will not continue to do so." Should he ask her? She had taken very little part in the investigation. She might consider the typhoid outbreak to be a more pressing need, and perhaps she was right. He had only the haziest idea how much disposable income she had for such things.

"Then I shall be happy to take care of the fee for as long as you believe there is purpose in continuing." She looked at him steadily. "Purpose with advantage to Mrs. Stonefield, that is, or to her children."

"Thank you," he said humbly.

"Did I overhear you say something about learning more of Caleb Stone?" she asked curiously. "And where he lives, when he can be said to live anywhere. From what I have heard, he spends a great deal of time moving from one place to another. Presumably to avoid his enemies, whom rumor would have to be legion."

"Yes. Anything you know, or have heard, might be helpful," he accepted. "I need to know where they might have been seen together that day. If I could produce a witness who saw them, and then Caleb alone, I should know where to search for a body. Even if I did not find one, it might be sufficient to make the police take up the case. Angus Stonefield was a well-respected man."

"I realize why you wish it, William." She rose to her feet heavily. "I may have spent the last week nursing the sick, but I have not lost my wits. I shall send Hester to you. She has spent more time with the people than I have, especially with Mary. I have been fighting with the frightened, bitter men at the local council, and all that they have said at enormous length and with enough words to fill a library, providing every book were the same, amounts to nothing whatever of the slightest use to man or beast." And before he could argue, she sailed out and he was left alone sitting on the bench in the light of one tallow candle, looking at the water-stained walls and waiting for Hester.

She was several minutes in coming, and by the time she did he was thoroughly uncomfortable.

She arrived and closed the door.

He stood up automatically, until she seated herself in the chair. She began straightaway, so obviously Callandra had explained his purpose.

"Everyone seems afraid of Caleb," she said gravely. "He seems to inhabit an area stretching from the East India Dock Road to the river—"

"The Isle of Dogs," he interrupted. "I know that much."

"On both sides," she continued, ignoring him. "And the Greenwich marshes as far as Bugsby's Reach. A great deal of the time no one knows precisely where he is. He sleeps in the dockyards, on barges, and sometimes with Selina Herries, which you already know."

"Yes, I do," he said impatiently. "I need to prove he was with Angus on the day he was last seen, and when and where."

"I know what you want." She was unruffled. "But you won't prove anything unless you can persuade someone to speak to you. I don't think anyone is going to betray Caleb unless they can be sure he won't take his revenge on them for it. And Selina won't, regardless. She may be frightened, but she loves him, in her own way."

There was a sound of buckets clanging on the far side of the door, but no one opened it.

He leaned forward. "How do you know? Do you know her?" It was foolish to get excited by the thought, but it would be the last chance, if he could find a way to gain her trust. "She may only be afraid as well."

Hester smiled. It lit her face, not removing the tiredness but overriding it.

"I don't doubt she is afraid of him," she agreed. "And I don't doubt she has cause, now and then. But by all accounts she also loves him, in her way, and is rather proud of him."

"Proud of him! In God's name, what for? The man's a failure in every way." As soon as he had said it, he wished he had not put it in such words. It was a damnation, and Caleb's vivid face with its rage and its intelligence was sharp in his mind. He could have been so much more. He could have been everything that Angus was. Instead jealousy had corroded his soul until in a passion of hatred he had committed murder and destroyed not only his brother but what was left of himself. The pity in Monk was tight and painful, fraught with loathing. And yet he knew rage himself. It was the grace of God that he had not killed. Could Angus conceivably have been a hypocrite too, a charming, predatory blackguard too clever for anyone to catch?

Hester did not interrupt his thoughts. He wished she would. Instead she simply sat staring at him, waiting. She knew him too intimately. It was uncomfortable.

"Well?" he demanded. "What could she be proud of him for?"

"Because no one cheats him or abuses him," she answered, her voice suggesting that it was obvious. "He's strong. Everyone knows his name. The fact that he chooses her makes her important. People don't dare to take advantage of her either."

He stood up and turned away, thrusting his hands into his pockets.

"And that's the height of her ambition? To be owned by the most hated and feared man in the Isle of Dogs! God, what a life!" He remembered Selina's beautifully boned face with its wide mouth and bold eyes, the proud swaying way she walked. She was worth more than that.

"It's better than most women, around here," Hester said quietly. "She isn't often cold or hungry, and no one knocks her around."

"Except Caleb!" he said.

"That's something," she replied calmly. "It's many people's dream to escape, but few ever do, except to the whorehouses up in the Haymarket, or worse."

He winced—at her language, not at the truth.

"Mary says one pretty girl did, Ginny something," she went on, though he was not interested. "Got married, she thought; but that's probably more a hope than a fact. Gentlemen don't marry girls they pick up in Limehouse."

It was a bare reality, and if he had said it himself he would have said it was simply the truth. From her lips it had a coarseness and a finality he resented.

"Do you know anything useful?" he said abruptly. "That Selina won't betray him doesn't help me."

"You asked me," she pointed out. "But I can tell you the names of a few of his enemies who would be delighted to see his downfall, if they can do it safely."

"Can you?" He could not hide his eagerness. He had not managed to turn up anything so definite himself. Of course, she was trusted in a way he never could be. She was living and working among these people, risking her life daily to tend to them in their extremity. He pushed that thought away. "Who? Where do I find them?"

She gave him a list of five names—one man, three women and a youth—and in all cases where he could find them.

"Thank you," he said sincerely. "That is excellent. If any one of them can tell me something, we may yet help Mrs. Stonefield. I shall begin immediately."


But he did not. That evening he had arranged to see Drusilla, and it was a pleasure he longed for. Not even to help Genevieve Stonefield could he forgo it and creep around the slums and rookeries of Limehouse in the dark and the cold. It could wait until tomorrow, when it would be both easier and safer. Caleb had to be aware Monk was still pursuing him. He was not a man to wait idly to be caught.

The weather had cleared and it was a dry, chilly evening with only the ever-present pall of smoke hiding the stars.

Half past seven found Monk superbly dressed, stepping out of a hansom cab to meet Drusilla on the steps of the British Archaeological Association in Sackville Street. She had requested that he meet her there because she had said she had promised to accompany a friend for dinner, which was a great bore. She had cancelled the arrangement, but in order to avoid lengthy and unnecessarily dishonest explanations, she could not be at home.

She appeared at exactly half past, as she had said she would. She wore a wide-skirted gown of silk the color of candlelight through brandy, and it complimented her marvelously. She seemed to glow in golds and tawny bronzes and her skin had a delicacy and a warmth unlike any he had seen before.

"Is something amiss?" she said laughingly. "You look terribly serious, William!"

The sound of his name from her lips was acutely pleasing. He collected his attention with an effort.

"No, nothing at all. I even have news which may help me even-tually to find where poor Angus Stonefield met his death."

"Have you?" she said eagerly, taking his arm and falling into step as he matched his pace to hers. "It does seem terribly tragic. Did he do it merely from jealousy, do you suppose? Why now? He must have been jealous of him for years." She gave a little shiver. "I wonder what happened which suddenly made such a difference? I don't sup-pose it really matters, but don't you long to know?" She turned to look at him curiously. "Don't you think it is one of the most inter-esting subjects in the world, why people do what they do?"

"Yes, of course it is." She could not know the nerve her question had struck in him, how many of his own acts he had learned from the evidences left of his life, and yet could not remember, so did not know why he had done them. So much can be understood, even ex-cused, when one understands.

"You look sad." She was searching his face with her wide hazel eyes. "Where shall we go, so I can cheer you up? Do you still think the widow is innocent? Do you think she may have known Caleb, recently?"

The idea was funny. He could not imagine the socially correct, money-careful, domestic Genevieve having the slightest thing in common with the violent, lonely Caleb, who lived from hand to mouth, never knowing what he would eat next or where he would sleep.

"No, I don't!"

"Why not?" she pursued. "After all, he must look very much like her husband. There must have been something in him which could have attracted her." She smiled, her eyes close to laughter. "I know you say Angus was very worthy, and virtuous in every way." She shrugged her shoulders. "But perhaps he was just the slightest bit te-dious? Some of the most worthy people are, you know."

He said nothing.

"Don't you know some very worthy women who are crashingly dull?" She looked at him sideways, a little through her lashes.

He smiled back. If he had denied it she would not have believed him for a moment. And perhaps Angus was everything Genevieve wanted and needed in a husband, but he could indeed have been a bore.

"If it were so, where do you suppose they might meet?" she asked thoughtfully. "Where would a respectable woman, with a limited knowledge of the less salubrious sides of society, go in order to meet a lover?"

"That would depend upon whether the lover were Titus Niven or Caleb," he replied, not taking the idea seriously, but thinking it would be fun to humor Drusilla. It would be a far more entertaining evening than sitting in some musical concert, or listening to a lecture, however profound the subject.

They crossed the road and he held her arm a trifle more tightly. It was a pleasing feeling, a warmth even in the raw wind that was blowing down the street and funneling between the buildings, carrying the smell of a thousand smoking chimneys.

He entered into the spirit of it.

"She could want something that was fun," he said cheerfully. "If Angus were a bore, then definitely she would seek something he would not do."

"A music hall," she said with a laugh. "A penny arcade. A marionette show, maybe Punch and Judy? A band or a street musician? There are so many things that a stuffy man wouldn't do which could be marvelous—don't you think? How about a hurdy-gurdy? A bazaar?" She gave a little giggle. "A peep show? A bare-knuckle fight?"

"What do you know about bare-knuckle fights?" he asked in surprise. It was such a brutal sport, as well as illegal.

She waved a hand. "Oh, nothing. I was thinking of her doing something really daring, where Angus would never think of looking for her, and none of his social circle would ever see her either," she reasoned. "After all, it would have to be somewhere where no one she knew would ever see her. They might talk, and she couldn't afford that, the more especially if she was party to his murder."

"It wouldn't matter if she was seen with Caleb," he pointed out. "In the lamplight and shadow, half-decently dressed, anyone would simply assume it was Angus."

"Oh." She bit her lip. "Yes, of course. I'd forgotten that." She was silent for a space of about fifty yards or so. They came to a crossroad and he guided her around Piccadilly Circus and along the far side towards the Haymarket. Most of the possibilities they mentioned were offered here, in Great Windmill Street or Shaftesbury Avenue.

Already in the glare of the gas lamps and the illumination of shop windows among the theater crowds and sightseers, they noticed women walking slowly with an arrogant set to their shoulders and swinging their hips in invitation. Skirts swayed, and now and then an ankle was visible.

They were all sorts of women: young and fresh-faced from the country; pale and sophisticated; those who had been milliners or dressmakers, or in domestic service, and lost their positions through seduction; older women, some already riddled with venereal disease.

Young gentlemen sauntered by, well-dressed, taking their pick. Others were older, even silver-haired. Every now and again two would disappear, arm-in-arm, into a doorway to some house of accommodation.

Carriages passed, hooves clattering, occupants laughing. Gaudy theater signs advertised melodrama and titillation. Monk and Drusilla passed a brazier roasting chestnuts and the wave of heat engulfed them for a moment.

"Would you like some?" he asked.

"Oh yes! Yes. I'd love some," she accepted quickly. "I haven't tasted them for ages."

He bought threepence worth, and they shared them, nibbling carefully not to burn their lips or tongues, now and then glancing at each other. The chestnuts were delicious, the more so for being a touch charred on the outside and too hot in the bitter evening.

Around them swirled laughter and a spice of danger. Some men hurried by with coat collars drawn up and hats pulled down over their brows, bent on pleasures for which they preferred to be anonymous. Others were quite open and swaggered brazenly, calling out comments.

Drusilla moved closer to Monk, her eyes bright, her face smooth and glowing with an inner excitement which gave her skin a kind of radiance and made her even lovelier. She was full of laughter, as if she were on the edge of some wonderful joke.

They passed a peep show. It rose to his mind to point out that they could not actually accomplish anything, because they had no way of learning if Genevieve had ever been here, or with whom. He had no likeness of her to show. But to say so would have spoiled their fun, and that was what actually mattered. It was conceivable that Genevieve had connived at Angus's death, but he did not believe it. Without a body, she had nothing to gain and everything to lose.

An hour later as they walked up Greek Street towards Soho Square, the subject arose, and he was obliged to answer it.

"But maybe the body will turn up?" she said, stepping up the pavement from the road. She swaggered a couple of steps, mimicking the prostitutes, and burst into laughter again. "I'm sorry!" she said happily. "But it's such fun not to care a fig for an evening, not to worry if everything is correct, who is looking at you or listening to you, if old Lady So-and-So will disapprove, and who she will repeat it to. Such freedom is terribly sweet. Thank you, William, for a unique evening!" And before he could reply, she hurried on. "Perhaps they are keeping it hidden for a reason?"

"What reason?" he asked amusedly. He was enjoying himself too much to care about the illogicality of it all. Tomorrow would be time enough to pursue the real. Tonight was his own, and Drusilla's.

"Ah!" She stopped suddenly and swung around, her eyes wide and dancing with excitement. "I have it! What if Angus turns up again, alive and well, saying he was hurt in a terrible fight with Caleb, in which he was injured, perhaps knocked on the head, and was unable to contact anyone. He was insensible, delirious. He thinks Caleb is dead. . . ."

"But he's alive," Monk pointed out. "I've seen him, and he admitted having killed Angus. In—"

"No, no," she interrupted eagerly. "Wait! Don't keep stopping me! Of course he is—and he did! Don't you see? The Angus who turns up is really Caleb. He and Genevieve have done away with Angus, and when it is too late to tell them apart, and the body has"—she wrinkled her nose—"decomposed sufficiently, all the doctors can say is that it was one of the brothers! By that time there will be no firm flesh in the face to recognize, no uncallused hands, clean fingernails, anything like that. If she says the man who returns is Angus, who will argue with her?" Her hand tightened on his arm. "William, it's brilliant. It explains everything!"

He searched for a flaw in it, and could not see one. He did not believe it, but it was perfectly possible. The longer he thought about it, the more possible it grew.

"Doesn't it?" she demanded eagerly. "Tell me I'm a brilliant detective, William! You must take me into partnership—I'll find the theories to fit all your cases. Then you can go and find the evidence to prove them."

"A wonderful idea," he said with a laugh. "Would you like dinner on it?"

"Yes, yes I would. With champagne." She looked around at the brightly lit street with its inviting windows. "Where shall we dine? Please let us make it somewhere exciting, disreputable and utterly delicious. I'm sure you must know such a place."

He probably had, before his accident. Now he could only guess. He must not take her where she could be bored, or where anything would happen which would embarrass or disgust her. And of course he could hardly expect Callandra to pay the bill for this. For a start, she would disapprove. She would consider it a betrayal of Hester, no matter how absurd that was. And it was absurd. His relationship with Hester was not one of choice but of circumstances which had thrown them together. There was no romance in it, only a kind of cooperation in certain areas—almost a business relationship, one might say.

Drusilla was waiting, her face full of expectancy.

"Of course," he agreed, not daring to expose his ignorance. "A little further along." With any luck, he would see something within the next two or three hundred yards. It was an excellent area for cafés, taverns and coffeehouses.

"Wonderful," she said happily, turning to walk forward again. "You know, I am really hungry. How unladylike of me to admit it. That's another thing about this evening I enjoy so much. I can be hungry! I can even drink what I please. Perhaps I shan't have champagne. Perhaps I shall have stout. Or porter."

They had an excellent meal at a tavern where the landlord told mildly bawdy jokes and laughed uproariously, and one of the regular customers lampooned various politicians and members of the royal family. The atmosphere was homely and warm and a multitude of odors, almost all of them pleasant, wrapped them round in an island from all the day-to-day reality of their separate worlds.

Afterwards they walked nearly to the end of the street back to Soho Square before picking up a hansom to take her home, and from there he could take it on to Fitzroy Street himself.

He realized with surprise he had no idea where she lived, and he was interested when she gave the driver an address on the edge of Mayfair. They sat close together in the alternating darkness and light as they bowled along Oxford Street westwards, then turned left down North Audley Street. He could not remember having felt more perfectly at ease in anyone's company, and yet never for an instant bored or irritated. He looked forward intensely to the next time he should see her. He must think of other things to do which would entertain her when the business of Angus Stonefield was concluded.

They were passing a large house where some kind of party was coming to an end. The street was full of carriages and they were obliged to slow their pace. There were lights everywhere, torches and carriage lamps, the blaze of chandeliers from the open doors. At least a dozen people stood around on the footpath, and five or six more in the street. Liveried footmen assisted a woman to get her massive skirts into her carriage. Grooms held horses' heads, coachmen steadied the reins.

Suddenly Drusilla lurched forward. Her face had changed utterly. There was a blind hatred in her which made her almost unrecognizable. Her hands went to the bosom of her gown and with a convulsive movement she tore it open, ripping the fabric, exposing her pale flesh and gashing it with her fingernails till it smeared blood. She screamed, again and again, piercingly, as if in mortal terror. She beat her fists against his chest, forcing her way past him, then plunged headlong into the street, landing in a heap in the road. Immediately she clambered to her feet, still screaming, and ran towards the astonished footman, now trying to control a startled horse, which was taking fright at the commotion.

Monk was too stunned even to comprehend what was happening. It was not until another footman tried to climb into the hansom, his face contorted with outrage, shouting, "Blackguard! Beast!" that Monk electrified into life. He lifted his foot and sent the man sprawling backwards, then yelled at the cabby to drive!

The cab lurched forward, the driver perhaps more frightened than obedient, hurling Monk hard back against the seat. It was a moment before he regained his balance, and they were going at a very smart pace southwards.

"Fitzroy Street!" he shouted at the driver. "As fast as you can! Do you hear me?"

The driver shouted something back, and a moment later they turned. Monk's mind was numb. It was inconceivable. It was as if he had suddenly taken leave of his wits and plunged into some total insanity. One moment they had been the closest of companions, happy and at ease; the next she had changed as if she had ripped off a mask and exposed something hideous, a creature filled with hatred and consumed by it, deranged, prepared to risk injury by falling out of a moving carriage.

And the accusation she had made against him could ruin him. Only as he reached Fitzroy Street and the cab stopped did he realize the implications of what she had done. It was there in the cabby's face, the horror, and the contempt.

He opened his mouth to protest his innocence, and saw the uselessness of it. He thrust his hand into his pocket and paid the man, then strode across the footpath, up the steps and in the front door. He was cold to the bone.

# CHAPTER
# SEVEN

———

Monk woke the next morning and memory returned like a cold tide, almost choking him. He gasped for breath, and sat up, his body shaking. The evening had been wonderful, full of laughter and companionship. Then suddenly, without the slightest warning whatever, Drusilla had changed from the caring, intimate friend she had been, and became a screaming accuser, her face contorted with hate. He could remember it with fearful clarity, as if it were still in front of him, the lips drawn back, the ugliness in mouth and eyes, the triumph.

But why? He hardly knew her, and everything they had shared had been of the greatest pleasure. She was a sophisticated, delightful woman of society, dabbling in a few hours' amusement rather more daring than usual. She was bored with her own circle. She had chosen Monk to take her out of it briefly. And she had chosen him! Her interest had been perfectly plain from the moment they had met on the Geographical Society steps. Looking back on it now, she had bumped into him every bit as much as he into her. Perhaps he should have wondered then why she was so willing to court his company. Most women would have been more cautious, more circumspect. But he had assumed that she was bored with the restrictions society placed on her and longed for the freedom he represented.

Was she mad? Her behavior was more than unstable, it was unbalanced. This charge would ruin him, but if she insisted that he attempted to force his attentions on her, which she could not possibly believe, then she stood to be at best the subject of speculation as well as sympathy, and at worst the butt of less than charitable gossip. Perhaps she had escaped from Bedlam, or some other asylum for the insane.

He lay on his back staring at the ceiling.

No, that was stupid. If she were demented, then it would be a private matter, cared for by her family. That must be it. She had temporarily escaped her keepers. When she was found again, it would all be explained. They would understand. Quite probably she had behaved wildly before. Perhaps she had even done the same thing to some other unfortunate man.

He rose, washed and shaved. It was while he was staring at his face in the glass, its lean planes, the level gray eyes hard and clever, the wide lips with the faint scar beneath, that he remembered seeing the same face when he first came back from hospital. He had not known it then, not found it even faintly familiar. He had searched it then as he might a stranger's, looking for character, the weaknesses and the strengths, the marks of appetite, the signs of gentleness or humor or pity.

The next question was obvious. Was Drusilla Wyndham mad, or had she known him before, and hated him? Had he done her some injury which she could never forgive, and this was her revenge?

He did not know!

Slowly he cleaned his shaving things and put them away, his hands moving automatically.

But if he had known her, then she must surely have expected him also to know her now? How had she dared approach him as if they were strangers? Had she changed so much she had assumed he would never recognize her?

That was ridiculous. She was a remarkable woman, not merely beautiful but most unusual. Her carriage, her dignity, and her wit were unique. How could she expect any man to see her and then forget her so completely that in meeting again, seeing her repeatedly, speaking with her, hearing her laugh, he would still not remember?

He walked over to the window and stared out at the gray morning, carriages passing below with lamps still lit.

She must know of the loss of his memory.

But how? Who could have told her? No one knew except his personal friends: Hester, Callandra, Oliver Rathbone, and of course John Evan, the young policeman who had been so loyal during that first terrible case after the accident.

Why did she hate him enough to do this? It was no sudden impulse. She had lied and connived from the beginning, sought him out, charmed him, and deliberately placed him where he could be accused and had no defense. They were alone. Her reputation was intact, it was a situation in which it was quite justifiable to be. He could imaginably have assaulted her, and she had witnesses, at least to her distress and escape.

Who would believe his account?

No one. It made no sense at all. He could hardly believe it himself.

He dressed, and forced himself to eat the breakfast his landlady brought.

"You don't look well, Mr. Monk," she said with a shake of her head. "Do 'ope as yer not coming down wi' summink. 'Ot mustard poultice, me ma always used to say. Swear by it, she did. Any'ow, tell me if yer needs one, an' I'll make it for yer."

"Thank you," he said absently. "Think I'm just tired. Don't worry."

"Well, you mind yerself, then." She nodded. "Gets yerself ter some funny parts, you do. Wouldn't be surprised if yer picked up summink nasty."

He mumbled a noncommittal reply, and she busied herself clearing away.

There was a knock on the outside door and Monk rose to answer it. The blast of cold air chilled him. The daylight was damp and gray.

"Letter for you, mister," a small boy said, smiling at him from beneath an oversized cap. "Fer Mr. Monk. That's you, innit? I knows yer. I seen yer abaht."

"Who gave it to you?" Monk demanded as a glance at the writing showed it unfamiliar. It was elegant, feminine, and not Hester's, Callandra's or Genevieve Stonefield's.

"Lady in a carriage, guv. Dunno her name. Give me threepence ter give it yer."

His stomach leaped. Perhaps this was some explanation? It would all make sense. It was a mistake.

"Lady with fair hair and brown eyes?" he demanded.

"Fair 'air, dunno about eyes." The boy shook his head.

"Thank you." Monk tore the letter open. It was dated that morning.

Mr William Monk,

I had never assumed you to be a gentleman of my own station, but I had imagined you to have the rudiments of decency, or I should never have consented to spend a moment's time in your company, other than as ordinary courtesy demanded. I found your differences entertaining, no more. I am bored with the narrow confines of my own place in society, stifled by the rules and conventions. You offered a stimulating view of another level of life.

I cannot believe you so misunderstood my courtesy that you imagined I was willing to allow our acquaintance to be more. The only explanation for your behaviour lies in your disregard for the feelings of others, and your willingness to use people to achieve your own satisfactions, regardless of the cost to them.

I can never forgive you for what you have done to me, and I shall do all in my power to see that you pay to the uttermost farthing. I shall pursue this through the law, by word of mouth, and through the civil courts if need be. You shall know with every breath you take that I am your enemy, and you will rue the day you chose to use me as you have. Such betrayal will always find its punishment.

Drusilla Wyndham

He read it again. His hands were shaking. It was incredible.

But on second reading it was exactly the same.

"Y' all right, mister?" the boy said anxiously.

"Yes," Monk lied. "Yes, thank you." He fished in his pocket and took out threepence. He would not have her pay more than he.

The boy took it with thanks, then changed his mind, painfully. "She already gimme."

"I know." Monk breathed in, trying to steady himself. "Keep it."

"Fank yer, guv." And before his good fortune could vanish, the boy turned and ran down the street, his boots clattering on the cold pavement.

Monk closed the door and went back to his inner room. His landlady had gone. He sat down, the letter still in his hand, although he did not look at it anymore.

It could not possibly refer to last night, or any other time over the last week. She could only mean some acquaintance they had had in the past.

It always came back to the past, and that great void in his memory, the darkness where anything might exist.

She had used the word *betrayal*. That implied trust. Was he really a man to do such a thing? He had never betrayed anyone since the accident. Honor was one virtue he possessed. He had never broken his word. He would not let himself down by such an act.

Could he have changed so much? Had the blow to his head not only obliterated all the past from his mind, but also altered his nature? Was that possible?

He paced the floor back and forth, trying to think of all the things he had pieced together about himself from before the accident, the fragments that had come back to him, the flashes from his childhood in the north, glimpses of the sea, its violence and its beauty. He recalled his eagerness to learn, fleeting impressions; a face, a sense of injustice and desperation, the man who had been his mentor, and who had been deceived and ruined, and Monk had been unable to help. Nothing he could do had saved him. That was when he had abandoned commerce and dedicated himself to the police.

That was not a man who would betray!

In the police he had risen quickly. He knew from a dozen minor evidences, people's faces when he met them again, remarks half heard. He had been cruel of tongue, critical, at times ruthless. Runcorn, his old superior, had hated him, and little by little Monk had learned it was not without cause. Monk had contributed to Runcorn's failures and inadequacies, he had undermined him steadily, even if Runcorn had at least in part brought it upon himself with his petty hatreds and his personal ambitions, which he was prepared to achieve on the backs of others.

Was that a kind of betrayal?

No. It was cruelty, but it was not dishonest. Betrayal was always eventually a kind of deceit.

He knew almost nothing about his relationships with women. The only one of whom he had any recollection was Hermione, whom he had thought he loved, and in that he was the loser. If anyone was betrayed it was he. It was Hermione who had been so much less than she promised, she who had been too shallow to grasp at love, who had preferred the comfortable, the unchallenging, the safe. He could still feel the hollowness of loss when he had found her again, so full of hope, and then the disillusion, the utter emptiness.

But he must have known Drusilla! That hatred on her face had some terrible reason, some foundation in a relationship where she felt so wronged she had been prepared to do even this to be revenged.

He had already read through all the letters and the bills he could find when he first returned home from the accident, trying then to reconstruct some framework to his life. There was little enough. He was careful with money, but extravagant as far as personal appearance was concerned. His tailor's bills were high, as were his shirtmaker's and bootmaker's, even his barber's.

There had been no personal letters except from his sister, Beth, and he had obviously been remiss in writing back to her. Now he searched through them again, but there was nothing in the same hand as Drusilla's letter. Admittedly there was nothing else personal.

He put them all back. It was a sparse record for a lifetime. There was no sense of identity in it, no feeling for the nature and personality of a man. There must be so much that he did not know, and probably never would. There must have been loves and hates, generosities, injuries, hopes, humiliations and triumphs. They were all wiped out as if they had never happened.

Except that for everyone else they were still there, sharp and real, still carrying all their emotion and pain.

How could he have known a woman like Drusilla, with her vitality, beauty, wit and charm, and simply have forgotten her so totally that even on seeing her again, being so happy with her, he still had no hint of memory? Nothing was familiar. Rack his brain as he might, there was no chord, no flash of even momentary recollection.

He stared out of the window at the street. It was still gray, but the carriage lamps were no longer lit.

It would be a delusion to think she would not proceed. Of course she could prove nothing. Nothing had happened. But that was immaterial. She could make the charge, and it would be sufficient to ruin him. His livelihood depended on his reputation, on trust.

He had no other skills. Perhaps she knew that?

What had he done to her? What manner of man was he—had he been?

Hester was still taking her turn nursing Enid Ravensbrook, who was now beginning the long, slow journey to recovery but still needed constant attention, or she could slip into relapse.

The same morning that Monk received his letter from Drusilla,

Hester returned from the makeshift hospital to Ravensbrook House, tired and thoroughly miserable. She ached from lack of sleep, her eyes stung as if she had grit or dust in them, and she was heartsick of the sights and sounds and smells of distress. So many people had died. The bare few who had recovered gave it all meaning, but it was small in the sight of so much loss. And no matter how hard Kristian tried, what arguments he put up in the local government council, nothing was done. They were frightened of the disease, frightened of the cost of new sewers, frightened of innovation or change, of new inventions which might not work, of old ones which had already failed, and of blame no matter what they did. It was an exhausting struggle, and almost certainly doomed to failure. But neither he nor Callandra could give up.

Hester had watched them day after day marshaling new arguments and returning to battle. Each evening they had retired defeated. The only good to come of it was the tenderness they shared with each other, and even that was fraught with pain. After the fever they would part again, to see each other only occasionally, formally, perhaps in meetings of the board of governors of the hospital where Kristian worked and Callandra gave her help voluntarily. These meetings would be in front of all the other governors, or if they were fortunate, perhaps a chance encounter in a corridor with the constant expectation of interruption. They would speak of anything and everything but themselves. In all probability it would always be so.

Hester was welcomed in by the parlormaid and told that a supper was prepared if she wished it, after she had seen Lady Ravensbrook and Mrs. Stonefield.

She thanked the girl and went upstairs.

Enid was propped up in bed, leaning against a pile of pillows. She looked gaunt, as if she had not eaten or slept in days. There were bruised hollows around her eyes and her skin looked discolored and paper-fragile. Her hair hung in lank strings around her shoulders and she was so thin the bones seemed in danger of hurting the flesh stretched across them. But she smiled as soon as she saw Hester.

"How are they?" she asked, her voice still weak, only lifted by the eagerness inside her. "Is it easing at all? How about Callandra? Is she all right? And Mary? And Kristian?"

Hester felt some of the tension slip away from her. The room was warm and comfortable. There was a fire in the hearth. It was a different world from the coldness and the dirt of the hospital, the guttering candles and the smell of too many people unwashed, close together in their pain.

Hester sat on the edge of the bed.

"Callandra and Mary are still well, though very tired," she replied. "And Kristian is still fighting the council, but I don't think he has won a yard of ground. And yes, I think the fever is lessening a little. Certainly there are fewer deaths. We sent two people home today, both well enough to leave."

"Who are they? Did I know them?"

"Yes," Hester said with a broad smile. "One is the little boy you were so fond of, the one you thought could never survive. . . ."

"He's all right?" Enid said in amazement, her eyes lighting. "He's recovered?"

"Yes. He went home today. I don't know what gave him the strength, but he survived."

Enid leaned back against her pillows, a great sweetness in her face, almost a radiance. "And the other?" she asked.

"A woman with four children," Hester answered. "She went home to them today as well. But how are you? That's what I came to know."

It was a question only of friendship. She would make her own determination. The improvement in Enid was great. Her eyes were clearer, her temperature down to normal, but the fever had wasted her and she looked at the very end of her strength.

Enid smiled. "Very impatient to feel better," she confessed. "I hate feeling so weak. I can barely lift my hands to feed myself, much less comb my hair. It's absurd. I lie here uselessly. There is so much to do, and I am spending three quarters of my life asleep."

"It is the best thing," Hester assured her. "Don't fight against it. It is nature's way of healing you. You will be better the faster if you submit to it."

Enid clenched her teeth. "I hate to surrender!"

"Military tactics." Hester leaned forward conspiratorially. "Never fight when you know your enemy has the advantage. Pick a time, don't let him do it for you. Retreat now, and return when the advantage is yours."

"Ever thought of being a soldier?" Enid asked with a giggle which turned into a cough.

"Frequently," Hester replied. "I think I could make a better fist of it than many who do it now. Certainly I could barely do worse."

"Don't let my husband hear you say that!" Enid warned happily.

Hester's reply was cut off by Genevieve's appearance. She looked less harassed than when Hester had seen her last, although she must have been tired, and Hester knew from Monk's remark that there had been no good news.

She greeted her, and after an exchange of necessary information regarding Enid, they both left to partake of the meal which had been set for them in the housekeeper's sitting room.

"The fever is definitely abating in Limehouse," Hester said conversationally. "I only wish we could do something to prevent it coming back again."

"What could anyone do?" Genevieve asked with a frown. "The way people live, it is bound to arise every so often."

"Change the way they live," Hester replied.

Genevieve smiled, bitterness and a kind of revulsion in it, not untouched by both anger and pity.

"You'd have more luck trying to stop the tide from turning." She speared a piece of meat in her steak and kidney pudding and put it in her mouth, then spoke again the moment after she had swallowed it. "You can't change people. Oh, one or two, maybe, but never thousands. They've lived like that for generations, never enough to eat, the bread's full of alum, the milk's half water." She gave a sharp laugh. "Even the tea is better for poisoning the rats than for humans drinking. Only working men get things like pigs' trotters or kippers, the rest of the family does without. Nobody has fruit or vegetables. Everybody in the street, in two streets, has to queue with pails for water from the wells, and half of them are contaminated by sewers, cesspits or middens. Even if they didn't use the one pail for everything!" Her voice was angry, bitter and racked with emotion. "They're born with disease, and they die with it. A few sewage pipes aren't going to change that!"

"Yes they can," Hester said slowly, her mind dizzy with the force of Genevieve's passion, bewildered by its suddenness and ringing sincerity. "It's the drains and the middens where the problem lies."

Genevieve's lip curled. "It's the same thing!"

"No it isn't!" Hester argued, leaning forward across the table. "If there were proper water-carrying sewers built, then—"

"Water?" Genevieve looked amazed and horrified. "Then it would go everywhere!"

"No it wouldn't—"

"Yes it would! I've seen that, when the tide turns, or there's a heavy rain, it all backs up, the middens overflow, the gutters run sewage! Even when it goes down again what it leaves behind sits in piles on the pavements! You can shovel it off!"

"Where?" Hester said slowly, an incredible idea taking form in her mind, something so ludicrous it could even be true, wild and absurd as it seemed.

"What?" Genevieve's face colored painfully. She fumbled for words and found none. "Well—perhaps I haven't seen. I should have said I had heard. . . ." She bent as if to resume eating her food, but only toyed with it, pushing it around with her fork.

"Caleb lives in Limehouse, doesn't he?" Hester remembered.

"I believe so." Genevieve's body tensed and her hands stopped moving her fork. "Why? I certainly haven't heard it from him. I only met him once or twice. I barely even knew him!" The fear and the horror were sharp in her face, and a loathing too great for words.

Hester felt ashamed for having brought up the name of the man who had taken so much from her. Instinctively she put out her hand and touched Genevieve's where it lay on the table.

"I'm sorry. I wish I had not spoken of him. There must be pleasant things for us to discuss. I met Mr. Niven in the hall yesterday as I was leaving. He seems a very gentle man, and a good friend to you."

Genevieve flushed. "Yes, he is," she admitted. "He was very fond of Angus, in spite of the . . . the business misfortunes which befell him because of Angus's greater skill. He really is quite able, you know. He has learned from his incautious judgments."

"I'm glad," Hester said sincerely. She had liked Niven's face, and she certainly liked Genevieve. "Perhaps he will yet find a position where he can mend his situation." Genevieve looked down. There was an awkwardness in her, but her short chin was set in determination, and there was tenderness and grief in her wide mouth.

"I . . . I am considering offering him the management of my business . . . that is . . . that is, of course, if I am permitted to." She gazed at Hester. "You must think me very cold. No one has yet proved what happened to my husband, although I know in my heart. And here I am discussing who I will put in his place." She leaned forward, pushing her unfinished plate out of the way. "I cannot help Angus anymore. I tried everything I knew to persuade him not to go to Caleb, but he wouldn't listen to me. Now I have to think of my children and what will happen to them. The world won't wait while I grieve." Her eyes were steady, and, gazing back at her, Hester realized some of the strength in her, the power of the resolve which had made her what she was and which now drove her on to rein in her own pain, guard and control it, for the sake of her children.

Perhaps some of her admiration was plain in her expression, because the defensiveness eased out of Genevieve and she smiled ruefully, a little at herself.

Genevieve seemed such a formal name for such a woman, almost an earthy woman, one with such a vivid reality. In the lamplight

Hester could see the shadow her lashes cast on her cheek and the very faint down on the skin. Had Angus called her Genny?

Genny . . . Ginny?

Was that where it all came from, the explanation for her acutely observed understanding of the people of Limehouse and their like, and the terror of poverty? Was it a dreadful familiarity which set her determination, that at almost any cost she would not allow her children ever to be cold, hungry, frightened and ashamed as she had been. The squalor and despair of the Limehouse slums was huge in her memory, and no present comfort would ever expunge it. Perhaps she was the girl Mary had spoken of, who had escaped Limehouse to marriage?

"Yes," Hester said quietly. "Yes, I see. I am sure Monk will do everything he can to prove Angus's death. And he is extremely clever. If he cannot do it one way, he will find another. Don't despair."

Genevieve looked at her, hope in her eyes, and curiosity. "Do you know him well?"

Hester hesitated. What was the answer to that? She was not sure she even knew it herself, much less that she was prepared to share it. What did she know of him? The areas she did not know were vast, cavernous; perhaps they were even areas he did not know himself?

"Only professionally," she replied with a tight smile, leaning back in her chair, away from Genevieve and the quick perception in her face. Her mind was filled suddenly with the memory of those few moments in the closed room in Edinburgh, of the feel of his arms around her and that one passionate, sublime kiss. "I have seen him work in other cases," she hurried on, knowing her face was hot. Could Genevieve see how she was lying? She thought so. "Do cling onto hope." She was talking too much, trying to turn the subject. "At least it seems he has learned the truth. He will find a way to prove it, sufficient for the authorities to—" She stopped.

Genevieve was smiling. She said nothing, but her silence was eloquent and full of pleasure.

Hester felt trapped, not by Genevieve but by herself.

"You came from Limehouse, didn't you?" she said quietly, as a matter of confidence, not accusation. Half of her knew it was an attack to defend herself.

Genevieve flushed, but her eyes did not evade Hester's, nor was there anger in them.

"Yes. It seems like another life now, it was so different, and so many years ago." She moved a little and the lamplight changed on the planes of her face, throwing the strength into relief. "But I won't let anything drive me back. My children will not grow up there! And I won't have Lord Ravensbrook feed them and clothe them, and dictate what manner of people they shall be. I won't let him hug them, to fill Angus's place."

"Would he do that?" Hester said slowly, picturing Ravensbrook's dark, patrician face in her mind with its arrogance and charm.

"I don't know," Genevieve confessed. "But I'm afraid of it. I feel terribly alone without Angus. You see, he understood me. He knew where I came from, and he didn't mind my occasional mistakes. . . ."

A whole vision of fear and humiliation opened up in front of Hester. With a breathtaking vividness she perceived what it would be like for Genevieve at Ravensbrook House night and day, watched at every meal, observed and quite soon criticized. Not only would Ravensbrook himself notice all the tiny errors in even the most carefully produced etiquette or grammar, but perhaps even worse, so would the staff, the careful butler, the supercilious housekeeper, the giggling maids. Only possibly Enid would not care.

"Of course," she said with intense feeling. "You must keep your own home. Mr.—"

She was interrupted by a brisk knock at the door and the housekeeper walking in, her face grim, the keys at her belt jangling.

"There is a person to see you, Miss Latterly," she announced. "You had better use the butler's pantry. Mr. Dolman says as he doesn't mind. Begging your pardon, Mrs. Stonefield."

"What kind of a person?" Hester asked.

The housekeeper's face did not change in the slightest, not a flicker of her expression moved.

"A male person, Miss Latterly. More than that you will have to find out for yourself. Please be advised we do not allow the female staff to have followers, and that also applies to you while you are resident here, whatever your purpose."

Hester was stunned.

But Genevieve felt no such restrictions.

"Miss Latterly is not a servant, Mrs. Gibbons," she said smartly. "She is a professional person who has given her time freely out of regard for Lady Ravensbrook, who might well have died if it had not been for her treatment!"

"If you can call nursing a profession," Mrs. Gibbons retorted with a sniff. "And it is the good Lord who heals the sick, not any of us, Mrs. Stonefield. As a Christian woman, I'm sure you know that."

Thoughts flashed across Hester's mind about the virtues of Christian women, beginning with charity, but this was not the time to enter into an argument she could not win.

"Thank you for bringing me the message, Mrs. Gibbons," she said, baring her teeth in a gesture that bore little resemblance to a smile. "How kind of you." And with a nod to Genevieve, she rose to her feet and left the room.

The butler's pantry was two doors along the passage, and she went in without knocking.

She was startled to see Monk standing there looking almost haggard. His face was pale and there were lines of strain unlike anything she had seen in him since the Grey case.

"What is it?" she asked, closing the door behind her, her stomach sinking with dread. "It can't be Stonefield, can it? It ... it's not Callandra." Pain almost dizzied her. "Has something happened to Callandra?"

"No!" His voice was strident. He controlled it with an effort. "No," he repeated more calmly. His face was full of emotion and he was obviously finding it extremely difficult to frame the words to tell her.

She forced back her impatience. She had seen both shock and fear before and she knew the signs. To have affected Monk this way it must be something very dreadful indeed.

"Sit down and tell me," she said gently. "What has happened?"

Temper flared in his eyes, then died away, replaced by the fear again. The very fact that he did not retaliate chilled her even more. She sat down on the drab, overstuffed chair and folded her hands in her lap, under her apron, where he could not see that they were clenched together.

"I have been accused of assault." He said the words between his teeth, not looking at her.

"And are you guilty?" she asked levelly, knowing his rage and his physical strength. She had not forgotten the body in Mecklenburg Square, beaten to death, and that Monk had once feared he had done it himself.

His eyes widened, glaring at her, his features twisted with outrage.

"No!" he shouted. "God in heaven, no! How can you even ask?" The words choked him. He looked as if he could never forgive her for the question. He was shaking with fury, his body so tensed he was even now at the edge of violence, simply to release what was becoming unbearable.

"Because I know you," she answered, feeling increasingly that perhaps she did not. "If someone angered you enough, you might—"

"A woman!" The cry strangled in his throat. "Assault a woman? Force myself on her?"

She was stunned. It was so absurd it was almost funny.

Except that he was obviously serious, and profoundly frightened. Such a charge would ruin him, she knew that only too well. Her own professional existence also rested on reputation, and she knew how nearly she had once lost that. It had been Monk who had fought for her, worked night and day to prove her innocence.

"That's ridiculous," she said gravely. "Obviously she cannot prove it to be so, but equally obviously you cannot prove it not to be, or you would not be here. Who is she, and what happened? Is she someone you rejected? Or has she some other reason for such a charge? Do you suppose she is with child, and needs to blame someone for it to claim her own innocence in the matter?"

"I don't know." At last he sat down as well, staring at the patched carpet on the floor. "I don't know why she has done it, except that it was deliberate. We were in a hansom, going home after an evening"—he hesitated, still looking down—"an evening of mild entertainment, a pleasant dinner. She suddenly tore open the bodice of her dress, then glared at me with the most violent hatred, screamed, and threw herself out of the carriage with it under way, in front of a score of guests leaving a party in North Audley Street!"

She felt a chill of fear touch her also. Such behavior held an element of madness. The woman had risked not only Monk's reputation but a good deal of her own as well. However innocent she claimed to be, there would be talk, speculation, tongues willing to be unkind.

"Who is she?" she asked again.

"Drusilla Wyndham," he said very quietly, still not looking at her.

She said nothing. A curious mix of emotions filled her mind: relief that after all he could not now love Drusilla, that Drusilla had failed him in every way, and her own hatred of Drusilla of a quite different nature from before, because now the woman threatened him. There was also fear for the injury Drusilla would do him, and anger for the injustice of it. She did not even think of curiosity as to why.

"Who is she?" she asked. "I mean socially. Where does she come from?"

He looked up at her, meeting her eyes for the first time.

"I don't know more than I could judge from her manner and her speech, which was enough. But what does it matter? Whoever she is, she can ruin me by the suggestion. She doesn't have to be related to anyone important." His voice rose again with impatience that she did not understand the point. "Any woman making the charge, except perhaps a servant or a prostitute—"

"I know that." She cut across him just as sharply, jerking her hand to dismiss the notion. "I'm not thinking of that, I'm thinking how to fight her. Know your enemy!"

"I can't fight her!" His voice rose in fury and desperation. "If she takes it to court I can deny it, but not if she simply does it by whisper and innuendo. What do you suggest? That I sue her for slander? Don't be absurd! Even if I could, which I couldn't, my reputation would still be ruined. In fact, the very act of calling her a liar would make it worse." He looked like a man on the edge of an abyss, staring destruction in the face.

"Of course not," she said quietly. "Who's your adviser? Lord Cardigan?"

"What in the hell are you talking about?"

"The charge of the Light Brigade," she answered bitterly.

She saw a glimmer of comprehension in his face.

"So what do you suggest?" he said, but without hope.

"I'm not sure," she replied, rising to her feet and walking to the one small window. "But certainly not a head-on charge at the enemy's guns. If they are dug into the high ground with breached cannons pointing at us, then we must either move them out of it or come at them by some other means."

"Stop playing soldiers," he said quietly. "Just because you nursed in the Crimea doesn't mean you know the first damn thing about warfare."

"Yes it does!" she said, swinging around. "The first damn thing about warfare is that soldiers get killed. Ask anyone who's been there! Except the bloody incompetent generals, of course."

He smiled in spite of himself, but there was only the humor of the grave in it.

"What a charming woman you are. What do you suggest in this particular battle? Shall I shoot her, besiege her, poison her water, or wait for the winter to freeze her out? Or hope that she contracts the typhoid?"

"Call on another woman," she answered, wishing the moment she had said it that she had not. She had no plans, no ideas, only a boiling determination to win.

He looked nonplussed. "Another woman? Whatever for? Who?"

"Me, of course, you fool!" she retorted. "You haven't the slightest understanding of women or how they think. You never have had. Obviously she hates you. How did you meet her?"

"I bumped into her on the steps of the Geographical Society. Or perhaps she bumped into me."

"You think she contrived it?" she said without great surprise. Women did such things far more often than most men realized.

"I do now. I didn't then." A bitter amusement lit his eyes for a moment. "She must have been surprised when I did not recognize her. She held me in conversation for several minutes. She must have been waiting for me to remember, and then realized that I didn't."

"You don't remember anything at all?" she pressed. "Not even an impression?"

"No! Of course I don't, or I would have said so. I have been through everything I can think of, but I can't remember anything about her. It's a complete blank."

She had a glimpse of his utter helplessness, the shadows and glimpses of cruelty within his memory, and the fears that would always be part of him. Then it evaporated. All she felt was tenderness and the determination to protect him whatever the cost.

"It doesn't matter anyway," she said, moving over and touching his head gently, just her fingers on his hair for a moment. "It is who she is now that matters. I'll think of a way to fight back. Don't worry. Just don't go anywhere near her again. Keep on looking for Angus Stonefield."

"At least I'm not likely to run into any outraged high society face down in the mud 'round the Isle of Dogs!" he said savagely. "A little rape might add to my credibility with the locals."

"I would mention it only if you intend to remain there," she replied tartly, turning to the door. "In the meantime, keep your powder dry."

He saluted sarcastically. "Yes, general, sir!"

But when he left Ravensbrook House, Monk did feel marginally better. The anger was scalding inside him, and the fear was just as real. Nothing had changed. Yet now he no longer stood alone. That took the despair away, the very worst of the pain.

He strode along the footpath, ignoring those he passed by, all but bumping into them. Even the smut-laden rain driving in his face was hardly heeded. He would find where Caleb had murdered his brother. He might not find the body, but he would prove his death, and he would see Caleb hanged for it. Somewhere there was a piece of evidence, a witness, a chain of events which would damn him. It was up to Monk to persist until he did. Wherever it was, whoever knew it, whatever it took to uncover it.

It was midday by the time he got to the Isle of Dogs and went again to the house in Manilla Street to speak to Selina. At first she refused to see him. She looked frightened, and he guessed it was not long since Caleb had been there. Her silence was a mixture of loyalty and fear. The fear at least was probably well grounded.

He stood in front of her in the small, cold, well-kept room.

"He killed Angus, and I'm going to prove it," he said viciously. "One way or another, I'll see him swing for it. Whether you prove it with me, or swing with him, is up to you."

She said nothing. She faced him defiantly, her head held cockily, as if she were sure of herself, one hip jutting out. But he saw her knuckles whiten, and heard the terror beneath her voice.

"You think he's a dangerous swine," he said grimly. "Cross me, and you'll think he's a model of the civilized man."

"It's his life," she retorted with contempt, looking him up and down, seeing the beautifully cut coat and the polished boots. "You don't even know what dangerous is."

"Believe me, I have little left to lose either," he said passionately.

She stared at him, looked into his eyes, and slowly her face changed. She saw something of the rage and despair in him, and the contempt died.

"I don't know where he is," she said quietly.

"I didn't expect you to. I want to know where he met Angus, every place you know of that they went together, or might have gone. He murdered Angus. Somebody somewhere knows about it."

"They won't tell you!" Her chin lifted again in defiance and a kind of pride.

"Yes they will." He laughed bitterly. "Whatever Caleb can do to them, the long wait of the last night, the eight o'clock walk in the morning to the hangman's rope, is worse."

She swore at him, and the hatred in her eyes reminded him of Drusilla. It robbed him of the pity he might have felt for her.

"Where did they meet?" he said again.

Silence.

"Have you seen a corpse after it's been hanged?" He looked at her slender throat.

"At the Artichoke, along by the Blackwall Stairs. But it won't do yer no good. They won't tell yer nothin'. I 'ope yer rot in 'ell. I 'ope they drown yer in a cesspool and feed yer body ter the rats."

"Is that what he did with Angus?"

"Gawd, I dunno." But beneath the paint her face was white and there was horror in her eyes. "Nah gits aht!"

Monk went back along Manilla Street in the rain, and turned east.

The landlord of the Artichoke served him a slice of eel pie and a glass of ale, but eyed him with suspicion. Men dressed as Monk presently was did not frequent such taverns, but money was money, and he took it readily enough.

After Monk had eaten he began his questions, civilly at first, but quickly gaining an undertone of menace. He learned only one piece of information which, if true, might prove of worth, and that was given as an incidental to an insult. But that had many times been the way. An angry man betrayed more than he knew. The landlord let slip that Caleb had several friends, whether by choice or mutual advantage, and one of them, another dangerous and greedy man, had a yard off Coldharbour, hard by the Cattle Wharf. Apparently he was a good friend, one whom Caleb could trust and who would, according to the landlord, avenge any wrong done Caleb by the likes of Monk.

Fifteen minutes later found Monk west again at Coldharbour, right on the bank of the river. It was now running hard and gray, carrying ships, barges and all manner of detritus on the outgoing tide. A dead rat floated by, and half a dozen rotted timbers. The smell of sewage clogged the nostrils. A clipper, half-rigged, was making its way majestically down from the Pool of London towards the open sea and the world beyond.

It was not hard to find the yard, but it served only as a starting point. If Caleb had intended from the beginning to murder his brother, he would have chosen a private place to do it. He would certainly not have risked a witness. There were far too many people up and down the river who would be only too happy to have the power to ruin Caleb Stone.

And if the act had arisen out of a quarrel which got out of control, then he would equally have needed somewhere out of sight to think what to do with the body. Simply to tip it into the river was too much of a risk, especially if it had been daylight. It would have to be weighted and set in midstream. Better still to take it to Limehouse and bury it as a typhoid victim. And all that took time.

There would be little purpose in being direct. He yanked the collar of his coat even higher and strode past the yard. He found all manner of laborers, derelicts, the hungry, cold, idle or sick, huddled in doorways, sheltering under sacking or canvas. He questioned them all. He walked from one end of Coldharbour to the other, and then across the bridge over the Blackwall Basin towards the stairs to the sibilant water.

He moved downriver slowly, picking his way over slippery stones and wet timbers, across patches of rotting shingle, through loading and unloading yards. He passed piles of merchandise, hauls of fish, lengths of rope and canvas. He climbed up and down steps and across gangways over dark, still water into a dozen larger or smaller slipways and docks. Always the stench was there, the sound of dripping and slurping, the creak of timber and straining ropes.

By dusk he was exhausted, angry and cold to the bone, but he refused to give up. Somewhere near here Caleb had killed Angus. Someone had seen or heard them quarreling, shouting voices, a cry of fury or pain, and then Caleb carrying the body. Perhaps there had been blood or a weapon. They were the same size, the same build. If it had come to a battle they must have been fairly evenly matched, even allowing for their different lives. What Angus lacked in physical exercise and the practice of fighting, perhaps he would at least partially compensate for with better nourishment and health.

Monk ate supper in a different tavern and set out into the dark. The rain had stopped and it was even colder. A mist was rising off the river, hanging in thin wreaths across the streets and dimming the few lights. The foghorns of barges drifted across the water, disembodied and mournful. On the corner of Robinhood Lane and the East India Dock Road two men were warming themselves by a brazier of roasting chestnuts.

Monk was drawn towards it because it was a refuge from the biting cold. It was human company and a light in the enveloping darkness, the endless sound of the creeping tide and the fine beads of moisture that gathered on everything and fell with myriad tiny sounds as if the night were alive.

As he drew closer he saw that one of the men was wearing an old seaman's jacket, too narrow across the shoulders for him, but at least waterproof. The other had on what at a glance he would have taken to be a tailored wool coat, had such a thing not been absurd in this place. And as his eyes followed the line of it down the man's body, he saw that it hung loosely, even shapelessly. When he moved his arm to poke the brazier, it was obvious the coat was so badly torn it was open at the sides, and there was a patch beneath one shoulder much darker. It was probably wet. Poor devil. Monk was cold enough in his fine broadcloth overcoat.

"Twopence for some chestnuts," he offered bluntly. He did not want to stand out as too obviously a stranger.

The man in the coat held out his hand wordlessly.

Monk put twopence in it.

The man picked out a dozen chestnuts expertly and left them in the ashes at the side to cool. His coat was of beautiful cut. The lapels set perfectly, the rim of the collar had been stitched by a tailor who knew his job. And Monk was a connoisseur of such things. The coat had been made for a man of Monk's height and breadth of shoulder.

Angus Stonefield?

He looked down at the man's trousers. In the light of the brazier's glow it was hard to see, but he judged they matched.

A wild idea came into his mind. It was a desperate throw. "I'll swap clothes with you for a guinea!"

"What?" The man stared at him as if he could not believe what he had heard. On the face of it, it was ridiculous. Monk had not changed since he left Ravensbrook House. His coat had cost him several pounds. He could not afford to replace it. But then if Drusilla went ahead with her intentions, he could end up no better off than this wretched man anyway. At least he would have the satisfaction of having caught Caleb Stone first. That would be one case of justice served!

"My coat for your jacket and trousers," he repeated.

The man weighed up his chances. "An' yer 'at," he bargained.

"The coat or nothing!" Monk snapped.

"What'll I do wi' no trouser?" The man demanded. "In't decent!"

"My jacket and trousers for yours, and I'll keep the coat," Monk offered. "And the hat." It was a better deal anyway. He had other suits.

"Le's see." The man was not going to take goods blindly.

Monk opened his coat so the man could judge his suit.

"Done!" he said instantly. "Yer daft, yer are, but a deal's a deal."

Solemnly, in the fog-shrouded darkness beside the brazier, they exchanged clothes, Monk holding very firmly to his coat, just in case the man had any ideas of theft.

"Daft," the man repeated again as he pulled Monk's warm jacket around him. It was too big, but it was a great deal better than the ripped one he had parted with.

Monk replaced his coat, nodded to the other man, who had watched the whole procedure with incredulity as if it had been some kind of drunken illusion, then he turned and walked away back along the East India Dock Road, to somewhere where he could find a hansom and go home.


Monk woke the following morning with his head reeling and his body feeling stiff and chilled, but also with a sense of anticipation, as if some long-sought success had finally been achieved. Then as he got out of bed and sneezed, he remembered Drusilla, and the joy drained out of him as if he had slit a vein.

He washed, shaved and dressed before bothering to look at the clothes he had acquired the previous night. His landlady brought breakfast and he ate it without tasting it. Five minutes afterwards he could not even remember what it had been.

Finally he picked up the clothes, jacket first, and examined it in the cold daylight near the window. It was made of a fine woolen cloth with a distinctive weave, beautifully cut in a conservative manner, with no concessions to fashion, simply quality. The tailor's name was stitched in the seam. More importantly as evidence, the sides were ripped as if someone had slashed it with a knife. There was a bloodstain about four inches across and some ten inches down on the left shoulder, roughly over where a man's heart would be, except it was at the back. There was also a small tear in the right elbow, no more than an inch long, and a scraping on the right forearm where several threads had been caught and pulled. Whoever had been wearing it had been involved in a serious fight, possibly even a fatal one.

And as he had observed the night before, the trousers matched the jacket. One knee was torn out, threads were pulled on both legs and there were stains of mud. The waist at the back was heavily soaked in blood.

He had only one choice. He must show them to Genevieve Stonefield. Without her identification of them, they were useless as evidence. The thought of subjecting her to such an ordeal was repellant, but there was no alternative. He could not protect her from it. And if anyone found the body, he would not be able to protect her from that either.

No one should face such an ordeal alone. There should be someone to offer her support, at least to care for her physically. There could be no comfort that would temper the cruelty of the truth.

But who? Hester was too busy with the typhoid outbreak, similarly Callandra. Enid Ravensbrook was still far too ill. Lord Ravensbrook she did not care for, or perhaps she was simply afraid of him. Arbuthnot was an employee, and one whom she would in due course have to instruct in what remained of the business.

There was only Titus Niven. Monk had suspected ill of him at one time, but he knew nothing to his discredit. The man was gentle, discreet, and too familiar with pain himself to treat it unkindly. Titus Niven it must be. And if he were party to Angus's death, then the fine irony of this was only one more element to compound the tragedy.

Monk wrapped the clothes in a bundle, put them in a soft-sided traveling bag and set out.

Niven was at home and received him with courtesy, but did not conceal his surprise. He was dressed in the same elegantly cut but slightly shabby clothes, and there was no fire in the grate. The room was bitterly cold. He looked embarrassed, but did not apologize for the temperature. He offered hot coffee, which Monk knew he could ill afford—either the coffee itself or the gas to heat it.

"Thank you, but I have only lately finished breakfast," Monk declined. "Besides, I have come on some business which would rob the pleasure of any refreshment at all. I would be most obliged if you could help me to break it to Mrs. Stonefield with as much gentleness as possible, and to be with her to offer any comfort you may."

Niven's face paled. "You have found Angus's body?"

"No, but I have found what I think may well be his clothes. I need her to identify them."

"Is that necessary?" Niven's voice was choked in his throat and his eyes pleaded with Monk.

"I wouldn't ask it if it were not," Monk said gently. "I think they are his, but I cannot pursue the matter with the police until I am certain beyond doubt. She is the only one whose word they would accept."

"The valet?" Niven asked thinly, then bit his lip. Perhaps he already knew Genevieve had dismissed all the servants but the children's nurse and the housemaid, so sure was she in her heart that Angus would never return. "Yes . . . yes, I suppose you are right," he agreed. "Do you wish me to come with you now?"

"If you please. She should not be told when she is alone."

"May I see them? I knew Angus well. Unless they are very new, I may be familiar with them. I do at least know his taste and style."

"And the same of his tailor?" Monk asked.

"Yes. Mr. Wicklow, of Wicklow and Harper."

It was the name in the suit Monk had worn back from the East India Dock Road. A dead man's clothes. He nodded, tightening his lips, and unrolled the package out of his bag.

Niven's face was ashen. He saw the blood, the stains of mud and water and the torn and slashed fabric. He swallowed with a convulsive movement of his throat, and nodded his head. He looked up at Monk, his blue eyes steady and filled with horror.

"I'll get my coat." And he turned away. Monk noticed that his hands were shaking very slightly and his shoulders were rigidly straight, as if he were making a deliberate effort to control himself and stand almost at attention.

They took a hansom and rode in silence. There was nothing to say, and neither of them made the pretense of conversation. Monk found himself hoping, so profoundly that it was almost a prayer, that Niven had had no part in Angus's death. The more he saw of the man, the more he both liked and admired him.

They alighted at Genevieve's home, but told the cab to wait. She might be at Ravensbrook House, and they might need to follow her there and very possibly bring her home immediately.

However, that proved not to be necessary. The housemaid who answered the door informed them that Mrs. Stonefield was at home, and when she recognized Niven, she had no hesitation in letting them in.

Monk paid the cab and dismissed it, following Niven within moments.

"What is it, Mr. Monk?" Genevieve asked immediately, dismissing the nursemaid and sending the two children with her. One look at Niven's face had told her the news was extremely serious. "You've found Angus. . . ."

"No." He would tell her as quickly as possible. Drawing it out only added another dimension to the suffering. "I have found some clothes which I believe may be his. If they are, and you have no doubt, it may be sufficient to cause the police to act."

"I see." Her voice was barely a whisper. "Allow me to see them."

Niven moved closer to her. Even at this anguished time, Monk noticed that he was not embarrassed. He had no self-consciousness. Perhaps it was because his thoughts were entirely upon her that he spared no part of his mind for himself. It was curiously comforting, a moment's warmth in the icy cold.

Monk opened his bag and took out the jacket. There was no need for her to see the trousers as well, and the blood soaking them. He unrolled it and held it up. He kept the shoulder towards himself, away from her, showing her only the inside and the tailor's mark.

She drew in her breath sharply and her hands flew to her mouth.

"Is it his?" Monk asked, although he knew the answer.

She was incapable of speech, but she nodded her head, her eyes filled with tears. She struggled against them, and failed.

Without a word, Niven put his arms around her, and she turned and buried her head in his shoulder.

There was nothing for Monk to say or do. He repacked the jacket, closed the bag and left without saying anything further, not troubling the maid to open or close the door for him.


This time the police did not argue. The sergeant regarded the jacket and trousers with a kind of vicious satisfaction, a slow smile spreading across his thin features.

"Got 'im," he said quietly. He regarded the bloodstain on the jacket with a shake of his head. "Poor sod!" He pushed them to one side of the desk and turned his head. "Robinson!" he shouted. "Robinson! Come 'ere! We're goin' to get a party together an' go after Caleb Stone. I want 'alf a dozen men wot knows the river, quick on their feet an' ready for a fight. Got that?"

From somewhere out of sight there was an answer in the affirmative.

The sergeant looked back at Monk.

"I'm obliged," he said with a nod. "We'll get 'im this time. Can't say as we'll make it stick, but we'll scare the 'ell out of 'im."

"I'm coming with you," Monk stated.

The sergeant sucked in his breath, then changed his mind. Perhaps an extra man would be useful, especially one with such a marked interest in success. And also, perhaps Monk deserved it.

"Right y'are then," he agreed. "We'll be off in"—he consulted his pocket watch, a handsome silver piece of considerable size—"fifteen minutes."

Half an hour later Monk was walking down Wharf Road beside a Constable Benyon, a lean young man with an eager face and a long, straight nose. The wind, smelling of smoke, damp and sewage, blew in their faces. They had begun on the east side of the Isle of Dogs, where the Greenwich Reach moves towards the Blackwall Reach, with instructions to follow the river downstream on the north shore. Two others were taking Limehouse, two more Greenwich and the south shore. The sergeant himself was coordinating their efforts from a hansom, moving from east to west. A further constable was detailed to cross the river and meet the team from Greenwich at the Crown and Sceptre Tavern at two o'clock, unless they were hot on the trail, in which case a message would be left.

"Reckon 'e'll be downriver, meself," Benyon said thoughtfully. "More like Blackwall, or the East India Docks. Else 'e'll be on t'other side. I'd a' taken ter the marshes, if I'd a bin 'im."

"He doesn't think we can touch him," Monk replied, hunching his shoulders against the chill coming up off the water. "Told me himself we'd never find the body."

"Mebbe we won't need one," Benyon said, willing himself to believe it.

They turned off Barque Street onto Manchester Road, passing a group of dockers going down towards the ferry. On the corner a one-legged sailor was selling matches. A running patterer jogged towards Ship Street corner, turned and disappeared.

"Wastin' our time 'ere." Benyon pulled a face. "I'll ask at the Cubitt Town pier. That's about the best place ter start."

They walked in silence past the Rice Mill and the Seysall Asphalt Company and made an acute right down to the pier. The cry of the gulls above the water came clearly over the rattle of wheels and the shouts of dockers handling bales of goods, bargees calling to one another, and the endless hiss and slap of the tide.

Monk hung back, not to intrude into Benyon's questioning. This was his area and he knew the people and what to say, what to avoid.

Benyon came back after several minutes.

"Not bin 'ere terday," he said, as if it proved his point.

Monk was not surprised. He nodded, and together they proceeded along Manchester Road past the Millwall Wharf, Plough Wharf, as far as Davis Street, then turned right and then left into Samuda Street. They stopped for a pint of ale at the Folly Tavern, and there at last heard news of Caleb Stone. No one admitted to having seen him at any specific time lately, but one little rat of a man with a long nose and a walleye followed them out and discreetly, at a price, told Benyon that Caleb had a friend in a tenement house on Quixley Street, off the East India Dock Wall Road, about three quarters of a mile away.

Benyon passed over half a crown and the man almost immediately disappeared across the alley and into the Samuda Yard with its piles of timber.

"Is that worth anything?" Monk asked dubiously.

"Oh yeah," Benyon replied with conviction. "Sammy 'as one or two 'ostages ter fortune. 'E won't lie ter me. We'd better find the sergeant. This'll need at least 'alf a dozen of us. If you'd seen Quixley Street yer'd not doubt that."

It took them over an hour and a half to find the pair from Limehouse and for all five of them, including the sergeant, to get to Quixley Street, which was a narrow throughway hardly a hundred yards long backing into the Great Northern Railway goods depot, just short of the first East India Dock. Two men were sent to Harrap Street at the back, and Benyon to Scamber Street at the side. The sergeant took Monk in at the front.

It was a large building, four stories high with narrow, dirty windows, several of them cracked or broken. The dark brick was stained with damp and soot but only one of the tall chimney stacks smoked, dribbling a fine gray-black trail into the cold air.

Monk felt a shiver of excitement, in spite of the filth and misery of the place. If Caleb Stone really was here, within a matter of minutes they would have him. He wanted to see him face-to-face, to watch those extraordinary green eyes when he knew he was beaten.

There was a man lying in the doorway, either drunk or asleep. His face had several days' growth of beard on it, and he breathed with difficulty. The sergeant stepped over him and Monk followed behind.

Inside the air smelled of mold and unemptied slops. The sergeant pushed open the door of the first room. Inside three women sat unraveling ropes. Their fingers were callused and swollen, some red with sores. Half a dozen children in various stages of undress played on the floor. A girl of about five was unpicking the stitching on a length of cloth which presumably had been a garment a short while ago. The window was boarded up. One candle relieved the shadows. It was bitterly cold. Obviously Caleb Stone was not here.

The next room was similarly occupied.

Monk glanced at the sergeant, but the grim look on his face silenced his doubts.

The third and fourth rooms were no more help. They climbed the rickety stairs, testing each stone before allowing their full weight on it. The steps rocked alarmingly, and the sergeant swore under his breath.

The first room on the next floor held two men, both in drunken sleep, but neither was Caleb Stone. The second room was occupied by a prostitute and a bargee, who hurled lurid abuse at them as they withdrew. An old man lay dying in the third, a woman keening gently beside him, rocking back and forth.

The third floor up was crammed with women sewing shirts, their heads bent, eyes straining to see, fingers flying with needle, thread weaving in and out. A man with pince-nez glasses balanced on his nose glared at the sergeant and hissed his irritation, wagging his finger like a school mistress. Monk longed to hit him for his meticulous cruelty, but he knew it would have done no good. One piece of paltry violence would not relieve anyone's poverty. And he was after Caleb Stone, not one wretched sweatshop profiteer.

The first room on the top floor up was occupied by a one-armed man, carefully measuring powder into a scale. In the next room three men played cards. One of them had thin gray hair and a stomach which bulged out over his trousers. The second was bald and had a red mustache. The third was Caleb Stone.

They looked up as the sergeant opened the door. For a moment there was silence, prickling cold. The fat man belched.

The sergeant took a step forward, and in that instant Caleb Stone saw Monk behind him. Perhaps it was some look of victory in Monk's face, maybe he recognized the sergeant. He climbed to his feet and lunged towards the window, throwing himself out of it with a shattering of glass.

The fat man rolled over onto all fours and charged at Monk. Monk raised his knee and caught him in the jaw, sending him reeling backwards, spitting blood. The other man was locked in a struggle with the sergeant, swinging backwards and forwards together like a parody of a dance.

Monk ran over to the window and smashed the rest of the glass out of the frame, then leaned out, half expecting to see the figure of Caleb broken on the pavement four stories below.

But he had forgotten the twists and turns of the stairs. They were facing the back of the building, and beneath him was the roof of a high wooden shed, not more than twelve feet away. Caleb was running across it, agile as an animal, making for the opposite side and a half-open window.

Monk scrambled over the sill and leaped, landing with a jar that shocked his bones. Within a moment he was on his feet and racing after Caleb, the shed roof rattling under his weight.

Caleb swung around once, his wide mouth grinning, then he jumped for the window and disappeared inside.

Monk went in after him, finding himself in another cold, suffocating room just like those he had left. Three old men sat with bottles in their hands around a potbellied stove smelling of soot.

Caleb flung the door open and charged across the landing and Monk heard his footsteps hard on the stairs. He dived after him, tripped on the fourth or fifth step, which was broken, and fell the remaining half dozen, landing bruisingly and only just missing cracking his head on the newel post. He heard Caleb's laughter as he clattered on down, a floor below him.

Monk clambered to his feet, furious with pain and frustration, and went down the rest of the stairs as fast as he could. He was just in time to see Caleb's back as he went out the door into Prestage Street and turned towards Brunswick Street, which ran all the way down to the river, Ashton's Wharf and the Blackwall Stairs.

Where the devil were the other constables? Monk yelled as loudly as his lungs would bear.

"Benyon! Brunswick Street!"

His elbow and shoulder were sore where he had hit them on the wall as he fell, and one ankle throbbed, but he charged along the footpath, barging into an old woman with a bag of clothes who was determined not to step aside for him. He knocked her against the wall, unintentionally, having been sure she would move. Her body felt heavy and soft, like a sack of porridge. She swore at him with a string of oaths he would have expected from a bargee.

Caleb had vanished.

Monk got into his stride again. Someone else was running along Harrap Street, coattails billowing. It must be one of the constables.

He swung around the corner and saw Caleb running easily, almost dancing as he turned around and waved, his face laughing, then scampered on towards the river.

Monk extended his pace, his lungs gasping, his blood pounding. It had been too long since he had been obliged to chase a man on foot. This was a hard way to discover it.

The constable caught up with him and forged ahead. Caleb was still twenty yards beyond them, and running easily, every now and then leaping, as if in mockery. They had passed the turning to Leicester Street and were approaching Norfolk Street. Where was Caleb making for?

Caleb passed the corner of Russell Street and there was nothing ahead of him but the dock and the stairs! A wild thought crossed Monk's mind that he was going to jump into the river. Suicide? Many a man would think it better than the hangman's rope. Monk would himself.

Then he would make for the wharf, not the stairs.

It was already mid-afternoon and the light was failing. A grayness crept up from the river and robbed everything of what little color there was. The mist deadened Caleb's flying footsteps as he raced across the stones to the edge of the water and the flight of steps downward. The constable was only a couple of yards behind him.

Monk's breath labored in his lungs but his ankle was easing.

Caleb disappeared down the stairs and the constable after him. Then there was a yell and a heavy splash, then a scream of fear, choked off almost instantly.

Monk reached the edge of the wall just as a second constable came behind him.

Caleb was on the steps, feet wide apart, balanced, laughing, his head thrown back. The constable was thrashing around in the water, sinking, dragged down by his boots and his heavy clothing.

"He'll drown!" Caleb shouted, looking at Monk. "You'd better pull him out! You can't leave him, Mr. Righteous!"

There was a barge about ten yards out, the first of a string moving slowly upriver with the incoming tide, low in the water, heavy with bales covered over with dark canvas. The bargee in the stern looked at the man in the water and threw his hands wide. He could not stop the impetus of his vessel. There were another dozen behind him, like railway carriages.

Monk hesitated only a moment. The constable was drowning. His face was white with terror. He had not the faintest idea how to swim and his own panic was killing him. There was a piece of timber lying on the edge. Monk threw it in and waited long enough to see it float.

The instant was enough. Caleb charged up the steps again, thrusting past him and onto the river wall, racing upstream towards the Artichoke Tavern fifty yards away.

The second constable arrived, swerving to go after Caleb and leave Monk to rescue the man in the water.

"Get him!" Monk shouted, jabbing his arm down the steps towards the water, and spun on his heel to run after Caleb.

The constable gasped, saw his colleague struggling, clasping for the wood, and swung around, plunging down the steps after him.

Monk sprinted along the hard pavement behind Caleb, who seemed to be veering away from the edge as if he would go around to the front of the tavern and the door. Why? Had he friends there? Reinforcements? He could hardly hope to hold off half a dozen police! There was no escape through the back—it fell sheer into the rising tide.

Monk was only fifteen yards behind him.

Then suddenly Caleb swerved again, turned on his foot and picked up speed, running straight towards the river. He was going to kill himself after all. He ran even faster and at the dock made an almighty leap. Only then did Monk realize what he meant to do. The barge was only twenty feet from the shore. He landed awkwardly, sprawled across the canvas, and all but pitched off the far side, but he was on it and already it was carrying him away.

With more rage than judgment, Monk backed off to give himself a launching distance, then in desperation leaped as well.

He landed with a numbing crash on the third barge. The breath was knocked out of him, and it was several seconds before he could even think to rise. When he did his hands were grazed and he found it hard to expand his lungs and gasp in the damp, darkening air. He could see the dim shape of the bargee, but he was barely aware of the sergeant on the river wall shouting and gesticulating, he was swearing wildly, his face contorted with fury. Certainly he did not even try to understand what he was saying. There was only one thought in his mind—get Caleb.

He straightened up and started to make his way forward, moving with his arms wide, keeping his foothold on the wet canvas with difficulty.

The barges were close, but there were still several feet of dark, filthy river water between the bow of one and the stern of another. If he fell he would be between the two, and would be crushed long before he could be drowned.

Caleb was on the lead barge, facing him, leaping up and down on the spot in mockery. He put his hands to his mouth to cup the sound.

"Come on!" he yelled. "Come and get me! Come on, Mr. Policeman! I killed Angus, didn't I? I destroyed him! He's gone forever! Finished! No more smart clothes, no more virtuous wife by the fireside! No more church on Sunday and 'Yes Sir,' 'No sir,' 'Aren't I a good boy, sir'!" He folded his arms across his chest, flat, hands down, then flung them wide. "Dead!" he cried. "Gone forever! You'll never find him. Nobody'll find him, ever! Ever!"

Monk started off towards him, floundering on the canvas piles, stumbling and regaining his balance, taking a wild leap across the dark water to the barge ahead, landing splayed and bruised on his hands and knees. He scrambled forward again, oblivious of pain or danger.

The bargee was yelling something but he ignored it.

They had passed the Blackwall entrance to the South Dock. Ahead of them was the Cubitt Town pier, then the curve of the river around the Isle of Dogs. He could no longer see the lights of Greenwich on the far side. The fog and darkness were closing in. The marshes to the left were a dim outline. There were other boats, but he saw them only from the corner of his eye.

He leaped to the front barge just in time to see Caleb apparently overbalance, land on his knees, then disappear over the side. Then he heard his laughter coming up from the water and just as he reached the edge himself, a rowing boat pulled away, one man heaving on the oars, another crouching in the stern, seemingly terrified.

Monk swore savagely. He swung around to the bargee, although even as he did, he knew it was pointless. The man had no way on earth of changing course. The heavily laden barges were tied together and going upstream on the tide.

"Monk!"

Where was the voice coming from?

"Monk! Jump, man!"

Then he saw the second rowing boat with the sergeant and another constable in it. Without a second's hesitation he jumped, landing in it and sending it rocking so violently it all but overturned. The constable at the oars let out an oath. The sergeant grabbed him roughly and forced him down on the duckboards at the bottom, and the boat righted itself and plowed forward again.

"After 'im!" the sergeant shouted unnecessarily.

They sat in silence, Monk still half crouched. The constable at the oars dug them into the water with all the strength he possessed, hurling his weight against them so violently that for several strokes the boat veered and bounced, then he settled down to an even pace and picked up speed.

There was hardly any light now. The late afternoon had drawn in and the overcast sky had robbed what little there was and the rising river mist distorted shapes. Foghorns sounded eerily. The lights of a clipper appeared, shadowed spars towering above them, drifting like giant trees in the sky. They rocked roughly in its wake.

"Where is the bastard?" the sergeant said between his teeth, peering forward through the gloom. "I'll get that swine if it's the last thing I do!"

"Bugsby's marshes," Monk answered, straightening his legs to sit up properly. "I'll wager he's going downriver again."

"Why?"

"He'll know we have men in Greenwich, and people who would say where he went. But he knows the marshes and we don't. We'll never get him once he's ashore there in the dark."

The sergeant swore.

The constable pulled harder on the oars, his back straining, hands rubbed to blisters. The boat sped over the misty, dark-running tide.

The shore loomed up before they were prepared. There were no lights, only the mud banks catching the last of the daylight in thin, shining strips, and the soft, seeping sound of the rising water in the marsh reeds.

Monk scrambled forward and jumped out into mud up to his calves. It took a surprising effort to pull himself loose from its ice-cold, sucking grip.

But twenty yards downstream he could see another figure on a firmer stretch, and the black shape of a boat pulling away, as if it had landed the devil himself and would flee for salvation.

The constable was out behind him, cursing at the mud. Together they squelched and struggled over the slime onto firmer shore, floundering towards Caleb, who was already trying to run.

No one shouted again. They all three plunged wildly through the deepening mist as the rising wind blew wraiths of it around them, then away again. The sergeant brought up the rear, dogged and determined, swinging inland a little, driving Caleb towards the point, cutting off his retreat back towards Greenwich.

It was another fifteen minutes of exhausting, heart-pounding, leg-aching pursuit before at last they cornered Caleb with his back to the river and nowhere else to turn.

He held his gloved hands up, open wide. They could no longer see his face, but Monk could imagine his expression from his voice in the darkness.

"All right! Take me!" he yelled. "Take me to your petty little courtroom, and your charade of a trial! What will you convict me of? There's no corpse! No corpse!" And he threw his head back and roared with laughter. The sound of it echoed across the dark water and was swallowed in the mist. "You'll never find a corpse—you fools!"

# CHAPTER
# EIGHT

———

The sergeant never for a moment hesitated about charging Caleb with the murder of Angus Stonefield. However, when the Crown Prosecutor came to consider the case, it was a different matter. He debated the evidence before him, and in the middle of the day sent for Oliver Rathbone.

"Well?" he demanded, when Rathbone had reviewed what they knew and heard the tale of Caleb's arrest. "Is there any point in bringing him to trial? In fact have we sufficient even to proceed with a charge?"

Rathbone thought about it for some time before replying. It was a rare bright winter day and the sun shone in through the long windows.

"I have some knowledge of the case," he said thoughtfully, sitting with his elegant legs crossed, his fingertips placed together. "Monk consulted me some time ago about the evidence necessary to presume death. He was acting for Mrs. Stonefield."

The prosecutor's eyebrows rose. "Interesting," he murmured.

"Not really," Rathbone answered. "Poor woman was convinced in her own mind of what had happened, and understandably wished to be in a position to appoint someone to continue the business, before it was too severely damaged by Stonefield's absence."

"So what do you know that might assist this case?" The prosecutor leaned back in his chair and regarded Rathbone steadily. "I'm inclined to believe Stone did kill his brother. I should very much like to see him answer for it, but I'm damned if I'll send to trial a case we cannot win, and which will leave the wretched man vindicated, as well as making us a laughingstock."

"Oh, indeed," Rathbone agreed heartily. "It would be sickening to have him acquitted for lack of evidence, and the moment after have the corpse turn up, with proof of his guilt, and not be able to do a damned thing about it. That's the trouble, we have only the one shot. It must hit the mark, there is no second chance."

"Considering that as children both men were wards of Lord Ravensbrook, it may well be a case which attracts some attention," the prosecutor went on, "in spite of Stone's present highly disreputable way of life. It will be interesting to see who defends him." He sighed. "If there is a need for defense."

"The wretched man has admitted killing his brother," Rathbone said grimly. "Boasted of it, in fact."

"It will still be very tight. We have no corpse, no absolute evidence of death . . ."

"But a great deal of circumstantial evidence," Rathbone argued, leaning forward. "They were seen together the day Stonefield disappeared, even seen quarreling. Stonefield's torn and bloodstained clothing has been found, and no one has seen him since."

The prosecutor shook his head. "Still possible he's alive somewhere."

"Where?" Rathbone demanded. "Jumped a ship and sailed to China or the Indies?"

"Or America?"

"But from a Pool of London quay, downriver, at what time?" Rathbone argued. "For America it would more likely be Liverpool or Southampton. Come to that, what time was it he was last seen? Was the tide going out or coming in? Couldn't jump a ship on the incoming tide, unless he ended up in London again. And why would he do that? He had nothing to gain and everything to lose." He sat back in his chair again. "No. You'd never persuade a jury he simply took flight. From what? He had no debts, no enemies, no incipient scandal. No, he's dead, poor devil. Probably buried in one of the common graves of the Limehouse typhoid victims."

"Then prove it," the prosecutor said grimly. "If his lawyer is worth his pay, you'll have a very hard job, Rathbone, a very hard job indeed. But I wish you luck."

When Rathbone returned to Vere Street he found Monk waiting for him. Monk looked appalling. His clothes were as immaculate as always and he was freshly shaved, but his face was haggard, as if he were ill and had not slept. When he stood up to follow Rathbone into his office, without permission, he moved as though his entire body ached. From his appearance he might have been in the later stages of rheumatism. Rathbone had very ambivalent feelings about him, but he would never have wished him ill . . . a slight reduction in arrogance and self-confidence, perhaps, but not this. It disturbed him more than he was prepared for.

"Close the door," he ordered unnecessarily. Monk was in the act of doing so, and stood against it for a moment, staring at Rathbone as he went around the desk and sat behind it. "You got Caleb Stone, I know. I've just come from the Crown Prosecutor's office. It would help a great deal to have more evidence."

"I know that!" Monk said savagely, moving away from the door and sitting painfully in the chair opposite the desk. "Maybe the police will set up a proper search and find the body. I imagine they'll go on dragging the river. Something I was hardly equipped to do. Although this much later, they'd have to be lucky to find it. They could always search the Greenwich and Bugsby marshes. For someone of Angus Stonefield's standing they'd think it worth it."

"They might also think it worth it to get a conviction, now that they have made an arrest," Rathbone said with a slight smile. "They have rather committed themselves. They won't want to be obliged to let Caleb Stone free. He'd be insufferable. He'd be a hero to every villain from Wapping to Woolwich. But you know that better than I."

"What does he think?"

"The prosecutor?" Rathbone raised his eyebrows. "A chance, but he's not optimistic. Would you like a cup of tea? You . . . look . . ." He hesitated, not sure how literal to be.

"No—yes." Monk shrugged. "Tea won't help." He made as if to stand up, too restless to wait, but then apparently found it painful, and reclined back into his chair.

"It was a rough chase?" Rathbone said with a dry smile.

Monk winced. "Very."

Rathbone rang his bell and when the clerk appeared he ordered tea.

"I want it, even if you don't. Now, tell me why you've come. It wasn't to know the Crown Prosecutor's opinion of the case."

"No," Monk agreed, then remained silent for several seconds.

Rathbone felt a chill inside. For something to have affected Monk this deeply it must be very ugly indeed. He had another appointment in twenty minutes. He could not afford delay, and yet he knew impatience would be clumsy, and he had no desire to add to the burden, whatever it was.

Perhaps Monk sensed his urgency. He looked up suddenly, as if having reached a resolve. His jaw was clenched and there was a muscle flicking in his temple. His words came out in a tight, level, carefully controlled monotone, as though he dared not allow any emotions through or it would all explode beyond his mastery.

"I met a woman some time ago, by chance, on the steps of the Geographical Society in Sackville Street. We became acquainted and I saw her several times after that. She was charming, intelligent, full of wit and enthusiasm." His voice was a flat concentrated monotone. "She expressed interest in the Stonefield case, because I was looking to find trace of Angus Stonefield. The long and short of it is we spent an evening together walking around Soho area looking for places where either Angus or Genevieve Stonefield might have met a lover. Of course we didn't find anything. I don't know if either of us expected to. It was an evening of enjoyment, away from the restrictions of society for her, and from the misery of poverty and crime for me."

Rathbone nodded but did not interrupt. It sounded very natural. He had no idea what was coming.

"I took her home in a hansom—" Monk stopped, his face white.

Rathbone said nothing to fill the silence.

Monk took a deep breath and gritted his teeth.

"We were passing along North Audley Street and were forced to slow because one of the large houses had been holding some social event and the guests were leaving. Suddenly she tore open the bodice of her gown, stared at me with passionate hatred, then shrieked and threw herself out of the moving hansom. She landed sprawled in the street, picked herself up and ran, screaming that I had assaulted her."

It was preposterous, but it was not a story utterly new to Rathbone. He had heard of hysterical women inviting advances and then suddenly and without the slightest warning that a man could see, losing their heads and accusing assault. Usually the matter could be kept private with a little sensible discussion and the exchange of money—or a promise of marriage. Money was preferable—it was a far cheaper price in the long run. But why would anyone do such a thing to Monk? She could hardly wish to marry him. No society woman could marry a private agent of inquiry. And he had no money. Although possibly she did not know that. He dressed like a wealthy man.

Monk had a letter in his hand. He held it out.

Rathbone took it and read it, then folded it up and laid it on his desk.

"That puts rather a different complexion on the subject," he said slowly. "It would appear from this that it is revenge she wishes. I assume you have no idea why, or you would have mentioned it."

"No. I've racked my memory, what there is of it." A bitter mockery passed over his face. "There's nothing at all. Not a shred. She's beautiful, amusing, a delight to be with, and there's not even a ghost, not a tiny thread, of familiarity." His voice rose, sharp in desperation. "Nothing!"

Rathbone caught a moment of the nightmare, the bitter horror of living inside a man you did not know. The one thing which in all eternity you could never escape was yourself. Quite suddenly and devastatingly he understood Monk as he never had before.

But if he were to be of use, he must quash emotion. A man clouded by feelings was less able to think rationally or to perceive the truth.

"Then perhaps it was not she you wronged," he said thoughtfully, "but someone she loved. A woman will often feel more passionately and take far greater risks to protect a loved one than she will to save herself."

He saw the sudden light of hope in Monk's eyes.

"But for God's sake, who?" he demanded. "It could be anyone!"

There was a light rap on the door, and they both ignored it.

"Well I know of no one better able to investigate it than you," Rathbone pointed out. "And it matters, Monk." He leaned forward, his elbows on the desk between them. "Don't delude yourself you can remain unharmed if she chooses to pursue this. Even if she proves nothing at all, such a charge, quite unsubstantiated, would still be enough to ruin you. If you were a gentleman in society, with means and family reputation, and she were a young woman seeking a husband, then you might ride it out. You could say she was hysterical, a lightly balanced woman, given to vapors or imaginings . . . even that she had imagined your favor and taken your rejection hard. But no one is going to believe that of a man in your position."

"Good God, don't you think I know that!" Monk said furiously. "If she were a young woman seeking a husband, and I were likely material, she wouldn't do it anyway. Think what it would do to her own reputation. What gentleman will look at her now? I'm not so damned ignorant I don't know what it will cost her. Nor is she. That's what makes it so terrifying. She hates me enough to destroy herself in order to destroy me."

"Then whatever you did to cause it is profound," Rathbone said. It was not meant in cruelty, but there was no time or space to deal in less than the truth, and he was aware of his desk just beyond the door, and his next appointment. "I'm not sure how much it may protect you to know," he went on, "but if you do search, I would begin by looking for someone who may have been unjustly convicted, or a person hanged, or jailed and perhaps died there. Don't begin with thefts or embezzlements, or the victims of petty crime. In other words, start with the result of the investigation, not the weight of the evidence or your own certainty that the prosecution was just."

"Will it help if I find it?" Monk asked, pinned between hope and bitterness.

Rathbone toyed with a lie, but only for an instant. Monk was not a man to give another an easy sop. He did not deserve it himself.

"Possibly not," he answered. "Only if it comes to trial, and you could prove she has a motive of revenge. But if she has as much intelligence as you suggest, I doubt she'll seek a prosecution. She'd be unlikely in that event to get one, certainly not a conviction, unless she had an extraordinary biased jury." His face tightened and his eyes were steady. "She will do far more damage to you, and leave you less chance of escape, vindication, or counterattack, if she simply passes the word around. She will not land you in prison that way, but she will ruin your career. You will be reduced to—"

"I know!" Monk snapped, rising to his feet abruptly, and with a sharp intake of breath as his aching muscles and bruised body hurt him. "I shall have to scrape a living working for people in the fringes of trade or the underworld, looking for errant husbands, collecting bad debts and chasing petty thieves." He turned his back on Rathbone and stared out of the window. "And I shall be lucky if they can afford to pay me enough for me to eat daily. There will be no more cases of any interest to Callandra Daviot, and she can't keep supporting me for nothing. I don't need you to tell me that. I shall have to move lodgings, and when my clothes wear out I shall be reduced to secondhand. I know all that."

Rathbone longed to be able to say something, anything, of comfort, but there was nothing, and he was increasingly aware of the faint noises from the office, and his next client waiting.

"Then for your own peace of mind at least, you had better do all you can to discover who she is," he said grimly. "And more importantly, who she was, and why she hates you so much she is prepared to do this."

"Thank you," Monk murmured as he went out, closing the door behind him and all but bumping into the clerk hovering until he should leave, and he might show in the gentleman waiting impatiently at his elbow.

Of course Rathbone was right. He had not really needed anyone to tell him, it was simply a release of the loneliness of it to hear the words from someone else, and someone who, for all their past differences, at least believed his account. And his advice regarding where to search was sound.

He walked along Vere Street deep in thought, oblivious of other pedestrians or carriages passing him by.

There was only one course open to him, and deeply as he loathed the prospect, he dared not delay. He must search his past records of cases and try to find the one in which Drusilla had been involved, albeit indirectly. At least Rathbone's suggestions gave him somewhere to start. It would be impossible to approach Runcorn. He would be only too delighted to add to Monk's predicament by denying him access. He had no rights to police information anymore, and Runcorn would be legally justified in refusing him. The irony of it would be the sweetest taste of victory for him at last, after all the years that Monk had trodden on his heels, mocked him and bettered him in case after case. And he would have to admit his amnesia. He had never known for certain how much Runcorn guessed, but no acknowledgment had ever passed between them. Runcorn had never had the satisfaction of being certain, and of knowing that Monk knew he knew.

Monk turned from Great Wild Street into Drury Lane.

John Evan was a different matter, as different as could be. He had not known Monk before the accident, and he had guessed the truth, working with him so closely in that first dreadful case. He had proved a good friend, loyal, despite all the odds, in the hardest of circumstances. He was young, full of charm and enthusiasm, a country parson's son with no money at all, but the casual ease of one born to what in better times had been minor gentry. Evan had admired him. He had chosen to see the best in him. That was why it was peculiarly painful now to have to tell him of this problem and seek his help in uncovering its cause.

In fact, he almost changed his mind about going to him at all. Perhaps it would do no good, and all he would do would be to lose Evan's regard before he had to.

That was not only the coward's way out, it was the fool's. Evan would learn sooner or later. Better now, and from Monk. Better at least to see him fight than allow defeat by surrender. He hailed a hansom and took it as far as the corner nearest his old station.

It was a bright morning. He had barely noticed. The sun had already melted the rime of ice on the footpath, and the harness of passing carriages winked and glistened. An errand boy was whistling as he walked with a swing in his stride.

Monk reached the police station and went straight up the steps and inside. To hesitate might lose him his courage.

"Mornin', Mr. Monk," the desk sergeant said with surprise. "What can we be doin' for you?"

"I'd like to see Mr. Evan, if you please?"

"About a crime, is it, sir?"

The man's face was unreadable, and Monk could not remember their relationship. It was probably not cordial. Monk was his senior, and the man was middle-aged. Monk had probably treated him with impatience, considering him second-rate. He winced now at what he imagined.

"I'm not sure whether it is or not," he said as smoothly as he could. "I need rather more information, and perhaps advice. Is Mr. Evan in the station?"

241

"You won't be needin' ter see Mr. Runcorn, then?" the sergeant said sententiously, a very slight smile touching his lips.

"No, I won't, thank you." Monk met his eyes without a flicker.

"Thought not." The sergeant's smile widened a fraction. " 'Aven't forgot the Moidore case, sir, I 'aven't."

Monk forced himself to smile back. "Thank you, Sergeant. A very nice memory you have, tastefully selective."

"Yer welcome, sir. I'll fetch Mr. Evan for yer." And he turned and disappeared behind the door, to reappear less than a minute later. " 'E'll meet you in the coffee shop 'round the corner, sir, in five minutes. Wiser that way, sir."

"I admire a man of wisdom," Monk agreed. "Thank you, Sergeant."

When Evan came into the coffee shop his long, humorous face with its aristocratic nose and rueful mouth looked full of anxiety. He sat down opposite Monk, ignoring the coffee placed there for him.

"What is it?" he asked. "It must be important to bring you to the station." He searched Monk's face. "You look awful. Are you ill?"

Monk drew a deep breath, and as briefly as possible without omitting anything essential, he told him the story.

Evan did not interrupt, but his expression grew more and more distressed as the account neared its climax.

"What can I do?" he said finally when Monk finished. "Surely she won't try to prosecute? She'd be ruined as well . . . and she'd never prove anything! The worst—" He stopped.

"Yes?" Monk said, biting his lip. "You were going to say the worst that could happen is that her own circle would believe her? It isn't. Even those who don't believe her will deny me the benefit of the doubt."

Evan had barely touched his coffee, and they were both unaware of the bustle and noise around them, the hum of chatter and aroma of food.

"No, actually I was going to say the worst that happened to her was that her gown was torn. She was in no way harmed in her person. But I suppose a torn gown is enough. It indicates an intention to do a great deal more." Evan regarded his cold coffee with distaste. He had not touched it. "We must find out who she is, and why she is prepared to take such a violent and costly revenge. Tell me all you know about her, and I'll search all your past case files. Her name is Drusilla Wyndham? How old is she? What is her appearance? Where does she live? Whom does she associate with?"

Monk realized how idiotically little he did know. He felt foolish and the embarrassment of it burned up his cheeks.

"I don't even know if her name is correct," he said grimly. "I never saw her in company of anyone else. I would hazard she is in her early thirties. She is very small, slender, dainty but with a fine figure. She has a beautiful face. . . ." He winced as he said it. "Fair brown hair, hazel eyes, and a charming voice with a little catch in it when she laughs. I have no idea where she lives, or with whom she associates, except that the Geographical Society would appear to be one place she frequents. She dresses very well, but not extravagantly. The chief charm of her appearance is her grace and her poise."

"Not a lot," Evan said with a look of concern. "You said she was in her early thirties, and yet presumably unmarried? Is that not odd for such a charming young woman? Could she be widowed?"

"I don't know." Monk had been too delighted in her company to tax himself with such questions. He realized now what a self-indulgent oversight it was.

"I presume she was well-spoken?" Evan continued. "That would narrow it at least to one class of person."

A couple sat down at the table next to them, still side by side, and laughing.

"Yes . . . she is well-bred," Monk agreed.

"But hardly a lady," Evan added with a sudden twist of dry humor. "Doesn't give us a great deal to help. I'll start with the cases where someone was hanged, or died in prison, and where there was a woman of that general description involved somewhere, a relative or close friend, some other victim of the tragedy."

"Of course, it could be someone I didn't catch," Monk said with sudden thought. "Perhaps a case I didn't solve, and the crime went unpunished. Perhaps she thinks I failed justice."

Evan rose to his feet, leaning a little on the table.

"Don't make it harder than it has to be," he said quietly. "Let's begin with the more obvious. Anyway"—he smiled—"I don't think you had many unsolved cases, from what I hear of you."

Monk said nothing, and watched Evan as he made his way out, turning once at the door to give a tiny salute of courage.

Monk spent the afternoon with the police as they continued dragging the river around the Isle of Dogs and across Bugsby's Reach, and searched the docks and inlets and the slums and alleys along the water's edge. They even searched some of the pigsties and middens or cesspits. They found much that was filthy, violent and tragic, including two dead bodies, but neither of them could have been Angus Stonefield. One was a child, the other a woman.

Monk went home in the dark close to despair. He had never seen such an accumulation of human misery, and he was weary, his body ached and he was cold to the bone. His feet were soaked and he no longer had any sensation left in his toes. He would not go with them again. Reluctantly he felt a new respect, deep and painful, gouging out undiscovered parts of himself, for men who could see such things day after day and still keep their courage and their innate kindness and sense of hope. All he felt was anger, and since he could change nothing, his brain told him that was useless, but his stomach still knotted inside.

The following morning he woke early, long before the light, and lay in bed planning what he would do to find Drusilla Wyndham. It might not save his reputation or his livelihood, but he had to know to answer the fears and the darkness within himself. What manner of man was he? That was the one truth which was inescapable. And there were increasing times when the dread of that answer was worse than the answer itself, because his imagination covered them all.

He rose at seven and ate a solitary breakfast, then before eight, left and walked for almost an hour, his head bent in thought, heedless of passersby, of carriages clattering within feet of him, idlers, street sellers, crossing sweepers, neatly suited office clerks hurrying to business, fashionable rakes and gamblers returning from a night's pleasure.

Finally just before nine he took a hansom to the Geographical Society, and went in at the entrance to seek some official of whom he could inquire.

He was uncharacteristically nervous. Usually his confidence intimidated people. He had only to meet their eyes and ask curtly in his precise diction, and he was answered. Today he felt at a disadvantage even before he spoke.

How far had she spread the accusation? Had these people already heard? He did not feel like a villain, only a fool!

"Good morning, sir?" the porter said inquiringly. "May I be of service? Were you seeking information regarding any particular meeting, or speaker?"

Monk had already composed his lie. It was the sort of thing he had done often enough before, when it mattered infinitely less personally. It had been so much easier then.

"Actually I met a lady on the steps as she was leaving here nearly two weeks ago," he began with acute self-consciousness. "She was kind enough to recommend several other societies and groups to me, but unfortunately I have mislaid the piece of paper on which I wrote them, and I do not know her well enough to call upon her. Indeed, I do not know her address." Was he talking too much—answering what had not been asked? "It was a chance meeting because she bumped into me, quite literally, and so we fell into conversation." He searched the man's face, but it was perfectly bland. There was not a shred of suspicion or disbelief in it.

"Indeed, sir. Perhaps I can be of assistance. I do know of several other societies which have similar areas of interest, although I must say, none of them, to my knowledge, deal in such an erudite manner, or have so fine a group of speakers."

"That is what the lady said. She was very dainty, almost . . . so tall." Monk drew a level at Drusilla's height. "She had very hand-some fair-brown hair and the most remarkable hazel eyes, very wide and candid, a most direct glance." He hated the description, but it was as she had seemed to him then. "She seemed to me to be of con-siderable intelligence and ease of manner. An unusual person, and most admirable. I would have judged her to be just above thirty."

"Sounds like Miss Wyndham," the porter said, nodding his head. "Very well-spoken young lady."

"Wyndham?" Monk raised his eyebrows as if he had not heard her name before. "I wonder, would that be Major Wyndham's daugh-ter, from the Hussars?" As far as he knew, there was no such person.

The porter pursed his lips doubtfully.

"Er, no, sir, I don't think so. I rather recall overhearing some snatch of conversation suggesting Miss Wyndham came from Buck-inghamshire, and her father was in the clergy, before an early demise, poor man. Very sad. He cannot have been an elderly gentleman."

"Sad indeed," Monk agreed, his mind racing. Buckinghamshire. It should not be so difficult to trace a well-to-do clergyman who had died recently. He must have been more than a mere parson, and pre-sumably his name was also Wyndham.

"I suppose it happened a few years ago now?" he said, trying to make his voice conversational.

"I really don't know, sir. It was spoken of with some sadness, but then it would be. And she was not in mourning."

"I only wish to know so that I did not intrude, and if I should mention it if I have to write," Monk explained. "Would it be possible for you to give me the lady's address, then I could request a new list of the places she recommended?"

"Well, sir, I hardly think that would be proper," the porter said regretfully, nodding to two gentlemen who passed and touching his hat in a gesture of respect. He turned back to Monk. "You see, sir, I'm afraid the society would not sanction such a practice. I'm sure

246

you understand. But if you care to write a letter and leave it with us, there would be no bar to me forwarding it to her."

"Of course. I understand. Perhaps I shall do that," Monk accepted because he really had no alternative. A trip to Buckinghamshire seemed indicated, unless he could find some record of the late Reverend Wyndham without recourse to travel. He left the Geographical Society, if not with hope, then at least with a sense of purpose.

But even the most diligent search of the appropriate register of the clergy yielded no Reverend Wyndham in Buckinghamshire, or in any other part of the country. He began to walk very slowly along the footpath away from the library, disappointment deep inside him like the cold and the damp of the afternoon.

Perhaps he had been naive to have thought it might be so easy. Either the information was incorrect, an invention for the benefit of whoever she was telling, or else it was basically true, but she had changed her name, presumably to avoid the disgrace of whatever crime had brought her across Monk's path.

He ignored a flower seller and a boy with the latest edition of the newspapers.

Perhaps the whole thing was nothing to do with his profession. Maybe he had met her purely personally. Her sense of injury might spring from some sexual betrayal he had committed.

His heart went cold at the thought. Had they been lovers and he had deserted her? Had there perhaps been a child, and he had left her, rather than take responsibility? It was not impossible. Men had done that from time immemorial. God knew, there were illegitimate children all over the country, and bungled abortions as well. He had seen them himself, even since the accident, let alone before. If that were true, she could not hate him any more profoundly than he would hate himself. He deserved the ruin she wished him.

He passed a seller of hot pies, and for a moment the savory aroma tempted him, then his stomach revolted at the thought of eating.

He had to know the truth. At any cost, whatever labor or pain, he must know.

And if he was guilty of such a thing, how could he tell Hester? She would not forgive him for that. She would not stand by with her courage and spirit, and help him fight his way back.

Neither would Callandra. Nor John Evan, for that matter.

He had to be the first to know.

But where to turn next? If Drusilla had changed her name, it could have been anything before, any of a million names.

He stepped off the curb and avoided the traffic and the horse dung.

Except almost all people wanted to keep some sense of identity, some link with the past. There was often a connection, a link of sound, of initial letter, or some other association in the mind. At times it was a family name, a mother or grandmother's maiden name, for example.

He reached the far pavement just as a landau missed him by no more than a yard.

Perhaps the part about Buckinghamshire was true? Or about the church?

He turned on his heel, back across the road again, and strode back to the library where the directory of all clergy was lodged, and asked to see it again. This time he searched the incumbents of Buck-inghamshire for any senior clergyman who had died within the last ten years.

But there were none whose names suggested any connection, however tenuous, with Drusilla Wyndham.

"Is this all?" he asked the clerk who was hovering anxiously. "Is there any way one might have been missed? Perhaps I had better look further back than ten years."

"Of course, sir, if you think it will help," the clerk agreed. "If you could be a little more precise as to what it is you are searching for, perhaps I could be of some assistance." He adjusted his spectacles and sneezed. "I do beg your pardon."

"I'm looking for a clergyman who died in Buckinghamshire, probably within the last ten years," Monk replied, feeling foolish and desperate. "But I have been given the wrong name."

"Then I don't know how you can find it, sir," the clerk said, shaking his head unhappily. "Do you know anything else about him?"

"No . . ."

"Do you not have even the least idea what his name is? Not even what it may have sounded like?" The man appeared to be pressing the issue simply for something to say. He looked most uncomfortable.

"It may have sounded like Wyndham," Monk replied, also only for civility's sake.

"Oh, dear. I am afraid I can think of nothing. Of course, there was the Reverend Buckingham, who died in Norfolk." The clerk gave a jerky, bitter laugh, and sneezed again. "In a place called Wymondham, which of course is pronounced 'Wyndham,' at least locally. But that is hardly of use to you—"

He stopped, startled because Monk had risen to his feet and clapped him on the back so sharply his spectacles flew off his nose and landed on the floor.

"You are brilliant, sir!" Monk said enthusiastically. "Quite brilliant! Why did I not think of that myself? Once you see it, it is as obvious as daylight. Thank God for one man with brains."

The clerk blushed furiously and was quite unable to frame any reply.

"What can you tell me about him?" Monk demanded, picking up the spectacles, polishing them and handing them back. "Where was he living? What was the cause of his death? How old a man was he? What family had he? What, precisely, was his position?"

"Good gracious!" The clerk blinked at him like an owl, his spectacles in his hand. "Well . . . well, I can certainly find out for you, sir. Yes, yes indeed. May I inquire why it is you must know? Is he perhaps a relative?"

"I believe he may be a relative of someone of the utmost importance to me," Monk replied truthfully, if deviously. "Someone who holds my very life in their hands. Yes, please tell me everything you can about the late Reverend Buckingham, and his family. I shall wait here."

"Ah—well—I may be . . . yes, of course." He sneezed again and apologized. "To be sure." And he scurried off about his task.

Monk paced the floor until the clerk returned some twenty-five minutes later, pink-faced and brimming with triumph.

"He died some eight years ago, sir, on the twenty-eighth of March, 1851." He frowned. "The cause of death was listed as chill, rather unspecific. He was not an elderly man, indeed only in his fifty-sixth year, and apparently had been in good health until that time."

"His family!" Monk said urgently. "Did he have children?"

"Why yes, yes he did. And he left a widow, a Mary Ann."

"Names of the children!" Monk demanded. "What were their names? What were their ages?"

"My goodness, sir, don't distress yourself so! Yes, there were children, indeed there were. One son named Octavian, which is curious, since apparently he was the eldest—"

"Curious?"

"Yes sir. Clergymen often have large families, and Octavian means eighth, you know. . . ."

"Daughters! Did he have daughters?"

"Yes, yes he did. Eldest named Julia, second named Septima. Poor man really cannot count! Quite amusing . . . yes! Yes! I am coming to the rest. Another son named Marcus . . . all very Roman. Perhaps it was an interest of his, a hobby. Yes! And a last daughter named Drusilla—ah!" This last gasp was because Monk had again clapped him on the back and driven the air out of his lungs. "I take it that is the lady whom you are seeking?"

"Yes, yes. I think it is. Now—the living. What was his position, and where?"

"Wymondham, sir. It is only a small village."

"Was he simply the parson?" It did not seem to fit what he had seen of Drusilla. Could it be no more than an extraordinary coincidence, and after all, have no meaning?

"No sir," the clerk replied with growing enthusiasm himself. "I believe he had an attachment to the Norwich Cathedral, or he had had in the recent past. A distinguished scholar, so my informant tells me."

"Ah—thank you." Hope surged back up again. "Is there anything else you know? About the family, for example? The widow? The daughters? In what circumstances do they find themselves now?"

The clerk's face fell.

"I'm sorry, sir, I have no idea. I daresay you would have to travel to Norfolk for that."

"Yes, of course. Thank you. I am enormously obliged to you." And indeed he was. He raced out of the building and flung himself into the first vacant hansom that passed, shouting to the driver to take him to the police station, where he could find John Evan and tell him what he now knew.

But he was obliged to wait nearly three hours before Evan returned from the case he was on, by which time it was long after dark and had begun to rain. They sat together in the coffee shop, warming themselves with hands around hot mugs, sipping slowly at the steaming liquid, a babble of noise around them and constant movement as people came and went.

"Buckingham!" Evan said with surprise. "I don't recall the name."

"But there must be a case concerning a Buckingham!" Monk insisted. "Try eight years ago specifically." It was a cry of desperation. Terror gripped inside him that his wrong against Drusilla had been personal . . . and unforgivable not only to her but to himself as well.

"I went back over all your cases," Evan said with pain in his eyes. "There was no Buckingham that I can remember, either charged or accused. But of course I'll try again. I'll look specifically for the name."

"Perhaps I'd better go to Norfolk." Monk stared beyond Evan without seeing the thronged room or hearing the laughter. "That's where they lived."

"Why would you have gone to Norfolk?" Evan was puzzled. "You only dealt with London cases. If it happened there, the local police would have handled it, not you." He shrugged very slightly, and shivered as if someone had opened an outside door, although the coffee shop was almost too hot, with its crowded atmosphere and steaming drinks, and the fire leaping in the hearth. "I suppose it could have started in London, and there have been witnesses—and suspects, for that matter—in Norfolk. I'll try." He frowned, knowing he was speaking only for comfort. "Don't worry, if it's there, I'll find it."

And if it is not, Monk thought, then any injury to her was personal, and how in God's name do I learn that? How will I ever know my own view of it, why I did whatever it was, what I thought or felt, what there is in mitigation for me?

He finished his coffee and stood up. He had not the heart even to meet Evan's eyes. What would he think or feel when he knew the truth, what bitter disillusion and sense of betrayal? He was so afraid of it, it was as if it had already happened.

"Thank you," he said with his voice choking in his throat. He wanted to add more, but could think of nothing. "Thank you."


Hester was also deeply afraid for Monk, not for what he might have done—she had not concerned herself with that—but for the ruin it would bring him when Drusilla made her charges public. The fact that she could not prove them was immaterial. She had chosen her time and place to be melodramatic with great skill. Not a man or woman emerging from the party in North Audley Street would forget the sight of her pitching headlong out of the moving cab, her clothes torn, screaming that she had been assaulted. Whatever reason told them, they would relive the emotions, the horror and the sense of outrage. And they would be totally unprepared to accept that they had been duped. It would make them foolish, and that would be intolerable.

Something must be done to help him, something practical and immediate. There was little use trying to limit the damage after it was done.

She and Callandra had talked about it sitting late at night in the small room in the Limehouse hospital, in the few moments when they were not either working or asleep. Callandra was deeply distressed, even in the face of the disease and death around her, and Hester realized with a quick uprush of pleasure how fond she must be of Monk. Callandra's regard for him was far more than mere interest, and the adding of a new dimension to her life.

But she had been able to offer no practical counsel.

Now Hester sat in the warmth and clean, sweet-smelling comfort of Enid's bedroom in Ravensbrook House and watched Enid's frail form, at last peacefully asleep. Genevieve had gone home, weary with grief and the mounting anxiety and loneliness of her loss, dreading the trial of Caleb which must shortly begin.

Hester tidied a few things which were hardly out of place, then returned to her seat. It was so different from just a few days ago. Then Monk faced no greater danger than failing on a case which had seemed hopeless from the beginning. Two weeks ago Enid had been delirious and fighting for her life. She had tossed from side to side, moaning in pain as her body ached and her mind wandered in nightmare and delusion, mixing past and present and distorting everything.

Hester smiled in spite of herself. One heard some very strange things in a sickroom. Perhaps that was one of the reasons certain people were wary of taking nurses rather than a lady's maid, who presumably already knew a great many of her mistress's secrets.

Enid had rambled about many things, snatches of thoughts, old griefs and loneliness, longings she had never realized and perhaps

253

would never have given words in her conscious mind. There had been fear in her, and half-guessed-at disillusion. She had also referred more than once to letters which were quite openly declarations of love. Hester hoped Enid had not kept them. She doubted very much they were from Lord Ravensbrook. Nothing in what she had seen of him suggested such fluency or ease of expression. He seemed a very formal man, even stilted when it came to speaking of feelings— which did not, of course, mean that his emotions were less, or that his physical expression of them was not as profound as any other man's.

She had debated whether to mention it to Enid, and warn her that she was capable of indiscretion in her illness, and therefore perhaps in her sleep, if she should ever become feverish again. Then she had decided it might be seen as an impertinence and place a barrier of embarrassment between them. If Enid had managed so far to conduct her marriage without such a disaster, then it might very well continue so, without Hester's advice.

She looked across at Enid's sleeping form now. She seemed utterly at peace; in fact, there was a very slight smile on her face, as if she dreamed of something pleasant.

Perhaps she was thinking of some of those past letters. They might still give her happy memories, days when she knew she was admired, found beautiful. Love letters were strange; they could do so much good, if kept discreetly . . . and in the wrong hands so much damage.

Hester had received very few herself, and most of them had been formal, more a statement of ardent hope than any real understanding or knowledge of her nature. Only those from soldiers had had any meaning, and they were romantic, heartfelt, but in some measure cries of desperation and loneliness from young men far from home in an alien and dreadful circumstance, and who simply found a gentle touch and a listening ear, a single spark of beauty in the midst of pain and loss, and the fear of loss. She had treasured them for what they were, not reading into them more.

She winced with embarrassment as she recalled one she had received long ago, before the Crimean War had even begun, from a young man her father had considered a very acceptable suitor. It had been couched in ardent terms, and far too familiar, in her opinion. It had stated a love which had appalled her, because he did not even see her, only what he could turn her into. She prickled with discomfort even now at the thought of it. She had never wanted to meet the man again.

In fact, she could remember vividly the next time they had met. It had been at the dinner table in her father's home—her mother was quite unaware of her feelings, and had sat smiling at the foot of the table, blandly staring at her across a sea of linen and crystal, making optimistic remarks about domestic happiness, while Hester squirmed, her face scarlet, willing to give anything at all to be elsewhere. She could still feel that wretched young man's eyes on her, and the thoughts she imagined must be in his mind as he sat there. In some ways it had been one of the worst evenings of her life.

If only he had not written, she would never have suffered so much. She might even have found him quite tolerable. He was not personally displeasing, quite intelligent, not too opinionated—in fact, altogether an agreeable person.

What ridiculous harm a letter could do if it overstated the intimate, or pressed a case too far, too soon.

It was as if the room had suddenly blazed with light. Of course! That was the answer! Not perhaps in the highest moral standard . . . in fact, definitely quite questionable. But Monk was in a desperate situation.

The problem was to whom she should send them. It must be the people of Drusilla's own social circle, or it would hardly accomplish the purpose. And Hester had no idea who composed the current fashionable society, because it had not interested her much for some years.

Now it was of the utmost urgency.

However, she thought on reflection that Callandra would probably not be much more knowledgeable than she. If she knew, it would be by chance, not design. If ever there was a woman who did not give a whit about fashionable company, or who dined or danced with whom, it was Callandra Daviot.

Genevieve was not of that social standing. Her husband was in business, albeit a very respectable one. But gentlemen only dabbled, they did not actually work.

She looked across at Enid. There was the answer.

Of course she could not possibly tell her why she wished to know, not because she needed to protect Monk—Enid would not have believed it of him without better proof than there was so far. Anyway, Hester could always moderate the story somewhat at this point. But Enid would certainly have the gravest doubts about what Hester intended to do about it. In fact, it might very well be suffi-cient to keep her from providing the information altogether.

It must be obtained without the reason for it given. And perhaps that might not be so very difficult? Hester could ask her about the last party she attended, who was there, what they wore, who danced, who flirted, what was served to eat. In fact, she could ask her to de-scribe several parties. Enid did not know her well enough to be aware that normally she had no interest whatever in such things.

She could do it. She could begin as soon as Enid awoke. Monk himself could find the necessary addresses, if there were no better way of obtaining them. She could begin with ten or a dozen. There was no time to be lost.

"You must have been to some wonderful parties," she began with enthusiasm when Enid awoke and she puffed up her pillows and brought her a little light food. "Please tell me about them. I should love to hear."

"Would you?" Enid said doubtfully. "I would not have thought such things would interest you in the slightest." She looked at Hester narrowly, amusement in her eyes.

"People are always interesting," Hester said truthfully. "Even peo-ple with whom one would not necessarily wish to spend great periods of time. Please tell me about the last big society party you went to. Who was there? What did they say? What did they do?"

"Who was there?" Enid repeated thoughtfully, staring past Hester at the curtains. "Well ... I remember John Pickering, because he told that awful story about the bishop, and ..." She reminisced with a short smile and a dry, not unkind observation, and gradually Hester knew from her what she needed, committing every relevant fact to memory.

The next day she found Monk at home, looking weary, irritable and frightened. She might have tried to comfort him, had she had time and not been so afraid he would somehow realize what she meant to do, and stop her.

"Do you still have the wretched letter that woman wrote to you?" she asked hastily.

He was standing by the fire, effectively shielding her from the warmth, although that had probably not occurred to him.

"Why?" he asked. "I've read it several times. It doesn't give any clues at all as to why it is she hates me, or who she really is, beyond the obvious."

"Do you have it or not?" Hester said sharply. "Please don't argue with everything I say. There really isn't time."

"You haven't said anything else," he pointed out.

"And I won't have time to, if you keep on being so persnickety. Do you have the letter?"

"Yes!"

"Then may I see it please?"

"What for?" He did not move.

"Get it!" she ordered.

He hesitated, as if to argue further, then decided it was not worth the emotional effort. He went to the bureau drawer and took out the letter, passing it to her with a look of distaste.

"Thank you." She put it into her pocket, then unfolded the piece of paper on which she had written the addresses of eighteen gentle-men who would serve her purpose. "I need the London addresses of as many of these as you can find, unless they are in the country at present," she instructed, holding it out to him. "Then it will be no use. I want at least twelve, and by tomorrow midday, if you please. It is of the utmost importance. You may leave them at my lodgings, in a sealed envelope. Don't fail." She turned to leave. "I am sorry I cannot remain, but I have a great deal to do. Good night."

"Hester!" he shouted. "What for? What on earth do you want them for? What are you doing?" He strode to the door after her, but she had her hand on the knob already.

"I have told you, I have no time to discuss it now," she replied briskly. "I shall explain it all later. Please do as I have asked you, and as rapidly as possible. Good night."

She began as soon as she reached her lodgings, where her landlady was quite surprised to see her, as she had been there so little of late. Hester spoke to her graciously, said how pleasant it was to be home again, and announced that she would spend the evening writing let-ters. In the unlikely event anyone should call, she was not available to receive them.

Her landlady looked both alarmed and fascinated, but did not let down her own dignity sufficiently to ask for an explanation. It was beneath a lady, and she wanted to be thought a lady, which pre-vented her exhibiting anything so vulgar as curiosity.

As soon as she had eaten, Hester began her task, doing her best to imitate Drusilla's flowery, erratic hand.

My dearest love,
I am still on fire from the joy of our last meeting. Of course I do understand the necessity for secrecy, at least for the time being, but the tenderness of your eyes was enough to thrill me to my very heart . . .

This was quite fun to write in such an unbridled strain. She would never in the world write like this if she were putting her own name to it, no matter what she felt. She continued.

I long for the time when we may be alone together, so that this pretense may no longer be, when you can take me in your arms and we can give ourselves to each other with the passion which I know you feel, as I do, tearing me apart. I ache for you. My dreams are filled with the sight of you and the sound of your voice, the touch of your skin against mine, the taste of your mouth . . .

Oh, dear! Had she gone too far?

But the aim of this was to be as excruciatingly embarrassing as possible. The man who received this must regard Drusilla Wyndham with an abhorrence verging on terror.

She proceeded.

I know all the things you dare not say. I do not misunderstand your occasional coldness towards me when we chance to meet in public. I burn inside, my heart melts to be able to tell the world that we are lovers, albeit yet to dare the final act, but I shall wait, knowing it will not be forever, and that soon, soon my darling, you will cut the ties that bind you to your wife now, and we shall be free to be together for ever.

Your one true love,
Drusilla

There now! If that did not make the man squirm, then he was a rake and a cad and possessed of no decency at all!

Naturally she had chosen only married men, or those about to be.

She reread what she had written. Perhaps it was a bit extreme?

What Drusilla had done was appalling, but such a letter might damage her irreparably, several almost certainly would, which would make Hester morally no better than Drusilla herself. And she realized with a wave of misery that even Monk was not sure that he had not somehow caused her hatred.

She tore up the letter and put the little pieces into the wastebasket, and began again.

This one was much more moderate, inviting misinterpretation, but phrased in such a manner that it could, at a stretch of the imagination, and with a great deal of charity, be explained reasonably innocently.

That was better. Please heaven she had not softened it too much, and it would still cause the necessary misgivings, and mistrust of anything Drusilla might say, the flickers of personal fear, the fellow feeling with another man who had had his words or his actions misconstrued by a vain and overeager woman.

She wrote several more. By the time she put her pen down at a quarter to ten, her hand ached and her eyes were stinging.

Two days later Lord Fontenoy opened his mail at the breakfast table. It appeared the usual collection of bills, invitations and polite letters of one sort or another. There was none which occasioned any unusual interest, and certainly no alarm . . . until he came to the last one.

Lady Fontenoy, who had been reading a letter from her cousin in Wales, heard him splutter, and looked up, then with some anxiety forgot her own mail entirely.

"My dear, are you all right? You look quite unwell. Is it distressing news?"

"No!" he said overloudly. "No, not at all," he amended. "It is something quite trivial." He strove to invent a plausible lie, something to account for his pale face and shaking hands, and yet not excite her curiosity so that she expected to read the wretched thing . . . which of course he could refuse, but he did not wish her suspicion aroused. He had a really most agreeable domestic life, and desired intensely to keep it so. "No, my dear, it is simply a most foolish letter from someone who desires to make trouble in a quarter I had not foreseen. It's unpleasant, but nothing to cause undue worry. I shall deal with it." Perhaps he was reacting too strongly. He recalled the phrases used. They had initially appalled him, but on second thought, they were ambiguous, capable of less demanding intent.

"Are you sure?" Lady Fontenoy pressed. "You do look very pale, Walter."

"I swallowed my tea a little hastily," he replied. "I fear it did not go quite the right way. Uncomfortable. Please don't distress yourself. How is Dorothea? That is a letter from Dorothea, is it not?"

She realized that was the end of the conversation. She accepted that he would not mention it again, but she knew perfectly well that the letter he had received had shaken his composure very thoroughly, and she was not at ease for the rest of the day.

Sir Peter Welby was also highly upset by his morning mail. Being still a bachelor, now on the brink of a very fortunate marriage, he breakfasted alone, apart from the distant presence of his manservant.

"Good God!" he expostulated, when he had read the alarming missive. If that should fall into the wrong hands, it could be very damagingly misconstrued. It could all become very ugly indeed, if read by someone unkindly disposed.

"Sir?" his manservant said questioningly.

His reaction was to tear it up, into many pieces, and those as small as possible, then put it all on the breakfast room fire. He remembered the woman quite clearly. He had danced with her, several times. She was very comely and had an air about her which was highly attractive. She had wit and, he had thought, intelligence. But she must be out of her senses to have perceived his very slight flirtation as anything more, and supposed that he had even the remotest intent to pursue the relationship, now of all times!

If she really did mean what she seemed to, then he must convince her he had no such thought in mind, nor ever had had.

But then perhaps she had merely expressed herself unfortunately? Better not to mention it at all—to anyone. Let it blow over. He must be a great deal more careful in the future. Handsome women of a certain age were the very devil.

The Honourable John Blenkinsop read his mail with total disbelief. He refolded the letter hastily and was in the act of replacing it in its envelope when his wife, who had no mail this morning, interrupted his train of thought. She had news of her own to discuss, which she had heard the previous evening, only she had retired before he had returned from his club and thus had had no opportunity to pass it on.

"Did you know, John, the most dreadful thing happened in North Audley Street the other day." She leaned forward over the toast and marmalade. "Poor Drusilla Wyndham, such a lovely creature, was assaulted in a hansom. Can you imagine anything so perfectly dreadful? She had asked some man's assistance in a matter, and the man, a very ordinary person, by all accounts, mistook her civility for encouragement and attempted to force his attentions on her! John, are you listening to me?"

"Force his attentions?" he repeated confusedly. "You mean kiss her?"

"Yes, I suppose so," she agreed. "He even went so far as to tear her gown open at the bosom. The whole thing must have been a nightmare for her, poor creature. She only escaped him by hurling herself out of the hansom, as it was moving, mind you, and fell into the road. How she was not injured, I cannot think."

The letter burned in his hand.

"I wouldn't put too much weight to it, my dear . . ." he began.

"What?" She was aghast. "How can you say such a thing? What on earth do you mean? The man behaved unpardonably!"

"Possibly, my dear, but some women do imagine things to be quite—"

"Imagine?" She was nonplussed. "The man put his hands on her, John! He tore her gown! How can she have imagined that?"

"Well . . . perhaps he merely brushed against her, the motions of the cab, and all that . . ." He thought of his own brush with Drusilla, and the absurd interpretation it seemed she had put upon that. His sympathy was entirely with this fellow, whoever he was. He broke out in a sweat thinking how easily he could have been in his place. "Rather a hysterical woman, my dear," he added. "Don't like to distress you, but I wouldn't accept all she says, if I were you. Single women in their thirties and all that. Given to fancies of a rather heated nature. It can happen. Misunderstood a civility for something much more. Easy enough."

She frowned. "Do you really think so, John? I find it hard to believe."

"Of course you do, my dear." He forced a smile, although it felt painted onto his face. "Because you are a woman, and properly married with a home of your own, and all that goes with it. You would never imagine such things. But not all women are as you, you must appreciate that. Be advised, Mariah. A good friend of mine, whose name I will not mention to avoid his embarrassment, has had a similar experience with a young woman, and he was as innocent as the day, I assure you. But in the heat of her . . . her imagination, she totally misread him, and accused him of . . . well . . . it is not fit for you to hear."

"Oh, my goodness!" She was totally taken aback. "Well, I never. I really had not thought . . ."

"It does you credit." He rose and left the table. "But I urge you to dismiss the matter altogether, and on no account be drawn into discussion of it. Now you must excuse me, my dear. Please do not let me disturb you." And as he passed the fire he dropped the letter into it and hesitated long enough to see the flames consume it, to his infinite relief. It would not be spoken of again.

# CHAPTER
# NINE

---

Four days later the trial of Caleb Stone began in the Central Criminal Court in the Old Bailey. For the prosecution was Oliver Rathbone, for the defense Ebenezer Goode. Goode was also a Queen's Counsel of flair and skill. He had taken the case not for the fee, there was none, but for the high profile of the issue, and perhaps even more for the challenge. Rathbone knew him slightly. They had appeared in opposition to each other before. Goode was a man in his mid-forties, tall and rather gangling, but the most remarkable things about him were his prominent, very bright, pale blue-gray eyes and his broad, startling smile. He was full of enthusiasm and had a highly eccentric sense of humor. He was also inordinately fond of cats.

The spectators' seats were not as crowded as for a trial where the accused was a member of high society, or the victim a more colorful character than Angus Stonefield. There was no hint of sexual scandal, and apparently no money involved. And since there was no corpse, the question of murder was one of the issues yet to be proved. Those who had come were there largely to witness the duel between Rathbone and Goode to prove that very point. They were connoisseurs of the adversarial procedure.

It was a fine, blustery day outside. Shafts of sunlight brightened the windows and shone in hazy beams across the wooden panels of the walls, the floor and the carved panoply of the judge's seat. The jurors were ready, twelve carefully chosen men of solemnity, proven worthiness, and of course the appropriate qualifications of property ownership.

Rathbone called his first witness, Genevieve Stonefield. There was only the mildest stir of anticipation as she crossed the court and climbed the steps to the witness-box. On Rathbone's advice she was wearing not black, but a mixture of dark gray and navy. It was sober, unostentatious, and extremely flattering. She looked tired and strained, but the essential passion and intelligence in her face were heightened, and as she turned at the top of the steps and looked towards the room, there was a sudden rustle of interest. One man drew in his breath in surprise and a woman clicked her teeth.

Rathbone smiled. Genevieve Stonefield was that sort of woman. She caused emotions, perhaps of envy, in the female members of the crowd, even if they did not quite know why. There was something in her yet to be awakened, something more elemental than in most women. He must handle it with the utmost care. Perhaps it was a fortunate thing a jury could only ever be composed of men.

She was sworn in and gave her name and address, staring solemnly at Rathbone as if there were no one else present. Not once did her eyes stray to the judge or the jury, not even to the clerk who gave her the Bible.

Rathbone rose to his feet and approached the high witness stand, but stopped some distance away so he did not have to crane his neck to see her. He began quietly.

"Mrs. Stonefield, would you please tell the court all you can remember of events on the last day you saw your husband. Begin with your conversation at breakfast."

She took a deep breath, and her voice was almost steady when she replied.

"There was nothing remarkable in the post," she said. "A few letters from friends, an invitation—" She stopped and had to make a considerable effort to control herself. It was not visible, no tears or trembling, no groping for a handkerchief, just a long hesitation before she resumed. "It was to a musical evening, in three days' time, which he said we should accept. It was a violin recital. He was particularly fond of the violin. He found its tones emotionally very stirring, in a way nothing else quite touched."

"So you wrote to accept?" Rathbone interrupted. "Believing he fully intended to be there?"

"Yes." She drew in her breath. "I never excused myself. They must think me most rude! It quite went out of my head."

"If they did not understand at the time, I am quite certain they will now," he assured her. "Please continue."

"Angus received one or two household bills which he said he would attend to when he came home, then he left for his business. He said he would be home for dinner."

"Have you seen him since, Mrs. Stonefield?"

Her voice was very quiet, almost a whisper. "No."

"Have you had any communication from him whatever?"

"No."

Rathbone walked a pace to the left and shifted his weight a little. He was acutely aware of Ebenezer Goode leaning back in his chair, a slight smile on his face, his eyes bright and watchful. He was at ease, confident, but never so careless as to take anything for granted.

In the dock, Caleb Stone stood motionless. His hair was long and thick and curled wildly, adding to the reckless look of his face with its wide mouth and brilliant green eyes. His very lack of movement drew the gaze in a room where everyone else fidgeted now and then, shifting position, scratching a nose or an ear, turning to look at someone or something, whispering to a neighbor. The only person who did not even glance his way was Genevieve, as if she could not bear to see his face with its mirrorlike resemblance to the husband she had loved.

"Mrs. Stonefield," Rathbone proceeded, "has your husband ever been away from home overnight before?"

"Oh, yes, quite often. His business necessitated traveling now and then."

"Any other purpose that you are aware of?"

"Yes . . ." She stared at him fixedly, her body rigid in its navy and gray wool and trimming silk. "He went quite regularly to the East End of the city, to the Limehouse area, to see his brother. He was . . ." She seemed lost for words.

Caleb stared as if he would force her to look at him, but she did not.

Several of the jurors were more attentive.

"Fond of him?" Rathbone suggested.

Ebenezer Goode stirred in his seat. Rathbone was leading the witness, but this time he did not object.

"In a way he loved him," Genevieve said with a frown, still keeping her head turned away from the dock. "I think also he felt a kind of pity, because—"

This time Ebenezer Goode did rise.

"Yes, yes." The judge waved his hand in a swift motion of dismissal. "Mrs. Stonefield, what you think is not evidence, unless you give us the reasons for your belief. Did your husband express such a sentiment?"

She looked at him with a frown. "No, my lord. It was my impression. Why else would he keep on going to see Caleb, in spite of the way Caleb treated him, unless it was loyalty, and a sort of pity? He defended him to me, even when he was most hurt."

The judge, a small, lean man with a face so weary he looked as if he could not have slept well in years, regarded her with patient intelligence.

"Do you mean his feelings were wounded, ma'am, or his person?"

"Both, my lord. But if I cannot say what I know by instinct, and because I knew my husband, but only what I can prove by evidence, then I shall say only that he was injured in his person. He had sustained bruises, abrasions, and more than once shallow knife wounds, or some other such sharp instrument."

Rathbone could not have planned it better. Now there was not a man or woman in the whole courtroom whose attention was not held. All the jurors were sitting bolt upright and facing the witness stand. The judge's lugubrious face was sharp. In the crowd Rathbone saw Hester Latterly sitting beside Lady Ravensbrook, who was ashen-skinned and looked as if she had aged ten years in the last weeks. Monk had said she'd had typhoid fever. It had certainly taken its toll. Even so, she was a remarkable woman and nothing could rob her features of their character.

Ebenezer Goode bit his lip and rolled his eyes very slightly.

In the dock, Caleb Stone gave a short burst of laughter, and the guards on either side of him inched closer, their disgust plain.

The judge glanced at Rathbone.

"Do we understand, Mrs. Stonefield," Rathbone picked up the thread again, "that your husband returned from these trips to see his brother, with injuries, sometimes quite serious and painful, and yet he still continued to make these journeys?"

"Yes," she said steadily.

"What explanation did he offer you for this unusual behavior?" Rathbone inquired.

"That Caleb was his brother," she answered, "and he could not desert him. Caleb had no one else. They were twins, and it was a bond which could not be broken, even by Caleb's hatred and his jealousy."

In the dock, Caleb's manacled hands, strong and slender, grasped the railing till his knuckles shone white.

Rathbone prayed she would remember precisely what they had discussed and agreed. So far it was going perfectly.

"Were you not afraid that one day the injuries might be more serious?" he asked. "Perhaps he might be crippled or maimed for life?"

Her face was pale and tense, and still she stared straight ahead of her.

"Yes—I was terrified of it. I implored him not to go again."

"But your pleas did not change his mind?"

"No. He said he could not abandon Caleb." She ignored Caleb's snort of derision, almost anguish. "He could always remember the boy he had been," she said chokingly. "And all that they had shared as children, the grief of their parents' death . . ." She blinked several times and her effort to maintain control was apparent.

Rathbone restrained himself from looking at the jury, but he could almost feel their sympathy like a warm tide across the room.

In the crowd, Enid Ravensbrook's haggard face was softened with pity for the distress she imagined so clearly. There was such a depth of feeling in her, Rathbone could not help the fleeting thought that perhaps she too had known such loneliness as a child.

"Yes?" he prompted Genevieve gently.

"Their sense of total loneliness," she continued. "And the dreams and fears they had shared. When they were ill or frightened, they turned to each other. There was no one else to care for them. He could not forget that, no matter what Caleb might do to him now. He was always aware that life had been good to him, and for Caleb it had not proved so fortunate."

In the dock Caleb let out a sound, half groan, half snarl. One of his gaolers touched him gently. The other sneered.

"Did he say that, Mrs. Stonefield?" Rathbone demanded. "Did he use those words, or is that your surmise?"

"No, he used those words, more than once." Her voice was clear and decisive now. It was a statement.

"You were afraid that Caleb might harm your husband seriously, out of his envy at his success, and the hatred arising from that?" Rathbone asked.

"Yes."

There was a murmur around the room, a shifting of weight. The sun had gone and the light was grayer across the wood.

"Did he not understand your feelings?" Rathbone asked.

"Oh yes," she affirmed. "He shared them. He was terrified, but Angus was a man who set duty and honor above all, even his own life. It was a matter of loyalty. He said he owed Caleb a debt for the past and he could not live with himself if he were to run away now."

269

One of the jurors nodded his approval and his determination deepened. He glanced up at the dock with bitter contempt.

"What was that debt, Mrs. Stonefield?" Rathbone asked. "Did he say?"

"Only a matter of Caleb having defended him on occasions when they were children," she replied. "He was not specific, but I think it was from older boys, from teasing and bullying. He did imply that there had been some boy who had been especially brutal, and Caleb had always been the one to take the brunt of it and protect Angus." The tears momentarily spilled down her face and she ignored them. "Angus never forgot that."

"I see," Rathbone said softly, smiling a little. "That is a sentiment of honor I imagine we can all understand and admire." He gave the jury a moment or two to absorb the idea. Again he did not look at them. It would be far too unsubtle. "But you believe he was frightened, all the same," he continued. "Why, Mrs. Stonefield?"

"Because before he went he would be restless and withdrawn," she answered. "Quite unlike his usual manner. He preferred to spend time alone, often pacing the floor. He would be pale-faced, unable to eat, his hands would shake and his mouth be dry. When someone is as deeply afraid as that, Mr. Rathbone, it is not hard to observe it, especially if it is someone you know well, and love."

"Of course," he murmured. He was acutely conscious of Caleb crouched forward over the railing, and of two jurors staring at him as if he were a wild animal, and might even leap over upon them, were he not manacled. "Was there anything else?"

"Sometimes he dreamed," she replied. "He would cry out, calling Caleb's name, and saying, 'No! No!' And then he would wake up covered in perspiration, and his whole body shaking."

"Did he discuss with you what was in these dreams?"

"No. He was too distressed." She closed her eyes and her voice quivered. "I would simply hold him in my arms until he went to sleep again, as I would a child."

There was total silence in the court. For once even Caleb had his head bent forward so his face was hidden. In the crowd there were only a few sighs of pent-up breath being let go, emotions tight.

Enid looked as if she might weep, and her hand clung to Hester's.

"I appreciate that this can only be painful for you," Rathbone resumed after a moment, allowing Genevieve time to master herself. "But there are questions I must ask. When your husband did not return, what steps did you take?"

"The following day I went into his place of business and asked Mr. Arbuthnot, the senior clerk, if perhaps Angus had been called away on business, and somehow the message to me had been lost. He said that had not happened. He—" She stopped.

"Yes, please do not tell us what Mr. Arbuthnot said." Rathbone smiled at her very slightly. "We shall ask him in due course. Tell us merely what you did yourself, as a result of his information."

"I waited two more days, then I called upon an agent of inquiry who had been recommended, a Mr. William Monk."

"I shall be calling both Mr. Arbuthnot and Mr. Monk, my lord," Rathbone said, then turned back to Genevieve. "What did you say to Mr. Monk?"

"I told him I feared my husband had gone to see his brother, and that Caleb had murdered him." She hesitated only a moment, gripping the edge of the railing hard, straining the fabric of her navy gloves. "I instructed him to do all he could to find proof of what had occurred. He promised to do so."

"And as a result of his efforts in this cause, Mrs. Stonefield, did he bring you certain articles of clothing?"

Her face grew even paler and this time her voice was beyond her ability to control. She gulped, and when she spoke it was huskily.

"Yes . . ."

Rathbone turned to the judge. "May it please your lordship, the prosecution exhibits one and two."

"Proceed." The judge nodded in assent.

The clerk produced the coat and trousers Monk had brought

back from the Isle of Dogs. They were just as he had presented them to the police, soiled, bloodstained and badly torn.

"Are these the clothes he brought you, Mrs. Stonefield?" Rathbone asked, holding them up so not only she must see, but the whole room. There was a gasp of indrawn breath. He glimpsed Titus Niven, white as a sheet, his eyes blazing with anger, sitting two rows behind Enid Ravensbrook. He saw Hester wince, but knew she at least understood.

Genevieve swayed and for an instant he thought she was going to faint. He stepped forward, although with the height of the witness stand above the floor, he could not practically have assisted her.

One of the jurors groaned audibly. If the verdict had depended upon sympathy rather than fact, and Ebenezer Goode were not to speak, Rathbone could have won at that moment.

The only person in the room who seemed unmoved was Caleb. He seemed merely curious and slightly surprised.

"Would you look at these clothes, Mrs. Stonefield, and tell the court if you recognize them?" Rathbone said very gently, but so his voice carried to every last person in the room. There was not a breath or a rustle to detract from him.

She looked at them for no more than an instant.

"They are the clothes my husband was wearing the last time I saw him," she said with her eyes on his face. "Please don't make me touch them. They are covered in his blood!"

Ebenezer Goode opened his mouth and closed it again. No one had proved it was Angus's blood, but he knew better than to argue the point now. He shot Rathbone a bright, warning glance. Battle would commence at the due time, but he had never doubted that. And Genevieve would not be spared, only treated with the caution necessary not to injure his own cause.

"Of course," Rathbone murmured. "As long as you have no doubt they are his?"

"None." Her voice was husky, but quite clear. "I have already read the tailor's label on the inside, when Mr. Monk first brought them to me."

"Thank you, Mrs. Stonefield. I have no need to distress you further, but please remain where you are, in case my learned friend for the defense wishes to speak to you." He smiled at her, meeting her eyes for a moment and seeing them remarkably steady, before returning to his seat.

Ebenezer Goode rose to his feet, smiling with dazzling benevolence. He approached the witness stand almost deferentially. There was a rustle of interest around the room. Only Caleb seemed not to care. He avoided looking at him.

"Mrs. Stonefield," Goode began, his voice resonant, caressing the ear, "I am truly so sorry to have to put you through this ordeal, but you do understand that grieved as we all are for your tragedy, it is my duty, specifically mine, to see we do not compound it by blaming someone who is not truly guilty. You see that, I'm sure." He raised his eyebrows hopefully.

"Yes, I understand," she answered him.

"Of course you do. You are a generous woman." He thrust his hands into his pockets, staring up at her. He was still smiling. "I do not doubt that the relationship between your husband and his brother was a troubled one, and that they quarreled occasionally. It could hardly be otherwise, when their paths had become so very different." He freed his hands, and gestured with them. "Your husband had everything life can afford: a beautiful and virtuous wife, five healthy children, a well-cared-for, comfortable home to return to every evening, a profitable business and the regard and esteem—indeed, the friendship—of the world, both socially and professionally."

He shook his head and pursed his lips. "Whereas poor Caleb, for whatever reasons, has none of these things. He has no wife, and no children. He sleeps wherever he can find shelter from the cold and the rain. He eats irregularly. He owns little beyond the clothes in which he stands. He earns his living as and where he can, too often by means other men would despise. And indeed he is rejected and despised among men, feared by some, I'll grant, as perhaps are many whose circumstances drove them to despair." He smiled at the jury. "I shall not try to depict him as an admirable man, only as one who may justly be pitied, and perhaps one whose occasional anger and resentment of his more fortunate brother is not beyond our limit to understand."

He had turned a little to face the crowd. Now he spun around to stare at Genevieve again.

"But Mrs. Stonefield, you say that in these visits of your husband's to the East End, perhaps to Limehouse, or the Isle of Dogs, that he returned home battered and bruised, and sometimes even injured! You did say that, didn't you?"

"Yes." She was puzzled, guarded.

"As if he had been in a fight, perhaps quite a serious one? That was what I understood you to mean. Was I correct?"

"Yes." Her glance strayed almost to Caleb, then jerked away again.

"Did he say, specifically, that it was Caleb who had injured him, Mrs. Stonefield?" Goode pressed. "Please think carefully, and be precise."

She swallowed, turned to Rathbone, who deliberately looked away. He must not be seen to have any communication with her. She must be alone, utterly alone, if her evidence were to carry its fullest might.

"Mrs. Stonefield?" Goode was impatient.

"It was Caleb he went to see!" she protested.

"Of course it was. I had not considered other possibilities," Goode conceded, thereby making sure the jury were aware that there were other possibilities. "We do not even need to consider them, at least for the time being. But did he say it was Caleb who had injured him, Mrs. Stonefield? That is the crux. Is it not possible that Caleb was in some struggle, and your husband, as a loyal brother, went to his assistance? Come, ma'am, is that impossible?"

"No—not—not impossible, I suppose," she said reluctantly. "But . . ."

"But what?" He was immeasurably polite. "But Angus was not a brawler?" He raised his eyebrows. "Not a man to get into a scrap? Not as you know him, I'm sure, but have you ever seen him in a public house in the Isle of Dogs? Sometimes it takes a very peaceable man, or even a coward, to avoid a fight there. Is Caleb a fighter, ma'am? Could he have instigated these brawls, or have been the focus of them?"

Rathbone rose to his feet. "Really, my lord, how can the witness possibly know such a thing? As my learned friend has pointed out, she was never there!"

Goode smiled at Rathbone with exaggerated courtesy, and not without humor.

"Alas, hoist with my own petard. I concede." He turned back to Genevieve. "I withdraw the question, ma'am. It was absurd. May I ask, from what your husband said to you, is it possible that he was injured in a fight, or a series of scraps, in Caleb's company, or even on his way to or from visiting him, but not actually by Caleb? Or is that impossible?"

"It is possible," she conceded, but everything in her face and the stance of her body denied it.

"And the regrettable blood upon these clothes," Goode said, his face twisted with distress, "which I willingly accept are his. May I be optimistic, even filled with hope, that it is not in fact his blood at all, but that of some other poor soul, and that he shed them simply because they became spoiled in this manner?"

"Then where is he?" she leaned forward over the railing, her face pleading. "Where is Angus?"

"Alas, I have no idea." Goode's expression was one of genuine sorrow, even apology. "But when they were found he was not in them, harmed or unharmed, ma'am. I agree, it does not look fortunate for him, but there is no need to despair, and certainly no proof of any tragedy. Let us keep courage and hope." He inclined his head slightly, and with something of a flourish returned to his seat.

The judge looked at Rathbone. There was the merest hint of weary humor in his eyes. "Mr. Rathbone, is there anything further you can usefully ask of your witness before I adjourn the court for luncheon?"

"Thank you, no, my lord. I believe she has told her story plainly enough for all to understand." There was nothing he could do but make her repeat what she had already said. It was a matter of judgment as to what would swing the jury one way or the other. He believed restraint was the better part. He had studied their faces, their reactions to Genevieve. He should not overdo it. Let them form their own opinions of her, paint her as they wished to see her. Her spirit to defend the interests of her children might be misperceived and mar the image.

The court rose. Caleb was taken down, the crowd spilled out to purchase whatever refreshment it wished, and Rathbone, Goode and the judge partook of an excellent meal, all separately, at a nearby tavern. They returned early in the afternoon.

"Proceed with your next witness, Mr. Rathbone," the judge directed. "Let us get to some meat in this matter."

Rathbone spent the rest of the day calling the Stonefield servants to corroborate what Genevieve had said regarding Angus's absences from home, which were considerable, although only when returning from seeing Caleb was he ever injured. On two of these occasions the wounds had necessitated considerable treatment. He had refused to call a doctor, in spite of the apparent seriousness, and Mrs. Stonefield had attended to him herself. She had some skill in that area.

Had Mr. Stonefield been long in recovering?

On one occasion he had been obliged to take to his bed for over a week. It seemed he had lost a great deal of blood.

Had he given any cause for his injury?

No. But the butler had overheard Mr. Stonefield speak of his brother, and Mrs. Stonefield had made no secret of her assumption that Caleb was the assailant.

The jurors' faces made the belief plain, and their contempt for Caleb, who ignored them almost as if they were irrelevant.

The butler was very straightforward. He offered Goode no opportunity to trip him, and Goode was far too wise to be seen to embarrass such a plain man. He was courteous and complimentary. All he could achieve was another reminder to the jury that the precise dealing of the wounds was still all surmise. Angus had never said in so many words that Caleb had stabbed him. And he did not labor that. Every man and woman in the room believed it was Caleb; it was in their faces when they looked at the dock, and at Caleb's jeering, insolent stare back at them.

The first day of the trial closed with a conviction of the mind, but no evidence which the judge could direct as law, only massive supposition and a crowd filled with a frustration of loathing.

Rathbone left and almost immediately found a hansom. Without thinking he directed the driver to Primrose Hill. That was where his father, a quiet, studious man with a gentle manner and an alarmingly sharp perception, lived.

His father was sitting by a large log fire with his feet on the fender and a glass of red wine by his side when Oliver arrived and was shown in by the manservant. Henry Rathbone looked up with surprise and then a shadow both of pleasure and concern.

"Sit down," he offered, indicating the chair opposite. "Wine?"

"What is it?" Oliver sat down, feeling the warmth of the fire creep over him with intense satisfaction. "I don't like that burgundy you have."

"It's a claret," Henry replied.

"I'll have a glass."

Henry nodded at the manservant, who departed to bring the wine.

"You'll burn your feet," Oliver said critically.

"Scorch the soles of my slippers, perhaps," Henry argued. He did not ask why Oliver had come. He knew he would be told in time.

Oliver slid a little farther down in the armchair and accepted the claret from the manservant, who went out and closed the door with a quiet snick.

The ash settled in the fire and Henry reached forward and put on another log. There was no sound in the room but the flickering of the fire, no light but the flames and one gas lamp on the far wall. The wind outside was inaudible, as was the first beginning of the rain.

"I'm thinking of getting a new dog," Henry remarked. "Old Edgemor has some retriever pups. One I like in particular."

"Good idea," Oliver said. He was going to have to open the subject himself. "This trial is troubling me."

"So I gathered." Henry reached for his pipe and put it in his mouth, but did not bother to light it. He seldom did. "Why? What is not as you expected?"

"Nothing, I suppose."

"Then what is there to be distressed about?" Henry looked at him with his clear, light-blue eyes, so unlike Oliver's own, which were very dark, in spite of his fairish hair. "You are off balance. Is it your mind, or your emotions? Are you going to lose when you should win, or win when you should lose?"

Oliver smiled in spite of himself. "Lose when I should win, I think."

"Summarize the case for me." He took the pipe out of his mouth and pointed the stem at Oliver absentmindedly. "And don't address me as if I were the jury! Just tell me the truth."

Oliver gave a jerky little laugh, and listed the bare, literal facts as far as he knew them, adding his feelings only as he believed they were relevant to some interpretation and not furnished by evidence. When he had finished he stared at his father waiting for his response.

"This is another one of Monk's," Henry observed. "Have you seen Hester again? How is she?"

Oliver found himself uncomfortable. It was not a subject he wished to contemplate, much less discuss.

"It is exceedingly difficult to get a jury to convict for murder without a body," he said irritably. "But if ever a man did deserve to hang, it is Caleb Stone. The more I hear of Angus, the more I admire him, and the worse Caleb appears. The man is violent, destructive, sadistic, an ingrate."

"But . . ." Henry raised his eyebrows, looking at Oliver with piercing gentleness.

"He seems to have not a shred of remorse," Oliver went on. "Even looking at his brother's widow, and knowing there are five children, and what will happen to them now—" He stopped.

"Do you doubt his guilt?" Henry asked, sipping his claret.

Oliver picked up his own glass. The firelight shone ruby in it, and the clean, slightly sharp aroma of it filled his head.

"No. He is just so vividly alive. Even when I am not looking at him, which is almost all the time, I am aware of his emotions, his rage . . . and his pain. And I am aware of his intelligence."

"And if you win, he will be hanged."

"Yes."

"And that offends you?"

"Yes."

"And if you lose, he will be a free man, guilty, and vindicated."

"Yes."

"I cannot help you, except to a quiet evening by the fire and another glass of claret. You already know everything I would say."

"Yes, of course I do. I suppose I simply do not want to say them to myself alone." He drank from the glass and the taste of it filled him. At least until it was time to leave, he could let the matter go.

Monk had not been in court. He would be called as a witness, so he could not attend until after he had given evidence, and he had no desire to wait around in corridors catching snippets of news.

He had no further word from Drusilla Wyndham. If she intended drawing the police into the matter of his alleged assault, she had apparently delayed her complaint. He thought it far more likely she knew the futility of such a prosecution, and would ruin him by innuendo, a slower, subtler form of torture, and far more likely to be successful. He would have to wait with the sword hanging over his head, never knowing when it would fall.

He went to see Evan, only to find he had been sent to Crouch End to interview a burglary suspect and would not be back until tomorrow. There was little he could do to help Monk until he knew at least what case, if any, was involved.

Monk strode the cold pavements almost oblivious of the gusts of wind blowing in his face. A carriage passed too close to the curb, its wheels splashing through the gutters and soaking him. His trousers flapped wetly around his ankles.

What had he done to Drusilla? What had he done to any woman? He knew so little about his personal life. He had not written regularly to his sister, Beth. He knew that from the few letters of hers he had kept. He had loathed Runcorn, and been at least partially responsible for the aggressive, self-serving way in which he now behaved. Runcorn had felt Monk's contempt all his professional life. His original mild dislike of him had hardened into fear, not without cause. Monk had sensed his weaknesses, and played on them.

There was nothing in that to admire.

Granted, Runcorn was an unattractive man, narrow, self-absorbed and a coward with no generosity of soul. But he was the poorer for having worked with Monk, not the richer.

Who else was there? No one from the past that he knew. Perhaps he had treated Hermione well? It seemed it was she who had let him down. But if he had known her longer, if she had not so bitterly disillusioned him, would he in time have hurt her also?

That was a futile line of thought.

He crossed the road, ignoring the horse droppings which had not been swept.

What of the present, the brief span of two years since the accident? He had behaved honorably with Evan. He was perfectly sure of that. And with Callandra. Callandra was fond of him; she quite genuinely liked him. The knowledge of that was one of the most pleasant of all his possessions, and he clung to it with a fierceness which he would not have believed possible even a month ago.

But Callandra was in her fifties. A far truer mirror would be Hester. How had he treated Hester, who had stood with him against such terrors in the past, and who had been unquestioningly brave and loyal in the teeth of failure and opposition?

He had been there, unfailingly, when she was in danger. He had never for an instant doubted her honor or her innocence. He had worked night and day to save her. He had not even had to think about it: it was the only possible course he could follow. No other had entered his thoughts.

But how had he behaved towards her as a woman?

If he were honest, he had been consistently abrasive and critical, even offensive. He had done it intentionally, wanting to hurt her, because in some indefinable way—what? Why did she make him so uncomfortable? Because there was some elemental truth in her he did not want to know, some emotion within himself she touched and he could not afford to feel. She was demanding, uncomfortable, critical. She demanded of him what he was not prepared to give—change, uncertainty, pain. She had the difficulties of a man without the virtues, the ease that went with them. She required friendship.

But Drusilla was utterly different. How he regarded Hester was irrelevant to this.

He crossed the next street, dodging a dray.

He had been happy with Drusilla, enjoying her company without shadow. She was fun, lighthearted, witty, feminine. She had made no intellectual demands, no moral judgments. There was nothing in her which irritated or discomforted him. Certainly, Hester was irrelevant.

But had he hurt Hester? Was he innately selfish, cruel? And had he always been? That was not totally irrelevant . . . indeed, it was the entire point.

He did not admire selfishness in others. It was ugly from every aspect, a spiritual weakness which soured every other virtue. Even courage and honesty were marred by it in the end. Is that what he was? Basically a man with no generosity of soul? Everything began and ended with his own interest?

What utter and abominable isolation. It was its own punishment, more terrible than anything imposed from outside.

He must know! Why did Drusilla hate him?

There was nothing he could do until Evan returned and he knew for certain whether it was a case or not. If it was not, then the next thing was to travel to Norfolk, but he could not leave London until he had testified in the Stonefield trial.

He could join the police in their further search of the river for Angus's body. Not that there was much hope of finding it now, but it was still worth every effort. It would almost certainly close the case against Caleb, and God knew, he deserved that. If ever a man warranted hanging, it was Caleb. More importantly, it would free Genevieve from the emotional and financial prison of not knowing. When he thought of her suffering, and her courage, her loss, he was barely aware of his own dilemma, or the gray street around him.

It was a clear, cold afternoon when he stood in the small boat setting off from the Shadwell Dock Stairs and started downstream with the wind in his face. They took the north bank. Another boat was searching the south.

It was a long, bitter day, filled with the smell of tide and sewage, the endlessly moving filthy water, the sound of lapping and slurping as the wake of the larger ships washed against the shingle or the pier stakes and stairs, and cargo boats, and barges bound for the east coast, passenger ships for France and Holland, clippers for every part in the Empire and the world.

They went in and out of every dock, every yard and stair, poked every pile of wood or canvas, every hulk, every shadowed stretch of water, lifted every drifting piece of flotsam. They scoured carefully through the pier stakes where long ago those convicted of piracy on the high seas were tied until the morning tide drowned them.

Monk was frozen. His feet and trousers were wet from where he had jumped ashore onto the shingle. His body ached, his knuckles were skinned, as were his palms from the wet ropes, and he was hungry.

As dusk drew over a clear sky, the air began to prickle the skin with cold and on shore the rime of moisture on the cobbles was turning to ice. The tide was rising again. They were beyond Woolwich and the Royal Arsenal, down as far as the end of Gallion's Reach. Ahead of them was Barking Reach.

"Nothing," the sergeant said with a shake of his head. "We're wasting our time. If 'e went in at all, 'e's long gone now. Poor devil." He waved his arm, rocking the boat slightly. "Right, men. Might as well go 'ome. Gawd knows, it's going ter freeze as 'ard as the 'obs o' 'ell tonight. Pass 'round that tot o' rum. It's far enough 'ome, dammit."

"We'll find 'im somew'ere," one of the others said laconically. "Sea gives up its dead, sooner or later."

"Mebbe," the sergeant agreed. "But not tonight, lads."

They turned in a wide circle and leaned their weight into the oars, too tired to bother talking. The shore was only a greater density in the night, lit by yellow lamps, carriage lights moving slowly. Sounds were faint across the water, a rattle of wheels, a shout, the creak of spars in midstream.

It was a good hour later when they bumped into the mass in the water and the man in the bow called out. It took them another twenty minutes, working by lamplight, awkward with the small boat tipping and the sodden heaviness of it, to haul the body into the bottom and examine it.

Monk felt his stomach knot, and then churn with revulsion and he thought for a moment he was going to be sick.

It was the remains of a man in his late thirties or early forties, as much as one could tell. He had been dead for some time, in Monk's judgment well over a week. His features were badly decomposed by the river and its natural inhabitants. What was left of his clothes were beyond recognition except that they must once have been a shirt and some form of trousers, but of what quality or color it was impossible to say.

"Well?" the sergeant asked, looking at Monk. "This 'im?" There was a dry smile on his mouth, and hopelessness in his eyes. "Geez! Poor devil. No 'uman bein' should come ter this."

Monk steeled himself and looked at the body more closely. He was surprised his stomach had settled again although he was shuddering with cold. He must have done such things before, perhaps often. The man was tall, strongly built. His hair was thick and dark. There was nothing to disprove it was Angus Stonefield.

"I don't know. It could be," he said with a sense of sadness which all but overwhelmed him, as if up to that moment he had in some way still believed Angus might have been alive.

The sergeant sighed. "I suppose we'll 'ave ter ask the wife, although Gawd 'isself knows 'ow yer could expec' any woman ter look at that . . . the more so if it's 'im."

"Take him to the morgue," Monk said quietly, loathing what he was doing even as he heard his own voice. Suddenly it seemed easy to hang Caleb. The anger was not enough even for that. "I'll bring her. It has to be done. There may be some mark on the body where the clothes have protected it, something she can recognize . . . or which makes it possible."

The sergeant searched his face in the moon of the lamplight, then nodded slowly. "Right y'are, sir. We'll do that. C'mon now, boys, put yer back inter them oars. D'yer wanter be stuck 'ere in the middle o' the damn' river till yer freezes solid?"


"Yes, Mr. Monk?" Genevieve looked at him, her face creased with anxiety, fear already at the back of her eyes. He had been admitted to the parlor. She was not using the larger, more formal rooms, probably to save the cost of heating them. She looked exhausted. He knew she had been in the courtroom all day, and in the witness-box a great deal of it, testifying in an attempt to prove her husband's death. Watching Caleb, so physically like him, must have been the worst ordeal of her life. And now he was possibly going to add to it the final horror.

Yet it could not be avoided. No one else could do this. If his face were undamaged, recognizable, perhaps Ravensbrook or Mr. Arbuthnot could have spared her. As it was, only she could know the intimacies of his body which were left.

Monk was not often at a loss for words, but even though he had thought of this since their grim find in the river, he still did not know how best to tell her.

"What is it, Mr. Monk?" Her eyes did not leave his face. "Have you found Angus? Is that what you cannot bring yourself to tell me?"

"I don't know." It was ridiculous that she should be helping him, when he should somehow be easing it for her. It was her grief, her loss, not his. "We have found a body, but it will require someone who knows him well to identify it."

"I don't understand. . . ." She swayed a little bit. "What are you trying to say?" She swallowed. "Is it Angus, or not? You have seen Caleb. I can see a multitude of differences between them, but to you they will be so alike you must know if it is Angus or not!" There was a rising panic in her voice and her eyes. "Please! This . . . this uncertainty is worse than knowing would be." She stood with her hands knotted in front of her, her body so tight she was shaking.

"If I knew, Mrs. Stonefield, I would not subject you to this!" he said desperately. "If even Lord Ravensbrook could have told, I would have asked him. But the river has done its damage to the face. Only where the clothes have protected it is it unharmed. That is why you alone can tell."

She drew in her breath with a gasp, tried to speak, and made no sound at all.

He ached to be able to touch her, in some manner lend her physical strength. But it would have been an impossible intrusion.

"Would you like me to have someone come with you?" he asked. "Have you a maid? Or shall we collect Mr. Niven on the way? I imagine you would not care for Lord Ravensbrook?" It was a question, but he knew her answer from the stiffening of her neck.

"No . . . no thank you. I think I prefer to be alone, except for you. If you will be so kind? I have seen dead bodies before, but not of my own husband, nor . . . damaged . . . as you say."

"Of course." He offered his arm immediately. "Are you ready to come now, or would you prefer to take a sip of brandy first?"

"I do not take spirits, thank you. I shall have my maid bring my cloak, then I shall come. It is better done quickly."

They rode in silence. There was nothing of relevance to say, and anything irrelevant now would have been both painful and absurd. They clattered through the darkness past the shimmering street lamps reflected on the mist and smoke and the swaying lights of other coaches and carriages passing. There was no sound but the clatter of hooves on stone and the swish of wheels and occasional splatter of water as they struck a particularly bad gutter.

They reached the morgue and pulled up with a jolt. Monk climbed out and helped her alight. They crossed the pavement and went up the steps. A single constable was waiting for them, pale-faced and unhappy. He led them inside.

The place smelled clean and stale, with an indefinable odor that was a mask for something else, the washed and deeply decaying flesh of the dead.

The attendant took them to a small room where a body lay on a wooden table, covered with a sheet. It was customary to remove the sheet and show only the face. In this instance it was the one part of the man most disfigured. Someone had taken the forethought to cover the head separately. The attendant unfolded the cloth from the neck down, showing the shoulders, upper arms, chest and abdomen.

Genevieve stood absolutely still, as if she could not move from the spot. Monk was afraid that if she did she would collapse, and yet from where she was she could not see sufficiently well to know more than that it was the upper torso of a well-built man. Unless there were some major abnormality in Angus, she would have to come closer to know if this were him or not.

He took her arm.

"Mrs. Stonefield?" he said gently. "Your distress is natural, even a revulsion, but we do not know if this is your husband or not. Without your help, we will never know. Please . . . use all your courage, and look."

She took a step forward, still with her eyes closed, then another step, and a third. Monk restrained her. She was close enough.

They stood together in the silence, not a sound from outside penetrated the room. There was no motion of breath. Even the lamps seemed to burn without a hiss, as if the air swallowed them.

Genevieve opened her eyes and looked down at the naked chest in front of her.

"No," she whispered, and the tears spilled over her eyes in both relief and despair. "It is not my husband. Please put back the cover over the poor man. I do not know who he is."

"It is not Angus?" Monk insisted. "You are quite sure?"

"Yes." She turned away from the body. "There are no scars on him. Angus had a unique pattern of scars on the side of his chest where he was hurt, a stab wound, once when he was with Caleb. I know exactly where it is. I stitched it myself. It is not there in that man."

Monk guided her towards the doorway out. "I'm sorry to have brought you here," he said bitterly. "I would have spared you this, could I have known." He nodded to the morgue attendant and the constable followed them out.

"I know you would, Mr. Monk," she answered with a little cough. She put her hand over her face and swayed. He steadied her and the constable came quickly to the other side. He guided her to the entrance and the sharp night air.

"Thank you." Monk looked at the constable. "I'll see Mrs. Stonefield home."

"Yes sir. Good night sir. Ma'am."


When the trial of Caleb Stone recommenced the following day, Rathbone was aware of the preceding night's events. He regretted profoundly both Genevieve's ordeal and the fact that it had not been Angus's body. He was also moved by it. She could so easily have claimed him. It was extremely unlikely anyone would have challenged her, and the poor man, whoever he was, would almost certainly not be identified by anyone else.

"Surely the temptation crossed her mind?" he said to Monk as they walked in the rain up the steps into the Central Criminal Court. "She could hardly have been prosecuted for such an error, even if it were ever proved. It could have answered all her immediate needs."

"And ours," Monk agreed grimly, following Rathbone in through the massive doors and shaking his umbrella before he folded it. "But no. She looked just once and pronounced it not him. She had no doubts. What she thought about in the journey there, or for the few moments before she looked at him, we shall probably never know. If she was tempted, she had overcome it by then."

"Remarkable woman," Rathbone said quietly, taking off his hat. "I wish I could feel more certain of an outcome for her."

"Little hope?" Monk asked.

"Not as it is," Rathbone replied. "But I shall do my best. We are certainly not beaten yet."

The first witness of the day was Monk himself. He testified of his search for Angus, which had taken him eventually to finding Angus's clothes on the beggar in the East India Dock Road, and his exchange of his own in order to obtain them.

Then he told of his pursuit of Caleb, with the police, and the arrest in the marshes. Rathbone did not mention their earlier encounter, since all that Caleb had said was inadmissible, being hearsay, and unwitnessed. Archie McLeish had been out of earshot beyond the other makeshift door.

When Rathbone had finished, Ebenezer Goode rose to his feet. He looked at Monk carefully, meeting his gaze. He recognized a professional. His eyes gleamed and his lips parted in a wolfish smile, brilliant, all teeth, but he was far too wily to attack where he could not win.

"Do you know where Angus Stonefield is now, Mr. Monk?" he asked very gently, as if they had struck up a casual conversation in some tavern over a pint of ale.

"No," Monk replied.

"Do you know, for certain, Mr. Monk, irrefutably, whether he is alive or dead?"

"No."

Goode's smile grew, if possible, even broader.

"No," he agreed. "Neither do any of us! Thank you, that is all."

Rathbone rose and called Lord Ravensbrook. There was a stir of interest, but only slight. The case was slipping away, and Rathbone knew it.

Ravensbrook took the stand with outward calm, but his body was rigid, his eyes staring straight ahead. He might have faced a firing squad with the same tight, unhappy courage. Enid was there in the crowd again, with Hester beside her, but he did not appear even to be aware of her, much less to seek her.

When he had been sworn, Rathbone approached him and began.

"My lord, you have known both brothers since their birth, have you not?"

"Not since birth," Ravensbrook corrected. "Since their parents died. They were then a little over five years old."

"I beg your pardon." Rathbone rephrased the question. "You have known of them. They are related to you, are they not?"

"Yes." Ravensbrook swallowed hard. Even from where Rathbone stood, he could see his throat tighten and the difficulty with which he answered. For a man of his nature—proud, intensely private, drilled to keep his feelings under control and seldom to express them in words, even when appropriate—this must be an experience close to torture.

"When they were left orphans . . ." Rathbone continued, loathing having to do this, but compelled. Without this background there was no case. Perhaps even with it there was none. Was he putting this man through such a refinement of public pain for nothing? "You took them into your home and cared for them as if they were your own, is that not so?"

"Yes," Ravensbrook said grimly. His eyes did not move from Rathbone's face, as though he were trying to blot out the rest of the room and convince himself they were alone, two men having an acutely personal conversation in the privacy of some club. "It seemed the obvious thing to do."

"To a benevolent man," Rathbone agreed. "So from the age of five years, Angus and Caleb Stonefield lived in your home and were raised as your sons?"

"Yes."

"Were you married at that time, my lord?"

"I was a widower. My first wife died very young." There was barely a flicker of expression on his face, just a shadow of grief, then it was gone again. It was not done to display one's vulnerability before others. "I married my present wife several years after that. Angus and Caleb had already grown to adulthood and left home." Still he did not look towards Enid, as if to do so would somehow draw her into his tangle of pain, or leave him more exposed.

"So you were all the family they knew?" Rathbone persisted.

Ebenezer Goode moved restlessly in his seat.

Caleb stretched his hand away from the gaoler beside him, and his manacles clanked against the railing.

The judge leaned forward. "Is this leading somewhere, Mr. Rathbone? So far your questions have seemed to elicit only the obvious."

"Yes, my lord. I am about to ask Lord Ravensbrook about the relationship between the two brothers, as he observed it from childhood. I am merely seeking to establish that he is an expert in this field."

"You have done so. Please proceed."

Rathbone bowed, and turned back to Ravensbrook.

"When you first knew them, my lord, were they fond of each other?"

Ravensbrook hesitated only a moment. His face held a curious look of puzzlement and distaste, as if he found it distressing to answer the question.

"Yes, they were extremely . . . close. At that time there was no division between them."

"When did you first notice a division?"

Ravensbrook did not reply. His face reflected a pain and a distaste which was hardly surprising. To remember that time when Angus and Caleb had loved one another was a peculiarly bitter contrast with the present. The sympathy for him was palpable in the room.

"My lord," Rathbone pressed, "when did you first notice the beginnings of a division between the two brothers? We need to know, and you are the only one who can tell us."

"Of course," Ravensbrook said grimly. "It was almost three years after their arrival. Angus was always a . . . a quiet child, studious, obedient. Caleb appeared to resent it. He was far less easy to discipline. He would take correction very poorly. He had an unfortunate temper."

In the dock, Caleb jerked his head up, and the movement caught the eye of several of the jurors. They looked at him with a new interest.

"Was this division between them on both sides?" Rathbone inquired.

Again Ravensbrook hesitated for so long Rathbone was obliged to repeat the question.

"It did not appear so," Ravensbrook answered at last. "Certainly as time passed, Angus became more . . . diligent in his studies, more of an agreeable companion—"

Caleb let out a snort which was almost a cry. There was rage in it, but an undertone of pain as well, and Rathbone suddenly felt the weight of rejection in it, even all those years after, the confusion and realization of the less favored son. He thought of his own father, and the bond between them. He could not recall ever feeling it threatened. Jealousy was unknown to him.

"And Caleb was not?" he prompted.

Ravensbrook's jaw tightened and his face was very pale.

"No," he said flatly. "He was rebellious, argumentative, a perverse child."

"Did you love him?" It was not a question he had intended to ask. It served no purpose to his case. He spoke without forethought, only a sudden overwhelming emotion, which was inexcusable, totally unprofessional.

"Of course," Ravensbrook answered, his dark eyebrows raised very slightly. "One does not withdraw one's loyalty or regard from a member of one's family simply because they are of a difficult nature. One hopes that with care they will grow out of it."

"And did Caleb grow out of it?"

Ravensbrook did not reply.

"Did he grow out of the envy of his brother?" Rathbone persisted. "Did they regain their earlier closeness?"

Ravensbrook's face was tight, bitterly inward, as if he exercised an iron control.

"It did not appear so to me."

In the dock Caleb let out a short bark of derisive laughter and the judge swiveled around to glare at him, breath drawn in to reprove him if he should make another sound.

Among the jurors a man frowned, another shook his head and pursed his lips.

Ebenezer Goode stiffened. It was the first negative sign to his case, although he must surely have known that Caleb's manner, the very expression on his face, was the greatest single factor against him. There was no evidence, at least so far; it was a matter of emotion and belief, a question of interpretation.

Rathbone pursued the line of inquiry.

"Lord Ravensbrook, will you draw for the court the pattern of the relationship between these two brothers as they grew up in your house. Were they educated similarly, for example?"

A bitter smile touched Ravensbrook's chiseled mouth, then vanished instantly.

"Exactly the same," he replied. "There was one tutor who taught one set of lessons. It was only their response which was different. In every regard I treated them equally, as did all the rest of the staff."

"Everyone?" Rathbone affected surprise. "Surely there would have been those who had favorites? As you say, the boys became increasingly dissimilar."

Caleb leaned forward in the dock, his face eager, listening intently.

Ravensbrook must have been aware of it, but he stood without the slightest movement. He could have been carved in bone. He was a man wading through a nightmare, and it showed in every line and angle of his body.

Enid's eyes seemed never to leave his face.

"Lord Ravensbrook!" Rathbone felt he needed to attract his attention before there was any purpose in repeating his question.

Ravensbrook looked at him slowly.

"Lord Ravensbrook, you have told us how unlike these two boys became. Surely others who know them must have felt differently towards them? Angus had every virtue: honesty, humility, gratitude, generosity; while Caleb was aggressive, lazy and ungrateful. If that is so, can people truly have regarded them with equal affection?"

"Perhaps I was speaking more for myself than for others," Ravensbrook conceded grudgingly, his face stiff. "I did my best not to permit it, but it may have existed in the village. I had no control over that."

"The village?" Rathbone had omitted to ask Ravensbrook where the brothers had spent their childhood. He should have realized it would not have been in London.

"My country home in Berkshire," Ravensbrook explained, his face suddenly white. "It was a better atmosphere for them than the city. Learned to ride, hunt, fish." He took a deep breath. "Manly pursuits. Learned a bit about the land, and a man's responsibilities towards his fellows."

There was a murmur of assent from one or two people in the room. Enid looked puzzled, Caleb bitter.

"A very privileged childhood, by the sound of it." Rathbone smiled.

"I gave them all I could," Ravensbrook said without expression, except perhaps for a certain gravity which might have been sadness, or merely an effect of the light in his impassive face, with its patrician features and dark, very level eyes under their short brows.

"You speak of a jealousy growing between them," Rathbone continued. He was battling with a witness who was all but hostile, and it was like drawing teeth. He could understand it. Having to expose his most private family life to the gaze of the public in general, and the seekers of sensation in particular, was something no decent man would wish, and to one like Milo Ravensbrook it was like facing enemy fire. But if there was to be justice it was unavoidable, not only punishment for Caleb, but a decent acknowledgment for Genevieve and her children. "Would you give the court an example of any evidences of these you can recall? Instances of behavior, resentments, quarrels . . ."

Ravensbrook looked somewhere over the heads of the crowd.

"I should prefer not to."

"Naturally," Rathbone commiserated. "No one wishes to recall such events, but I am afraid it is necessary if we are to discover what is the truth of this present tragedy. I am sure you wish that." He was not perfectly sure. Perhaps Ravensbrook would rather it went unknown, and could fade from memory as a mystery. But he could not say so.

There were several minutes of silence. One of the jurors coughed and produced a large handkerchief. Another shifted his weight as though embarrassed. The judge stared at Ravensbrook. Ebenezer Goode looked first at Ravensbrook, then at Rathbone, his face expectant.

But it was Caleb who broke the tension.

"Forgotten, have you?" he called down, his lips drawn back in something close to a snarl. "Forgotten how Angus was afraid of that damn black horse of yours—but I rode it! Forgotten how angry you were—"

"Silence!" The judge banged his gavel, but Caleb ignored him, leaning forward over the railing of the dock, his beautiful, manacled hands gripping the railing. His eyes glaring. His expression was one of such blazing hatred it struck a note of fear, even though he was imprisoned by the height of the dock above the floor of the court and had warders on either side of him. There was a power and a rage in him which could be felt across the space as though it might actually touch and darken the mind.

". . . because I could make it behave, and you couldn't?" Caleb finished, ignoring the judge. It was as if no one existed in the room but himself and Ravensbrook. "Remember how you beat me because I took the peaches from the conservatory?"

Goode was on his feet, but powerless.

"That was seven years earlier," Ravensbrook replied, not looking at Caleb, but staring straight ahead of him still. "You took every peach. You deserved punishment."

The judge banged his gavel again.

"Mr. Goode, either keep your client's behavior appropriate to this court or I shall have him removed and continue the case in his absence. Make that plain to him, sir."

Caleb swung around, his face twisted with fury. "Don't talk to me through a third party, as if I weren't here, damn you! I can hear what you're saying and I can understand you. What bloody difference does it make whether I'm here or not anyway? You say what you want about me. Believe what you want. You'll believe what suits your idea of the way you want things to be!" His voice rose even more. "What does the truth matter? What do you care who killed whom, as long as your world stays the same, with the same comfortable, reassuring lies? Cover it all up! Bury it! Put a white cross over it and say a prayer to your God that he'll forgive you, then go away and forget. I'll see you all in hell, be sure of it! I'll be there and waiting for you!"

The judge looked tired and sad. "Take the prisoner down," he instructed the warders.

Caleb sank down suddenly, his head in his hands.

Ebenezer Goode rose and walked at least halfway towards the bench.

"My lord, may we have a brief adjournment so I may advise my client? I believe I can persuade him to keep silence."

"There's no need," Caleb interrupted, jerking his head up. "I shan't speak again. There's nothing else to say."

The judge glanced at Rathbone.

"I am ready to proceed, my lord," Rathbone replied. He had no desire to break the mood by an adjournment.

"Another outburst and I will act," the judge warned.

"Yes, my lord." Goode returned to his seat without looking towards the dock.

Rathbone faced Lord Ravensbrook again.

"I think part of my question has already been answered, but if you could mention one or two other instances, it would give the court a fuller picture. For example, how did the two brothers fare in their academic studies?"

Ravensbrook's body was as rigid as if he were in a military parade.

"Angus was excellent at his work, especially mathematics, history and geography," he said, staring ahead of him. "He was less interested in Latin and the classics, but he studied them because I wished it. He was a most admirable boy, and abundantly repaid me all I ever did for him."

A ghost of a smile crossed his face and vanished again.

"I believe in later years he grew to appreciate the value of Latin, at least. It is such a superb discipline for the mind. He always understood the need for that. Caleb never did. He was always unruly, desiring to rebel, to overthrow, even to destroy. It was something in him I could never govern. I tried everything I knew, and everything failed."

"Did he say anything about Angus's success?" Rathbone asked.

Ravensbrook's voice was hard and low.

"To begin with he merely expressed resentment. Later his feelings grew into a positive hatred, a jealousy he seemed unable to control."

"Did he ever resort to physical violence?"

Ravensbrook's face was filled with an emotion so deep he seemed to shake very slightly and his skin was pale and tight across his high, narrow cheekbones. But to Rathbone at least, it was unreadable. There could have been anger in it, frustration, knowledge of failure, guilt, or nothing other than a deep, aching grief.

"I cannot answer you of my own knowledge," Ravensbrook said almost under his breath, and yet his words carried in a silent room where not a man or woman moved. Not a boot creaked, not a skirt rustled. "If they fought, I had not seen them."

"Did either of them ever sustain injuries you could not account for otherwise?" Rathbone pursued the inevitable.

Caleb was still motionless in the dock, his head bent, face hidden as though he had accepted defeat.

"I don't recall," Rathbone answered. "Youths will climb trees, ride horses, drive carriages and gigs dangerously." The set of his jaw made it obvious he could be drawn no further.

"Naturally." Rathbone bowed and accepted defeat. "At what age did they leave home to go their separate ways, my lord?"

Ravensbrook winced as if he had been struck.

"Angus joined a company of dealers in the City just after his eighteenth birthday. They were acquaintances of mine, and were keen to have him." There was pride in his tone, a slight lift to his head. "It seemed an excellent opportunity, and he grasped it eagerly. He did extremely well. It was not long before he rose within the company, and as you know, eventually founded his own business."

"And Caleb?" Rathbone said.

"Caleb left shortly before that. He simply walked out. I heard rumor that he had been seen in the village, stories of drinking, brawling." Ravensbrook remained silent for a moment. There was not a sound in the room. "Then they ceased," he finished. "I presume that was when he went to London."

"But he did not take up any position, any calling?"

"Not that I know of."

"Did you seek to find any position for him?"

Ravensbrook winced. "I could not recommend him to anyone. It would have been dishonest. He was a violent and deceitful man, and appeared possessed of very few skills that were of any use."

In the crowd Enid Ravensbrook sat with such a pity in her face one might have thought it was that which had ravaged her rather than disease. Hester slid her arm around her and held her with a tenderness as if she might break.

"I see," Rathbone murmured. "Thank you, my lord. Did he at this time express any hatred or jealousy towards his brother, who sounds to have and to be everything he was not?"

"Yes, frequently," Ravensbrook acknowledged. "He both hated and despised his brother."

"Despised him?" Rathbone affected surprise.

Ravensbrook's face was bitter. "He thought Angus weak and dependent, lacking in either courage or individuality. He thought him a coward, and said so. I imagine it was his way of excusing his own failure, in his mind."

"Possibly." Rathbone nodded. "We are, most of us, loath to admit fault in ourselves. Thank you, my lord. That is all I have to ask you. Would you be so good as to remain for my learned friend to speak with you."

Ebenezer Goode was courteous, and at least outwardly genial. He rose to his feet and strolled into the center of the floor, his startling face full of interest.

"All this must be deeply distressing for you, Lord Ravensbrook. It would be for any man. I shall be as brief as I am able." He sighed. "You have painted a vivid picture of two brothers who began with a deep bond between them and grew apart, one favored, obedient, talented; the other rebellious, unconventional, and rightly or wrongly, feeling himself less favored. It was not surprising he should express a resentment and a jealousy." He glanced at the jury with his dazzling, wolfish smile. "Brothers do fight with each other at times. Any family man will tell you that. Yet you say that you never witnessed any of their fights?"

"That is correct." There was no expression on Ravensbrook's face.

"And the resultant injuries, whether from fights or other youthful masculine pursuits," Goode pursued, "such as climbing trees, riding horses and so on, were they serious? For example, were there ever broken bones, concussions, dangerous bleeding?"

"No, merely abrasions and some severe bruising." Ravensbrook remained expressionless, his voice flat.

"Tell me, my lord, did either brother suffer these injuries very much more severely than the other?" Goode inquired.

"No. No, as far as I can remember, they were fairly equally matched."

Goode shrugged. "And nothing was serious, nothing that you would consider a wounding, never intent to maim or permanently to damage?"

"No."

"In other words, much as you or I may well have sustained in our youth?"

"Yes, if you will," Ravensbrook agreed, his voice still without lift or interest, as though the entire subject were tedious.

"So in your knowledge, this regrettable jealousy never resulted in anything more than words?" Goode pressed.

"Not in my knowledge."

Goode gave the court his wide, gleaming smile.

"Thank you, my lord. That is all."

And so the trial progressed, and continued throughout the afternoon and the following day. Rathbone called Arbuthnot, who testified that Angus had come into the offices on the day of his disappearance, that a woman had visited him, after which he had declared that he was going to visit his brother, and expressed his intention to return, at least by the following day.

Ebenezer Goode could not shake him, and did not try.

Next followed a procession of witnesses from Limehouse and the Isle of Dogs, all adding their small pieces to the picture. It built slowly, indistinctly. It was all indicative, nothing conclusive. But the picture was dark, the setting for tragedy, and everyone in the courtroom could feel it like a coldness in the air.

Rathbone was aware at the edge of his mind of Hester sitting next to Enid Ravensbrook, of their faces as they watched the parade of frightened and troubled people one by one adding their few words, their tiny addition of color, to the story, still so full of gaps and shadows. He forced it to the edge of his awareness. Their feelings must not matter. Nor must those of Caleb, now sitting forward in the dock, staring down towards the crowd, although whose face he watched, Rathbone could not know, but his expression was still the same mixture of anger, pain and triumph.

Ebenezer Goode questioned them also, and showed just how fragmentary was their evidence. The picture remained partial, distorted, illusionary. But he could not dispel the ever-growing awareness of hatred, darkness, and the conviction that Angus Stonefield was dead, and by whatever means it was the man in the dock, with his passion of suppressed violence, who had accomplished it.

# CHAPTER
# TEN

———

After he had finished his evidence, Monk left the court. There was nothing he could accomplish there, and his own inner fear drove him to pursue the truth about Drusilla Wyndham. It was no longer a matter of what she could do to ruin his reputation and his livelihood, it was the question within himself as to what manner of man he was that she wished to, even at such a cost to herself.

She had accused him of assaulting her, of trying to force himself upon her. Was it possible that although he had certainly not done so this time, on some occasion in the past he had?

The thought was repulsive to him. He could not imagine any pleasure whatever in taking a woman against her will. It would seem a degrading performance to both parties, devoid of tenderness or dignity and with no communication of the mind, nothing shared beyond the most rudimentary physical contact, and afterwards the shame and the regret, and the sense of futility.

Had he really done such a thing?

Only if he were then a completely different man.

But the fear plagued him, waking him in the night with a choking in the throat and a sudden coldness. Perhaps the fear was as bad as a reality?

On leaving the Old Bailey he went straight to find Evan. He must see the records for himself, even if he had to be smuggled into the police station after hours, as a witness or a suspect, so he could read the files of all his old cases which had ended in the ruin or death of anyone.

Again he had to wait for Evan. He paced back and forth, unable to sit down, his muscles jumping, his mind tormenting him with frustration.

The desk sergeant looked at him with a certain pity.

"Yer look right tore up, Mr. Monk," he observed. "If it's real urgent, like, I can tell yer w'ere Mr. Evan is?"

"I should be most grateful," Monk added. He tried to smile at the man, but he knew it ended as a grimace, his lips pulled over his teeth.

"Twenty-five Great Coram Street, just orff Brunswick Square. Know where that is I 'spec'?"

"Oh, yes." It was opposite Mecklenburg Square, where they had found the body of the man he had so nearly killed before the accident. He could not ever forget that. "Yes, I do, thank you." The man's name flashed into his mind. "Parsons."

The sergeant's face lit with a smile. He had not realized that Monk remembered him.

"Welcome, sir, I'm sure."

Monk raced out and caught a hansom at the end of the street, swinging himself up and shouting the address at the driver as he threw himself into the seat.

He was then obliged to wait standing in the icy wind in Great Coram Street while Evan concluded his business, but when he emerged he saw Monk and recognized him instantly, perhaps because men dressed as he was seldom stood idly on pavements in late February.

"I found it!" he said triumphantly, striding across towards him, hunching his shoulders and pulling his greatcoat collar higher, shivering a little, but his face radiated success.

Monk felt a kind of breathlessness, a hope so painful it almost choked him. He swallowed before he could speak.

"Found it?" He dared not even make it plain he meant the reference to Drusilla, in case it was not. He might have meant merely something concerning his present investigation. It was hard for Monk to remember there were other matters, other crimes, other people's lives.

"Well, I think it is," Evan qualified it very slightly, moving smartly away from the curb as a brougham clattered by. "The name Buckingham is there." He touched Monk on the arm and turned to walk against the wind along Great Coram Street towards the square with its bare trees outlined against the sky. "The reason it took me so long to find," he went on, "was that it wasn't a capital case at all, only an embezzlement, and not of very much."

Monk said nothing. His footsteps rang on the cold stone. It made no sense, at least not so far.

"A Reginald Sallis embezzled some funds from the church," Evan continued the tale. "A matter of about twenty pounds or so, but it was reported to the police and investigated. It was unpleasant, because the money was from an orphans' fund, and suspicion fell on a lot of people before the case was proved."

"But it was proved?" Monk said urgently. "We didn't get the wrong man?"

"Oh no," Evan assured him, keeping pace. "It was definitely the right man. Good family, but a bit of a rake. Apparently very handsome, or at least had a fine way with women."

"What makes you say that?" Monk asked quickly. They had turned into the square and were walking across the grass towards Landsdowne Place and the Foundling Hospital, which lay ahead of them. They must skirt around it to Guildford Street.

"The evidence of his involvement was rather carefully concealed by two young ladies, both of them apparently in love with him," Evan replied. "Or more accurately, one of them felt very deeply, the other, her sister, was merely flirting."

"This doesn't explain anything!" Monk said desperately, brushing past a hussar in uniform. "A romantic rivalry between sisters, a petty embezzlement for which a young rake got . . . what? A year? Five years?"

"Two years," Evan answered, his face suddenly tight and his eyes full of pity. "But he died of gaol fever in Coldbath Fields. He wasn't a particularly pleasant young man, he robbed the charitable funds of the church, but he didn't deserve to die alone in prison for it."

"Was that my fault?" Monk felt the same wrench of pity. He had seen the Coldbath Fields prison and would not have wished it on any living thing. He could remember the cold that ate into the bones, the damp of the walls as if they were forever weeping, the smell of mold and sour places that are never open to the air. One could taste the despair in it. He could close his eyes and see the men, shaven-headed, in the backbreaking exercises of passing the shot, endlessly, pointlessly moving cannon balls from one place to another, around in a ring, or the treadmill, the cages graphically known as the "cock-chafers." The enforced silence beat in his ears, where all human exchange was forbidden.

"Was that my fault?" he demanded again with sudden violence, stopping Evan by grasping his arm so he winced and was forced to swing around to face him.

"It was your doing," Evan said without deviating his gaze at all. "But the man was guilty. The sentence was the judge's to give, not yours. What Drusilla Buckingham could not forgive you for, I should imagine, was that you used her to catch Sallis. You told her he was betraying her with her own sister, Julia. In rage and hurt she gave you what you wanted."

Monk felt the cold bite into the core of his body. He was no longer aware of his feet on the pavement or the carriages coming and going along Guilford Street, the clink of harness.

"And was he?"

"I don't know," Evan answered him. "There's nothing to suggest it."

Monk let out his breath slowly. He hated the misery in Evan's eyes, the refusal to excuse him, but he had no argument. He felt the same revulsion for himself. The man might have been guilty, but why had he pushed the hurt so far? Was it worth using a woman's jealousy to betray her lover to the Coldbath Fields, for a few pounds from the church funds, albeit the poor box?

He wouldn't do it now. He would let it go. The shame would be enough. If the vicar knew, even if Drusilla knew in her heart, was that not all it really needed?

"It's past," Evan said quietly. "You can't undo it. I wish I knew how to stop her now, but I don't."

"I didn't recognize her," Monk said sincerely, as if it meant something. "I spent hours with her, and nothing returned in my memory at all."

Evan started to walk again and Monk kept up with him.

"Nothing!" Monk said desperately.

"It's not so surprising." Evan looked straight ahead of them. "She's changed her name, and it was several years ago. Fashions are different now. I daresay she altered her appearance somewhat. Women can. It was a very trivial offense, to our eyes, but it was a scandal at the time. Sallis was trusted, and the romance came out too. Both girls' reputations were ruined."

All sorts of thoughts boiled up inside Monk, excuses that died before they were formed, self-disgust, remorse, confusion. None of it found easy words, and perhaps they were better unsaid anyway.

"I see." He kept pace with Evan, their footsteps making a single sound on the pavement. "Thank you."

They crossed Guildford Street and turned down Lamb's Conduit Street. Monk had no idea where they were going, he was simply following, but he was glad it was not Mecklenburg Square. He had too many nightmares already.

That evening Drusilla Wyndham, as she was now known, attended a musical soiree at the home of a lady of fashion. She had dressed with great care, to set off her considerable beauty, and she fully expected to create an effect. She swept in, head high, skin glowing with the inner triumph which burned in her mind, the knowledge that the cup of revenge was at her lips, the first taste on her tongue.

And she did create an effect, but it was far from the one she had intended. A gentleman who had always shown her gallantry looked at her with alarm, and then turned his back as if he had suddenly seen someone else he must speak with immediately.

She did not take it seriously, until Sir Percy Gainsborough also effected not to have seen her, when he quite plainly had done.

The Honourable Gerald Hapsgood positively spilled his champagne in his urgency to avoid her, apologized in alarm to the lady next to him, and then in most unbecoming haste, trod on the edge of her gown and only saved his balance by catching hold of Lady Burgoyne.

The Duchess of Granby gave her a stare which would have frozen cream.

Altogether it was a most unpleasant evening, and she went home early, confused and very put out, not having said a word of what she had meant to.

Rathbone entered the courtroom of the Old Bailey for the third day of the trial with little more confidence than he had had in the beginning, but his resolution undiminished. He had hoped the police might find Angus's body, since they had turned their full efforts towards it, but he had always known it was an outside chance. There were so many other possibilities, and Caleb's defiance of Monk in the Greenwich marshes should have warned him. He had said they would never find Angus.

Looking at Caleb as he stood in the dock while the judge entered and took his place at the bench, and the last whispering ceased, Rathbone saw the jeering triumph in him again, the violence so close beneath the surface. Every angle of his body suggested arrogance.

"Are you ready to proceed, Mr. Rathbone?" the judge inquired. Was that a faint shred of pity in his face, as if he believed Rathbone could not win? He was a small man with a lean, weary face, full of lines that had once been pugnacious, but were now too tired for the effort.

"Yes, may it please the court, my lord," Rathbone responded. "I call Albert Swain."

"Albert Swain!" the usher repeated loudly. "Call Albert Swain!"

Swain, large, awkward and mumbling so badly he had to repeat almost everything, told how he had seen Caleb on the day of Angus's disappearance, bruised, his clothes badly torn and stained. Yes, he thought it was blood. Yes, his face was bruised and swollen and his cheek gashed. What other wounds were there? He could not say. He had not looked.

Did Caleb appear to limp, or carry himself as if some limb were paining him?

He did not remember.

Try harder, Rathbone urged.

Yes, Caleb had limped.

Upon which leg?

Swain had no idea. He thought it had been the left. Or the right. Rathbone thanked him.

Ebenezer Goode rose to his feet, toyed with the idea of demolishing the man, and decided it would be impolite. Cruelty seldom paid, and it was against his nature.

And, surprisingly, having made his statement, the witness could not be shifted from it. He had most definitely seen Caleb Stone looking as if he had been in a fight, and that was no mistake. He would not be pushed further. He would not retreat. He drew no conclusions. He was perfectly certain it was the right day. He had earned two shillings, and redeemed his blanket from the pawnbrokers. That was not an event to forget.

He was rewarded by a nod from the judge and a sad pursing of the lips from the foreman of the jury.

"Ah, indeed," Goode conceded. "Thank you, Mr. Swain. That is all."

Rathbone called his final witness, Selina Herries. She came very much against her will and stood in the witness stand clutching the railing, stiff-backed, her head and neck rigid. She was dressed in drab clothes, a plain stuff dress of respectable cut, modest at neck and sleeve, and she had a shawl wrapped around her so that one could only guess at her waist. Her bonnet hid a great deal of her hair. Nevertheless, her face was fully visible, and nothing could detract from the strength and the spirit in the high cheekbones, the bold eyes and generous mouth. In spite of the fact that she was afraid, and desperately unwilling, she stared straight at Rathbone and awaited whatever he should say.

In her seat on the public benches Genevieve turned slowly, reluctantly, and gazed at her. In some faint way this was her mirror image. This was the woman who loved the man who had killed Angus. Their lives were opposite. Genevieve was a widow, but Selina stood on the brink of bereavement too, and perhaps a worse one.

Rathbone, looking from one to the other, could see an uncrossable gulf between them, and yet a spark of the same courage and defiance gave both faces the same fierce warmth.

He could not help also looking at Caleb. Would the sight of Selina waken anything in him of regret, of understanding not only of Genevieve's loss, but of what he too was about to pay in retribution? Was there anything of human passion or need or gentleness in the man?

What he saw as Caleb leaned over the rail, balancing his manacles on the wood, was utter despair, that absolute absence of hope which knows defeat and makes no struggle at all.

Then in the public benches Lord Ravensbrook moved, and Caleb caught sight of him, and the old scalding hatred returned, and with it will to fight.

"Mr. Rathbone?" the judge prompted.

"Yes, my lord." He turned to the witness stand. "Miss Herries," he began, standing in the center of the open space of the floor, his feet a little apart, "you live on Manilla Street, on the Isle of Dogs, is that so?"

"Yes sir." She was not going to commit herself to anything whatsoever that she did not have to.

"Are you acquainted with the accused, Caleb Stone?"

Her eyes did not flicker. Certainly she did not look across at Caleb.

"Yes sir."

"How long have you known him?"

" 'Bout . . ." She hesitated. "Six, seven years, I s'pose." She swallowed nervously and ran her tongue over her lips.

"Six or seven years is quite close enough." Rathbone smiled, trying to reassure her. "Approximately how often do you see him?" Her face clouded and he hastened to help. "Every day? Or once a week, perhaps? Or once a month?"

" 'E comes and goes," she said guardedly. "Sometimes 'e's around fer two or free days, then 'e'll be gorn again. Mebbe gorn for weeks, mebbe back sooner. I'nt reg'lar."

"I see. But over the years, you have come to know him well?"

"Yer could say—"

"Is he your lover, Miss Herries?"

Her eyes slid to Caleb, then away again quickly.

There was no readable expression in his face. A juror frowned. Someone in the crowd sniggered.

"May I rephrase the question?" Rathbone offered. "Are you his woman?"

Caleb grinned, his green eyes bright. It was impossible to read his thoughts, or even whether his tense, almost wolfish expression was amusement or unworded threat.

Selina's chin came up a fraction. She avoided meeting the glance of anyone in the crowd beyond Rathbone.

"Yeah, I am."

"Thank you for your candor, ma'am. I think we may take it that you do know him as well as anyone may be said to?"

"I s'pose." She remained careful.

There was almost silence in the room, but one or two people stirred. This was of little interest. She was acknowledging the obvious.

Rathbone was aware of it. She was his final witness, and his last chance. But for all her fear of the court, she would not willingly betray Caleb. Not only were her emotions involved, and whatever memories she might have of moments of intimacy, but if he were to be found not guilty, then his vengeance would be terrible. Added to that, she lived on the Isle of Dogs; it was her home and they were her people. They would not look with tolerance on a woman who sold out her man, whether for gain or from fear for herself. Whatever price the law exacted for loyalty, the punishment for disloyalty must be worse. It was a matter of survival.

"Have you met his brother Angus as well?" Rathbone asked, his eyebrows raised.

She stared at him as she would a snake.

"Yeah." It was a qualified agreement, made reluctantly. There was warning in her voice that she would go little further.

Rathbone smiled. "Mr. Arbuthnot has testified that you called at his place of business and saw him on the day of his disappearance. Is he correct?"

Her face tightened with anger. There was no way out.

"Yeah . . ."

"Why?"

"Wot?"

"Why?" he repeated. "Why did you call upon Angus Stonefield?"

" 'Cos Caleb told me ter."

"What passed between you?"

"Nuffink!"

"I mean what did you say to him, and he to you?"

"Oh. I don' 'member." It was a lie, and everyone knew it. It was there in the low mumble from the onlookers, the slight shaking of the heads of the jurors, the quick shift of the judge's eyes from Selina to Rathbone.

Selina saw it too, but she assumed she had beaten Rathbone.

Rathbone pushed his hands into his pockets and looked at her blandly.

"Then if I were to say that you gave him a message that Caleb wished to see him urgently, that day, and wished him to go immediately to the Folly House Tavern, or the Artichoke, you would not be able to recall differently?"

"I . . ." Her eyes blazed with defiance, but there was no way out. She was loath to entrap herself by argument, or excuses which might rebound on her again. She had been caught once.

"Perhaps that has stirred your memory?" Rathbone suggested, carefully ironing all the sarcasm out of his voice.

She said nothing, but he had scored the point, and he knew it from the jury's faces. Once she had established that she was prepared to evade, or even lie, to protect Caleb, it would prejudice anything she might say in his defense.

"Did you see Angus Stonefield later that day, Miss Herries?" Rathbone resumed.

She said nothing.

"You must answer the question, Miss Herries," the judge warned. "If you do not, I shall hold you in contempt of court. That means that I can sentence you to prison until such time as you do answer. And of course the jury are free to take any meaning they will from your silence. Do you understand me?"

"I saw 'im," she said huskily, and swallowed hard. She stared straight ahead of her, her head rigid so she could not, even in the corner of her eye, see Caleb leaning over the railing of the dock, his eyes on her.

Rathbone affected interest, as if he had no idea what she was going to say.

Now there was total silence in the room.

"At the Folly House Tavern," she said sullenly.

"What was he doing?"

"Nuffink."

"Nothing?"

" 'E were standin' around, waitin' fer Caleb, I s'pose. That's w'ere I told 'im ter be."

"Did you see Caleb arrive also?"

"No."

"But he told you earlier that he intended to be there?"

"Not that time special. That's where 'e said Angus were to go for 'im always. Same place. I didn't even see 'em together, an' I never saw 'em quarrel, an' that's the truth, whether yer believe me or not!"

"I do believe you, ma'am," Rathbone conceded. "But did you see Caleb later on that day?"

"No, I didn't."

One of the jurors shook his head, another coughed into his handkerchief. There was a rustling in the public benches.

Rathbone turned away from the witness stand, and his glance caught Ebenezer Goode's and saw him smile ruefully. The case still hovered on the knife's edge, but however unwillingly, Selina's evidence might be all it needed to topple it against Caleb. Goode had very little with which to fight, and they both knew it. It would be a desperate gamble to call Caleb himself. Even Goode could not know what he might say. There was a recklessness in the man, a well of emotion too dangerous to tap.

Rathbone turned the full circle before he faced Selina again. His eye caught Hester, near the front of the crowd, and beside her, Enid Ravensbrook, looking pale and tense. Her face was strained with pity and the terrible waiting for the evidence to unfold as they came nearer and nearer to the moment when the hatred and jealousy of years must finally explode in murder. Caleb had already left home when she had married Ravensbrook, but she must still have inherited some feeling for him, sensitive to her husband's long involvement, to all he had given, the years of struggle and finally the failure.

Certainly she knew both Angus and Genevieve, and was only too familiar with their loss.

Milo Ravensbrook sat on the other side of her, his face so pale he seemed bloodless, his dark eyes and level brows like black gashes on gray-white wax. Could a man see a more hideously painful revelation than that one child had killed the other? He would be left with nothing.

And yet from the moment that Angus's bloodstained clothes had been identified, was there anything else they could have done, any other course to follow?

Enid turned to him, her expression a mixture of anguish and almost an expectation of hurt, as if she already knew he would reject such intimacy, yet she could not help offering herself. She put her hand on his arm. Even from where Rathbone stood, he could see how thin her fingers were. It was only three and a half weeks since she had passed the crisis of her illness.

Ravensbrook remained frozen, as if he was not even aware of her.

There was silence in the room.

Rathbone looked again at Selina.

"Miss Herries, when did you see Caleb again? Consider your answer very carefully. An error in judgment now could cost you very dearly."

Ebenezer Goode half rose to his feet, then decided an objection would achieve nothing. The question had been too carefully worded to be considered a threat. He sank back.

In the crowd someone dropped an umbrella, rustled for an instant, then left it where it lay.

"Miss Herries?"

Selina stared at Rathbone and he remained fixed on her gaze, as if he could see into her brain, read her fears and weigh them one against another.

The judge moved his hands, then refolded them.

"Next day," Selina said almost inaudibly.

"Did he mention Angus?"

"No . . ." Her voice was a whisper.

"Will you please speak so we may hear you, Miss Herries?" the judge directed.

"No."

"Not at all?" Rathbone pressed.

"No."

"He didn't say that he had met him?"

"No."

"And you didn't ask?" Rathbone allowed his eyebrows to shoot up. "Did you not care? You surprise me. Was it not the money for the rent of your home which Angus was to bring? Surely that was a matter of the utmost importance to you?"

"I took the message," she said flatly. "Wot else weren't up ter me ter ask."

"And he didn't tell you? Reassure you, for example? How boorish. Perhaps he was in too foul a temper."

This time Ebenezer Goode did rise.

"My lord, my learned friend is making suggestions for which he has had no grounds, and they are the merest speculation. . . ."

"Yes, yes," the judge agreed. "Mr. Rathbone, please do not lead your witness with such remarks. You know better than that. Ask your question and have done."

"My lord. Miss Herries, was Caleb in a bad temper when you saw him again?"

"No."

"Just a little hurt?"

"Hurt?" she said suspiciously.

"Stiff! Bruised?"

"Yeah, well . . ." She hesitated, weighing how far she dare lie. Her glance slid once towards Caleb, then quickly away again. She was frightened, weighing one danger against another.

Rathbone was sorry for her, but he could not relent. There were facets of his professional skills he did not enjoy.

It would be overdoing it to draw the jury's attention to her dilemma. They had seen Caleb's face. They knew her position. Better to allow them to deduce it than to patronize them, risk having them think he was too eager.

"I do not ask you to tell us how he obtained any injuries he may have received, Miss Herries," he helped her. "If you do not know, simply say whether he was injured in any way, or not. You are surely in a circumstance to know. He was your lover."

" 'E were 'urt, yeah," she conceded. "But 'e didn't say 'ow, an I don't ask. There's lot's o' fights in Lime'ouse an' Blackwall. Fights any night, an' most days. Caleb often got 'urt, but 'e never killed no one, far as I know." Her chin came up a fraction. "Not that anyone got the best of 'im neither."

"I can well believe it, ma'am. I have heard suggestions he is a very powerful man with an excellent skill in defending himself, and considerable physical courage."

She stood a little straighter, her head high.

"That's right. No one beats Caleb Stone."

Her pride caught him with a knife stab of pity, and he knew, almost without letting his eyes stray to the jury, that it was also the last fragment needed to tip the thin balance of belief towards conviction.

"Thank you, Miss Herries." He turned to Goode. "Your witness, sir."

Goode rose slowly, as if he were tired, uncurling his long legs. He ambled across the open space of the floor and stopped before the witness stand, looking up at her.

"Ah, Miss Herries. Allow me to ask you a few questions. They will not take long." He smiled at her dazzlingly. From the look in her face she may well have found that more unnerving than Rathbone's elegance. "Nor prove painful," he added.

"Yeah."

"Excellent. I'm most obliged." He tucked his thumbs under the armholes of his waistcoat beneath his gown. "Did Caleb tell you why he was prepared to ask his brother for money, considering the feeling between them? Or indeed, why his brother was willing to give it?"

"No, 'e don't tell me things like that. I'nt my bus'ness. Angus always gave 'im money, if 'e wanted it. Guilt, I reckon."

"Guilt for what, Miss Herries? Was Angus responsible for Caleb's misfortune?"

"I dunno," she said sharply. "Mebbe 'e was! Mebbe 'e poisoned the old man's mind agin' Caleb. 'E were all goody goody. Butter wouldn't melt in 'is mouf. 'Ow do I know what 'e felt? I jus' know 'e came any time Caleb sent for 'im."

"I see. And was Angus at all apprehensive when you gave him Caleb's message?"

"Wot?"

"I apologize. Did he seem to you to be worried or fearful? Was he reluctant to go?"

"No. Well . . . I s'pose 'e didn't want ter leave his bus'ness. But he never did. That ain't 'ard t'understand—'oo'd waana leave a nice warm office uptarn ter go ter some public 'ouse on the Isle of Dogs?"

"No one, indeed," Goode agreed. "But beyond that natural reluctance, he was as usual?"

"Yeah."

"And he had often met with Caleb before?"

"Yeah."

"He did not, for example, offer to give you the money, to save himself the journey to Limehouse, and in fact the necessity to see Caleb at all?"

"No." She did not add anything further, but there was surprise in her face, as well as antagonism.

Goode hesitated, seemed to consider a further question, then discard it.

Rathbone had a sudden flash of intuition as to what it was. He determined to ask it himself on reexamination. Goode had led the way for him.

"And when you saw Caleb the day after?" Goode resumed. "He made no reference to Angus, is that right?"

"Yeah. 'E din't say nuffin' at all abaht 'im." Her face was pale; Rathbone was sure she was lying. He looked across at the jury and saw reflected in their faces exactly what he felt. No one believed her.

"Do you know if he killed his brother, Miss Herries?" Goode's voice cut across the silence.

There was a gasp of indrawn breath around the room.

Caleb let out a short cry of derision, almost like a bark.

"No," Selina said, shaking her head from side to side, as if to be rid of something that caught at her. "No, I don't know nuffin' like that, an' you got no right to say as 'e did!"

"I'm not saying it, Miss Herries," Goode assured her. "I am doing my utmost to persuade these gentlemen here"—he waved his hand in the general direction of the jury—"that there is no proof whatever even that Angus is dead—no absolute proof at all—let alone that they can hold his brother responsible for it! There are a dozen other possibilities as to where Angus Stonefield may be—and why!"

Rathbone stood up.

The judge sighed. "Mr. Goode, this is not the time to address the jury, either directly or indirectly, as you well know. If you have any further questions for this witness, please put them to her. If not, then allow Mr. Rathbone to redirect, if he so chooses."

"Of course." Goode bowed with formal, if rather ostentatious courtesy, and returned to his seat. "Mr. Rathbone."

Rathbone faced Selina. He smiled. "You just confirmed to my learned friend that Caleb had often met with Angus before, and you were aware of this. You also said that on the occasion we are specifically referring to, the last day on which Angus Stonefield was ever seen, that Caleb was not in a temper any different from usual."

"Yeah." She had already admitted as much, and it seemed a favorable thing to acknowledge.

"Yet he sent for his brother, and his brother dropped all his matters of business, and came—to a public tavern on the Isle of

Dogs—so far as you know, simply to pass over money, which since it was for your rent, he could easily have given to you. And as you say, who would willingly leave a warm office in the West End, to—"

The judge did not wait for Goode. "Mr. Rathbone, you are retracing old ground. Please, if you have a point, come to it!"

"Yes, my lord. I do have a point, indeed. Miss Herries, you are telling us that for Caleb to send for his brother, for him to come, and for Caleb to be bruised, stiff, injured, scarred, perhaps bleeding in places, but nonetheless jubilant, having won a fight, was a perfectly normal pattern of behavior for him. And you have also said no one beats Caleb Stone. That 'no one' must include his unfortunate brother, who has not been seen since! Only his bloodstained clothes have been found on the Isle of Dogs!"

Selina said nothing. Her face was as white as the paper on which the court clerk wrote.

In the dock Caleb Stone started to laugh, wildly. It soared in pitch and volume until it seemed to fill the room and reverberate from the wooden paneling.

The judge banged his gavel and was ignored—it was no more than an instrument beating time to the uproar. He demanded silence, and no one even heard him. Caleb's hysterical laughter drowned out everything else. The gaolers grabbed at him, and he flung them off.

In the gallery journalists scrambled over each other to get out and grab the first hansom to race to Fleet Street and the extra editions.

Enid rose to her feet amid the clamor, looking one way, then the other. She tried to speak to Ravensbrook, but he ignored her, staring at the dock as if transfixed. He did not seem to see what was in front of him, the frenzy and the farce, only some terrible truth within him.

The judge was still banging his gavel, a sharp, thin, rhythmic sound without meaning.

Rathbone waved his hands to indicate that Selina Herries might be excused. She swiveled around and descended the steps to the floor, her head always turned towards Caleb.

Finally the gaolers overpowered him and he was led down. Some semblance of order was restored.

Red-faced, the judge adjourned the court.

Outside in the corridor Rathbone, considerably shaken, ran into Ebenezer Goode, looking shocked and unhappy.

"Didn't think you could do it, my dear fellow," he said with a sigh. "But from the jury's faces, I would wager now that you'll get a conviction. Never had a client been so hell-bent on his own destruction."

Rathbone smiled, but it was a gesture of amiability, not of any pleasure. His victory would bring a professional satisfaction, but it was curiously devoid of personal triumph. He had thought Caleb Stone totally despicable. Now his feelings were less clear. The force of his instability, the awareness of his emotions in the room, even though he had not yet spoken, became tangled in his judgments, and he found himself awaiting his testimony with far less certainty of the outcome than Goode.

Lord and Lady Ravensbrook were standing a few yards from them. She looked ashen, but determined not to give way. She was supported by her husband. Hester must have been temporarily dismissed, perhaps to summon the carriage.

Ravensbrook did not hesitate to interrupt.

"Goode! I must speak with you."

Goode turned politely, and then he saw Enid. His expression altered instantly to one of amazement and concern. Apparently he had not met her, but he surmised who she was.

"My dear lady, you must still be far from recovered. Please permit me to find you some more comfortable place to wait."

Ravensbrook recognized his own omission with a flicker of anger, and introduced them hastily. Goode bowed, not taking his eyes from Enid's face. In the circumstances the quality of his attention was a compliment, and she smiled, in spite of herself.

"Thank you, Mr. Goode. I think I shall wait in my carriage. I am sure Miss Latterly will return in a few moments, and I shall be quite all right until then. It is very kind of you to think of it."

"Not at all," he assured her. "We cannot permit you to stand, even until your carriage should come. I shall fetch a chair." And so saying, he ignored Ravensbrook and Rathbone, marched some ten yards away, and returned carrying a large wooden chair, which he placed near the wall, and assisted Enid into it.

The matter dealt with, Ravensbrook turned to Goode again, ignoring Rathbone, although he cannot have failed to know who he was.

"Is there any hope?" he said bluntly. His face was still stiff and blurred with shock.

Rathbone moved a step away, in courtesy, although he was not beyond earshot.

"Of finding the truth?" Goode raised his eyebrows. "I doubt it, my lord. Certainly not of proving it. I daresay what happened to Angus will always be a matter of surmise. If you mean what will the verdict be, at present I think a conviction of some sort is not unlikely, although whether it will be murder or manslaughter I would not venture to say." He took a deep breath. "We must first hear Caleb's story. That may now be different from earlier. He has heard evidence which may prompt him to speak more openly of the meeting with his brother."

"You intend to call him?" Ravensbrook's body was rigid, his skin like paper. "Do you not fear he will damn himself out of his own mouth, if he has not already done so? I ask you in compassion not to. If you leave it as it is, plead a quarrel which got out of hand, on his behalf, then the jury may return manslaughter, or even less, perhaps only the conceding of a death." Hope flickered boldly in his dark eyes. "That would surely be in the best interests of your client. He is quite apparently insane. Perhaps the only place for him is Bedlam."

Goode considered it for several moments. "Possibly," he conceded, pulling down his brows, his voice very quiet. "But the jury is not well disposed towards him. His own behavior has seen to that. Bedlam is not a place I would send a dog. I think I must give him the opportunity to tell the story himself. There is always far less likelihood of the jury believing it if he will not tell it himself."

"Rathbone will destroy him!" Ravensbrook accused in a sudden flair of temper. "He will lose control of himself again if he is pressed, and he is frightened. Then he'll say anything, simply to shock."

"I will make the judgment when I have spoken with him," Goode promised. "Although I am inclined to agree with you."

"Thank God!"

"Of course it is his decision," Goode added. "The man is being tried for his life. If he wishes to speak, then he must be allowed."

"Cannot you, as his legal adviser, protect him from himself?" Ravensbrook demanded.

"I can advise him, that is all. I cannot deny him the opportunity to speak in his own defense."

"I see." Ravensbrook glanced at Rathbone's profile. "Then I think he has very little chance. Since I am his only living relative, and once he is convicted I may have no further opportunity to speak with him, I would like to see him, alone. Today, at least, he is still an innocent man."

"Of course," Goode agreed quickly. "Would you like me to arrange it for you?"

"I shall seek your help if it is necessary," Ravensbrook answered. "I am obliged for your offer." He glanced at Rathbone, then at Enid on her chair.

She looked at him in a long, curious, pleading gaze, as if there were a question she did not know how to frame.

If he understood, there was no reflection of it in his expression or in his bearing. He did not offer any further explanation.

"Wait for me in the carriage," he told her. "You will be more comfortable there. Miss Latterly will be back in a few moments."

And without anything further, he took his leave, walking rapidly towards the stairs down to the cells.

Some twenty minutes later Rathbone was outside on the entrance steps to the street, talking to Monk, who had just arrived. Ebenezer Goode came striding down, his hair flying, his face ashen. He pushed past a clerk, almost knocking the man off his feet.

"What is it?" Rathbone said with a sudden upsurge of fear. "What's happened, man? You look terrible!"

Goode seized him by the arm, half turning him around.

"He's dead! It's all over. He's dead!"

"Who's dead?" Monk demanded. "What are you talking about?"

"Caleb," his voice was hoarse. "Caleb is dead."

"He can't be!" Rathbone knew even as he said it that it was stupid. He was trying to deny reality, because it was ugly and he did not want to believe it.

"How?" Monk asked, cutting across Rathbone. "What happened? Did he kill himself?" He swore viciously, clenching his fist in the air. "How could they be so damnably stupid? Although I don't know why I care! Better the poor devil does it himself than drag it out to the long torture of a judicial hanging. I should be glad." He said the words between his teeth, hard and gutteral. "Why can't I be?"

Rathbone looked from Monk to Goode. The same conflicting emotions tore inside him. He should have been grateful. Caleb had in effect confessed. Rathbone had succeeded. The Duke of Wellington's words rang in his ears about the next most terrible thing to a battle lost being a battle won. There was no taste of victory whatever.

"It wasn't suicide," Goode said shakily. "Ravensbrook went in to see him, as he asked. Apparently Caleb was concerned he was going to be found guilty. He said he wanted to write a statement. Perhaps it was a confession, or an indication of something, who knows? Ravensbrook came out for a quill and a paper for him. He took them back in. Apparently the quill was poor. He found his penknife to re-cut it . . ."

Rathbone felt sick, as if he knew the words before they came.

"Caleb suddenly lurched forward, seized the knife, and attacked Ravensbrook," Goode said, his eyes going from Rathbone to Monk, and back again.

Rathbone was startled. It was not what he had thought after all.

"They fought," Goode went on. "Poor Ravensbrook is cut quite badly."

"God help him," Rathbone said quietly. "That was not the ending I wanted, but perhaps it is not the worst. Thank you, Goode. Thank you for telling me."

# CHAPTER
# ELEVEN

———

Rathbone was stunned by the news. It was preposterous, even if not all the elements were tragic. He had never known such a thing to happen before, certainly not in this manner.

Monk was standing stock-still, his face dark.

"Come on," Rathbone said gently. "It's all over."

Monk did not move. "No it isn't. I don't understand it."

Rathbone laughed abruptly. "Do you ever? Do any of us? If you thought he was going to tell you what he did with Angus, or why he killed him now, instead of sometime in the past years, you were dreaming. The wretched man was mad. Dear God, wasn't that evidence enough? Jealousy had driven him insane. What more is there to understand?"

"Why he attacked Ravensbrook now," Monk replied, turning and standing to climb the steps back up. "What good would it have done him?"

"None at all!" Rathbone said impatiently, following rapidly after him. "What good did killing Angus do him? Nothing except release his hatred. Perhaps he felt the same way about Ravensbrook. He had nothing to lose. Can't hang him twice."

"But they weren't necessarily going to hang him at all!" Monk said sharply, striding through the door and into the hallway. "Goode hadn't even begun. He's a damned clever lawyer." They passed a group of dark-suited men talking quietly, and almost bumped into a clerk hurrying in the opposite direction. "We know Caleb killed Angus," Monk went on. "Or at least I do . . . because I heard him admit it, even boast about it. But that's not proof. He still had hope."

"Maybe he didn't know that. I'm a damned clever lawyer too!" Rathbone said at his elbow.

"Is this what you wanted?" Monk demanded, matching Rathbone pace for pace along the corridor, coattails flying. "Can't prove he was guilty, so deceive the poor devil into committing another murder, right there in his cell, so we can hang him for that, without a quibble? Even Ebenezer Goode couldn't defend him from that!"

It was on the edge of Rathbone's tongue to give back an equally bitter response, then he looked more closely at Monk, the confusion in his face. It was not all anger. There was doubt and pain in it as well.

"What?" he demanded, swinging to a stop.

"Are you deaf? I said—" Monk began.

"I heard what you said!" Rathbone snapped. "It was sufficiently stupid—I shall ignore it. I am trying to fathom what you meant. Something puzzles you, something more than simply the questions we were asking before, and now we shall almost certainly never answer."

"Ravensbrook said Caleb attacked him." Monk began walking again. "And he fought him off. In the struggle Caleb was killed . . . accidentally."

"I heard it," Rathbone agreed, going down the steps towards the cells. "Why? What are you thinking? That it was actually suicide, and Ravensbrook is covering it up? Why?" They were obliged to walk in single file for some distance, then at the bottom Monk caught up again. "It makes no sense," Rathbone went on. "What reason could he have? The wretched man is dead, and guilty by implication, if not proof. What would he be saving him? Or anyone?"

"Legally he's innocent," Monk said with a scowl. "Not yet proven guilty, whatever we know, you and I. We don't count."

"For God's sake, Monk, the public knows. And as soon as the

court reconvenes, they'll have him for trying to kill Ravensbrook as well."

"But as a suicide he'd be buried in unhallowed ground," Monk pointed out. They were just outside the main door to the cells. "This way he's not convicted of anything, only charged. People can believe whatever they want. He'll go down in posterity as an innocent man."

"I should think if it's a lie at all," Rathbone argued, "it is more likely Ravensbrook doesn't want to be accused of deliberately allowing the man to take his own life, morally at any time, legally while he's in custody and on trial."

"Point," Monk conceded.

"Thank you," Rathbone acknowledged. "I think it is most probable he is simply giving a mixture of what he knows in the confusion, and what he hopes happened. He is bound to be very shocked, and grieved, poor devil."

Monk did not reply, but knocked sharply on the door.

They were permitted in with some reluctance. Rathbone had to insist in his capacity as an officer of the court, and Monk was permitted largely by instinct of the gaoler, who knew him from the past, and was used to obeying him.

It was a small anteroom for the duty gaolers to wait. Ravensbrook was half collapsed on a wooden hard-backed chair. His hair and clothes were disheveled and there was blood splattered on his arms and chest, even on his face. He seemed in the deepest stages of shock, his eyes sunk in their sockets, unfocused. He was breathing through his mouth, gasping and occasionally swallowing and gulping air. His body was rigid and he trembled as if perished with cold.

One gaoler stood holding a rolled-up handkerchief to a wound in Ravensbrook's chest, a second held a glass of water and tried to persuade him to drink from it, but he seemed not even to hear the man.

"Are you the doctor?" the gaoler with the handkerchief demanded, looking at Monk. In his gown and wig, Rathbone was instantly recognizable for what he was.

"No. But there's probably a nurse still on the premises, if you send someone to look for her immediately," Monk replied. "Her name is Hester Latterly, and she'll be with Lady Ravensbrook in her carriage."

"Nurse'll be no use," the gaoler said desperately. "Nobody about needs nursin', for Gawd's sake. Look at it!"

"An army nurse," Monk corrected his impression. "You might have to go a mile or more to find a doctor. And she'll be more used to this sort of thing than most doctors around here anyway. Go and get her. Don't stand around arguing."

The man went, perhaps glad to escape.

Monk turned to look at Ravensbrook, studied his face for a moment, then abandoned the idea and spoke instead to the remaining gaoler.

"What happened?" he asked. "Tell us precisely, and in exact order as you remember it. Start when Lord Ravensbrook arrived."

He did not question who Monk was, or what authority he had to be demanding explanations. The tone in Monk's voice was sufficient, and the gaoler was overwhelmingly relieved to hand over responsibility to someone else, anyone at all.

" 'Is lordship came in wi' permission from the 'ead warder for 'im ter visit wi' the prisoner," he responded. " 'Im bein' a relative, like, an' the prisoner lookin' fit ter be sent down, then like as not, topped."

"Where is the head warder?" Rathbone interrupted.

"Goin' ter speak wi' the judge," the gaoler replied. "Dunno wot 'appens next. Never 'ad no one killed in the middle o' a trial afore, leastways not while I were 'ere." He shivered. He had taken the glass of water, theoretically for Ravensbrook, and it slurped at the edges as his hand shook.

Rathbone took it from him and set it down.

"So you opened the cell and allowed Lord Ravensbrook in?" Monk prompted.

"Yes, sir. An' o' course I locked it be'ind 'im, the prisoner bein' charged wi' a violent crime, like, it were necessary."

"Of course it was," Monk agreed. "Then what happened?"

"Nuffink, for 'bout five minutes or so."

"You waited out here?"

"O' course."

"And after five minutes?"

" 'Is lordship, Lord Ravensbrook, 'e knocked on the door an' asked ter come out. I thought it was kind o' quick, but it in't none o' my business. So I let 'im aht. But 'e weren't through." He was still holding the rolled-up handkerchief at Ravensbrook's chest, and the blood was seeping through his fingers. " 'E said as the prisoner wanted ter write 'is last statement an' 'ad I any paper and a pen an' ink," he went on, his voice hoarse. "Well, o' course I don't 'ave it in me pocket, like, but I told 'im as I could send for 'em, which I did. I'nt that right, me lord?" He looked down at Ravensbrook for confirmation, but Ravensbrook seemed almost unaware of him.

"You sent for them. Who did you send?" Monk pressed.

"Jimson, the other bloke on watch wi' me. The feller wot yer sent for the nurse."

"And you locked the cell door?"

"O' course I locked it." There was indignation in his voice.

"And Lord Ravensbrook waited out here with you?"

"Yeah, yeah 'e did."

"Did he say anything?"

Ravensbrook neither moved on his chair nor made any sound.

"Wot, ter me?" the gaoler said with surprise. "Wot would a lord-ship talk ter the likes o' me abaht?"

"You waited in silence?" Monk asked.

"Yeah. Weren't long, three or four minutes, then Jimson came back wi' pen an' paper an' ink. I gave 'em ter 'is lordship, opened the cell door again, and 'e went in, an' I locked it."

"And then?"

The man screwed up his face in concentration. "I'm trying ter think as if I 'eard anythink, but I can't recall as I did. I should 'ave . . ."

"Why?"

"Well, there must 'a bin summink, mustn't there?" he said reasonably. " 'Cos arter a few minutes like, 'is lordship banged on the door an' shouted fer 'elp, shouted real loud, like 'e were in terrible trouble—which o' course 'e were." He took a deep breath, still staring at Monk. "So me an' Jimson, we both went to the door, immediate like. Jimson unlocked it, an' I stood ready, not knowin' what ter expec'."

"And what did you find?"

He looked over towards the cell door about ten feet away, and still very slightly ajar.

" 'Is lordship staggerin' an' beatin' on the doors wi' 'is fists," he answered, his voice strained. "An' 'e were all covered in blood, like 'e is now." He glanced at Ravensbrook, then away again. "The prisoner were in an 'eap on the floor, wi' even more blood on 'im. I can't remember wot I said, nor wot Jimson said neither. 'E 'elped 'is lordship out, an' I went ter the prisoner." He kept his eyes fixed on Monk's face, as if to block out what was in his mind. "I knelt down by 'im an' reached for 'is 'and, like, ter see if 'e were alive. I couldn't feel nothin'. Although ter be 'onest wif yer, sir, I dunno as 'ow I weren't shakin' so much I wouldn't a' knowed anyway. But I think 'e were dead already. I never seen so much blood in me life."

"I see." Monk's eye strayed involuntarily towards the half-open cell door. He forced his attention back to the man in front of him. "And then what?"

The gaoler looked at Ravensbrook, but Ravensbrook gave him no prompt whatsoever; in fact, from the fixed expression on his face, he might not even have heard what they said.

"We asked 'is lordship what 'ad 'appened," the gaoler said unhappily. "Although anyone could see as there'd bin a terrible fight, an' some'ow the prisoner'd got the worst o' it."

"And when you asked Lord Ravensbrook, what did he say?"

" 'E said as the prisoner'd leaped on 'im and attacked 'im when 'e 'ad the penknife out ter recut the nib, and 'though 'e'd done 'is best ter fight 'im off, in the struggle, 'e'd got 'isself stabbed, an' it were all over in a matter o' seconds. Caught the vein in 'is throat and whoosh! Gorn." He swallowed hard, his concentration on Monk intense. "Don' get me wrong, sir, I wouldn't never 'ave had it 'appen, but maybe there's some justice in it. Don't deserve ter get away wi' murderin' 'is bruvver, like. No one do. But I 'ates an 'anging. Jimson says as I'm soft, but it in't the way for no man ter go."

"Thank you." Monk did not volunteer an opinion, but a certain sense of his agreement was in his silence, and the absence of censure in his voice.

At last Monk turned to Ravensbrook and spoke clearly and with emphasis.

"Lord Ravensbrook, will you please tell us exactly what happened? It is most important, sir."

Ravensbrook looked up very slowly, focusing on Monk with difficulty, like a man wakening from a deep sleep.

"I beg your pardon?"

Monk repeated his words.

"Oh. Yes. Of course." He drew in his breath and let it out silently. "I'm sorry." For several more seconds he said nothing, until Rathbone was about to prompt him. Then at last he spoke. "He was in a very strange mood," he said slowly, speaking as if his lips were stiff, his tongue unwilling to obey him. His voice was curiously flat. Rathbone had seen it before in people suffering shock. "At first he seemed pleased to see me," Ravensbrook went on. "Almost relieved. We spoke about trivialities for a few minutes. I asked him if he needed anything, if there was anything I could do for him." He swallowed, and Rathbone could see his throat tighten.

"Straightaway he said that there was." Ravensbrook was speaking to Monk, ignoring Rathbone. "He wanted to write a statement. I thought perhaps he was going to make a clean breast of it, some kind of confession, for Genevieve's sake. Tell her where Angus's body was." He was not looking directly at Monk, but at some distance of the mind, some region of thought or hope.

"And was that what he wanted?" Rathbone asked, although he held no belief that it could have been. It was only a last, wild chance that he might have said something. But what could it matter, except that Genevieve would have some clearer idea. And was that good or bad? Perhaps ignorance was more merciful.

Ravensbrook looked at him for the first time.

"No . . ." he said thoughtfully. "No, I don't think he even intended to write anything. But I believed him. I came out and asked for the materials, which were brought me. I took them back in. He grasped the pen from me, put it in the inkwell, which I had placed on the table, then made an attempt to write. I think he forced it. Then he looked up at me and said the nib was blunt and had divided, would I recut it." He moved his shoulders very slightly, not quite a shrug. "Of course I agreed. He gave it to me. I wiped it clean so I could see what I was doing, and then I took out my knife, opened it . . ."

No one in the room moved. The gaoler seemed mesmerized. There was no sound of the outer world, the courthouse beyond the heavy, iron door.

Ravensbrook looked back at Monk again, his eyes dark and full of nightmare. Then, almost as if closing curtains within his mind, he looked just beyond him. His voice was a little high-pitched, as if he could not open his throat. "The next moment I felt a ringing blow, and I was forced back against the wall, and Caleb was on top of me." He took a deep breath. "We struggled for several moments. I did all I could to free myself, but he had an extraordinary strength. He seemed determined to kill me, and it was all I could do to force the knife away from my throat. I made a tremendous effort, I suppose seeing the nearness of death in the blade. I don't know exactly how it occurred. He jerked back, slipped, and missed his footing somehow, and fell, pulling me on top of him."

Rathbone tried to visualize it, the fear, the violence, the confusion. It was not difficult.

"When I freed myself and managed to rise to my feet," Ravensbrook went on, "he was lying there with the knife in his throat and blood pouring from the wound. There was nothing I could do. God help him. At least he is at some sort of peace now. He'll be spared the . . ." He took another long, deep breath and let it out in a sigh. "The judicial . . . process."

Rathbone glanced at Monk, and saw the same look of distress in his face, and also the knowledge that there was no retreat or evasion possible.

"Thank you," Monk acknowledged Ravensbrook, then with Rathbone behind him, walked over and pushed the cell door wider and went inside. Caleb Stone was lying on the floor in a sheet of blood. It lay in a scarlet tide around his head and shoulders. The penknife, a beautiful silver engraved thing, was lying upside down against his neck, as if it had fallen out of the wound with its own weight. There was no question that he was dead. The beautiful green eyes were open, and quite blind. There was in his face a look of resignation, as if he had at last let go of something which was both a possession and a torture, and the ease of it had surprised him.

Monk looked for something to tell him some fact beyond that which Ravensbrook or the gaoler had said, and saw nothing. There were no contradictions, no suggestions of anything additional, anything unexplained by the account of a simple, stupid piece of violence. The only question was had he been impulsive, in a sudden overwhelming rage, perhaps like the rage that had killed Angus, or had it been a deliberately planned way of committing suicide before the hangman could take his life in the slow, exquisite mind-torture of conviction, sentence and hanging?

He turned to Rathbone, and saw an understanding of the same question in his face.

Before either of them could form it in words there was a noise behind them, the heavy clank of an iron bolt in a lock, and then

Hester's voice. Monk swung around and came out of the cell, almost pushing Rathbone forward into the outer room.

"Lord Ravensbrook!" Hester glanced once at the gaoler, still holding the blood-soaked handkerchief against Ravensbrook's chest, then moved forward and dropped to her knees. "Where are you hurt?" she said, as if he had been a child—quite soothingly, but with the voice of authority.

He raised his head and stared at her.

"Where are you hurt?" she repeated, putting her hand gently over the gaoler's and moving the kerchief away very slowly. No gush of blood followed it; in fact, it seemed to have clotted and dried already. "Please, allow me to take your coat off," she asked. "I must see if you are still bleeding." It seemed an unnecessary comment. There was so much blood he must still be losing it at a considerable rate.

"Should you, miss?" Jimson asked. He had returned with her and was staring at Ravensbrook dubiously. "Might make it worse. Better wait till the doctor gets 'ere. 'E's bin sent fer."

"Take if off!" Hester ignored Jimson, and started to pull on Ravensbrook's shoulders to ease the jacket away from him. He did nothing, and she moved his arm aside from where he had been holding it across his chest. "Take the other one!" she ordered Monk. "It will slip away if you hold it properly."

He did as he was bid, and gently she pulled the coat off, leaving it in Monk's hands. The shirt beneath was surprisingly white and not nearly as badly stained as Monk had expected. Indeed, there were only four marks that he could see, one on the front of the left shoulder, one on the left forearm, and two on the right side of the chest. None of them were bright scarlet or puddled in blood. Only the one on the shoulder that he had been holding was still shining wet.

"Doesn't look too bad," Hester said dispassionately. She turned to the first gaoler. "I don't suppose you have any bandages? No, I thought not. Have you cloths of any sort?"

The man hesitated.

"Right," she nodded. "Then take off your shirt. It will have to do.

I'll use the tails." She smiled very dryly. "And yours too, Mr. Rathbone, I think. I need a white one." She ignored Monk, and his immaculate linen. Even in this contingency she was apparently aware of his finances.

Rathbone drew in a sharp breath, and thoughts of voluminous petticoats floated into his mind, and out again. He obeyed.

"Have you any spirits?" she asked the gaoler. "A little brandy for restorative purposes, perhaps?" She looked at Ravensbrook. "Have you a hip flask, my lord?"

"I don't require brandy," he said with a very slight shake of the head. "Just do what is necessary, woman."

"I wasn't going to give it to you," she answered. "Have you any?"

He stared at her with seeming incomprehension.

"Yer feelin' faint, miss?" the gaoler said with concern.

The shadow of a smile touched her lips. "No thank you. I wanted to clean the wounds. Water will do if that's all there is, but brandy would have been better."

Rathbone passed her the glass of water Ravensbrook had declined. Monk moved forward and fished in Ravensbrook's jacket and found the flat, silver engraved flask, opened it and set it where she could reach it.

In silence they watched her work, cleaning away the blood first with cloths from the gaoler's coarse shirt, then with a little brandy, which must have stung when it was applied, from the involuntary oath escaping Ravensbrook, and the clenched teeth and gulp of pain.

But even Monk could see that the wounds were not deep, more gashes and cuts than genuine stabs.

She then bound them with bandages made from almost all of Rathbone's fine Egyptian cotton shirt, which she tore with great abandon and considerable dexterity, and, Monk thought, not a little satisfaction. He glanced at Rathbone and saw him wince as the cloth ripped.

"Thank you," Ravensbrook said stiffly when she was finished. "I am obliged to you again, Miss Latterly. You are extremely efficient. Where is my wife?"

"In your carriage, my lord," she replied. "I daresay she will be at home by now. I took the liberty of instructing the coachman to take her. She may become ill if she sits waiting in this chill. I am sure someone will find you a hansom immediately."

"Yes," he said after a moment. "Of course." He looked at Rathbone. "If you need me for anything, I can be found at my home. I cannot think what else there is to do now, or to say. I assume the judge will make whatever remarks he believes necessary, and that will be an end to it. Good day, gentlemen." He stood up and, walking very uprightly and with a slight sway, made his way to the door. "Oh." He turned and looked at Rathbone. "I presume I may have the liberty of giving him a decent burial? After all, he has not been found guilty of anything, and I am his only relative." He swallowed painfully.

"I can see no reason why not," Rathbone agreed, suddenly touched by a sense of overwhelming loss, deeper than mere death, a bereavement of the spirit, of the past as well as the future. "I will attend to the formalities, my lord, if you wish?"

"Yes. Yes, thank you," Ravensbrook accepted. "Good day." And he went out of the door. Now no longer locked, it swung to heavily behind him.

Hester looked towards the cell.

"You don't need to," Rathbone stepped in front of her. "It's most unpleasant."

"Thank you, Oliver, for your sensitivity," she said bleakly. "But I have seen far more dead men than you have. I shall be quite all right." And she walked in, brushing his shoulder. He had replaced his jacket and it looked odd with no shirt beneath.

Inside she stood still and looked down at the crumpled form of Caleb Stone. She stared at him for several seconds before she frowned a little, then with a deep sigh, straightened up and came out again. Her eyes met Rathbone's.

"What are you going to do?" she asked quietly.

"Go home and get a shirt," he replied with a twisted smile. "There isn't anything else we can do, my dear. There's no case to prosecute or defend anymore. If Mrs. Stonefield wishes me to act for her in the matter of formally acknowledging her husband's death, then of course I will do so. First we must deal with this matter, which I imagine the judge will do when court reconvenes tomorrow morning."

"Is there something which worries you?" Monk said suddenly, looking at her closely. "What is it?"

"I . . . I don't think I am quite certain . . ." She frowned in concentration, but seemed unwilling to add more.

"Then come to my house and dine," Rathbone invited her, and included Monk with a gesture. "That is, if you do not have to return with Lady Ravensbrook, or go back to Limehouse?"

"No." She shook her head. "The typhoid is past its worst. In fact, there have been no new cases for over two days, and many of those who are left are beginning to recover. I . . . I would like to think further on Caleb Stone."

Before even considering it they ate a surprisingly good meal. Rathbone's house was warm and quiet, furnished in the discreet fashion of half a century earlier, the excellent chair lines of the Regency. It made for comfort and a sense of space.

Hester had not thought she would wish to eat at all, but when the meal was placed before her, and she had not had to take any part in its preparation, she found that she was, after all, quite hungry.

When the last course was completed Rathbone sat back and looked across at her.

"Well, what is it that worries you? Are you afraid it was suicide? And if it was, does it really matter? Who would it help to prove it, even if we could?"

"Why would he commit suicide now?" she asked, fumbling

through the ideas jumbled in her mind, the memory of the words she had seen and the small, very sharp knife, almost like a scalpel, lying with the very end of its blade in Caleb's neck and its silver handle in the sheet of blood beside him. "His defense had not even begun!"

"Perhaps he had no hope it could succeed?" Monk suggested.

"You don't believe that," Rathbone said instantly. "Could he have killed himself in remorse? Perhaps hearing the evidence somehow brought it back to him. Or more likely it was seeing Ravensbrook, and knowing the grief it had brought him, and of course Genevieve."

"Genevieve?" Monk's eyebrows rose. "He loathed her. She was part of all that he despised in Angus: the comfortable, pious wife with her smiling, complacent face and her total ignorance of the tragedy and reality of the kind of life he led, the poverty and the hardship and the dirt."

"You don't know anything about Genevieve, do you?" Hester looked from one to the other of them, and saw the blank incomprehension in their faces. "No, of course you don't. She grew up in Limehouse. . . ."

Rathbone was astonished. He sat quite still, except for a slight parting of his lips.

Monk, on the other hand, gave a snort of disbelief and moved his hand sharply to dismiss the idea as preposterous, knocking his elbow against his empty wineglass and clinking it against its neighbor.

"Yes, she did!" Hester said sharply. "I've just spent nearly a month in Limehouse, and I know the people she grew up with. They remember her. Her name used to be Ginny Motson."

Monk looked astonished. His face was almost expressionless with surprise.

"I assume you wouldn't say that unless you were sure beyond question?" Rathbone said gravely. "This is not gossip, is it?"

"No, of course it isn't," Hester answered, the scene over the mistake clear in her mind. "She told me herself, when she realized I had guessed."

They sat silently for several minutes, turning over those new and amazing thoughts. The butler came in and removed the last of the dishes and brought the port, offering it to Monk and Rathbone. He bowed civilly to Hester, but disregarded her otherwise. She puzzled him, and his uncertainty showed in his face.

"It would explain a number of things," Monk conceded at last. "Her dread of poverty, above all. No woman who had not known it should fear it as she does. I thought it was simple love of comfort. I'm glad it isn't."

Hester smiled. She knew Monk's vulnerability where certain women were concerned. He had been a startlingly poor judge of character before, but she did not refer to that. It was a precisely delicate subject just now.

"Then was it Angus, or perhaps Caleb, who taught her to carry herself like a lady, and speak like one?" Rathbone mused. "If it were Caleb, then that may have been the catalyst which turned his rivalry with Angus into hatred. She met Angus when he came to see Caleb, and perhaps she fell in love with him, or less attractively, saw a chance to get out of the poverty and squalor of Limehouse into something far better, and she took it."

"And you think Caleb might have loved her?" Hester said, raising her eyebrows. "So much that after he had killed Angus, for having taken her away from him, he now felt such remorse, on looking at her face in the courtroom, that he killed himself halfway through the trial? And Lord Ravensbrook allowed him to, and is prepared to conceal it? No." She shook her head sharply. "She told me she was never Caleb's woman, and I believe her. She had no reason to lie, and I don't think she did. Anyway, it makes no sense. If what you are saying were true, he would have written whatever it was he sent for the paper and ink to say. Unless, of course you think Lord Ravensbrook took it? But why would he?"

Rathbone regarded his port, shining ruby red in the candlelight, but did not touch it.

"You're right," he conceded. "It doesn't make sense."

"And I don't see Caleb Stone taking his own life out of remorse, honestly," Monk added. "There was more than hatred in him. I don't know what, a terrible emotion that clawed at his heart or his belly, or both, but there was a wild humor in it, a kind of pain that was far subtler than remorse. And does it matter now?" He looked from one to the other of them, but the shadow in his eyes and the sense of un-happiness in him answered the question more vividly than words could have done.

No one bothered to affirm it. It was tangible in the air, the quiet candlelight of the dinner table gleaming on unused silver and wink-ing in the blood-red colors of the untouched port glasses.

"If it was not suicide, then either it was accident or murder," Rathbone stated. He looked at Hester. "Was it exactly as Ravens-brook said?"

"No." She was quite positive. "It may have been an accident, but if it was as he said, then why didn't he cry out when Caleb first at-tacked him?"

"He didn't," Rathbone said slowly. "He can't have. And accord-ing to his own account, he struggled with him for several moments, seconds perhaps, but there was obviously a struggle."

"In which Lord Ravensbrook tried to save himself from injury," Monk took up the thread. "And was in principle, successful. His wounds are minor. But Caleb was killed, by a freak mischance." He pulled a face.

"If Caleb attacked him, why did he not cry out straightaway?" Hester asked.

"I don't know. In some desperate hope of ending the matter without the gaolers needing to know?" Rathbone suggested. "It could be damning evidence if it were revealed in court, and even if no one introduced it, Ravensbrook's injuries would allow the conclusion eas-ily enough."

"Irrational, in the circumstances," Monk argued.

"People frequently are irrational," Hester said. "But I don't think they work out a chain of thought as complicated as that in the heat of an unexpected attack. Would you, if you were leapt upon when you least thought of such a thing? Would you think of anything more than defending yourself? If there were a weapon involved, and the attacker were younger and stronger than you, and you knew he had already killed one man, and was in danger of being hanged, so he had nothing to lose, even if he were caught, would you even think at all, or just fight for your life?"

Rathbone bit his lip. "If Caleb Stone attacked me, there'd be nothing in my mind but surviving," he admitted. His face twisted. "But I am not his father. . . ."

Monk shrugged, but there was a tightness of wounded enthusiasm in his eyes. "When I was chasing him down the river, I didn't think at all. There was nothing in my mind but a blind determination to catch him. I hardly even felt my own wrenches and bruises until afterwards."

Rathbone looked at Hester. "Are you sure he didn't cry out almost immediately, after the initial shock of the attack? It might take a moment in time to ward him off, and collect his wits."

"He had six separate wounds," she answered. "But they were all clean. He may well have bruises come up in the next day or two as well, and his clothes were torn a little, as if in a struggle. But Caleb had only one real wound, and that was the slash across his throat which killed him."

"What are you saying?" Rathbone leaned forward. "That Ravensbrook was mistaken, or that in some essential of importance, he lied?"

"I think so. Yes, I think he lied," she answered very deliberately. "I just don't know why."

Monk sipped his port, looking from one to the other of them.

"You mean there was a considerable struggle before he called out?" Rathbone persisted. "What reason would he have? If it was not suicide, and not an accident, then are you saying that Ravensbrook murdered him? Why on earth should he? Not just to prevent him from being hanged. That's absurd."

"Then there is something we don't know," Hester answered. "Something which would make sense of it . . . or if not sense, at least something understandable to one's feelings."

"People kill for various reasons," Rathbone said thoughtfully. "Greed, fear, hatred. If it is irrational, then it may spring simply from emotion, but if it is rational, then it will be as a result of something that has happened, and to prevent something else from happening, to prevent some loss or pain to themselves, or someone they love."

"What could Caleb do to Ravensbrook, apart from be hanged, which could be a disgrace, but he has already disgraced himself very thoroughly." Monk shook his head. "Hester is right. There is something crucial that we don't know, perhaps haven't even come close to." He turned to Rathbone. "What was going to happen next, if Caleb had lived?"

"The defense would have begun tomorrow," Rathbone replied slowly, his concentration suddenly sharpening, his wineglass ignored. "Perhaps we need to speak with Ebenezer Goode? I thought I knew what he was going to do, but perhaps I don't."

Monk stared at him. "What could he do? Plead insanity? The best argument he has is that it was an accident, that Caleb didn't mean to kill him, and then when he had, he panicked. Either that, or try to convince them there is not enough evidence to prove Angus is dead at all. And I don't think he will win with that."

"Then maybe that's it." Rathbone clenched his fists on the white tablecloth. "He was going to bring out some evidence to show Angus was not the just and honorable man we suppose. That would be worth killing him for. To protect Angus's name, and Genevieve's. Perhaps to prevent Caleb from telling some appalling truth about him? That would be a reason."

"Do you think Lord Ravensbrook would kill Caleb to protect Genevieve?" Monk looked skeptical. "I gathered from their behavior towards each other that their relationship was cool, at best."

"Then to protect himself?" Rathbone argued urgently, leaning farther forward. "Or protect Angus, or his memory of him. After all, he was the nearest to a son he had. One can love a son in a strange, passionate and possessive way, as if he were part of oneself. I've seen some very complex emotions between parent and child."

"And Caleb?" Monk asked, his lips drawn back in a hard smile.

"God knows." Rathbone sighed. "Perhaps it was to spare him the verdict and the hanging. I wouldn't wish hanging on anyone. It's an appalling way to die. It's not the actual drop, and the rope around the throat, jerking tight and breaking the neck as the trap opens, it's the deliberate hour-by-hour, minute-by-minute dragging it out to the appointed hour. It's a refinement of cruelty which degrades everyone involved."

"Then perhaps we should ask Mr. Goode?" Hester concluded. "If we want to know? But do we?"

"Yes," Monk said without hesitation. "I want to know, even if I don't want to do anything about it."

Rathbone's eyes widened. "Could you do that . . . know, and do nothing?"

Monk opened his mouth to reply, then changed his mind. He shrugged, and drank the rest of his port, looking at neither Rathbone nor Hester.

Rathbone rang the bell and the butler appeared within seconds.

"I want you to take a note to Ebenezer Goode, straightaway," Rathbone ordered. "It is vital we meet with him before court sits again tomorrow. I expect he will be at his home, but if he is not, it is worth pursuing him to wherever he is. Get your coat, and I'll have the note ready. Take a hansom."

The butler did not move a muscle; his face remained as impassive as if Rathbone had merely asked him to bring another bottle of port.

"Yes sir. Would that be the address in Westbourne Place, sir?"

"Yes." Rathbone stood up. "And make all haste."

It was over an hour and a half later when Ebenezer Goode strode in, his coattails flapping behind him, a broad-brimmed hat jammed on his head and a look of glittering expectation in his eyes.

"Well?" he said as soon as he was in the door. He swept a bow to Hester, then ignored her, staring at Rathbone and Monk. "What is it that possibly matters now, that it cannot wait until tomorrow morning and allow me a decent dinner? Have you found a body?"

"Yes, and no." Rathbone indicated an easy chair. They had retired to the withdrawing room and were relaxed in front of a brisk fire. "Do you know Miss Hester Latterly? She, of course, knows you."

"Miss Latterly. How do you do." Goode bowed perfunctorily. "What the devil do you mean, Rathbone? Have you found Angus Stonefield's body, or not?"

"No, we have not. But Caleb's death may not be nearly as simple as we had supposed."

Goode froze, still halfway to the chair.

"How? In what way. Is Ravensbrook more severely injured than they said?"

Goode sank into the chair.

"No," Hester answered him. "A few very minor cuts on his upper arms and shoulders. They will stay for a while, but none of them is serious."

Goode looked at her sharply.

"Miss Latterly is a nurse," Monk said rather quickly. "She was in the Crimea, and has tended more wounded men than you have had cases. She was close to the court, fortunately, and came to Lord Ravensbrook's assistance."

"I see." A flash of interest lit Goode's expression. "Do I take it from your tone of voice, and your curious choice of words, Miss Latterly, that there is something more to your opinion than you have said?"

"It is simply this, Mr. Goode," Monk explained. "We can think of no explanation which fits all the facts, therefore we feel that there must be some profoundly significant fact which we do not know."

Goode's eyebrows shot up. "And you think I do?" he said incredulously. "I have no idea at all why Caleb should attack Lord Ravensbrook. He may well have hated him, because he so obviously preferred Angus, and perhaps always had done, but that is all rather obvious. By the way, what facts does that not fit?" He looked again at Hester.

"The fact that Lord Ravensbrook did not cry out until after he had sustained six very minor wounds," she answered him. "And Caleb had sustained one fatal slash across the jugular vein and was already dead."

He leaned forward, staring at her intently.

"Are you suggesting, ma'am, that Lord Ravensbrook was a willing actor in Caleb's death, either by suicide or by murder?"

"Not quite. We do not believe it likely Caleb would have killed himself. Why should he? His defense had not even begun." She looked at him intently. "Had he not some realistic chance of escaping conviction, or at least conviction of anything worse than not reporting a fatal accident? If I were defending him"—she ignored Goode's sharp start of amazement—"I should plead a fight in which Angus had accidently been killed, perhaps fallen into the river, hit his head, and Caleb had been afraid to report it, since he could not prove what had happened, and knowing the quarrel between them, and his own reputation, expected no one would believe him. After all, there is no witness to say anything differently."

Goode leaned back in his chair and stretched his long legs.

"Would you indeed?"

"Yes," she said decisively. "Wouldn't you?"

A sudden, dazzling smile broke across his face. "Yes, ma'am, indeed I would, especially after the weight of evidence produced by the prosecution. I think trying to rebut it simply as not proven would be insufficient. The jury do not like Caleb Stone, and Mrs. Stonefield has aroused a considerable sympathy."

"Was that what you intended?" Rathbone demanded. "Were you going to call Caleb tomorrow?"

"Of course," Goode answered. "I have no one else. Why? What light can that throw upon his death?"

"None, unless we knew what he was going to say." Monk spoke

for the first time. "Plainly, was he going to say something about Angus which it would have been worth killing him to keep secret?"

"Ravensbrook?" Goode's voice rose almost to falsetto. "You think Lord Ravensbrook murdered Caleb in his cell to keep him silent?"

"Obviously you don't," Rathbone said dryly. "So you cannot know of anything such as we suggest."

"Or else he does not know its effect." Monk could not let go so easily. "Perhaps he knows what it is, but not its meaning, or what it could lead to." He swiveled around to face Goode. "What was he going to say?"

Goode bit his lip. "Well, with a normal client, I would know the answer, or I would not ask the question. But with Stone all I could do was guess. Certainly he told me he would say it was an accident, that the hatred was mutual and he had no more destroyed Angus than Angus had wished to destroy him." He crossed his legs and rested his elbows on the arms of his chair, making a steeple of his fingers. "You must understand he spoke elliptically and in paradoxes, and half the time he just laughed. If I thought it would have helped him, I would have pleaded the man mad." He regarded them each in turn, his face full of pity and question. "But who wants to spend his life in Bedlam? I think I'd rather be hanged. He was at times eminently sane. He was certainly highly intelligent and obviously well educated. When he chose to, he spoke beautifully. At other times he sounded like any other ruffian from the Isle of Dogs."

"So you don't really know what he would say?" Rathbone concluded.

"Would you? I only know what I intended to ask him."

"What was that?" Rathbone and Monk said together.

"About his quarrel with Angus, of course, and what led up to it," Goode replied.

"About Angus!" Monk clapped his hands on his knee. He twisted around to look at Hester. "Then we must find out what it was he was going to say, what their quarrel really was, if we want to know if it was worth killing him for. Do we?"

"I do," Goode said instantly. "Guilty or innocent, he was my client. If he was murdered, for whatever reason, I not only want to know, I want to prove it."

"To whom?" Rathbone asked. "The court isn't going to sit while we search for Angus Stonefield's youth."

"It's an unnatural death," Goode pointed out. "There'll be a coroner's inquest."

"A formality," Rathbone answered. "Ravensbrook will give his account. The gaolers will confirm it. The doctor will confirm the cause of death and it will be pronounced an unfortunate accident. Everyone will say 'What a shame,' and think 'What a relief.' The matter will be closed, and they will proceed to the next case."

"It will take us days, perhaps weeks, to find the answer to whatever Caleb was going to say which mattered so much," Monk said angrily. "Can't you delay it?"

"A while, perhaps." Rathbone looked across at Goode. "What do you think?"

"We can try." Goode's voice lifted a little. "Yes, dammit, we can certainly try!" He swung around. "Miss Latterly?"

"Yes?"

"Are you with us? Will you be as obstructive as possible as a witness to the events, as vague and as contradictory as you may? Give them cause to think, to question, to wonder and to doubt."

"Of course," she agreed. "But who will help Monk to trace Angus's life? He cannot do it all alone."

"We'll all do it, until the inquest begins," Goode said simply. "By then, surely we will have some idea of what it is we are seeking, and from whom."

"We must make the coroner believe there is a question of murder," Rathbone went on with rising eagerness. "If he thinks it is accident or suicide he will simply close the matter. And dammit, that is going to be hard. The only possible guilty party is Ravensbrook, and that won't sit easily with any coroner I know."

"So we had better begin now," Monk said decisively. He looked at Goode. "I assume you will demand a full coroner's inquest for your client, and time to gather evidence?" He turned to Rathbone. "And you will ask to represent the Crown, since you are the prosecutor?" He turned lastly to Hester, assuming her agreement without it crossing his mind to ask her. "You and I will begin to delve into Angus's past. We shall have to do it separately, because there is no time to do it together. You already know far more about Genevieve than I do." Humor and self-mockery flickered across his face. "And you seem to be a far better judge of her character. Find out all you can of Angus from her, including where, when and how they first met, and all she knows of his relationship with Caleb, and Ravensbrook. This time, the truth. I shall go to Ravensbrook's country home and see what I can learn there. That is apparently where the brothers grew up."

"What about the Isle of Dogs, and Limehouse?" Rathbone asked.

"I'll go there," Hester said immediately. "After I have seen Genevieve, and perhaps Titus Niven."

Goode was aghast. "You cannot go to Limehouse, Miss Latterly! You have not the faintest idea what it is like, or you would not entertain such a thought. A gentlewoman like yourself would be—"

"I have been nursing the typhoid victims there for more than a month, Mr. Goode," she said patiently. "I am in an excellent position to investigate in that quarter. I daresay I know more of the individual residents than anyone else. I could name you at least two hundred, and tell you their families and their ancestors. And I could tell you who they have lost recently. They will talk to me as they would not to any of you. That I can swear."

Goode looked taken aback, and considerably impressed.

"I see. Perhaps I had better stick to my own last. Would I be presumptuous to be concerned for your safety?"

"Not at all, but probably unnecessarily worried," she replied with a generous smile. "Since Caleb is dead, no one is going to feel the same urgency to defend him now, or fear the reprisals for betraying him by the truth."

Rathbone rose to his feet. "Think a good night's sleep is called for, before we begin. Let us meet here again in three days' time and discuss what we have learned."

"Agreed." Goode rose also. "Miss Latterly, may I find you a hansom and escort you as far as your home?"

"Thank you," she accepted graciously. "That would be most agreeable. It has been a somewhat exhausting day."

# CHAPTER
# TWELVE

———

Ebenezer Goode woke very early the following morning, unable to sleep any longer because his mind was churning over the extraordinary events of the preceding day. He had not liked Caleb Stone; indeed, privately he had had little doubt that Stone was guilty of the murder of his brother exactly as he was charged. But there had been an extraordinary vitality in the man, a core of passion which made his death unexpectedly hard to accept.

He lay with the blankets up to his chin, turning over and over in his mind what Rathbone had said, and that odd fellow Monk. Did the nurse really know what she was talking about? Was it conceivable that Milo Ravensbrook could either have willed Caleb's death, or worse still, have brought it about?

The thought was especially hideous when he remembered the remarkable face of Lady Ravensbrook, the strength in it, the power of feeling and imagination, even ravaged by recent disease as it was. There was something in her which awoke an extraordinary interest in him. He found even while he was thinking of ways and means of discerning the truth, and the near impossibility of proving it, it was her features impressed on his closed eyelids, her expression, her mouth, even her voice in his ears. She had said barely a dozen words to him, and every inflection remained.

He rose at half past six, while it was still dark, sent for water from a very surprised housemaid, then shaved, washed, dressed and requested breakfast by quarter past seven. His cook was not in the least amused, and allowed it to be known. He did not care in the slightest, although good cooks were not easy to obtain.

He left the house at eight and walked briskly, swinging his rather handsome stick, and so deep in thought he passed a dozen acquaintances without seeing them, and addressed two more by their fathers' names.

By five minutes past nine he was outside Ravensbrook House, and saw his lordship leave in his own carriage. Goode mounted the steps and pulled the brass bell knob.

"Good morning, sir," the footman said with only the merest surprise.

"Good morning," Goode replied with a charming smile. "I am sorry to disturb the family so early, but there are matters which cannot wait. Will you ask Lady Ravensbrook if I may speak with her? I shall await her convenience, naturally." He passed over his card.

"Lady Ravensbrook, sir?" The footman was uncertain he had heard correctly. It seemed absurd. What could the lawyer have to say to Lady Ravensbrook?

"If you please." Good stepped inside and took off his coat and gave the man his hat. He had no intention of being turned away, and he was used to pressing his cause. He had not become one of London's leading barristers by being easily refused or overridden. "Thank you. So good of you. Should I wait in the morning room? Yes?" He had been here only once before, but he recalled it was the second door to the left. He assumed consent, and strode across the hall, leaving the footman holding his clothes, and with little choice but to accede.

He was obliged to wait nearly three quarters of an hour in the calm, ornate room with its heavy curtains and shelves of books, but when at last the door opened, it was Enid Ravensbrook who stood there. Instantly he felt guilty. She looked desperately afraid. Her lavender-colored gown hung on her, in spite of the fact her maid had taken it in as much as was possible without recutting it altogether. Her hair had lost its luster and even the cleverest dressing could not conceal how much of it had come out in her illness. Her skin had no color at all, but nothing could dim the intelligence in her eyes or the underlying strength in the lines of her cheekbones and jutting nose and jaw. She looked at him with unwavering courage.

"Good morning, Mr. Goode. My footman tells me you wish to speak with me." She closed the door and walked quite slowly, as if she were afraid of losing her balance.

He made half a gesture towards helping her, and knew instantly that he should not. He ached to reach out and give her his strength, but it would be an intrusion. He did not need to meet her eyes to know it.

She reached the nearest chair and sat down, smiling at last.

"Thank you, Mr. Goode. I am obliged to you. I hate being an invalid. Now, what is it you wish to say to me? I presume it is to do with poor Caleb. I knew him very little, and yet I cannot help grieving that he should die so. Although, God knows, perhaps the alternative was worse."

"But you knew Angus," he said quickly. "With Lord Ravensbrook's regard for him, and his own gratitude and affection, he must have come here often."

It had been a statement, as if he did not doubt it, yet the look on her face was one of uncertainty and denial.

"No." She shook her head fractionally. "He came, of course, but not so very often, and he seldom stayed long. I am not sure if it was because Genevieve felt a certain . . . uncomfortableness here? I think my husband overawed her to a degree. He can be . . ." Again she hesitated, and he had a sudden sharp perception that it was not the words she was struggling with, nor even if she should express the thought to him, but the thought itself. It was something she had long avoided facing, because of its pain. He was stunned by how much it distressed him.

He hesitated. Perhaps it was not worth pursuing at such cost. It could all be left to the coroner to cover with polite decencies.

But the doubt lasted only a moment. He could not live with such cowardice, and it was not worthy of her.

He smiled, "Please, ma'am, tell me the truth as you feel it, as you saw it. It is not a time for lies, however gently meant, or seemingly kind."

"Isn't it?" She frowned. "Both Angus and Caleb are dead, poor creatures, and their hatred with them, whatever it was for. It is gone now . . . finished."

"I wish it were." He meant it profoundly. "But there will have to be an inquest into Caleb's death. We need to know why suddenly he launched himself into such a violent and hopeless act."

"Do we?" Her face was calm, her inner decision made. "What does it matter now, Mr. Goode? It seems he never lived in peace. Cannot he now at least be buried and left to rest in whatever ease his soul can find? And we with him. My husband has known little but grief of one sort or another since he first took them into his home."

"Even with Angus?"

"No. No, that was quite unfair of me. Angus brought him great joy. He was everything he could have wished."

"But?" he said gently, insistently.

"He was!"

"There is a shadow in your voice, a hesitation," he insisted. "What is it? What was it in Angus, Lady Ravensbrook, which made Caleb hate him so passionately? They were close once. Why did they grow so hideously far apart?"

"I don't know!"

"But you guess? You must have thought about it, wondered. Even if only for the pain it brought your husband."

"Of course I thought about it. I lay awake many hours wondering if there were some way they might be reconciled. I searched my mind. I asked my husband often, until I realized he knew as little as I, and that to speak of it gave him pain. He and Angus were not . . ."

"Not what?"

She spoke reluctantly. He was dragging the words out of her, and he knew it.

"Easy in each other's company," she admitted. "It was as if the shadow of Caleb were always there, a darkness between them, a wound that could never be completely forgotten."

"But you liked Angus?"

"Yes, yes I liked him." Now the shadow was gone, she spoke wholeheartedly. "He was extraordinarily kind. He was a man you could admire without reservation, and yet so modest he never put himself forward, was never pompous. Yes, I liked Angus enormously. I never saw him lose his temper or perform a cruel act." The marks of grief were plain in her face, but simple loss, without doubt or underlying darkness.

He hated himself for persisting, and yet the nagging anxiety was in his mind like a toothache, dull and ever present, and sometimes giving a stab so sharp it robbed the breath.

"Never?"

"No," she said as if she had not expected to feel so. "Never. I am not surprised my husband loved him. He was all he could have wished in a son, had he been granted one."

"He must have hated Caleb for destroying him," he said gently. "It would be understandable if he could never forgive such an act of treachery. Most especially since Angus still kept such loyalty towards Caleb."

She turned away, her voice even lower. "Yes, I could not blame him. And yet he does not seem to feel the anger I do. It is almost as if . . ."

He waited, leaning forward, the silence in the room prickling his ears.

She turned very slowly to look at him.

"I don't know what you expect me to say, Mr. Goode. . . ."

"The truth, ma'am. It is the only thing clean enough, the only thing which will in the end stand above all the pain."

"I don't know it!"

"It was almost as if . . . what?" he prompted.

"As if he had known one day it must happen, and it was like a blow he had long awaited, and the reality of it is the end of the tension, almost a solace. Is that a terrible thing to say?"

"No. It is merely sad," he said gently. "And if we were honest, perhaps something we might all say. One can become very tired."

She smiled, for the first time some brightness reached her eyes.

"You are very kind, Mr. Goode. I think perhaps you are well named."

For the first time in many years, he felt the color warm in his face, and a strange mixture of pleasure and an awareness of how lonely he was.

Oliver Rathbone was in court when it reconvened. The benches for the crowd were almost empty. The newspapers were blaring headlines that Caleb Stone had tried to commit another murder, this time of the man who had been a father and a benefactor to him, and a greater justice had prevailed—he himself had become the victim. The matter was ended.

The judge looked for Ebenezer Goode, saw his absence, and raised his eyebrows at Rathbone.

"There is no one to defend, my lord," Rathbone said with a shrug. He did not know where Goode was, and was privately a little disconcerted that he was not present. He had counted on his support.

"Indeed," the judge said dryly. "Not an entirely satisfactory explanation, but I suppose it will have to suffice." He turned to the jury and in formal manner told them what they all already knew. Caleb Stone was dead. There was no possibility of proceeding with the trial, since he could not now give evidence or speak in his own defense. Therefore there could be no verdict. A mistrial was declared, the jury thanked and dismissed.

Rathbone saw the judge afterwards in his oak-paneled chambers, the early March sunlight shone pale through the high windows.

"What is it?" the judge asked with some surprise. "You have no more interest in this, Rathbone. Whatever we may believe of him, we cannot pursue Caleb Stone any further. He has made the only escape which is beyond us to retrieve."

"I know that, my lord." Rathbone stood in front of him looking down to where the judge sat in his leather chair, a small man with lines under his eyes. "All I want is to be sure that his escape was either an accident or of his own planning."

"I don't understand you." The judge frowned. "Ravensbrook said it was an accident, but if it was suicide, are you really so passionate in prosecution you want it proved?" His mouth tightened. "Why, man? You want him buried in unconsecrated ground? It is unlike you to be so vindictive. It has nothing to do with providing for the widow, or allowing her to marry again, in due time, if she so wishes."

"I don't believe it was suicide," Rathbone answered.

"Murder?" The judge's rather tattered eyebrows rose in astonishment. "Did you not hear what happened? Lord Ravensbrook went in to see—"

"I know what he said," Rathbone cut across him. "I was there within a few minutes of it. I saw Ravensbrook and saw the body. I think there is a possibility Ravensbrook murdered him."

"Lord Ravensbrook?" The judge was not shocked, he simply did not believe it. "Do you realize what you are saying, Rathbone? Why on earth would Lord Ravensbrook murder anyone, let alone his own ward, appalling as the man was? And before the defense, which could conceivably have made a case for an accident."

"That is something I intend to find out," Rathbone said through his teeth. "I have Monk on the case now."

"You've taken leave of your senses," the judge said with a sigh, leaning back in his chair as if he needed the softness of its leather padding to cushion his bones. "The idea has no foundation whatever." His eyes narrowed. "Unless there is something quite extraordinary which you are concealing from the court. If there is, you place yourself in considerable jeopardy."

"There isn't," Rathbone replied with feeling. "I know nothing beyond what has already been revealed, but I believe that something exists. I would like the coroner to open the inquest, and then adjourn it so we may find the evidence to prove it."

"And you expect me to tell him this?" The judge's pale blue eyes were wide with incredulity. "I'm sorry, Rathbone, but even if I did, without some evidence to support you, he would think me as mad as I think you. You'll have three days at the most."

"It's not enough."

"Maybe that's as well. Now if that is all I can do for you, allow me to prepare for my next case. Good day to you."

Hester also rose early, and took a hansom to Genevieve's house. She had reason to believe she would be at home, since she was no longer required to help Enid, and there was no further business to be hoped for at the Old Bailey. In the prevailing tragic circumstances, she would hardly be either receiving social calls or making any. The business of Angus's death would have to wait upon legal procedure.

She was not disappointed. Genevieve looked pale and exhausted, but reasonably composed.

"How are you?" Hester said as she was led into the kitchen, the only room in the house with any warmth. It was spacious and full of agreeable smells of baking bread and fresh linen drying on the large airing rack across the ceiling, let up and down on a rope pulley fastened to the wall. There was no one else present. Presumably the cook had been allowed to go, in the interests of the increasingly stringent economy. A housemaid had answered the door, and perhaps there could be a woman come in to do the heavy work once or twice a week. No doubt the nurserymaid would be the last to be let go. A manservant would have been too expensive even to consider.

Genevieve smiled briefly, but there was an honesty in it.

"We shall manage. Once they grant that Angus is dead, we shall be able to appoint someone to manage the business and proceed with decisions. I daresay it will be difficult for a little while, but that will not matter." She met Hester's eyes with candor. "I have certainly been colder and hungrier before. The children do not find it easy to understand, but I shall explain it to them as well as I can."

"Will it be Mr. Niven you ask to manage the business?" It was really none of her affair, but Hester inquired because she hoped it was.

Genevieve colored very faintly, but there was no awkwardness in her answer. Without excusing herself, or explaining the necessity, she went over to the sink and started to peel potatoes. They were old, black in spots, and with too many eyes. There were also carrots and turnips on the bench.

"Yes. I have known him for a long time, and he is the most honorable of men," she answered frankly. "I think Angus would have approved."

"I'm glad." Hester tried to smile, to soften what she had to say next, even though Genevieve had her back to her where she sat at the scrubbed wooden table.

Genevieve turned around, the knife in her hand. "What is it? What else can have happened?"

"Nothing. It is simply that it is not yet over. We do not know the truth, not all of it. . . ."

"We never will," Genevieve said bleakly, glancing at the kettle on the range, then resuming her peeling. "But even with Caleb alive, I don't think we would have. All I hoped for was to have the authorities accept that Angus was dead. I could have borne it if Caleb had not been proved guilty, unjust though that would be."

"What was Angus like?" Hester said with sudden urgency. "How could he still care for Caleb, when Caleb hated him so much? Why did he keep going back to the East End? What childhood debt of honor, or guilt, kept him bound to someone who loathed him so passionately that he finally killed him?"

Genevieve stood rigid for several seconds, then put down her knife and moved to the large black cooking range. The kettle was beginning to steam. She took a black-and-white china teapot out of the cupboard, rinsed it with boiling water, then spooned tea out of the caddy and poured the rest of the water from the kettle and let it steep. She brought out cups and then milk from the larder.

"I don't know," she said at last. "I really don't. There were times when I thought he hated Caleb just as much, and I begged him never to see him again." She sat down in the chair opposite and began to pour the tea. "At other times he was sorry for him, and yes, perhaps almost a little guilty. Although he had no cause to be. Caleb could have had as much, had he chosen. It was not as if there were an inheritance and Angus had it at Caleb's expense."

"There was nothing from their parents?"

Genevieve shook her head.

"If there was, it was so little, it was used long ago. Do you care for milk? Certainly Angus began his business by joining a firm, as any young man might do." She passed the cup over. "Caleb could have done the same, except that he was so reckless, and so lazy in his studies, that he had not equipped himself to be of use. But again, that was his choice." She was staring at Hester now. "Sometimes I think Angus was sorry for Caleb, and there were times when I knew he was afraid of him."

Hester took the tea and thanked her. It was hot and fresh, and she was glad of it.

"It took a great deal of courage for Angus to return to Limehouse and find Caleb," Genevieve went on. "After he had been badly hurt—and he was, more than once. He was always tired, and depressed, and I begged him not to return. It is not as if Caleb cared for him, or was even grateful for the help Angus gave him. It made me so angry . . . and then that distressed him. He said he could not help it. Caleb was his brother, his twin, and he was bound by a tie which he could not break. When I realized how it hurt him, I ceased to speak of it."

She looked down again, ignoring her tea, her eyes brimming with tears.

"If you had known Angus, you would understand. There was a goodness in him, an honor unlike anyone else I have known. The only other man as gentle, and with anything like the same inward love of what is good, is Mr. Niven. I think that is why they were friends, and why I feel I can turn to him now. Angus would have understood that."

There was nothing further to pursue, except facts, and Hester was not even sure what use they would be. Nevertheless she asked Genevieve precisely in which street she had grown up, where and when she had first met Caleb, how she had met Angus, and all she could remember of that early relationship.

"I barely knew Caleb!" she said bitterly. "I swear to you that is the truth. He was a violent man, even for Limehouse. He frightened me. I think he frightened everyone. He was so like Angus in build and feature, and yet so unlike him in nature that no one could mistake one for the other. The way he walked, the way he stood, his voice, everything was wild and . . . I don't know how to describe it." She frowned, struggling with recollection. "As if he were always angry, as if there were something inside him so full of rage it was held in only by the frailest thread, and any provocation at all and it would explode and be free to hurt and destroy whatever stood in its path."

Hester did not interrupt her, but quietly sipped her tea and watched Genevieve's face.

"I suppose he must have had a gentler side," Genevieve went on, her voice lower. "That poor creature Selina seemed to have cared for him." She bit her lip. "I don't know why I speak of her like that. I started in the same place, just three streets away. I could easily have been there now, if I had never met Angus, and he had not had the patience and the love to teach me how to better myself, to speak well enough to pass as respectable, if not as a lady."

She smiled ruefully, and began her tea at last. "He taught me how to carry myself, how to dress, how to conduct myself with others. I would never have passed for gentry, and have entertained in my own home, but over the years I have learned more confidence, and I don't believe I ever embarrassed him in front of his colleagues. You see, he was the opposite of Caleb, he had endless patience. I cannot remember him ever losing his temper. He would have considered it wrong, that he was betraying the best in himself."

"I wish I had known him," Hester said sincerely. He might have been a trifle pompous, perhaps he lacked humor or imagination, but he must have been a man of immense kindness and an inner integrity which was both rare and beautiful. "Thank you for telling me so much." She rose to take her leave. "I am sorry to have had to ask you. It must have given you pain."

"And pleasure." Genevieve rose also. "I like to talk about him. It is very sad when people cease to mention someone when he is dead. It is almost like denying he ever lived. I am glad you wanted to know."

Monk already knew from Genevieve where Angus had grown up, and even before Ebenezer Goode had left his home, Monk was in a hansom bound for the railway station and the first train to the Berkshire village of Chilverley. It was a tedious journey, necessitating a number of changes and delays, moving from cozy waiting room with fire, to icy, wind-raked platforms, then chilly trains. It was quarter to eleven when he finally stepped off at Chilverley in a bright, hard wind.

"Chilverley Hall?" the stationmaster said obligingly. "Yes sir. About three miles north from here. That way." He pointed half behind him. "Know Colonel Patterson, do you? You look like a military man, if I may say so."

Monk was astonished. Had it not been so contrary to his own interests, he would have let his temper have full rein.

"Colonel Patterson?" he said grimly. "This is Chilverley?"

"Yes sir, Chilverley, Berkshire." He looked at Monk anxiously. "Who were you looking for, sir?"

"The family home of Lord Ravensbrook."

"Oh, bless you, sir. It is the family home of the Ravensbrooks, but he don't live here no more. Sold it. Moved up to live in London, so they say."

"I'm surprised it wasn't entailed," Monk said irrelevantly.

"Daresay it might have been." The stationmaster wagged his head. "But Lord Milo were the last o' the line. No reason why he shouldn't sell, if he wanted. Must have got a tidy sum for it." He touched his cap respectfully as two gentlemen, one in a Norfolk jacket, the other in a greatcoat, went by and through the gate to the road.

"No brothers, or even cousins?" Monk had no reason to ask, it simply occurred to him.

The stationmaster turned back to him.

"No sir. Had one brother, younger than him, but he was killed, poor soul. Accident it was, in Italy, or some such place." He shook his head. "Drowned, they say. Pity, that was. He were a very charming gentleman, if a bit wild. Very handsome, and a bit free with the ladies, and with his money. Still, a sad end for one so young."

"How old was he?" Again it hardly mattered.

"No more than thirty-one or thirty-two," the stationmaster answered. "It's all a long time ago now, well over quarter of a century, nearer thirty-five years."

"Would you know if any of the old servants are still at the house?"

"Oh no, sir. All left when his lordship did. Colonel Patterson brought his own household with him."

"Is there no one I could find who lived in the house then?" Monk pressed. "What about outside staff? Even a gardener, gamekeeper, coachman? Is it still the same vicar as it was then?"

The stationmaster nodded. "Oh, yes. Mr. Nicolson is still the vicar. Vicarage is opposite the church, just beyond that second stand of elms." He pointed. "Can't miss it. Just follow the road 'round. About two miles from here, sir."

"Thank you. I'm obliged to you for your time and your courtesy." And without waiting for any acknowledgment, Monk strode out in the direction the stationmaster had indicated.

The wind sighed through the bare branches of the elms and a cloud of rooks soared up into the air, disturbed by some predatory cat. Their black, tangled nests were low in the forks, towards the trunks. It had been a hard winter.

The vicar was an elderly man, but spry and bright-eyed. He greeted Monk over the hedge from where he had been looking hopefully at the green lawn and first spears of bulbs showing through.

Monk gave the briefest of explanations as to his purpose.

The vicar regarded him with a lively interest.

"Yes sir, of course I can. What a fine morning, isn't it? Won't be long before the daffodils come through. Love a good show of daffodils. Come into the parlor, my dear fellow. Got a decent fire going. Get the chill out of yourself."

He came to the gate and opened it for Monk to walk through. Then he led him up a chipped stone path to the door, which was heavily bowered with honeysuckle, now a dark tangle of stems not yet showing green.

"In fact, would you like a spot of luncheon?" he invited, showing Monk the way inside, where it was immediately warm. "Hate to eat alone. Uncivilized. Good conversation best for a meal, don't you think?" He went through the overcrowded hall and opened the door into a bright, chintz-curtained room. "Wife died five years ago. Have to grasp at all the company I can. Know everyone here. Have done for years. Can't surprise each other anymore. Gets tedious in the winter. Don't mind in the summer, enough to do in the garden. What did you say your name was?"

"William Monk, Mr. Nicolson."

"Ah, well, Mr. Monk, would you care for some luncheon, while you tell me your business here in Chilverley?"

Monk was delighted to accept. He was cold and hungry, and it would be far easier to stretch out a conversation over the table than sitting in even the most agreeable parlor.

"Good, good. Now please make yourself comfortable while I inform the cook!"

The Reverend Nicolson was so obviously happy to have company that Monk allowed at least half the meal to pass before he broached the subject of his journey. He swallowed the last of the cold mutton, pickles and vegetables and set his knife and fork down.

The maid appeared with hot, flaky apple pie and a jug of cream and set them on the table with evident satisfaction, taking away the empty plates.

Then the vicar began his tale and Monk listened with amazement, anger, and growing compassion.

# CHAPTER
# THIRTEEN

---

The coroner's inquest into the death of Caleb Stone opened two days later. The public benches were packed. It was an extraordinary incident, and people were curious to learn how such a thing had happened.

Lord Ravensbrook was obliged to attend and give evidence; indeed, he was the only immediate witness. Also to be called were the three gaolers, all sitting rigidly upright, embarrassed and profoundly frightened. Jimson was convinced they were all innocent, Bailey, that they were all to blame, and would be punished appropriately. The third gaoler, who had gone to report the matter, refused to have an opinion at all.

Hester was to be called, by Rathbone, if not by the coroner. There was also the doctor who had examined the body officially.

Enid Ravensbrook sat beside her husband, still pale-faced and gaunt, but steady-eyed, and less physically ill than the week before. Next to her was Genevieve Stonefield, and beside her, calm and resolute, Titus Niven.

Selina Herries sat alone, head high, face white and set, eyes hollow with shock. Rathbone looked at her, and felt an unaccountable grief for her. They had nothing whatever in common, no culture, no cause, no beliefs, barely even a common language. And yet the sight of her filled him with a sense of the universality of bereavement. He knew what it was to lose that which had been dear, in whatever manner, however mixed or confused the emotion.

Ebenezer Goode was not yet there. It was he who was officially to represent the interests of Caleb Stone. Rathbone had persuaded Genevieve to allow him to represent her, as sister-in-law of the deceased, and therefore the closest relative. Ravensbrook had been only his childhood guardian, and had never apparently adopted either boy, and Selina was not Caleb's wife.

The coroner was a large, genial man with a ready smile, but more of agreeability than humor, as was appropriate to his calling. He opened proceedings with formality, then called the first witness, the gaoler Jimson. The room was simple, not like the high court in the Old Bailey. There were no steps to climb to a stand, no carved and ornamental bench or thronelike chair for the coroner as for the judge. Jimson stood behind a simple rail which did little more than mark the position for him, and the coroner sat behind a fine oak table.

Jimson swore to tell the truth, then gave his name and occupation. He was so nervous he gulped and stumbled over his words.

The coroner smiled at him benignly.

"Now, Mr. Jimson, simply tell us what happened. There is no need to be so frightened, man. This is a court of inquiry, not of accusation. Now! Begin when the prisoner was put back in your custody after the trial was adjourned."

"Yes sir! M'lord!"

" 'Sir' will do very well. I am not a judge."

"Yes sir. Thank you, sir!" Jimson took a deep breath and swallowed hard again. " 'E were in a rare state, the prisoner, I mean. 'E were laughin' an' shoutin' an' swearin' fit ter bust. There was a rage in 'im like nothin' I ever seen afore, 'cepting it were all mixed up wi' laughter like there was some 'uge joke as only 'e knew. But 'e didn't offer us no violence, like," he added hastily. " 'E went easy inter 'is cell an' we locked 'im in."

"We?" the coroner inquired. "Can you recall which of you it was?"

"Yes sir, it were me."

"I see. Proceed."

There was almost silence around the room, only the slight sound of fabric rustling as someone shifted in a seat, and a whisper as a woman spoke to the person next to her. The journalists present wrote nothing so far.

"Then Lord Ravensbrook came an' asked if 'e could see the prisoner, 'im bein' 'is only relative, like," Jimson continued. "An' seein' as 'ow things was goin' bad with 'im in the trial. Guess like 'e thought as there'd be a verdict soon, an' then 'e wouldn't be allowed ter see 'im alone anymore, 'im bein' a guilty man then, an' still an innocent one now, leastways afore the law."

"I understand." The coroner nodded. "You do not need to explain, it is quite clear, and natural."

"Thank you, sir." Jimson did not look in the slightest relieved. "Well, it all seemed right ter us, Bailey an' Alcott an' me, so we let 'im in—"

"Just a moment, Mr. Jimson," the coroner interrupted. "When you let Lord Ravensbrook in, how was the prisoner? What was his demeanor, his attitude? Was he still in this rage you described earlier? How did he greet Lord Ravensbrook?"

Jimson looked confused.

"Did you see him, Mr. Jimson?" the coroner pressed. "It is necessary that you answer truthfully. This matter concerns the death of a man in your custody."

"Yes sir." Jimson swallowed convulsively, only too desperately aware of his responsibility. "No sir, I didn't go in with 'is lordship. I . . . I didn't like ter, 'im bein' family like, an' knowin' from the guard as 'ad 'im in court 'ow 'ard it were goin', an' as 'e were like ter be 'anged. I let 'is lordship in, w'en 'e said as 'e preferred ter be alone—"

"Lord Ravensbrook said he wished to see the prisoner alone?"

"Yes sir, 'e did."

"I see. Then what happened?"

"Arter a few moments, 'is lordship came out an' asked fer a pen an' ink an' paper, 'cos the prisoner wanted ter write a statement o' some sort, I forget exactly what." He fidgeted with his collar. It appeared to be too tight for him. "I sent Bailey fer 'em, an' w'en 'e brought 'em back, I gave 'em ter 'is lordship, an' 'e went back inter the cell wi' 'em. Then just a few minutes arter that there were a cry, an' a bangin' on the door, an' w'en I opened it, 'is lordship staggered out, covered wi' blood, an' said as there'd bin an accident, or summink like that, an' the prisoner were dead . . . sir." He took a breath and plunged on. " 'E looked terrible white and shocked, sir, poor gennelman. So I sent Bailey for 'elp. I think 'e got a glass o' water, but 'is lordship were too upset ter take it."

"Did you go to the cell to look at the prisoner?" the coroner demanded.

"Yes sir, 'course I did. 'E were lyin' in a pool o' blood like a lake, sir, an' 'is eyes were wide open an' starin'." He tugged at his collar again. " 'E were dead. Weren't nuffink more ter be done for 'im. I pulled the door to, didn't lock it, weren't no point. Alcott went ter report wot 'ad 'appened, an' I tried ter do what I could fer 'is lordship till 'elp come."

"Thank you, Mr. Jimson." The coroner looked for Goode.

"Where is Mr. Goode?" he asked with a frown. "I understood he was to represent the family of the dead man. Is that not so?"

Rathbone rose to his feet. "Yes sir, he is. I don't know what may have kept him. I ask the court's indulgence. I am sure he will not be long." He had better not be, he thought grimly, or we shall lose this by default!

"This is not a court of advocacy, Mr. Rathbone," the coroner said irritably. "If Mr. Goode does not favor us with his presence, we shall proceed without him. Have you any questions you wish to ask this witness?"

Rathbone drew in his breath to make as long-winded a reply as he could, and was saved the necessity by the doors swinging open wide on their hinges. Ebenezer Goode swept in, coattails flying, arms full of papers, and strode up to the front. He bestowed a dazzling smile upon the coroner, apologized profusely and took his seat, managing to disturb everyone within a ten-foot radius.

"Are you ready, Mr. Goode?" the coroner asked with heavy sarcasm. "May we proceed?"

"Of course!" Goode said, still with the same smile. "Very civil of you to have waited for me."

"We did not wait for you!" the coroner snapped. "Do you have questions for this witness, sir?"

"Yes indeed, thank you." Goode rose to his feet, upset his papers and picked them up, then proceeded to ask a lot of questions which merely reaffirmed what Jimson had already said. No one learned anything new, but it wasted considerable time, which was Goode's purpose. And Rathbone's. The coroner kept his temper with difficulty.

Bailey, the second gaoler, was called next, and the coroner elicited from him confirmation of everything Jimson had said, but briefly. There were no contradictions to explore.

It took all Goode's ingenuity to think of sufficient questions to stretch it out a further half hour, and Rathbone found it hard to add anything at all. He redescribed Caleb's words, his gestures, his tone of voice, his behavior earlier during the trial. He even asked Bailey what he thought Caleb felt and expected of the outcome, until the coroner stopped him and told him he was asking the witness to speculate beyond his ability to know.

"But sir, Mr. Bailey is an expert witness on the mood and expectations of prisoners charged with capital crimes," Rathbone protested. "It is his daily occupation. Surely he, of all men, may know whether a prisoner has hope of being acquitted or not? It is of the utmost importance in learning the truth that we know whether Caleb Stone was in despair, or still nurtured some hope of life."

"Of course it is, Mr. Rathbone," the coroner conceded. "But you have already drawn from Mr. Bailey, and Mr. Jimson, everything that they know. It is up to me to reach conclusions, not the witnesses, however experienced."

"Yes sir," Rathbone said reluctantly. It was only one o'clock.

The coroner looked at the clock and adjourned for luncheon.

"Have you heard from Monk?" Goode demanded when he and Rathbone were seated in an excellent tavern nearby and enjoying a meal of roast beef and vegetables, ale, apple and blackberry pie, ripe Stilton cheese, and biscuits. "Has he learned anything?"

"No, I haven't," Rathbone said grimly. "I know he went to Chilverley, but I haven't heard a thing after that."

Goode helped himself to a large portion of cheese.

"And what about the nurse, what's her name? Latterly?" he asked. "Did she learn anything of use? I see her in court. Shouldn't she be in the East End? We could have put off calling her today. She might have given us something!"

"She's already learned all she can," Rathbone said defensively. "She said there's nothing there we don't already know."

"What about Caleb, damn it!" Goode said angrily. "If this isn't an accident, then either it's suicide—and we've already decided that is unlikely—or it's murder. In the interests of human decency, never mind abstract concepts like truth, we need to know."

"Then we'll have to go further back than Caleb's life in Limehouse," Rathbone replied, taking another biscuit. "It lies in the relationship between Ravensbrook, Angus and him. That is in Chilverley. All we can do is stretch this out until Monk himself returns, or at least sends us a witness!"

Goode sighed. "And God knows what we'll learn then!"

"Or what we'll be able to prove," Rathbone added, finishing his ale.

The afternoon proceedings began with the coroner calling Milo Ravensbrook to the stand. There was instant silence around the room. Even the barest rustling of movement ceased and every eye was on him. His skin was sickly pale but his clothes were immaculate and his bearing upright. He looked neither right nor left as he took his place behind the rail and swore in a precise, slightly hoarse voice as to his name. His jacket was open and hung a little loosely, to accommodate the bandages where he had been injured. His jaw was tight, but whether it was clenched in physical pain or emotional distress no one could say.

There was a murmur of both awe and sympathy even before the coroner spoke.

Rathbone glanced at the crowd. Enid looked at her husband, and her eyes were shadowed with unhappiness and pity. Almost absently her hand strayed to Genevieve beside her.

"Lord Ravensbrook," the coroner began, "will you please tell us what happened on the day of Caleb Stone's death? You do not need to repeat anything before you actually went into his cell, unless you wish to do so. I have no desire to harrow your feelings more than is my duty and cannot be avoided."

"Thank you," Ravensbrook acknowledged without turning his head. He stared at the wall opposite him, and spoke as if in a trance. He seemed to be reliving the events in his mind, more real to him than the paneled room, the mild face of the coroner, or the crowd listening to his every word. All eyes were upon his face, which was racked with emotions, and yet curiously immobile, as if it were all held inside him with unyielding self-control.

"The gaoler opened the door and stood back for me to go in," he began in a level, careful voice. "I had sought permission to speak to Caleb alone. I know it might very well be the last time I had such an opportunity. The trial was not going in his favor." His hesitation was barely perceptible. "I . . . I had certain things I wanted to say to him which were of a personal nature. Probably it was foolish of me, but I hoped that for Angus's widow's sake, he might tell me what had happened between Angus and himself, and she could know that Angus was . . . at peace, if you will." The coroner nodded. There was a sigh around the room.

Genevieve caught her breath in a gasp, but made no other sound. She closed her eyes, as if she could not bear to see.

Rathbone glanced at Goode and saw a flicker of question in his eyes.

"Of course it was futile," Ravensbrook resumed. "Nothing I could say had any effect upon him, or softened the anger inside him."

"Was he in a rage when you first went in, Lord Ravensbrook?" the coroner asked, his eyes wide and gentle. "The gaoler seems not to know."

"He was . . . sullen," Ravensbrook replied, frowning slightly. If he were aware of Selina Herries staring at him as if she would imprint his features in her mind, he gave no sign of it at all. "I asked him, for Genevieve's sake, to tell me what had happened in that last meeting," he continued. "But he would not. I assured him I would not repeat it to the authorities. It was only for the family I wished to know. But he was adamant." His voice was level, but seemed tight in his throat, as though he had to force it out, and several times he licked his lips.

Rathbone glanced around the room again. Enid sat stiff-backed, leaning a trifle forward, as if she would be closer to him. Genevieve looked from the witness stand to Enid, and back. Selina Herries clenched her knuckles in front of her, and her bold face was filled with pain, but her eyes did not waver.

"He asked me for pen and paper," Ravensbrook said, resuming his account. "He said he wanted to write a last testament. . . ."

"Did he mean a will, or a statement, do you know?" the coroner inquired.

"He did not say, and I did not ask," Ravensbrook answered. "I assumed it was some statement, perhaps a form of last words. I hoped it would be his confession or contrition, for his own soul's sake."

In the audience Selina let out a little cry, then immediately stifled it. Another woman gave a stifled sob, but whether of personal grief or simply the emotion of the scene, it was impossible to say.

Titus Niven put his hand on Genevieve's, discreetly, very gently, and the tightness in her shoulders eased a fraction.

"So you asked the gaoler for a pen, ink and paper," the coroner prompted.

"Yes," Ravensbrook agreed. The emotion in the room did not seem to touch him; perhaps his own turmoil was too great. "When they came, I returned to the cell and gave them to Caleb. He tried to use the pen, but said it was scratchy. The nib needed recutting. I took out my penknife to do it for him . . ."

"You did not offer him the knife?" the coroner asked, leaning forward earnestly.

Ravensbrook's mouth tightened and his brows furrowed. "No, of course not!"

"Thank you. Proceed."

Ravensbrook stood even more rigidly. The desperate grip on his emotions, the fragility of his hold, was painfully apparent. He was a man walking through a nightmare, and not a soul in the room could be unaware of it.

This time even the coroner did not prompt him.

Ravensbrook took a deep breath and let it out in an inaudible sigh.

"Without the slightest warning, without saying a word, Caleb launched himself at me. The first I knew of it, he was at my throat, his hand clasping my wrist and attempting to seize the knife from me. We struggled—I to save my life, he to gain mastery over me, whether to kill me or to snatch the knife in an attempt to take his own life, I do not know, nor will I guess."

There was a slight murmur of assent, a sigh of pity.

"For God's sake, where's Monk?" Goode whispered to Rathbone. "This can't be strung out beyond tomorrow!"

Rathbone did not answer. There was nothing else to say.

"I cannot tell you precisely what happened," Ravensbrook started again. "It was all too quick. He managed to stab at me several times, half a dozen or so. We fought back and forth. It probably seemed for longer than it was." He turned to face the coroner, looking at him earnestly. "I have very little idea whether it was seconds or minutes. I managed to force him away from me. He slipped and my own impetus carried me forward. I tripped over his leg and we landed together. When I arose, he was lying on the floor with the knife in his throat."

He stopped. There was total motionless silence in the room. Every face was turned towards him, emotions naked in horror and compassion.

Selina Herries looked like a ghost, suddenly thinner, sadder, the brave arrogance leached away.

"When I could gather my senses," Ravensbrook said, taking up his account again, "and realized that I was no longer in danger from him, I leaned forward and attempted to find his pulse. He was bleeding very profusely, and I feared he was beyond help. I turned to the door and banged and called out for the gaolers. One of them opened it and let me out. The rest I believe you already know."

"Indeed, my lord," the coroner agreed. "I do not need to trouble you any further. May I offer you and your family my deepest sympathy in your double loss."

"Thank you." Ravensbrook turned to leave.

Goode rose to his feet.

The coroner made a motion with his hand to stop Ravensbrook, who looked at Goode as he would an enemy in the field of battle.

"If you must," the coroner conceded reluctantly.

"Thank you, sir." Goode turned to Ravensbrook, smiling courteously, showing all his teeth.

"By your own account, my lord, and by the evidence of your most unfortunate injuries . . ." he began. "By the way, I hope you are beginning to recover?"

"Thank you," Ravensbrook said stiffly.

"I am very glad." Goode inclined his head. "As I was saying, by your own account, my lord, you did not cry out for help until the struggle with Caleb had continued for some moments. Why did you not call immediately? You surely must have appreciated that you were in very considerable danger?"

Ravensbrook stared at him, his face white.

"Of course I knew that," he said, his jaw clenched, the muscles visible even from where Rathbone sat.

"And yet you did not cry out," Goode persisted. "Why not?"

Ravensbrook looked at him with loathing.

"I doubt you would understand, sir, or you would not ask. For all his sins and ingratitude, his disloyalty, Caleb Stonefield had been a son to me. I hoped I might deal with the matter without the authorities ever needing to know of it. It was the most tragic accident that it ended as it did. I could have hidden my own wounds until I was clear of the courthouse. He was, until the end, unhurt."

"I see," Goode replied expressionlessly.

He went on to ask all manner of further questions, sought explanations of the finest points. Rathbone did the same after him, until it was apparent he had lost all sympathy from the crowd and worn the coroner's patience threadbare. He conceded at quarter past four in the afternoon, and was called by the coroner to take the stand himself. The coroner elicited his evidence and dispatched him within twelve minutes.

Goode racked his brains, and could think of nothing further to ask him.

At twenty-nine minutes to five Monk was called, and found to be absent. Rathbone protested that he should be located. The coroner pointed out that since Rathbone himself had been in Monk's presence every moment of the relevant time, there was nothing useful that Monk could add.

Goode rose to his feet, and was also overruled.

The coroner adjourned the sitting until the following day.

Rathbone and Goode left the court together, deep in anxiety. There was no word from Monk.

———

The first witness of the morning was Hester Latterly.

"Miss Latterly." The coroner smiled at her benignly. "There is no need to be nervous, my dear. Simply answer the questions to the best of your ability. If you do not know the answer, then say so."

"Yes sir." She nodded and smiled back at him innocently.

"You were leaving the courtroom after attending the trial, when you were informed by the gaoler Bailey that someone was injured and needed medical assistance, is that correct?" He was not going to allow her to ramble by telling the story in her own words. He had summarized it for her most precisely.

Rathbone swore under his breath.

"If Monk doesn't come within an hour, it is all going to be over," Goode said. "Where in God's name is he? Is there an early train from Chilverley this morning? Should I go and look for him?"

Rathbone glanced around desperately. "I'll send a clerk," he said.

"Mr. Rathbone?" the coroner said with a frown.

"I beg your pardon," Rathbone apologized grimly.

The coroner turned to Hester. "Miss Latterly?"

"Yes?"

"Would you please answer the question?"

"I beg your pardon, sir. What was it?"

Very carefully the coroner repeated himself.

"Yes sir," she replied. "I had attended the trial with Lady Ravensbrook." She then repeated the entire procedure of her departure, Bailey's arrival, Enid's reaction, her own reaction, the instructions she had given to the coachman and her reasons for doing so, all the alternatives and why they were unacceptable, Enid's assurance that she would be perfectly able to manage and that she would indeed go home, and then her return with Bailey through the courtroom buildings and her arrival at the cells. Nothing the coroner could say—and he tried several times—would stop her. She seemed not to hear him.

Rathbone shot a sideways glance at Goode, and saw his incredulity, and the beginning of a bleak amusement.

"Yes," the coroner said grimly. "Thank you. What did you see when you arrived at the cells, Miss Latterly? Please confine yourself to what is relevant."

"I beg your pardon?"

"Please confine yourself to what is relevant, Miss Latterly."

"To what, sir?"

"To what is relevant, Miss Latterly!" the coroner said extremely loudly.

"Relevant to what, sir?"

The coroner controlled himself with some effort.

"To the matter of Caleb Stone's death, madam."

"I am afraid I don't know what is relevant," she replied without a flicker of expression in her face. "It would seem, from what I observed, that he was possessed by such a frantic hatred of his erstwhile guardian, Lord Ravensbrook, that he was prepared, at any cost whatever, even the certain sacrifice of his own life by hanging . . . surely a most damnable way to die, to inflict upon him some injury, even to wish his death. I am sorry. That is a very complicated sentence. Perhaps I had better rephrase it—"

"No!" the coroner shouted. Then he drew a deep breath. "That is not necessary, Miss Latterly. Your meaning is perfectly plain, even if not your reasons for believing so."

She launched into her reasons for believing so, impervious to his attempted interruptions. She seemed to be hard of hearing, verging upon outright deafness. She described in detail exactly how Lord Ravensbrook had appeared to her, describing every sign with clinical thoroughness, and drawing upon her experience of soldiers in shock in the Crimea to illustrate that her opinion was an expert one. Then she described his wounds, their appearance, her treatment of them, how she had been obliged to make use of Rathbone's shirt, and why the gaolers' shirts would not do, her apologies to Rathbone for the inconvenience and her belief that Ravensbrook would make good his loss. When she had finished that, without drawing breath, she went on to describe Ravensbrook's response to the treatment. By half past twelve she still had not reached the point where she had opened the cell door and seen the body of Caleb Stone.

The coroner adjourned the sitting for luncheon, and retired exhausted.

"Brilliant, if somewhat farcical," Goode said dourly, in the same tavern as the day before. "But unless Monk turns up with something this afternoon, it will achieve nothing. I think one of us should go to Chilverley and get him!"

"He would come if he had anything!" Rathbone said.

When the court reconvened, it was packed to standing room. No one offered an explanation as to why. Perhaps it was because it had not gone as expected, perhaps it was the hope of some revelation, possibly it was Hester's performance, and the sense of the absurd. Suddenly it had all become interesting.

The coroner had dined well. He was in a better mood for battle and he met Hester's resumption of evidence with a stern eye and a voice which was perfectly willing and capable of shouting her down.

"Would you please tell me if Caleb Stone was dead when you looked into the cell, Miss Latterly. 'Yes' or 'No' will suffice."

"Yes," she said with a smile of agreeability.

"He was dead?"

"Yes."

"How do you know?"

At some length she told him, explaining all the ways by which one might know that life is extinct.

"I am a physician and a lawyer, ma'am!" he shouted above her. "I am perfectly aware of the difference between life and death."

"I beg your pardon?" she said pleasantly.

He repeated what he had said.

"No." She shook her head. "I mean I am sorry for having told you what you already know, sir. Of course, I knew you must be a lawyer. I did not appreciate you were a physician also. If I have slighted you, I am very sorry."

"Not at all," he said graciously. "Thank you. I have nothing further to ask you." He looked at Rathbone and Goode meaningfully. "Your evidence has been most complete!" he added.

Nevertheless Goode rose to his feet and asked her to clarify as much as he could possibly misunderstand. He was drawing to the end of his wit and invention when an elderly gentleman in clerical garb made his way, with difficulty, to the front of the room and handed a letter to Rathbone.

Rathbone tore it open and read it, and let out an audible sigh of relief.

Goode turned to look at him, and saw the rescue in his eyes. He allowed Hester to draw to a close at last and be released with a sigh of gratitude from the coroner, and some disappointment from that part of the crowd who had known neither Caleb or Angus, and had no emotional involvement in the outcome.

The doctor who had examined the body was called. The coroner dealt with his evidence and dispatched him in less than a quarter of an hour. Neither Goode nor Rathbone could think of anything further to ask him. He had said that the cause of death was a slashing wound from the penknife which had caught the jugular vein, and the deceased had then bled to death. It was quite consistent with him having held the weapon in his other hand, and its being forced back into his throat in a fall or during a struggle. There was nothing more to add.


Rathbone rose to his feet. Where on earth was Monk? If he did not appear in the next few minutes they would lose by default. He could not spin this out any longer. The coroner's patience was stretched to breaking. "With respect, sir, while all this is both true and relevant, it still does not tell us whether his death was accidental or not."

"In the absence of proof that it was suicide, Mr. Rathbone," the coroner said patiently, "we shall have to assume that he attacked Lord Ravensbrook in the same jealousy and hatred which apparently possessed him with regard to his brother, only in this case his weapon was turned upon himself, and he became the victim."

Rathbone took a deep breath and laid his reputation in the balance.

"Or there is the third possibility, sir; that it was not Caleb who attacked Lord Ravensbrook, but that the outcome was exactly what was meant from the beginning."

There was utter silence, not even an indrawn breath of disbelief. It was as if life in the room were suspended. Enid was ashen-faced, Genevieve paralyzed.

Finally the coroner spoke.

"Mr. Rathbone, are you suggesting that Lord Ravensbrook intentionally killed Caleb Stone?"

"I am suggesting that it is a possibility, sir."

Goode closed his eyes and leaned back in his seat, anguish written all over his face.

Two spots of color touched Milo Ravensbrook's cheeks, but he neither moved nor spoke.

Selina Herries bit her knuckles and stared at Rathbone. "In God's name, man, for what conceivable reason?" the coroner asked.

The door opened at the back of the court and Monk came in, drenched with rain, tousled and exhausted for lack of sleep, but accompanied by an elderly man and a stout woman in black.

Rathbone felt weak with relief. His voice trembled as he answered the coroner.

"I will call witnesses to answer that question, sir. I shall begin with the Reverend Horatio Nicolson, of Chilverley, with your permission."

The coroner hesitated. He looked around the room, saw the

wide-eyed faces, the anticipation, the single journalist who was still present sitting with pencil in hand, face bright with eagerness. He could not disallow it.

"I shall stop you if for one instant there is irrelevance, or any attempt at unsubstantiated attack!" he warned. "Be very careful, Mr. Rathbone, very careful indeed! I will have no one's good name taken lightly."

Rathbone bowed his head in acknowledgment and called Horatio Nicolson to the witness stand.

Slowly, with deep regret and obvious embarrassment, the Reverend Nicolson mounted the witness stand and took the oath.

Rathbone began by establishing precisely who he was so that the court might understand his importance.

"So you knew Lord Ravensbrook and his family quite well at the time Angus Stonefield came to Chilverley?" he asked.

"Yes sir," Nicolson answered, his face grave.

"Did you come to know Angus?"

"Yes. I tutored him in Latin, beginning when he was about eight, I believe. He was an excellent student, intelligent, willing and quick to learn. A most agreeable boy, so thoughtful and well mannered." He smiled at the memory, in spite of himself. "My wife was especially fond of him. She worried about him. He was quite often ill, you know, and at times seemed very withdrawn." His voice dropped a little. "There was a sadness in him, especially when he was very young. Most rational, I suppose, having lost both his parents at such an early age."

"Did he continue to be such an excellent student, Mr. Nicolson?" Rathbone asked.

Nicolson's face pinched with grief.

"No. I am afraid he became very erratic. At times he was excellent, his old self. And then there would be occasions when I would hardly see him for several weeks."

"Do you know the reason for this?"

Nicolson drew in a deep breath and let it out in a silent sigh. "I asked, naturally. Lord Ravensbrook confided in me that he had become most recalcitrant at times, hard to discipline, and on occasion even openly rebellious."

There was a faint rustling in the room. No one was yet interested. Nicolson's head lifted. "Although I must say in his defense that Lord Ravensbrook was a hard man to please." He spoke as if he had not seen Ravensbrook in the room, nor did his eyes move towards where he sat, stiff and pale. "He was handsome, charming and talented himself," Nicolson continued. "And he expected those in his own family to come up to his standards. If they did not, he was harsh in his criticism."

"But Angus was not, strictly speaking, his own family," Rathbone pointed out. "Except distantly. Was he not the child of a cousin?"

Nicolson's face tightened, touched with a deep pity. "No sir, he was the illegitimate son of his younger brother, Phineas Ravensbrook. Stonefield was the young woman's name, which was all he was legally entitled to. But he was Ravensbrook by blood."

Rathbone heard the murmur of surprise around the room, the indrawn breath.

The coroner leaned forward, as if about to interrupt, then changed his mind.

"Why did Lord Ravensbrook not adopt him?" Rathbone asked. "Especially since he had lost his wife and had no children of his own."

"Lord Ravensbrook and his brother were not close, sir." Nicolson shook his head, a great weight of sadness in his voice, and in the gentle lines of his face. "There was tension between them, a deep-lying rivalry that could take no joy in the other's happiness or success. Milo, the present Lord Ravensbrook, was the elder. He was clever, charming and talented, but I think his ambition was even larger than his abilities, considerable as they were."

Memory lit his face. "Phineas was quite different. He had such vitality, such laughter and imagination. Everyone loved Phineas. And he seemed to have no ambition at all, except to enjoy himself. . . ."

The coroner leaned across his table.

"Mr. Rathbone! Is this of any relevance to Caleb Stonefield's death? It seems to be very old history, and of a very personal nature. Can you justify it in this court?"

"Yes sir, it is at the very core of it," Rathbone said with feeling momentary to passion. Something of the rage and the emergency in him must have been there in his voice and the angles of his body. Every eye was on him, and the coroner hesitated only a moment before permitting him to proceed.

Rathbone nodded to Nicolson.

"I am afraid he got away with much that perhaps he should not," Nicolson said quietly, but his voice carried even to the back of the room in the silence. "He could smile at people, and they forgot their anger. They forgave him far too much for his own good, or for Milo's. The sense of injustice, you see? As if all the pleasures and pains of life could be weighed against each other—only God can do that . . . at the end, when it is all known."

He sighed. "Perhaps that is why he was so harsh with poor Angus, to try to prevent him following in his father's footsteps. Such charm can be a terrible curse, undoing all that would be good in a man. It is not right that we should laugh our way out of justice. It teaches us all the wrong lessons."

"Was Lord Ravensbrook so very harsh, Mr. Nicolson?"

"In my opinion, yes sir."

"In what way?"

The coroner's face pinched, but he did not interrupt.

In the room there was a scrape of fabric on fabric, the squeak of a boot. Milo Ravensbrook fidgeted and moved as if to speak, but did not.

Nicolson looked wretched, but he did not hesitate to reply in a soft, steady voice.

"He seemed at times impossible to please. He would humiliate the boy for mistakes, for foolishness which was merely born of ignorance, or uncertainty, lack of confidence. And of course the more a child is embarrassed, the more mistakes he makes. It is a terrible thing to feel worthless, sir, to feel you owe a debt of gratitude, and instead of paying it, you have to let down those you most wish to please." He pressed on with difficulty through his obvious emotion. "As a small boy I saw Angus many times struggling to keep from weeping, and then the shame he felt when he could no longer help it, and was then chastened for that too. And he was bitterly ashamed of being beaten, which he was frequently. It terrified him, and then he felt himself a coward because of it."

In the crowd a woman stifled a sob.

Selina Herries had not wept for Caleb's death. It was still too new a shock for her, her feelings towards the man too mixed between pride, contempt, and fear of him. Now her feelings for the child he must have been were simple. She let the tears run down her face without shame or hindrance.

Enid Ravensbrook's face was ash-gray and set in lines of intolerable pain, as if some long-feared tragedy had at last struck her. She looked sideways at her husband, but her expression was unreadable. Not once did he turn to her. Perhaps he did not dare to see what was in her eyes.

Genevieve Stonefield was beyond weeping, but she clasped Titus Niven's hand as if she might drown if she let it go.

"Mr. Nicolson . . ." Rathbone prompted.

Nicolson blinked. "My heart ached for him, and I was moved to speak to Lord Ravensbrook on his behalf, but I fear I did no good. My interference only provoked him to be even stricter. He thought Angus had complained to me, and he regarded that as both cowardice and a personal disloyalty."

"I see." To Rathbone it was a picture of such pain he was lost for more powerful or appropriate words. What must have lain beneath the surface of Angus's honorable and upright character? Could he ever have forgiven Ravensbrook for those years of misery?

The coroner had not interrupted, nor had his eyes once strayed to the clock, but now, deeply unhappy, he was compelled to speak.

"Mr. Rathbone, this past distress is most harrowing, but it is still, so far, irrelevant to the death of Caleb Stonefield. I am sure you must be aware of that. Mr. Nicolson's evidence has addressed itself solely to Angus."

"That is because he never met Caleb," Rathbone replied. "If I may be permitted to call my last witness, sir, she will explain it all."

"I hope she can, Mr. Rathbone, otherwise you appear to have harrowed our emotions and wasted our time to no purpose."

"It is to a purpose, I assure you. I call Miss Abigail Ratchett."

Abigail Ratchett was a very stout woman with unnaturally black hair, considering that she must have been at least seventy-five. But apart from being hard of hearing, she was self-assured and quite in command of her wits. Every eye in the room was upon her.

"You are a nurse, Miss Ratchett?" Rathbone began, speaking clearly and rather above his usual pitch and volume.

"Yes sir, and midwife. At least I used to be."

The coroner's face tightened.

Goode groaned.

Rathbone ignored them both.

"Were you in attendance when Miss Alice Stonefield was delivered of her two sons, in October of 1829, the father being one Phineas Ravensbrook?"

Rathbone glanced at Ravensbrook. He looked like a death's-head.

"I were in attendance, yes sir," Miss Ratchett replied. "But it were just a normal birth like any other, no twins, sir, just the one child. Boy ... beautiful he were. Healthy child. Called him Angus, she did."

One could have heard a tin tack drop in the court.

"What?" Rathbone demanded.

The coroner leaned forward, peering at her.

"Madam, you are aware of what you are saying? There are people in this courtroom who knew both Angus and Caleb!"

"There were one baby, sir," Miss Ratchett repeated. "I were there.

Miss Alice had one baby. I were with her for all the time she nursed him. Knew him right until his poor mother were killed. Year after Phineas Ravensbrook died in some foreign place. It were after that as his uncle took him, poor little mite. Only five, he were, an' terrible took with his grief. Father never 'ad no time for 'im. Never owned 'im, he didn't, nor loved 'is mother neither." Her face betrayed her feelings for Phineas Ravensbrook.

"What you say makes no sense, madam!" the coroner cried desperately. "If there was only one child, where did Caleb come from? Who was he? And who killed Angus?"

"I don't know nothing about that," Miss Ratchett answered levelly. "I just know there were one baby. But I do know as children have a powerful imagination! I looked after a little girl once as 'ad a friend, all imaginary, and whenever she done something wrong, she said as how it were Mary what done it, not her. She was good, Mary was bad."

"An ordinary excuse any child might make," the coroner said. "I have children myself, madam. I have heard many such stories."

The Reverend Nicolson rose to his feet. "I beg your pardon, sir." He addressed the coroner respectfully, but he would not be denied. "But is it not possible that in his unhappiness, and his feeling of rejection, obligation and loneliness, that the boy created an alternative self which would take the blame for his failures, and which would also be free to hate his uncle as he wished to, as he did in his heart?"

He raised his voice above the mounting noise in the room, the groans and murmurs of horror, pity, rage or disbelief.

"Might it not begin as an escape within the imagination of an unhappy child's hurt and humiliation?" he asked. "And then grow into a genuine madness wherein he became two quite separate people, one who did everything to please, and earned the resultant rewards, and another who was free to feel, without guilt, all the anger and hatred for his rejection, because he was the son of a father who would not own him, and an uncle for whom he was never good enough, a reflection of the brother he envied, and upon whom he could no longer be revenged, except through the child?"

The coroner banged on his desk for silence. "Order!" he commanded. "That is a monstrous scene you paint, sir. May God forgive you for it. I should not be surprised if the Ravensbrook family cannot." He looked at where Milo Ravensbrook sat rigid, white-faced but for the scarlet daubs on his cheeks.

But it was Enid Ravensbrook's expression, the rage and the pity in her, which made the coroner draw in his breath, and from which Rathbone knew that Nicolson was not so far wrong.

"Absolute insanity," Ravensbrook said between his teeth. "For God's sake! Everyone here knows there were two brothers! This woman is either wicked or she has lost her wits. Her memory is fuddled with drink." He swung around. "Genevieve! You have seen both Angus and Caleb!" He was shouting now. "Tell them this is preposterous!"

"I have seen them," Genevieve said slowly. "But never together. I have never seen them at the same time. But . . . it couldn't be. They were utterly different. No." She looked at Abigail Ratchett. "No, you have to be mistaken. It was over forty-one years ago. Your memory is confused. How many babies have you delivered? Hundreds?"

"It was one baby!" Abigail Ratchett said fiercely. "I'm not drunk and I'm not mad, no matter what anyone says."

Genevieve turned to Monk, desperation in her face. She had to raise her voice to make herself heard. "You said someone saw them together on the day Angus was killed! Find that man and bring him here. That will solve it!"

The coroner banged again, demanding silence, then turned to Monk. "Well?" he said sharply. "Did you find such a witness? If you did, what is all the nonsense? It seems you are totally irresponsible, sir!"

"I went back," Monk replied, his voice quiet, hard. "I found the witness, and I had him stand exactly where he had seen Angus and Caleb face each other. I stood where he said they did."

Now, suddenly, there was not a sound in the room.

"I was before a mirror, sir," Monk said with a brilliant smile. "I fought with my own reflection in a glass, and the man watching me relived a mirage."

"That proves nothing!" Ravensbrook said thickly. "You have said Caleb confessed to murdering Angus. How can a man murder himself?"

"He said he had destroyed Angus," Monk corrected. "And that I would never find the body. That was the joke. That is why he laughed. Caleb knew of Angus, and despised him. I think Angus did not know of Caleb. He could not bear to. For him it was truly another person, a dark presence beyond himself, and he was profoundly afraid of him."

"Nonsense!" Ravensbrook retaliated, his voice rising. "You cannot prove such a wild and totally scurrilous story. Caleb was insane, certainly, and he murdered his brother. Then when he knew he would be convicted, and hanged, in a last frenzy of hatred, he attacked me too, because, God forgive me, I always loved Angus better. If I am guilty of a sin, it is that, and only that!"

The voice was rising again. People were moving about.

"It can be proved." Monk lifted his voice, staring at the coroner. "The body of Caleb Stone is in the morgue." He swung around to Selina. "Madam, do you know Caleb's body well enough to tell it from Angus's?"

"Yeah, 'course I do," she said without blushing.

He looked at Genevieve. "And you, Mrs. Stonefield, could you tell your husband's body from Caleb's?"

"Yes." Her voice was no more than a whisper, her face bloodless.

"Then let us put an end to this farce," the coroner commanded. "We shall take these two ladies to the morgue." He rose, his face set, his eyes unblinking. He did not even bother with the uproar in the court or pay the slightest attention to the journalists falling over one another to get out and find messengers.


The morgue attendant pulled back the sheet and uncovered the naked body as far as the groin. The room was cold, and smelled of water and death. The candlelight was yellow and left the corners in shadow.

Selina Herries leaned on Hester's arm, her face calm, almost beautiful, all the brashness and the anger gone from it. She looked at the face with its smooth brow, the chiseled mouth, the green eyes closed, then she looked down at the broad chest, scarred and marble white. The pattern of old injuries was quite individual.

"That's Caleb," she said quietly. She touched his cold cheek with her fingers, gently, as if he could feel her. "God rest him," she whispered.

The coroner nodded and Hester went out with her. A few minutes later she returned with Genevieve. Again the morgue attendant laid back the sheet. Genevieve stared hard at the same calm face with its closed eyes, and the same white body with its old scars.

Finally her eyes filled with tears and they spilled down her cheeks in an anguish of pity, wrenching at her with a pain she would never forget.

"Yes," she whispered so quietly that in any place but this room of death, it would not have been heard. "Yes, that is Angus. I know those scars as I know my own hand. I bandaged most of them myself. God make him whole, and give him peace at last." She turned slowly and Hester held her in her arms while she wept the grief of all the lost pain she could not heal, the child she could not reach.

"I'll conduct the prosecution of Ravensbrook for murder," Rathbone said with passion.

"You'll never prove it," Monk pointed out.

"That doesn't matter!" Rathbone clenched his jaw, his body rigid. "The charge will ruin him. It will be enough."

Monk leaned forward and picked up one of the dead hands. It was beautiful, perfect-nailed, and he knew now why Caleb had always worn gloves—to protect Angus's hands. He folded it carefully across the other. Perhaps no one else in the room could feel so deeply and with such an intimate pity for a man divided against himself, forever in fear of a dark half he did not know.

"Be at peace," he said. "What debts you cannot pay, we will."

ANNE PERRY's other William Monk novels include *The Face of a Stranger*, *A Dangerous Mourning*, *Defend and Betray*, *A Sudden, Fearful Death*, and *The Sins of the Wolf*. She is also the author of fifteen novels, beginning with *The Cater Street Hangman*, in another Victorian mystery series featuring Inspector Thomas Pitt and his wife Charlotte, the most recent of which is *Traitors Gate*.